THE
CULLING
Heroes of the Undead
Peter Meredith

Fictional works by Peter Meredith:

A Perfect America
Infinite Reality: Daggerland Online Novel 1
Infinite Assassins: Daggerland Online Novel 2
Generation Z
Generation Z: The Queen of the Dead
Generation Z: The Queen of War
Generation Z: The Queen Unthroned
Generation Z: The Queen Enslaved
The Sacrificial Daughter
The Apocalypse Crusade War of the Undead: Day One
The Apocalypse Crusade War of the Undead: Day Two
The Apocalypse Crusade War of the Undead Day Three
The Apocalypse Crusade War of the Undead Day Four
The Apocalypse Crusade War of the Undead Day Five
The Horror of the Shade: Trilogy of the Void 1
An Illusion of Hell: Trilogy of the Void 2
Hell Blade: Trilogy of the Void 3
The Punished
Sprite
The Blood Lure The Hidden Land Novel 1
The King's Trap The Hidden Land Novel 2
To Ensnare a Queen The Hidden Land Novel 3
Dead Eye Hunt
Dead Eye Hunt: Into the Rad Lands
The Apocalypse: The Undead World Novel 1
The Apocalypse Survivors: The Undead World Novel 2
The Apocalypse Outcasts: The Undead World Novel 3
The Apocalypse Fugitives: The Undead World Novel 4
The Apocalypse Renegades: The Undead World Novel 5
The Apocalypse Exile: The Undead World Novel 6
The Apocalypse War: The Undead World Novel 7
The Apocalypse Executioner: The Undead World Novel 8
The Apocalypse Revenge: The Undead World Novel 9
The Apocalypse Sacrifice: The Undead World 10
The Edge of Hell: Gods of the Undead Book One
The Edge of Temptation: Gods of the Undead Book Two
Tales from the Butcher's Block

Prologue
Wednesday, November 24, 2021

The line seemed to go on forever and that wasn't such a bad thing in Michael-13's mind. Any excuse to put off the inevitable for even a few minutes was okay with him.

It was the day before Thanksgiving and all around him were thousands of other travelers looking to get out of the heat of L.A. Nothing killed the desire for turkey more than an eighty-five-degree day. Nothing except maybe murder on a global scale, and Michael-13 wasn't hungry in the least.

He was a slight man with receding brown hair and soft quivering hands. Just then his complexion resembled curdled milk. He stood in the third of eight security lines that wound in tight loops towards the metal detectors where the dull-eyed TSA agents ruled like petty tyrants.

In another line thirty feet away was Monica-3. She was a tiny thing, not even five foot. Along with her diminutive stature, she had limp brown hair and a timid character, which made her the perfect person to be hung with the label of mouse, as in, "Monica Mouse." Before joining the Order, everyone called her that.

She was mostly hidden by a young backpacker, who flagrantly hoisted three immense carry-ons, in spite of the dozens of signs that forbade more than one. In contrast, both she and Michael-13 carried simple one-pocket satchels. Hers held only a few magazines, a boarding ticket damp with sweat, her driver's license and a thermos. Although the thermoses they carried didn't look like much, they were in fact special.

The two of them needed nothing else. They were in L.A. on business, the entirety of which was about to occur in the next minute. Theirs was an important mission. They, and a hundred couples just like them, were going to destroy the world, one thermos at a time.

Destroying the world was not an easy thing. Physically, it would be as simple as twisting the cap on their thermoses a half turn to the right and walking away. The difficult part was all mental. The hundred couples had to accept that their actions would kill eight billion men, women, and children.

Each of them had killed before. Each had jabbed a syringe full of bleach into a person as part of their training. It had been terrible watching their victims squirm in misery, and cry, and froth at the mouth. Terrible, but necessary. When the time came, there could be no cold feet or half measures. The future was too important to trust to chance.

Michael-13 had wept and squirmed along with the grizzled old man they had scooped up off the street with the promise of a meal. Killing him went against everything he had been taught since joining the Order, and yet, when it was done, he had not wavered. Magnus had asked him personally to be a part of the mission and although the great man had explained at length the need for a new start for humanity, he really hadn't needed to. Michael-13 would stab himself in the eye for Magnus.

Others had wavered. In fact, the majority of the volunteers had failed, either before, during, or after their first killing. None had been blamed or scolded. That was not the way.

The way forward was beautifully simple: be the best person you can be. For Michael-13, a one-time school teacher, it seemed that being a mass murderer was the best he could be.

It also made his stomach heave.

Ahead of him in line was a man and his five-year-old daughter. With her button-nose and oversized eyes, she was precious. Looking at her made him want to run out of there, screaming.

He stared across at Monica-3 instead, and she stared back at him as they progressed forward, one step at a time. His line was the quicker. In front of him were the conveyor belts and the grey bins. The five-year-old dropped down onto the thin carpet to pull off her sneakers. She had to pull them off like everyone else— *Why? Because she is a terrorist?* thought Michael-13.

A mad laugh began to build inside him. It threatened to explode from his mouth, so he turned away.

Now in front of him was *the* garbage can.

At every airport and in every security line, there was always that last chance garbage can. It was half-filled with water bottles and soda cans. Sitting among these were a sprinkling of make-up containers and shampoo bottles. There were a few paper bags as well. Michael-13 had always assumed these held drugs or booze. Or maybe porn.

"You gonna go?" the man behind Michael-13 asked. He had slick, oiled hair that ran straight back over his great dome of a head. There was mustard at the corners of his mouth. He wore a suit coat over a Hawaiian shirt and teal shorts.

Michael-13 stared, his mouth hanging open. The man and his outfit were incongruent. He made no sense and Michael-13's mind flailed in uncertainty. Then his watch chimed and he found his voice. "No. You go."

The alarm on his watch went off a second time. It was time. A hundred couples around the world were looking at their watches at that exact moment. Some were at airports and some were at subway or train stations. None were where they were by chance. Magnus had a plan. He always had a plan.

With damp, sweaty hands, Michael-13 opened the satchel and produced the thermos. There was nothing obviously special about it. From the outside, there was no way for anyone to know that the fate of humanity lay inside.

A long sad breath escaped him as he turned the cap a half turn to the right.

Across from him, Monica-3 had reached her own trashcan. Like Michael-13, she had been somewhat lost in life before meeting Daniel Magnus. Her degree in literature had meant nothing. Her friends had been directionless partiers who had drifted away after graduation. She had once been religious, however the concept of God had been so thoroughly abused by her teachers and the mainstream culture that she pretended to be an atheist. It was just easier.

Then she had met Magnus, and to her, he was a god.

God or not, she was trembling inside when her alarm went off. Her hands were shaking so badly that she dropped her thermos. She sucked in a quick breath and took a step back as if it might explode. It wouldn't, of course. The only thing inside was what looked and tasted like dry ice. And it was mostly dry ice. Mostly.

"Let me get that for you." Monica-3 froze as a TSA agent dipped and picked up the thermos. "Last chance," he said, handing it to her. Her mouth moved up and down but no sound came out. He grinned at her odd behavior and said, "Nothing over two ounces from here on."

"Yeah, right" she answered, suddenly relieved. He gave her a smile that she saw right through. He wasn't just some friendly man in a uniform, he was part of the system, the same system that was responsible for so much misery in the world. They all were—everyone around her.

Without another thought, she turned the lid on her thermos. There was the expected click and the top began to slowly twist.

The spring inside had enough resistance for it to take five full minutes before the cap popped off. Then the dry ice would begin to sublimate, changing directly from a solid to a gas. When the molecules lifted away, they would take with them tens of thousands of tiny viral-like cells, and no one would know.

Dry ice only gave off the fog cloud in the presence of water. Without water, the gas was invisible. In twenty minutes, there would be an unseen cloud of death, around the trashcan. Hers and Michael-13's.

Only he was still standing by his trashcan, staring down at his thermos. Something was wrong. She dodged through the travelers until she was steps away. She couldn't bring herself to get closer. "What are you doing?" she hissed, glancing back at the TSA agents.

"It didn't click."

A man brushed into Monica-3 and she flinched. "Can you hear anything going inside?" He listened, but with the background noise of a thousand people crowded into a small area, he could hear nothing. He shook his head.

As more people swept around them, the two stared at the thermos until she asked, "What are you going to do?"

"Follow the plan. I guess." The contingency plan for a malfunctioning thermos was simple: manually open the thermos, walk through the airport with it and then die. There was no cure for what was coming and Michael-13 knew that anyone with symptoms would not be allowed back inside the compound. Of course, he could simply leave the thermos and board his flight, but…

"I'd be nothing to the Order," he whispered. Sucking in a harsh breath, he grabbed the cap like he was going to tear it off.

"Hold on," Monica hissed. "Not yet." She eyed the thermos nervously as she eased towards him. A few people glanced their way, but no one really cared about the stressed-out couple. It looked like they were in the middle of a low-key spat and it was none of their business.

Monica gripped his thin arm; he was shaking. She couldn't bring herself to get close enough to hug him. "Magnus will know what you did here. You'll be a hero."

This was little consolation. "No. I've lost my chance." Those who made it back from the mission would be given the opportunity to advance, to become one of the Chosen. They would be gods among men…if they survived the process. Only one in five made it through, but the reward was worth the risk.

Now he would just die, the first of billions.

The thought made him feel weaker and smaller than ever. He tried to give her a smile, but it was frail and twittered at the edges. "You better go."

She backed slowly away before turning for the conveyors. Her shoes came off in a blink and her satchel was thrown into the bin. The crowds seem to part like magic and she breezed through the checkpoint. Just as she retrieved her shoes on the other side, she looked back. Michael-13 was gone.

He had popped the top off his thermos and after a deep shaky breath, had looked inside. A part of him expected to see a vile witch's brew of sickening green sludge, but there was nothing in it except a large cube of gently smoking dry ice.

It looked harmless, and yet he felt suddenly sick. Although he was already breathing in the disease, it was an irrational sensation. It would be a couple of hours before he even felt the change. Then it would be another hour before he became infectious, and it was anyone's guess before he turned completely. According to his briefing, the test subjects had taken between four and six hours to transform.

"Oh, God," he whispered as he tottered off.

The first hour went by in a blink as he walked around the airport, holding the open thermos out away from him. People stared at the sweat dripping from his chin. They knew there was something wrong with him but they were too shallow and wrapped up in their own unimportant lives to ask if he need help.

At the end of the hour, the ice was gone; he had done all he could. A thousand people had been infected—he pictured the five-year-old and her button nose. His stomach twisted and he had to fight the acid puke gurgling up the back of his throat.

He spent the next hour at an airport bar, drinking and feeling every breath go in and out. He kept waiting for something terrible to happen. In his mind, he was sure there would be a sudden onslaught of pain, or vomiting, or his heart would start to chug like an old engine; however the change actually started as a rash on his palms. It took fifteen minutes of absently scratching himself before he realized that this was it. This was the beginning of his death.

"Where's the nearest hospital?" he asked the portly, sagging bartender. A shrug was his reply. Michael-13 stared in disbelief at the man, but only for a few seconds. Then he smiled ruefully. That ugly, inhumane shrug of complete apathy was exactly the sort of thing he was destroying. That was Magnus' plan.

In a moment of extreme passive-aggression, Michael-13 tripled what he normally would've tipped the man. Then he went looking for a taxi to take him to the nearest hospital. He knew what was coming. It would be painful and it would be violent.

The pain started in his joints and worked its way into his head, where it began a fire. By the time the cab made it to the emergency room, he was drenched in sweat and writhing on the floor of the backseat. The cabby leapt out of the vehicle and stood back from it pointing and calling for help until the EMTs rushed from the building. Within minutes, Michael-13 was given an IV and pain meds. And then more pain meds. Doctors rattled off orders and blood was drawn.

"There's something wrong here," a nurse named Natalie Gere said. She held up a vial of the darkest blood any of them had ever seen. The room grew quiet as the staff stared, first at the vial and then at Michael-13. His flesh was grey and his eyes were sunken and terribly dark.

Natalie hesitated before taking a step away. That one second of indecision doomed her.

Michael-13 was gone and in his place was a monster, one with a ravenous appetite. He snapped out a long arm and grabbed her wrist. Instinctively, Natalie ripped her hand away, leaving skin under his nails. The scratches weren't deep, and yet they were deep enough, as the microscopic cells swarmed over her flesh and then slipped inside.

She fell back as other nurses darted in to try to calm him. He was beyond calm. He was beyond the capacity for rational thought. Like a wild thing, he attacked the women. His strength was a shock to them and with ease, he pinned them to a wall by the throat, one per hand. Their screams were loud but when he tore a chunk from the face of one, they went beyond shrill. The terrifying sound filled the emergency room and in seconds, orderlies and doctors were grappling Michael-13 in a wild melee.

Half a dozen were bitten and more were scratched before they managed to pin him down and tie him to a gurney. Even then, he wasn't done infecting people. In his madness, he bit his tongue nearly in half and soon he was spitting blood as he raged.

It took the equivalent of a horse tranquilizer to sedate him. By the time it took effect, Natalie was complaining of a headache. She was the smallest of those who'd been injured and the first to feel the effects of the cells replicating throughout her system. She left work early, hoping to get home quickly and lie in the dark. But this was the day before Thanksgiving and the freeways were gridlocked even beyond L.A. standards.

The sound of the first horn was like a knife in her skull. By the hundredth, she was downing Midol by the handful. Then a shiny green Honda Civic cut in behind her. The driver, bone-thin Jun Bae, had his bass thumping, and the pulse coming from the four 20-inch subwoofers caused the air to shimmer.

It made Natalie's eyes quiver in their sockets. She screamed a dozen curse words at Jun and flipped him off. He smiled at her reaction and proceeded to turn up the sound until his windows danced along to the beat. It was a little loud even for him, but he had some grass and after firing up a joint, the sound and the creeping traffic was all good.

His eyes were half-lidded and the world was in a fine haze when Natalie appeared at his door. In vain, she ripped at the handle, but the door was locked. So, she stepped back and crashed the heel of her sneakered foot into the green door, denting it badly.

"What the fuck!" Jun Bae's face was twisted in anger as he shouldered his door open. Halfway out, his fury turned to surprise as Natalie dove into the car and slammed into him, throwing him back. She was all claws and teeth, and spitting rage. Jun was a thin man and he found himself wedged between the console and the passenger seat. There was no way he could defend himself or fight back.

He tried to push her away, but she was viciously strong for someone so small, and she forced him down. Then he tried to punch her and she bit off two of his fingers. For the first time since he was a little kid, he screamed.

Jun lost two more fingers and a chunk of his left forearm before she was wrestled away by two very large men, both of whom were bitten. Three others were scratched and a police officer was kicked in the mouth. His lip was split and a minute later, he was infected when Natalie screamed like a hellion into his face.

An ambulance was called for Jun Bae, but with the traffic blocking everything, it took an hour for it to arrive and another hour for it to roll up to the closest hospital, which just happened to be the one where Natalie worked and by then it was on fire. Ten others who had been infected right around the same time as Natalie had been, were rampaging through the building, attacking anything that moved.

It was a running fight that was going in every direction. Those ten infected nearly seventy others before the police gunned the last of them down. Although none of the ten survived, their tainted blood coated the building.

Michael-13 had started a fire in Los Angeles and by midnight it was spreading out of control. Los Angeles was doomed, but it was not the only city that was dying. London, Moscow, Beijing, Tokyo, Calcutta...every major city had been marked for destruction. And that even included the Order's home city of New York.

New York City was a powder keg to begin with and when it went off, it would take half the country with it.

Chapter 1
Three days earlier—November 21, 2021
Massachusetts Institute of Technology

Security cameras picked up the two men in dark suits even before they entered the Whitehead Institute. This was a hundred-times-a-day occurrence and the bored man on surveillance didn't blink an eye. It was only after the front desk security guard rang up Lab 338 that things started moving.

On average, the front desk called that lab exactly zero times a year. It had never happened, and yet the call triggered an alarm in a small room two floors up. The room was set aside exclusively for visiting researchers. Almost exclusively. A pair of FBI agents had been roosting in it for the last two weeks.

The room smelled of Fritos and old French fries. In front were a few desks and a cubicle wall. Thrown on the floor in back were a couple of mattresses and a like number of suitcases, each gaping and spewing clothing.

Lying on one of the mattresses and snoring softly was the large ungainly form of FBI agent Stanley Plinkett, while in front, sitting at a desk and trying to stay awake was Agent Griffin Meyers. At twenty-eight, Griff was the junior agent by more than a decade. Still, his blue eyes were puffy from staring endlessly at the three live feeds he had going on one screen. On a second monitor, he was playing a game of solitaire. He was in the middle of losing, again, when the sound of a phone ringing over the speakers made him jump.

A canned voice answered, "Hmm, yes?"

"Hi, this is Ron from down in the lobby. Dr. Carter has a couple of guests."

"Guests? For Carter? Okay. I'll send him down."

As Griff jotted the time down on a pad of paper, he barked, "Plink! Get up. It's Bryce."

"Just Bryce?"

"So far."

Plinkett groaned as he struggled to sit up. The two had a running bet on which of the three-hundred scientists at the institute would be contacted. Bryce Carter had been Griff's third pick in their NFL-style draft.

"There's still time," Plinkett said as he came around the cubicle wall and leaned over Griff. Age and too many stakeouts had given Plinkett a bit of a paunch. With his thinning blonde hair and owlish expression, he looked more like an insurance salesman than an FBI agent. He squinted at the camera feed that covered the lobby. He pointed at the two men in suits. "Does that look like Seven and Eight?" The reference was to the nine pairs of recruiters that Magnus Enterprises were using to suck in some of the nation's best scientists, doctors, engineers and artists.

"I'll be able to get a good capture when they're leaving. Oh. There's Bryce. Look a him. He looks like he thinks he's in trouble." Bryce was Griff's age, but dressed as he was in khakis and a plaid shirt he looked like a middle-aged nerd. It didn't help that he was short and thin, with a perfect part on the right side of his head. "Here's the handshake, and the name drop. Look how his mouth fell open. And now for the card."

On the screen, Bryce stared at the business card for six seconds then looked at the back of it. Recruiter number Eight then held up a black envelope but didn't hand it over. He gestured to the lobby doors and the three headed outside where they were picked up by another camera.

"That's them," Plinkett muttered. "Eight has that ring of hair around his head."

Subconsciously, Griff ran a hand through his own thick dark hair. "Why the hell doesn't he just shave it off completely? Better to be bald if you ask me."

Plinkett shrugged. "Because he's an idiot. You better get going. Be cool. Don't spook him."

Griff unfolded his six-foot frame from the chair he'd been sitting in for the last three hours and stretched. "Bryce is a mouse. He's gonna spook no matter what. I just won't say anything until we're in the elevator."

Three minutes later Griff was in the lobby, watching the door. Trying to fit in among the undergraduates, he had dressed in old jeans and a t-shirt; he had a satchel slung across his shoulders. His disguise was a failure. The t-shirt did nothing to hide his muscles and the satchel only highlighted the breadth of his shoulders. He was also more *aware* than any of the students schlepping through the lobby. In short, he looked like a cop.

Still, Bryce didn't even notice him until the two were alone in the elevator together. Bryce wore a happy/stunned look and couldn't stop staring at the black envelope. He even sniffed it.

Griff pressed the five and then put out a hand to stop Bryce from hitting the three.

13

"You'll be getting out with me," Griff said. "I'm FBI and we need to talk about your upcoming trip."

Bryce backed to the wall of the elevator, holding a protective hand up to the throat of his plaid shirt. "M-my trip?" When he was frightened, his voice turned high and reedy. "How did you know about that? They just told me. They just told me two minutes ago. I-I-I think I need to see some ID or a warrant or something."

"When we get upstairs."

For a moment, Bryce looked like he wanted to say something more, but Griff was a head taller than him and an unspoken but innate promise of violence hung in the air around him. The two rode in a long silence that gripped Bryce and seemed to infect him with a malaise. Minutes before, his life was hitting a pinnacle. He was being wooed by none other than Daniel Magnus, the eighth richest man in the world. And now he had the FBI after him.

He was numb by the time he made it into the FBI's borrowed room.

Once inside, first Griff then Plinkett produced their IDs. "When's the limo coming for you?" Griff asked.

Should I demand a lawyer? Bryce wondered. He had the feeling they wouldn't let him call one. They were standing very close. "The day after tomorrow. At ten. What's this all about?"

"Daniel Magnus," Griff answered. "Something is happening with him and we need to know what. He's been collecting people. Scientists, artists, doctors. All young. All highly intelligent."

Bryce shrugged. "So? Didn't Edison do the same thing? And what about the Manhattan Project? That was our own government."

Plinkett slapped a heavy hand down on Bryce's shoulder and glared down at him. "This is different. You know that group of buildings he bought in New York City?"

"The Magnus Plaza? That's where I'm going. On his private jet. And it's perfectly legal." Bryce hoped so, at least. His head was spinning and his normally precise thoughts were nebulous and hard to grasp.

"Are you sure?" Griff asked. "Something's happening there. Something that doesn't make sense. We estimate Magnus has seven thousand people living in those buildings. They go in, but they don't come out."

This brought Bryce up short. "Ever? That's impossible."

"You'd be surprised," Plinkett said. "He has deliveries brought in. Truckload after truckload, every day. It's true, a few people do go out. Like those recruiters. When they do get out, the first thing they do is contact their families; to warn them."

Bryce's stomach dropped. "About what?"

Griff stared hard at the young scientist before answering. "We've had eleven family members contacted so far. The threat is never spoken of directly, but they were all told to leave their homes. Half were told to go north; as far north as they could go. Some were told to get up into the Rockies. Another was told to take a vacation to Tahiti."

Breathless, Bryce said, "Eleven is not really a lot."

Plinkett spun Bryce so the scientist faced him. "That's only the ones that contacted us. How many others simply heard the warning and took off? And more likely, how many of these people had no family at all? More than you'd think and it should worry you. In the last four months we've had a spike in missing persons with a few characteristics in common; young, intelligent, scientifically educated, few to no family members, and all had been in contact with Magnus. Like we said, they go in, but they don't come out."

No family members? This struck particularly close to Bryce, who had been an only child and had lost his mother the year before.

"So…so, what do you think he's doing? You think he's starting a cult? Or planning to go David Koresh? No way. This is Daniel Magnus! *The* Daniel Magnus."

Plinkett sat back on the desk, knocking one of the monitors with his elbow. "We have no idea what he's really doing in there. It's why we're talking to you and others like you. We're going to need you to go in, find out what he's up to and get out again. You'll be perfectly safe. We'll have eyes on you every step of the way. Except for when you're inside, obviously. Once inside, you'll have three hours to get the information and get out. If you don't come out by then, we'll spring a search warrant on them."

A search warrant? For Daniel Magnus? People did not serve Daniel Magnus with a search warrant. "This is crazy. What you're asking is…Wait. Why don't you just go in now? You just said that there were missing persons."

Plinkett sighed. "We tried that once and they produced the person in a snap, almost as if the judge had warned them ahead of time. And it didn't matter either way. The guy wouldn't say a word. He sat like a stone even when we threatened to charge him with sedition. He didn't fucking blink at the idea of the death penalty."

Before Bryce could say anything, Griff spun him around. "That man had been inside for six weeks. Let that sink in. It took only six weeks for him to give up his life. Look, Bryce, your country needs you."

"Potentially," Bryce corrected. "What happens if he's working on something important and needs my help. You don't know this but I've just made a breakthrough in my…"

Griff spoke over him, "In your research into chromosomal protein pairings. We know all about it, which means Magnus knows. It's why he wants you, or rather, why he wants your work."

Bryce's eyes narrowed. "You think he's going to try to steal it?" When it came to his research, Bryce was extremely guarded, almost to the point of paranoia. Just the idea that Magnus was after his work made him rethink everything. He tapped his lip absently before asking, "I'll be safe?"

"Perfectly," Plinkett said.

Griff nodded in complete agreement and then held up a hand. "Except, like I said, we need to know what's happening in there and we won't find out unless you take a few chances. Walk around. Talk to people. Insist on it. If Magnus is really trying to recruit you, wouldn't you want to find out everything you could before you gave him your answer?"

"I suppose, but what if my answer is yes? What if he really is legit? It's Daniel Fucking Magnus."

Griff stepped right up to Bryce and looked down his nose at him. "At least eleven people told their parents to run far away from what's coming. No. Let me rephrase that. Eleven *scientists* told their parents to run far away. It scared them enough to call us. What would cause you to do that? Something legitimate or something terrible?"

Plinkett stood as well. "And if things do go sideways and you're on the wrong side, we'll make sure to find the right judge to pin as much of it on you as humanly possible. I wouldn't rule out the death penalty."

"Christ! It was a hypothetical question," Bryce replied.

"Hypothetical or not," Plinkett said, "we chose you for a reason. According to your file you paid for some of your schooling by playing poker. That right?"

Normally, Bryce would've gone into exquisite detail concerning his poker skills, but just then he was miserable and could only nod. Griff put a hand on his thin shoulder. "We're going to need you to carry a bluff from the moment you get picked up by the limo, to the second you walk out the front doors. Can you do that?"

"You want me to try to bluff one of the smartest men in the world?"

"Exactly," Griff said. "Just remember, he's like everyone else. He sees only two things: what he wants to see and what he expects to see."

Chapter 2
November 24th, 2021
The Day the World Ends
JFK Airport

"That was fucking awesome," Bryce Carter whispered beneath the sound of the plane's engines throttling down. He figured it was a guarantee that the plane was bugged, and even if it wasn't, he had to stay in character. The Gulfstream had a price tag of a hundred-million dollars and was worth every penny. The interior was spacious, and with its gold inlays and shining teak, it reminded him of a luxury yacht instead of a plane.

The real Bryce Carter, PhD would have reveled in the chance to fly on a private jet. He would've been giddy, and he would be a bit sad at the idea of having to leave it. This fake Bryce sighed and thumped the armrest with the meaty part of his small fist before he stood and forced a grin at the pretty stewardess. She was a fake, too. No woman had ever smiled so much at Bryce in his life.

At the door of the jet, he paused to adjust his cuff—normally, this would be for the visual effect alone. His cuff was fine, but this was what powerful men did...at least according to the magazines. Bryce only did it so the FBI could get a good look at him. His eyes flicked around, hoping to spot a man up on the roof of a hanger with a pair of over-sized binoculars, or a baggage handler in dark sunglasses, talking to his wrist.

Ahead of him, a servant in a nicer suit than his own, carried his bag to a helicopter that was waiting to whisk him off to his meeting with Daniel Magnus. *THE* Daniel Magnus. Bryce couldn't stop thinking of him that way, with the "*THE*" in capitals and in italics.

Magnus was the Henry Ford of his time and the next Bill Gates. He was the future of technology as much as he was its present. He was the epitome of cutting edge in a dozen fields, including work in molecular biology and the Human Genome project. And somehow, he had come across Bryce's name.

The "real" Bryce would've felt like the king of the world as he sauntered off the private jet, the wind plucking at the lapel of his suit. He would've had to hide the grin that kept wanting to bloom across his face. He would have a manic feeling of success, of having "made it" before he was even thirty. It would bubble up inside him and demand to burst out.

Bryce had to fake all this. He had to keep from muttering: "Fucking FBI." They had ruined this moment, potentially the greatest moment of his life.

The helicopter blades were already spinning, causing his brown hair to ripple and wave like fire. Normally, he wouldn't care, however, there was a woman sitting in the back. He assumed that she was nothing more than an expensive bit of blonde eye-candy, like the stewardess had been.

It was only when he climbed in next to her that he recognized the woman as Maddy Whitmore. For the most part, she hadn't changed in four years; her cheeks were a little chubbier, and her round chin a little rounder. Her sharp grey eyes were deeply set in fleshy folds, making them appear smaller than they were. Her hair was cut into a brown bob which was a vast improvement over the dreadlocks she had once sported.

"Mad Maddy! My God, it's you. Wait, is it Maddy, or are you still going by that tribal name you adopted at Harvard? Mgbaila-something wasn't it?"

Maddy's round face turned wooden and her lips practically disappeared. "Bryce. I see you're still waiting on that growth spurt. If you're the kind of person Magnus is looking to hire, this is even a greater waste of time than I envisioned."

"Yeah, why are you here? You know Magnus has a bad habit of actually making a profit while delivering goods and services to customers at a fair market value. Last I heard, you were going to go work for Cuba in their socialist paradise."

Before she could answer, the pilot leaned back so that her blonde hair spilled down one shoulder—Magnus sure liked his blondes. In her blue uniform, she was stern, but pretty. She pointed at the headsets. "You'll need to put the headgear on. If you'd like to speak to each other, there's a microphone built in."

Maddy picked one up. "Mine comes with an off switch. Must be my lucky day." As the engine began to spool up, she placed the headset over her ears, and with a final insincere smile, she turned to look out the window.

Bryce muttered, "Oh, how will I ever cope with the rejection?" He was actually disappointed. Seeing Maddy and slipping into their old antagonistic bantering had been the only natural thing he had done that day. Everything else had been a calculated act, and the stress of keeping it up was already wearing on him.

Even in the helicopter, he kept asking himself: what would Bryce do?

He would grin and enjoy the moment as the helicopter gently lifted into the air. From a thousand feet, New York City was far more alluring than at ground level. The trash and the graffiti disappeared, leaving only the canyons of concrete and steel, the rivers of cars, and the endless flow of humanity. It all washed over Bryce without leaving an impression. He was anxious...no, he was scared.

Up to this point, his act had been only a warm up. The limo driver, the stewardess, the pilot; none of them had the genius-level intellect of Daniel Magnus. They hadn't sat before Congress or been grilled on *60 Minutes*. They were just people...and they saw what they wanted to see.

"Just like Magnus," he whispered under his breath. But was that true? Magnus was known for spotting talent. He knew the goods when he saw it, which suggested he also knew crap when it wore a fake smile and put out a damp, frightened hand to shake.

Bryce was just wiping his hand on his coat when he saw that they were already landing. "Shit," he whispered as the helicopter set down, feather light, atop a skyscraper on the upper West Side of Manhattan. The engines cut out and the moment the blades slowed, a long-legged woman with masses of black hair, stepped from an elevator. She wore a white silken pantsuit and a calm smile. Maybe it was the smile but she seemed ageless and her light grey eyes were utterly beguiling. Bryce had to wipe his hand a second time before he stuck it out.

Unlike Bryce's, the woman's hand was soft, cool and dry. "I'm Katherine 6, one of Daniel's personal assistants. Your bags will be brought down."

She gestured Bryce and Maddy into a glass-walled elevator; the door whispered shut behind them.

Maddy, an odd look on her face, tilted her head way to take in the taller woman. "Did you say your name is Katherine 6. Like the number six?"

"No. Not like the number. It is the number. There are a lot of Katherine's running around here." Maddy and Bryce shared a look. Katherine nodded in agreement. "Yes, it's strange, but freeing. Hopefully, you'll see."

Before either Maddy or Bryce could say a word, a male voice came through a speaker. "What floor would you like?"

"Fifty please."

It was only then that Bryce noticed there were no numbered buttons or a control panel like on a normal elevator. The implication of this crept over him as the car dropped—the elevators could only be used with permission. Would access to the stairs be the same? Almost certainly. He was already trapped.

The FBI was right. A shiver struck Bryce. He glanced to see if either woman had noticed. Neither had, but what about the cameras? There had to be cameras. He swallowed loudly and then smiled broadly—both actions felt incorrect.

The doors chimed as they slid open onto a spacious hallway with plush, purple carpet. Paintings in gilded frames hung from the walls at regular intervals. Each was softly lit from above. As expected, everything was perfectly clean, perfectly beautiful, perfectly perfect.

Almost.

Right in front of the doors were a man and a woman, both in white. They were young with wide smiles and odd, open faces, which gave them a strange alluring quality. They were happy. Happy to be in the hall. Happy to see Maddy and Bryce. Happy to be alive. It was weird.

"Good morning," the woman said, cheerfully.

"Good morning," Katherine 6 answered.

Bryce stared, not knowing what the "real" Bryce would say. Maddy was equally weirded out and could only mutter, "Hi."

The awkward moment ended as the couple entered the elevator. "This way," Katherine 6 said and walked down the hall, passing more and more of the same sort of people. Everyone was pleasant and young, and *everyone* said good morning until it almost felt like there was a joke being played on the two.

Finally, they came to a conference room where a large, thickset man held the door open. His black suit was stretched tight around his muscled shoulders, and although he too had a friendly smile, there was something that spoke of danger in his eyes.

"Good morning," the guard said. Friendly and deadly; that was the guard.

"Good morning," Katherine 6 answered as she strolled past. Once inside she paused by the door. "If you'll wait here, Magnus will be in shortly. There are drinks in the fridge. Help yourself."

She closed the door and the *click* as the lock engaged was loud and unsettling.

"Was that weird, or is it just me?" Maddy asked.

Bryce hesitated before realizing that he would've thought that was weird, FBI or no FBI. "It was weird, alright. Is Magnus a Mormon?"

Maddy went to the window, saying over her shoulder, "No. He's agnostic. But there is something cultish about this place, that's for certain. How long has he owned this building?"

Three years. Bryce knew that for a fact. For the last couple of days, he had studied everything he could about the man. For the sake of the cameras, he shrugged. "Who knows? I thought he was still on his island." He went to the refrigerator and looked inside at an assortment of soft drinks and fruit juices. Picking out a Coke, he turned. "And if there's a cult feel, it's no wonder. The guy is a rock star. He's like Midas. Everything he touches turns to gold."

"That's the problem. All he cares about is…"

Maddy swallowed her words as the door suddenly swung open. Daniel Magnus marched in, filling the room with his tremendous presence. His tan was perfect. His teeth were white and ruler-straight. He was far taller than either of them had expected, making Bryce feel runty in comparison.

His ice-blue eyes were a force that had Bryce shaking inside and held Maddy in place. She couldn't move as he walked right up to her. "Doctor Whitmore. It's a pleasure." He took her limp hand and shook it.

"Yes," she said, breathlessly. He indeed had a rock-star's vibe and she was suddenly shy. She was never shy.

Bryce wiped his hand on his carefully pleated pants, and advanced with it out in front of him. He felt like he was somewhere between a dream and a nightmare as Magnus' big hand engulfed his. Through numb lips, he blurted out, "Dag Manulous…I mean Daniel…*Mister* Magnus. I really am your biggest fan. I've been following you since I was a kid."

Magnus smiled warmly, putting Bryce at ease. "And I've been following you since you submitted your doctoral thesis on chromosomal variation codes. It was very impressive. So impressive that I lifted entire sections of it as a primer for some of the work we're doing in the human genome."

This brought Bryce up short. "Lifted? Do you mean stole?"

"Or plagiarized, word for word. Either way works." Magnus smiled broadly at Bryce's stunned look. "Yours was a very important contribution toward our work. And yours as well, Maddy. May I call you Maddy? And you can call me Magnus. I think we might have thirty Daniels, but only one Magnus."

"Do you not use last names here?" Maddy asked.

"And perpetuate the patriarchy? No."

At this Bryce's frown deepened. "The patriarchy. Really?" *Was this a joke? Did he know about the FBI and is making some sort of example out of me?* "And you just stole my work without asking? Without compensation?"

"If I had asked, it wouldn't have been stealing then, would it?" Magnus laughed and clapped Bryce on the shoulder. He sat down at the table and waved for them to do the same. "You'll see we do things differently within these walls. We have a different vision for the future of humanity here. And I would like the two of you to be a part of it."

"I'm under contract at MIT for the rest of the year," Maddy said.

He waved this away with a flick of his hand. "Outside contracts are meaningless to us. I guarantee that nothing will come of you breaking it. And since we're on the subject, we don't use contracts ourselves. At all. You will stay with us for as long as you wish. You may leave any time."

Bryce drummed his fingers on the gleaming wood. The real Bryce wouldn't have been happy. Was this how Magnus did things? He stole a man's hard work? It was criminal. The thought reminded him that he had a duty to perform. "And what would you have us do here?"

"Specifically, I want you to continue your work on isolating weak chromosomal protein pairings. I firmly believe it may be one of the biggest game changers the human race has ever seen, and I'm not just talking about reversing Downs Syndrome or Patau's, or any replication disorder for that matter." Filled with energy, he jumped up and leaned over Bryce. His excitement was sudden and somewhat alarming. "With a full understanding of protein pairings, there isn't a genetic disorder we can't treat."

Magnus understood, Bryce realized. He got it. He had just articulated why Bryce had gotten into the field in the first place. "Exactly."

"And there's more!" Magnus said, grabbing Bryce's shoulders from behind. "The blueprint to build a more perfect person is all there in the DNA."

Bryce was just envisioning this when Maddy said, "Is that what your end goal is? You want to create the perfect race?"

"Yes. We have taken great strides towards that goal, great strides, but there are still improvements to be made."

Silence. The simple answer had stunned the two scientists.

"Would this perfect race be the master race?" Maddy asked, eventually. Bryce's eyes shot to Maddy as she went on, "Sorry to be so blunt, but there is a distinct vibe about this place. We passed thirteen people on the way from the elevator. None wore rings, wedding or otherwise. The women were completely unadorned. Not a one of them wore make-up. Not even lipstick."

"And no one had a cellphone," Bryce added. "Or a purse or a wallet."

"And yet they were all happy," Magnus remarked. "I understand that you're afraid that you've stepped into the headquarters of some sort of cult. And you have. You really have. But it's not what you think. Welcome to Utopia."

Chapter 3

Maddy and Bryce shared a look.

"Utopia," Maddy deadpanned. "That's somewhat disappointing. I expected more from you."

Instead of being upset, Magnus gave her a shrewd look. "And I, you. I thought I would get more of an uproar from Bryce."

"Oh, you will," Maddy assured him. "Bryce's personality is as derivative as his theories. Give him five minutes and he'll be riding whatever wave is strongest."

Forgetting the FBI for a moment, Bryce glared at her. Before he could think of a scathing reply, Magnus sighed. It was an unfeigned, sad sound. "I have gotten off on the wrong foot and yet, I won't lie to you. This is the beginning of a utopia." Standing, he went to the window. "Somewhere along the line, God's creation has gone awry."

"And there it is," Maddy declared. "You started off your career by unleashing the power of technology, which led to you discovering the ungodly power of money. And now you wish to unlock the Holy Grail of control: religion."

"All true," Magnus replied. "To create a utopia…a heaven on earth, if you will, it will take a leap of faith unlike anything you can imagine. You will have to embrace the idea of no more wars, no more hunger, no more murder, no more of the petty bickering that fills our lives."

Bryce's smile dipped and reformed as he struggled with the concept. Like Maddy, he was disappointed with Magnus. "The idea of a utopia is nice, but it's unfeasible. No murder? Come on."

Magnus turned and unfurled his beautifully warm smile. "In all of Iceland, there was only one murder last year and none so far this year. Yes, you will have outliers but a standard of no murder is perfectly feasible."

Once more Bryce was thrown for a loss. "But…but that's Iceland. The demographics are far different than in America."

"Who said I was going to create my utopia in America? One of the first things we're going to have to learn is that to end war, we're going to have to end the concept of nations and borders."

Bryce sighed inwardly. He had heard the adage: *Never meet your heroes*, and now he knew why. "I think the Chinese might have a problem with that. How do you plan on convincing them? Two at a time, like with us?"

"The first step to convincing anyone of anything is to believe it whole heartedly, yourself."

"You didn't answer his question," Maddy blurted. "Which is sad because you had me going for just a moment there. Without a plan, 'no borders' is just something to stick on a bumper sticker to make college kids think they're deep. Maybe we should cut to the chase. You want us to join your little group, and for this great honor do you expect us to sell our cars or give you the deeds to our houses? Sign over our 401Ks?"

"Quite the opposite. I don't want or need your money. Money will very soon be a thing of the past."

Bryce felt a cold spike in his stomach—something bad was coming. Eleven families had come forward with the same warning. "How soon?" The question just jumped out. He had hoped to be more subtle. Then again, the "real" Bryce wouldn't have been. He would want to know the score right off the bat.

Magnus looked at him openly, without the least bit of suspicion. "Sooner than you'd think." He glanced out the window and took a sighing breath before turning back. "Suffice to say your needs will be met and your wants addressed. I won't give you a Corvette but you'll have your own lab and your own team of researchers. You'll be safe, well fed and happy. In return, all I ask is that you help me stamp out the diseases that plague mankind. You'll get full credit, of course. This goes for you as well, Maddy. Your work in mylar synthesizing is the stuff of genius."

Other than the Corvette and a yacht brimming with bikini-clad babes, Magnus had nailed Bryce's desires. Maddy's as well, judging by her slow blinking, stunned look.

"But…" was all she could say. In the simplest term, her mind was boggled.

For Bryce, the list of "buts" was long. He could handle no last names, maybe. Though it begged the question: how was he going to be recognized for his work? Would he just be called: *Bryce*…like Prince or Madonna?

And no money? *Is this his way of legally stealing my work? My intellectual property?* It sure seemed that way. And no borders and no war? Under almost any circumstances, these were a pipe dream. The only exception Bryce could think of was if Daniel Magnus was involved. Even then it sounded too good to be true, especially with the FBI investigating him.

He was trying to figure out his next move when Maddy smirked and shook her head. "How soon will money be a thing of the past?" she demanded, forcing the issue. "Really? You dodged that question just like you dodged the question on borders."

"I'm sorry," Magnus answered. "I truly am. I have so many things going on today that I'm rushing this. Normally, I like to ease people in. The idea of flipping the world on its head takes some time to get used to. And time is just something we don't have a lot of right now."

"Why?" Bryce asked. "What's going to happen?"

Magnus's blue eyes narrowed as he looked Bryce up and down. "Like I said, I'm very busy. I'm going ask Katherine-6 to give you a tour of the facilities, including your labs. Trust me, you'll love them. They are state of the art in every way. I'd do it myself, but I have another twenty people just like you to talk to. Maybe we can get together for dinner tomorrow…"

"How soon will money be a thing of the past?" Maddy asked again. "You said you wouldn't lie to us." She paused, her bushy unplucked eyebrows halfway up her forehead. "Well? How soon do you think money will be a thing of the past?"

Magnus stood slowly. He towered over them and suddenly the aura around him changed. He was no longer the benevolent demi-god who allowed mortals to bask in his glory. There was now a dangerous edge to him. "Sometimes it's a mistake to reveal too much, too soon," he said. "Even when it's in their favor, people rebel against change."

Maddy was undeterred. Fearlessly, she demanded, "How soon? Your best guess." The two locked eyes. Three seconds passed before she grinned. "That's what I thought. You're peddling utopia with nothing but sound bites. You know what you remind me of? One of those TV evangelists. You know, a mega-church preacher. Sure, it may not be money you're after, but you want something from us."

The anger in Magnus dissipated. "In truth, I want you to be happy. And you will be. I'm sure of it. Now, let me get Katherine-6."

"No," she said. "I think I'll be leaving and I'll be taking my research with me. I bet your hackers weren't too happy that I used a double code to conceal my work."

"They were impressed by your thoroughness," Magnus admitted. "Yours as well, Bryce."

Maddy grunted in amazement. "You admit it. Just like that."

"Proudly," he answered. "Like I said, I don't lie. I am trying to create something great here. If it means stealing, then I'll do it. If it means...*detaining* you for a few days, I'll do that, too."

"Detaining?" Bryce asked. "Is that your way of saying kidnapping? What happened to being able to leave whenever we wanted?"

Magnus grimaced as if in pain. "Please stay. Just for the night. Just to give us a chance. I know it seems like we're after you for your work, but we don't want to lose you as individuals. I like to think that everyone who walks through our doors becomes one of us."

"You mean part of the collective?" Maddy asked. "Or part of the hive? I don't believe giving up one's personality is the kind of utopia I'm looking for. Thank you, though." She headed for the door; it was locked. Maddy turned back, her grey eyes flinty. "Open the door. Open the fucking door, or else!"

"I'm sorry, Maddy, but there's really nothing you can threaten me with. I insist that you stay the night for your own safety. I believe that tomorrow will bring new light to the situation. Until then, I can see you to your rooms or you csn go on the tour, or you can..."

Maddy shook the knob and screeched, "Let us out, now!"

This only made Magnus sigh again. Bryce tapped on the table. Then knocked on it. It was solid. It was real. Everything else felt like a terrible dream. At least he had been warned. If he hadn't, he might've been worse off than Maddy.

"I can do more than threaten," he said.

This made Magnus smile. The two could not have been more different in size and shape. Magnus looked capable of bending Bryce over his knee and spanking him.

"Do you think you can call the police?" Magnus asked. "If you take a look at your phone, you'll see that you don't have service." Bryce slid his phone out of his pocket and checked. Maddy did as well. Magnus went on. "Yours are the only two phones in the building. The elevators are under my control as are the stairwell doors. You are stuck here until I say otherwise, so let's try to settle down."

"Fuck you," Maddy hissed.

"You'll find that uncouth language is frowned upon here. I think that maybe you need some time alone. Ron-2!" Maddy jumped back as the burly guard opened the door. "Escort Maddy to her room. You may restrain her if she gets out of hand, physically. Let her yell and curse if she wishes."

Bryce stood up. "No." The word came out sharply, but high-pitched. "She'll remain with me. And yes, I have plenty to threaten you with, Magnus. I work for the FBI."

He hoped that this would make more of an impact than a frown from Magnus. "Yes, the FBI," Bryce added with a little more authority.

Magnus stepped closer and stared down at Bryce, who quailed and shrank back. A sudden need to apologize swept over him. This was followed by an urgent desire to run away. Magnus locked his eyes on Bryce's; the smaller man froze in place. Magnus did not just have a "presence," there was something physical in his stare. Bryce felt like his mind was being opened and his thoughts explored.

He had played poker against some heavy hitters who could read a man's cards by the way he sat or how close his elbows were held into his body. This was far worse. At the poker table, Bryce knew that the only way to combat such perception was to disregard his own cards completely. In this case he had to forget his thoughts, his fears, and even his own memories of Agents Stanley Plinkett and Griffin Meyers.

Bryce drove them from his mind by studying his opponent with his own perception.

What was Magnus hiding? He had twice used the word safe in their brief conversation. It was a word that Bryce might use once a month. Something was coming, just like the FBI said. Was it an asteroid? A plague? A…

"Well," Magnus said, leaning back. "That's interesting and a little upsetting." Bryce knew better than to answer. He held his tongue, knowing that anything he said would only give Magnus more information. "I did not see that in you, Bryce. Impressive. Very impressive."

Maddy had regained a bit of her composure. "What? What's impressive?" To her, he was the same old over-bearing, half-grown Bryce Carter he had always been.

"He is working *with* the FBI. Not for the FBI like he said. As an informant? A snitch?"

Bryce tried to keep the words: *As a spy,* from forming, but they did anyway. He pulled his eyes from Magnus. There was sweat in Maddy's hair and a tiny bit of hope in her eyes. It was a feeling Bryce didn't share, though he tried to rally.

"They think you're kidnapping people. And you are, clearly. They asked me for help on the case and I…"

"So, you were sent to spy on me," Magnus said. "You're a cool customer, Bryce. I like that. I also like how you stood up for Miss Whitmore. That was very gallant. What do you think, Ron? Should I reward this sort of behavior?"

"Your instincts are generally correct, Magnus," Ron-2 said, without taking his eyes from Bryce. "But I wonder if he'll back up his words with his fists. Should I test him?"

The guard took a step towards Bryce, who went pale. Bryce brought up small, shaking hands and balled them into equally small fists. He held them close to his face so that he looked as if he were peeking from behind them.

A laugh burst from Magnus. "Again impressive. You may not be a warrior-king, Bryce but you have something. I like it, and I like you, Bryce. Normally, I would toss you on your ear and let you deal with the coming storm in your own pathetic way, but I think we should give you a chance. Both of you."

"What's that supposed to mean?" Maddy asked.

"I'd much rather have you join us," Magnus said, "but since you won't, I'll settle for the encryption key for your work. If you give it to us, I will let you walk right out the front door."

Maddy hesitated, but Bryce was more willing to fight for his work than he was for his life. "The answer is no. You can't do anything to us."

"We'll see about that," Magnus replied.

"What's that supposed to mean?" Maddy asked a second time.

His smile turned enigmatic. "I have Bryce's response. What about yours? Will you show more of that backbone? Will you tell me to fuck-off again or scurry away with your tail between your legs?"

"Fuck-off." This came out in a whisper.

In unexpected excitement, he slammed the table with his fist. "That's what I wanted to see. You have a fighter inside you as well." His smile was genuine but brief. He marched from the room, bellowing for Katherine-6. Maddy and Bryce stood in uncomfortable silence with Ron-2 standing placidly by the door.

Bryce was sure the goon wore the same calm expression when he was choking his victims to death.

Bryce's head went light at the thought.

Minutes ticked by.

"What's he going to do?" Maddy finally asked Ron-2.

"He's giving you a chance, like he said."

"A chance at what?" Bryce whispered.

Ron-2 shrugged his broad shoulders. "A chance to join us, perhaps. If it is just a chance, it'll be a long painful journey. But maybe that's what you need. Some people are slow to see the world for what it is."

"And what is it?"

"Hell."

The moment Ron-2 said this, Magnus returned with Katherine-6, five very large men, a pair of nurses and two syringes.

"The FBI will be here any moment," Bryce said, pushing Maddy behind him. "You're in enough trouble without…without any of that." He had no idea what was about to happen and whatever gallantry remained in his frail bones was seeping out of him fast. He didn't even try to fight when two of the men latched onto his arms and smashed him to the floor.

"Magnus! Stop this. I demand…" One of the men put a knee on his back and crushed downward, driving the air out of Bryce's lungs. He was pinned like a butterfly in a book.

Magnus dropped down next to him, a syringe in hand. "Katherine, if you'll note that this is Serum-21, syringe number six-one." Katherine-6 had a small blue notebook. Her hand stopped almost before it started and her eyes shot to Magnus. He nodded. "Yes, Serum-21. Test subject is named Bryce Carter. Age twenty-eight. Five-feet, five inches. Weight: a hundred and forty-five pounds. Time 10:32 a.m. Good luck, Bryce."

He jabbed the needle into Bryce's arm and pushed a syringe filled with fire into his muscle.

Chapter 4

The dead came over the wall just as the sun set. There was only a soft golden glow in the west, which was nothing compared to the inferno raging to the north. The Bronx was on fire—all of it.

For some reason, the dead swarmed at sunrise and sunset. They grew manic and would charge at a flapping screen door or attack a swirl of leaves. It took rock-steady nerves to remain motionless when a dozen bloody creatures came roaring in a man's direction. Or a woman's, Maddy thought. There was a high scream and suddenly the dead were everywhere. Hiding was no longer an option. Maddy let the first few pass before she stepped out from behind a van and swung her bat. It felt light in her hand and yet it had enough weight behind it to crush a skull.

She reversed her grip and whipped the bat left-handed at the next of the frothing-mad creatures. Just as she did, its foot came off the sidewalk and it dipped. The bat clipped the top of its greasy head, tearing a chunk of diseased flesh away. It wobbled in place, its eyes losing focus for just a second.

This gave Maddy enough time to swing the bat again. Tank! Its skull cracked like an egg and shards of bone went deep.

Maddy spun, moving with a grace that only a dream could give. Down went another of the black-eyed beasts. And another. But when one fell, two took its place. She was being swarmed from all directions and no amount of grace or quickness would save her. She reached for the gun at her hip.

To shoot would be a death sentence for most of her group. Instead of a hundred beasts, they would be neck-deep in a thousand. Her hand hesitated as the morality of her action struck her. But there was no time for hesitation. A clawed hand slashed at her neck, drawing blood. Another beast slammed into her.

It tripped on the curb and as it stumbled, it pulled her down as well. Something fell across her legs and now the gun was out. She aimed, but as she did, a shadow swept over her. Bryce stood over her, looking tall and golden in the last light as he swung his axe in a...

"Bryce?" the word slithered from her aching throat as she woke. Her grey eyes flicked open and a groan escaped her. At least it started out as a groan, but it then turned into a whimper.

Every part of her was in misery. Her joints most of all…no, now that they were open, her eyes were the worst. They felt huge and thick. They pulsed in their sockets.

Above her, the lights were unpleasantly bright. Slowly, her neck creaking, she turned her head to the side and saw the IV stand; it held three different bags of fluids. What sort they were, she didn't have a clue. The writing was fuzzy.

Mounted on the wall behind it was a monitor that showed her vital signs. She could read the tiny words "heart rate" perfectly. The rhythmic up and down of a normal pulse was not in evidence. The beats on her monitor were racing each other faster and faster, without pause.

Unbelievably, her pulse was 162 beats a minute. As bad as that was, her blood pressure was worse at 224 over 140.

As a woman who had been "pleasantly plump" for her entire life, she knew the dangers of such high blood pressure. A blood vessel in her brain could explode and she'd be a vegetable in a blink. The very idea of being helpless and trapped in her own body like it was a flesh coffin, shook her to her core.

With the bones of her neck grinding together, she turned her head back the other way and felt clammy coldness on her cheek. Her pillow was wet with sweat, as was her entire bed. She was drenched.

"What happened?" The two words clawed their way from her throat in a whisper.

Something stirred down past the foot of her bed. With another moan, she lifted her head and saw that she had a visitor. A rumpled, balding man in his forties, slept in an awkward position draped across two plastic chairs.

"FBI," Maddy said. Somehow, she knew this as a fact even though her memory was disjointed and twisted. Nothing was in focus and nothing made sense. She had been on a helicopter, and there had been a purple hallway—no, the carpet had been purple. And Magnus was there. "And Bryce." She remembered Bryce as being tall, strong, fierce. "No, that was a dream."

The paunchy man sat up. "Miss Whitmore?"

"It's *Ms*. Whitmore." She felt stupid the moment she said this. As far as she could tell, she was on the verge of dying. At this point, what did it matter if she was called Miss or Ms?

"What happened?" she asked.

"I was going to ask you the same thing," Plinkett said. "You and Bryce met with Daniel Magnus at his plaza and were in the building for maybe a half an hour before an ambulance was called."

"An ambulance?" Fear rippled through her at the thought. The last thing she could remember about being in Magnus' tower was being afraid, but didn't know why. She looked down at herself. Her gown was plastered to her body with sweat. A quick check beneath it showed the same pale flesh that kept her out of the sun at all costs. There wasn't a single bruise on her.

Plinkett rubbed his scruffy jaw before answering, "Yes. You were on LSD. You and Bryce. They said you two showed up acting a little strange. It then exploded into some sort of panic attack and that's when they called 911."

"I didn't take any acid. And Bryce…Bryce on drugs? No way. He can't handle a jalapeno. Back in school, his drink of choice was a strawberry wine cooler. No. No, they did something to us. I remember Bryce getting mad." The word *gallant* floated through her mind, though she couldn't connect it to anything.

"I have the test results. It's true. And there were other drugs in your system. Still are, I should say. LSD, meth and pot. It's a weird combination. You and Bryce are lucky to be alive."

Maddy grimaced as she pushed herself up. "Where is he? I need to talk to him. Something happened in there." She stopped, her face slack. "Hold on. Bryce was working for you. For the FBI. He tried to stop them from…no, Bryce tried to stop *him*. Bryce tried to stop Magnus from taking our work."

She remembered Magnus clearly. He had been huge and strong, and gloriously handsome. Even there in the bed, sweaty, aching and sick, she felt a strange tingle for the man.

"Was there anything else?" Plinkett asked. "Did he mention terrorist attacks? A viral outbreak? No? Shit. Okay, what about kidnapping?"

The word set off an echo in her head that went nowhere. She was trying to chase it down when Agent Griffin Meyers burst in. He paused at the sight of Maddy. He stared at her for half a second before blurting out, "There's been another one. London. Turn on the TV."

"Another one what?" Maddy asked.

Plinkett, fiddling with the remote, replied, "A terrorist attack. It started in L.A. two hours ago. Then Chicago. Then Mexico City."

The images on the television were of burning buildings and people running. It made no sense to Maddy, and it hurt her eyes. The agents' phones began to ring. The sound drilled into her ears. While the agents spoke in hushed, nervous tones, she rang the nurses call button.

"I need something," she told the nurse who came hurrying in. At first glance, Maddy saw she had velvety dark skin that made her seem like she was twenty instead of her real age of thirty-five. When Maddy looked closer, she saw the woman's individual pores and the tiny cracks around her eyes and mouth. The woman was clearly harried, busier than she was used to, and yet she was also hesitant, with a wary look on her face.

"Sorry, hun. You're on everything we can give you. We can't have you going into liver failure on us."

"Liver's fine," Maddy gasped. "It's everything else." Now that she was concentrating on the pain, it was like her body was filled with shards of broken glass.

The nurse gave her a sympathetic shrug. "Let me check with the doctor. He'll want to see you either way. Just hang in there."

Once the nurse left, Maddy turned her attention back to the TV. There were fires now in Moscow as well as London. It was a "Breaking Report," but it felt like more of the same. Without knowing why, she crawled out of bed and stood on shaking legs. Pulling off her leads set off alarms. She cringed from the sound and wheeled her IV stand out of the room and into a crowded hallway.

It was only then that she realized she was in an ICU. Across from her was an open bay where six beds and an uncountable amount of medical machinery were set at regular, but close, intervals. Each bed was occupied, as were two gurneys that were set against the wall.

Two nurses were in sight. One, heavy-set with a fake blonde mane, was opening drawer after tiny drawer in a med closet, and the other was the lady who had denied her more meds. She had a phone cocked to her ear as she typed furiously on a computer. Above her was the white board where patient information was open for everyone to see.

Maddy saw her own name first. Her diagnosis was cardiac dysrhythmia. The letters O.D. were circled in red. Below her name was Bryce's. He was in room 317, the next room over.

"You have to get back in bed," the fake-blonde nurse snapped. "We'll get to you when we can."

"Sure, got it." Maddy turned slowly, but instead of going into her room, she slipped into Bryce's.

A single sheet covered his spare frame; his face was obscured by an oxygen mask. Unlike her, he wasn't drenched in sweat, and his heart rate and blood pressure weren't through the roof. He looked to be sleeping.

"Bryce," she hissed. Easing forward, she shook his foot. "Bryce!"

"He's in a coma." It was the black nurse again. Her dark eyes were hard, harder than they needed to be. "Leave him alone and get back into your room." She was thin and stringy but exuded strength. She was ready to fight…somehow Maddy knew this…no, not somehow. It was all there: the tense muscles, the increased respiration, the gritting of her teeth, the dilated pupils.

Maddy was in no position to do much of anything, least of all fight. "I just wanted to see how he was doing. I was worr…" His foot jerked beneath her hand and she snatched it back. "Bryce?"

He woke like she did, moaning, though in her ears he sounded pitiful. "Bryce. Hey, look at me. Try not to think about the pain." She hobbled around to the side of the bed.

"What happened?" He sounded like a frog croaking. "Where are we?"

"The hospital. They did something to us. Magnus drugged us, I think. He told the cops that we were on LSD, but that never happened. Did it?"

Before he could answer, the nurse pushed between them. "That's enough Miss Whitmore. I need to let the doctor know that Mr. Carter is awake."

"Then get calling. No one's stopping you." Maddy was in a sour mood from the pain and wasn't going to be bossed around by anyone. She glared the nurse out the door and then turned back to Bryce. He was whimpering as he tried to open his hand.

"This can't be what LSD feels like," he said. "Who would ever do it? Oh God, it hurts. My joints…like there's glass in them."

Maddy grabbed his arm and he stifled a cry. "You have to move. The more you move, the better you'll feel." She bent his thin arm without warning.

"Fuck!"

"Don't be a baby." He was clearly overreacting. There was no way his pain could be as bad as hers. His vital signs were basically normal.

He was red-faced, and there were tears in his eyes when the two FBI agents marched in, followed by the black nurse and a stern, grey-haired man. Maddy assumed he was a doctor by the white coat he wore over green scrubs.

"Thank goodness you're awake," Griff said. "The shit's hitting the fan out there, and we need to know what you found out. What is Magnus doing?"

Before Bryce could catch a shaky breath, the doctor intervened. "Enough! This patient just emerged from an altered cognitive state. He will not be interviewed until I clear him of any…"

Plinkett barked, "Shut your mouth. Griff, get him out of here. The nurse, too." The doctor let out a cry of outrage as Griff shoved him from the room. He only had to look at the nurse to get her moving. When they were gone, Plinkett gave Bryce a strained smile. "What happened in there?"

"We just talked. We didn't do drugs, I swear." He looked to Maddy and she nodded with tiny painful jerks of her head. "Everything was fine at first, then Magnus said he stole our work. Then he threatened to hold us there overnight."

"To keep us safe," Maddy added. "But he never said what from."

Bryce nodded, then grimaced. "He said safe *twice*."

Plinkett looked from one to the other, waiting for them to go on. "And? Come on. I need something actionable."

"I don't remember," Bryce admitted. "He threatened to hold Maddy against her will. I remember that. I know I should've let him and continued on with the mission, but he was acting scary and I thought he was going to do something to her. Either way, I told him that I was working with you guys and he left…I think." Everything from the moment Magnus had left was fuzzy and made no sense. "He said something about giving us a chance, and that's it. Then I woke up here."

"That's it?" Plinkett snapped. "There are terrorists attacking fourteen American cities. Concentrate! What was he keeping you safe from? What was the chance he was talking about?"

Maddy felt a sudden shock of guilt. She had screwed up. Instead of holding in her temper, she had told Magnus to fuck off—and now there were terrorists attacking multiple cities. How the two were connected, she didn't know.

"He never said," she answered. "Look, I can go back and try to talk to him. I can wear a wire if you want. He knows about Bryce working with you, but he knows I wasn't."

Plinkett chewed his lip for a moment. "Maybe. It'll be a long shot and we'd need a good excuse for you to go in. I bet we can get a warrant expedited. What do you think, Griff?"

Griff was at the window, staring out in something of a trance. He had slowly become aware of a low mewling noise that had been constantly in the background for the last hour or so. Curious, he had gone to the window and was shocked to see dozens of flashing lights scattered across the small swath of the city that was in sight.

There were police cars racing chaotically in all directions. The firetrucks were more orderly, moving in little squads towards a dozen plumes of smoke. On the street five stories below, a scrum of ambulances pushed around each other, cutting one another off in a hurry to unload their casualties.

"I don't know if we have time for any of that," Griff said.

Chapter 5

As Griff watched, a police car careened around the corner, its siren warbling. It missed hitting an ambulance by inches and would've struck an EMT if the driver hadn't yanked the wheel to the right, sending the cruiser onto the sidewalk.

In the back of the car was a raving Bree McDaniels. Mad black eyes peered from a window that was smeared with God only knew what. There was blood in her hair and on her chin. There were curls of flesh beneath her fingernails. Her once pert nose was quashed and her lips were swollen and split.

Five hours earlier, she had boarded the Number 7 Train in Queens and experienced a New York rarity when a rag-covered bum sat down next to her. Right away, she noticed that his hair wasn't crawling with lice. Even more surprising, he didn't stink like piss. As miraculous as this was, he still wasn't normal.

He rocked back and forth, muttering to himself and holding a thermos with both hands, treating it as if it were some sort of idol.

Slowly, she eased as far away from him as possible, afraid that he would get angry if she simply hopped up and ran from him. Thankfully, he staggered to the door as the train pulled into the next stop. Bree let out a long sigh of relief, but then happened to glance down and saw he had left behind his thermos. For just a moment, she considered grabbing it and taking it to the bum. She even had her hand out to it, but her fingers recoiled as she pictured his lips on it.

He left and she said nothing. She and the thermos were still there, gently rocking back and forth, five minutes later when the cap popped off on its own. It rolled away like a little wagon wheel. She watched it until it came to rest against the boot of a sleeping construction worker. Then her eyes were drawn to the thermos—would there be brown liquor inside? Murky questionable soup? The moldy, rotting remains of a child's ear?

At first, all she saw was a wisp of grey fog lifting from the opening. Then she saw an oblong chunk of ice…and that was it.

Bree McDaniels essentially died right then.

Yes, she felt fine for the next couple of hours as she worked the swing shift at a paleo juice bar, but gradually a raging headache sent her into the back room. The darkness helped, as did the weed and the oxycontin. But even these had their limits and soon she stormed out into the lobby, screamed in an incoherent rage at the room-full of customers and attacked the store's sound system.

With each punch, plastic flew. "It's too…fucking…early… for…Christmas…music!"

When Tenisha, the manager, shouted at her to stop, Bree launched herself on the bigger girl and tore flesh from her face before blinding her with her claws. Screeching at the top of her lungs, Tenisha tore herself away from Bree and flailed away, one hand clutching her face, the other out in front waving at the air.

Next, two customers jumped in. She bit the throat out of one and got punched in the face by the second. Richie Orr, who had arms like twigs and a concave chest, had never been in a fight in his life and the only punch he'd ever thrown was when he hit his sister in the sixth grade.

Bree didn't feel the blow land. Nor did she feel him grab a fistful of her hair. But she tasted his blood when she bit down on his wrist. He screamed high and piercing and he began slapping at Bree with his left hand. Three other customers joined in the melee and held her down.

"Someone call the fucking police!" Richie cried.

The police were dialed, but they were dealing with a hundred calls much worse than one relatively small, crazy girl. Six blocks away, a man was rampaging through central park, stabbing anyone he came across. Another man burst into St. Patrick's Cathedral and attacked nuns and school children. A third tore through Macy's killing a half-dozen people and wounding a score more before being brought down in a hail of bullets.

The moment the police dealt with one of these crazies, two more took their place…then five more…then ten. The calls about Bree varied between a cat-fight and someone freaking out on meth. Bree was given a low priority and then forgotten about.

An hour passed. After such a long wait, one of the men holding Bree down relaxed his grip a little too much and she spun like a greased leopard, sinking her teeth into his bicep and tearing out a mouthful of meat.

The shop was basically closed at that point. The blind manager had been whisked away by cab and other than the three men holding Bree down, there weren't any other customers left in the building. The rest had since slipped away. One of the two employees left in the store suggested that they tie Bree up, using an electrical cord. This was agreed to without hesitation.

The men bound her wrists and ankles, and cinched the cords down tight enough to bite into her flesh.

Unfortunately, none of them had been in the scouts, and the knots weren't as secure as they could've wished. Bree snarled and hissed as she fought her bonds, and it wasn't long before she had one foot free, then, a minute later, a hand. By then, one of the employees had snuck out the back, and two of the customers had made excuses and left.

"Fuck it," the last employee said as she untied her apron. "This job was never worth this." She chucked the apron at Bree and walked out the front door.

This left only a bank teller named Andrew, who lost his nerve and rushed out as well. Once outside he summoned enough courage to put his shoulder to the door, thinking he could hold back such a small woman. The street was crowded with people, all rushing back and forth. Things were getting weird and the sight of a man fighting to hold a woman in a juice bar just added to it.

No one asked if he needed help.

The door shuddered as the two struggled in their strange battle. Andrew prevailed and was just barely strong enough to hold the door closed. Inside, Bree raged, screaming so loud she shredded her vocal cords. She threw herself against the door, no longer wishing to open it. She wanted to destroy it, and for a moment, Andrew was afraid it would come apart.

But it held and there was a pause.

"Thank God," Andrew whispered. His relief was honest and yet he knew better than to relax. The girl was something out of a horror film and he had seen enough of those to know you never relaxed until the monster/killer was reduced to ashes, and even then, it made sense to make a paste out of it with Holy Water. He was right to be afraid.

The undead creature that had once been Bree McDaniels couldn't think as she once had, but her mind wasn't completely destroyed. She still had murky memories and some part of her could reason out the very simplest puzzles. She fixated on the window and somewhere inside the darkness of her mind she saw a vision of glass breaking.

Grabbing a chair, she hammered it against the window. It took six strikes before the glass shattered. By then Andrew was already gone. After the first hit, he fled into a city that had changed a great deal in the last few hours. There was panic in the air…and screams—these filled Bree with malevolent energy as she jumped through the remains of the window. Her dark eyes locked onto a woman across the street who was in the Thanksgiving spirit and wore a festive orange blouse and brown pants.

Ignoring the cars filling the street and the people in them, Bree charged at the woman, who screamed at the sight of her bloody clothes and ran. The woman blazed past an old man with a cane, a yamaka, and no peripheral vision. He never saw Bree coming.

"Watch where you're go…" he started to say just before Bree crashed into him.

He was dead in seconds.

In the next hour, Bree killed three more people and infected seventeen, including the police officer who had wrangled her into the squad car which Agent Griffin Meyers saw trundling up the sidewalk towards the hospital. It was becoming clear that jailing people like Bree was the wrong tactic. All over the city, jail cells were turning into murder rooms painted in blood and decorated with the flesh of the dead. Someone thought it was a good idea to attempt to use chemical restraints instead of physical ones and now ERs were being flooded with murderous cannibals.

Griff watched Bree smash at the car's windows with her forehead. "It's happening here. Whatever's going on in L.A. and Chicago is happening here, too. We could go to a judge, but we both know that could take hours."

"We *are* going to a judge," Plinkett barked. "And it'll take as long as it takes. If we show up without a warrant, Magnus will just lock his doors. He's under no obligation to do jack-shit if we don't have a warrant. And if he is behind this, he might just have a small army with him."

"Look at this," Griff said, jabbing a finger at the window. "Look out there. A judge'll take too long. Do you hear that?" They all cocked an ear. Below the mewling could be heard a smattering of small arms fire.

Plinkett nodded, making his soft under-chin bounce. "Yeah, I hear it." He went to the window; his eyes shot back and forth, and as they did, his lips pursed until they disappeared. "Shit."

Maddy hobbled to stand next to him, and like Plinkett, her eyes zipped to every flashing light, and there were a lot of them. "Magnus said we'd be safe if we stayed. Maybe we should've."

Bryce tried to sit up far enough to look out, but it hurt too much and he wilted down. "I can go back. I'll tell Magnus I changed my mind. He'll take me. My work is important."

"No more than mine is," Maddy said, sharply. "Besides, you may not come out again. You sound a little desperate if you ask me. A little scared."

"We're in this mess because I was too brave," Bryce answered her, glaring.

Plinkett slammed his palm against the window. "Shut up, both of you. Why would they take you back, Bryce? They know you're working with us." He turned, hands on his hips. His gun was just visible beneath his jacket. "I'll go get the warrant. Griff, you'll stay here with them. Get a full statement and email it to my phone, asap."

When Plinkett left, Griff didn't immediately start the interview. The three of them sat without speaking, listening to the city. Blaring horns and the wail of sirens were always something of a constant in the city, but now they were on a level that surpassed anything they had ever heard. With every passing second, the decibel level climbed and the sounds were merging into a strange rumble that was punctuated by the pop, pop, pop of handguns. These would come in short bursts. Interspersed, here and there, was the boom of a shotgun.

"This is crazy," Bryce said through gritted teeth. He had finally gotten out of the bed and stood hunched in on himself at the window. He couldn't move without sucking in a gasping breath. "Magnus never said anything like this was going to happen. He said he could keep us safe. How? We're going to be in the middle of World War 3 any moment."

This turned out to be a wild over-exaggeration. No one, on any level of government, knew what was going on. They were as blind, and as blind-sided as the average person. Terror attacks was the fallback guess most people had, but that didn't jibe with the footage being broadcast on every channel. The talking heads at the networks were all over the board. They had "experts" who were also arguing that the water supply had been drugged by the government, that aliens were attacking, that the Chinese were using advanced mind control, and that the South had risen again!

Nothing made sense and that included the answers Maddy and Bryce gave to Griff. They spoke over each other, snarked back and forth, sat in sullen silences, and generally had no idea what had happened to them.

Griff was in the middle of writing what felt like a useless report when Bryce frantically grabbed the television remote and aimed it at the TV. "Read the chyron! Area hospitals and police stations are believed to be the focal points for the attacks. Mayor warns citizens not to…"

The current feed jumped to another expert, this one on the psychology of climate change, and the chyron changed to a report on the crashing markets.

"What?" demanded Maddy. "What did the mayor say?"

"Does it matter?" Bryce asked in a whisper. "Listen."

There were screams coming from down the hall. It sounded as if someone was being eaten alive. Griff hurried to the door and snatched it open just as the two nurses flashed past. They charged into a room three doors down and were followed by a pair of burly orderlies dressed in all white. Two more orderlies stood across from Bryce's room. They were big, thick men and looked more like wrestlers than anything else.

"No one out of their room," one growled.

"I'm not a patient," Griff explained. "I'm FBI." He flashed his badge, but neither man bothered to look at it.

"You're a patient now. This floor has been quarantined. Get back in your room."

Griff noted how loose their white coats were and how each man had their right hands held close to their hips. It was an unnatural stance unless they meant to pull a gun. These were not orderlies.

Chapter 6

For a moment, Griff thought about going for his gun. He was fast and his aim was deadly, but...

There were a number of "buts" that stayed his hand. Was the quarantine real? Were these men trained to a higher standard than a couple of bored bank guards? And where were the other two orderlies? Were they armed as well? He had to assume they were.

"Quarantine, huh?" Griff said. "That makes sense. I guess." He gave the man a friendly nod and received a cold stare in return. Shutting the door behind him, he paused for a moment staring at the faux wood, unable to answer any of the questions that had popped into his mind. When he turned, he saw that Bryce and Maddy were frozen in place, gaping at him; he didn't need to ask if either had heard.

"Magnus did this," Bryce said in a frightened whisper. He was so quiet that they had to lean in to hear him. "He did something to us and now he's trying to keep us locked up here so he can keep an eye on us. Or...or to study us."

"You think he's using us as guinea pigs?" Maddy asked. Her hands went to her damp gown. Beneath it, her stomach was starting to churn in fear. Together, their fear was like an electric current running between them and as that current went back and forth, it grew.

Bryce had never considered himself an overly brave person. The one flash of courage he'd shown in Magnus' tower had come with the full backing of the FBI. Now all he had was one young agent. It didn't feel like near enough.

Maddy had a shrill courage that relied almost wholly on the civilized nature of her fellow man. Deep down, she was sure that no one would ever *really* hurt her. For her, true evil was a rarity, a threat for those in the hood or the trailer park, but not to someone firmly ensconced in the top 2%, and certainly not someone with an Ivy League education. This thinking was a gossamer shield that she pretended didn't exist.

The horrid screams sifting up through the building were beginning to erode that imaginary shield. The TV caught her eye. The news station was showing footage of a small woman attacking an old man. The flesh of his neck was loose and sagging, and when she bit into it and pulled back, it stretched like taffy. "Is that going to be us?" Maddy asked.

Bryce stared at the TV in horror. "God, I hope not."

When another expert replaced the bloody footage, they all looked away. Griff went to the window. There were even more flashing lights, strobes of red and blue in the darkness. People were running on the street. A few blocks away, there was a building on fire. It was a rectangle of steel and glass jutting thirty stories into the air. Around its waist was a belt of flame and smoke. *How many people were trapped inside?*

"Hundreds." And yet there were only two fire trucks visible and no ambulances. None. Looking down, Griff saw there were still over a dozen on the street below. "This is all wrong. This isn't a terrorist attack. It would've taken hundreds, if not thousands of men…suicidal men and women, to do this."

"And it's not mind control," Maddy noted. "That thing on the TV didn't have a mind. So, is it a plague unleashed by Daniel Magnus?"

"He said he wanted to create a utopia," Bryce muttered. "Did he screw up, or is this all on purpose? And where do we fit in? He did this to us but…but I think we're different from all of them out there going crazy. If a thousand people in New York had been suffering like us, it would've been news. Someone would've noticed a bunch of full ICUs. Right?"

Before answering, Griff glanced up at the TV—for the last hour, his eyes had been constantly drawn to it. "Yeah, someone would've noticed. We get alerts when things are strange and I didn't get anything about ICUs. At five, we had alerts of ERs being targeted in California, but that's it. Two hours later, everything is fucked. I think we need to see if this quarantine is legit."

He pulled his cell phone and was greeted with the message: *All Circuits Are Busy. Please Try Again Later*. "Shit. Do either of you have your phones?"

Bryce looked around and found that he didn't have his phone, his wallet, or his clothes. He also saw that his IV had run dry. He pressed the call nurse button. "Maybe the nurse can tell us something." The nurse took twenty minutes to answer the ringing chime, and when she came in, her eyes were dark with anger.

"What?" she demanded, staring straight at Bryce without blinking. "What is it? What the fuck is everyone calling and calling about? Huh? What? What do you want!"

Her voice was a high screech that had him instantly regretting calling her. With a shaking hand, he pointed up at his IV bag, which sagged, completely deflated. "It's empty. I didn't know if that was bad." It seemed bad, especially as his bright red blood was beginning to seep up into the tube. Her eyes latched onto the blood.

"It ain't nothing," she said, quieter now. She seemed mesmerized by the blood. "None of it. This is all nothing. None of it matters. Not the money. Not the job. Not my pounding head. My head is the worst of all." As she spoke, she walked to the edge of Bryce's bed, the whole time, staring at the tube. "There's only one thing that matters now."

Bryce eased back and covered the lower end of the tube with a pillow. "Hey, it's okay. The IV is okay the way it was."

She finally blinked and for a few seconds, a normal person stood in front of him. "They're watching you, but I guess that don't matter now either." She sighed then grimaced as if even breathing hurt. Just before she turned away, she grabbed the exposed tube and yanked it out of his arm. "There. All fixed."

It stung like a wasp sting and he hissed in a breath. The nurse didn't notice. She walked from the room and shut the door behind her.

"She's the one that needs to be quarantined," Bryce snapped. He was bleeding from where the catheter had been ripped from his skin. "The good news is at least we know we weren't on drugs. Magnus wouldn't bother watching a pair of druggies."

"But he did *something* to us," Maddy said. She looked down at her own IV and then frantically began to tear at the tape holding it in place. When the catheter was exposed, she ripped it out and rushed to the sink, where she furiously scrubbed her arm until it was red. As she was rinsing off, she paused, her face going pale. "Maybe we should be quarantined. It only makes sense if we're going to be like them."

They all looked up at the TV.

Griff backed away a few steps. Bryce snapped at him, "Stop. You're supposed to be the tough one. And we're not like those people on TV. Is Magnus watching them? No. At least, not like this he isn't. He did something…special to us. Maybe in the end, we'll be like them. Or maybe he's using us to test a vaccine against whatever all that is. I don't know. If we are special, we need to escape and find a real hospital."

"This is a real hospital," Griff said.

"You know what I mean. One that doesn't have goons."

"And one far away from here," Maddy added.

"How do we escape?" Griff asked.

Bryce shrugged and Maddy frowned. "You're the gun expert," she stated, as if this alone meant he should be able to formulate plans in a blink.

"And you two are geniuses," he shot back. After another glance at the screen where stalled cars on a Santa Monica freeway were being attacked, he muttered, "For now, at least." He eased around Maddy and went to the little sink. In the cubby beneath it, he found a box of masks and another of latex gloves. He donned a mask and a pair of gloves, then tossed some to the other two. "Just in case you don't have what they have."

Maddy slipped the mask over her face only to reverse the move a second later. "Do you smell that? Is that smoke?"

Bryce breathed deep until he caught just a slight tang of something acrid. "It is."

Griff pulled his mask far enough back to take a few whiffs. "I don't smell anything." He went to the door and sniffed there as well. He was just putting his mask back in place when an alarm began to ring somewhere deep in the building. "Shit. This day just keeps getting better and…"

He was interrupted by gunfire from two floors down. Bryce drew his feet off the floor and sucked his hands to his chest, while Maddy stepped closer to the bed. They acted as if it were some sort of magical island of normalcy that could protect them.

"Don't mo…" Griff started to say, but stopped at the sight of them. They clearly weren't going anywhere. He pulled his pistol and slowly opened the door, keeping the gun hidden.

One of the orderlies stood against the far wall, a hand beneath his white jacket. He had military cut brown hair, cold grey eyes and was a twitch away from pulling a gun. The second orderly was behind the nurses' desk, his hands out of sight.

Other than the two men and a few empty gurneys, the hallway was empty.

Griff nodded to the orderly across from him. The man made no move. He only stared. "There's a fire." Griff said this calmly, in the same way he might comment on the weather.

"It's a drill."

Cold silence.

Griff tried again, "The quarantine has failed. Have you looked out the window? Do you see what's happening out there?"

"No. My business is right here and only right here. Your business is getting back in that room." When Griff didn't move, the man added, "I don't know if you've guessed this or not, but you are extraneous. Unneeded. Try not to become unwanted."

The two men eyed each other, while to the side, the presence of the other orderly loomed. Griff wouldn't be able to get them both. All three knew it.

Griff slowly shut the door. The room was so quiet, that when he tried his phone again, they could all hear the same message play. "Okay, we're fucked," he told them. "We can wait until my partner gets back, or we can hope the hospital staff comes for us, or we shoot our way out. That's it. Those are our choices."

They were awful choices. Griff didn't think they could afford to wait with a fire in the building. And what would happen if Bryce or Maddy turned raving mad? And shooting their way out was suicide. *Maybe* he could get the orderly guarding the door, but there was no way he'd be able to take down the second one. And where were the other two he had seen earlier?

It was a given that they weren't real either. Magnus could afford an entire battalion of fake orderlies.

"There's got to be another way out," Maddy said. Her tone suggested that this was a fact, and that if it wasn't, she was going to need to speak to a manager. She waddled around, grunting in pain, checking drawers, the security of the windows, the width of the air vents—all were too small to fit her girth. Increasingly wild, hair-brained ideas flashed into her mind; each came with the whisper of the old movie line: *That's so crazy it just might work!*

In the end, they waited, listening to the horns and the sirens, the guns and the screams, the volume of which swelled with each passing minute. They made escaping seem even more deadly than simply staying put.

But that was an illusion. The fire in the building grew and grey smoke began to fill the halls. Someone on their floor began to beg to be untied. Then the person began to scream in madness.

She was still screaming when the elevator opened with a plume of smoke. The doors were barely open before a violent fight spilled out into the hallway. Two black-eyed men were attacking three women, punching, biting, tearing their hair out by the roots. One of the women was screeching in terror, but the other two were in the pain-maddened phase of turning, and were fighting back, ripping open faces with their long, salon-toughened claws.

The orderly at the desk, Don Boggs, stood, Sig Sauer in hand, and waited. They were killing each other; he figured there was no reason to waste bullets. He and the other mercs had received a quick briefing three hours before and when he heard the type of "altered" humans they'd have to deal with: hyper-aggressive, immune to pain, cannibalistic, reduced cognitive ability, he had simply said, "You mean zombies, right?"

"If that's how you want to classify them, that's fine with me," their captain answered. "Just as long as you realize that they're not people."

Boggs was an ex-soldier, an ex-cop and a full-time asshole; he didn't care one way or another, as long as the check cleared at the end of the day.

Chapter 7

The little battle in front of Boggs ended as the men eventually prevailed, killing the one uninfected woman and breaking the neck of one of the others. It was then that the remaining three saw him standing there.

Ignoring the gun in his hands, they charged over and through the front desk, knocking it down. Generally, center mass was Boggs' way of thinking, but if these were zombies, he had to go for the head. At this range—almost within arm's reach—he couldn't miss. The first man went down with a hole, neat as you please, in the center of his forehead.

The next took one in the eye, and the third shifted slightly at the last moment and had his ear blown clean off. Boggs followed it up by putting a nine-millimeter hole between his eyes.

The man fell but did not die. Bullets did strange things sometimes. They spun, tumbled, and ricocheted in the oddest manners. After striking the very lower edge of the frontal bone, the bullet took an immediate dive and blasted down through the nasal cavity, passed through the mouth and exploded out the bottom of the jaw. The man dropped.

In line with Boggs' training, he was just ejecting his old magazine to replace it with a full one, when the man lurched upward in a clumsy attack. Clumsy or not, the two fell backwards over the chair Boggs had been sitting in. They went down in a twist of arms and legs. The magazine fell away and his second was still on his belt, pinned behind him.

Boggs was a brute of a man and very strong. He was able to lift his attacker off of him, but it cost him his right thumb, which was bitten off.

"Christ!" The pain was like nothing he'd ever felt before. Even though his thumb was the problem, his entire right arm seemed to go flaccid and the creature fell onto him. "Wilkes! Get him off of me!"

Wilkes, the cold-eyed orderly, abandoned his watch on the door and ran to help his comrade. A single shot was all it took, but by then Griff was in the hall, his pistol aimed at the back of Wilkes' head.

Griff had heard the commotion and had been waiting for something like this to happen. "Don't you fucking move!" he barked at Wilkes. "Slowly, get those hands up. Come on. I will shoot you." Cursing under his breath, Wilkes raised his hands. When he did, Griff said, "Bryce, get out here. Get his gun."

"Me?"

Maddy, who was in the doorway next to Bryce, elbowed him and they both grimaced. Their intense pain was only slowly fading and any quick movement brought it right back. "Fine," Bryce grumbled. He was barefoot and squeamish about stepping in any of the blood; he had no idea what was contaminated and what wasn't. The floor wasn't just dappled, it was a gory mess.

He tiptoed through it as if he were walking through a minefield. Then, when he got close to Wilkes, he was struck numb with fear. This was a trained killer. In every movie he had ever seen, they were fast as lightning and always seemed able to turn the tables on someone as meek as Bryce.

Stretching out his arm from ridiculously far away, he snatched the pistol and grabbed it in both hands.

"Careful," Wilkes said, looking back over his shoulder. "That thing's ready to go. Maybe put the safety on?"

"Maybe he doesn't," Maddy replied. She would've been a lot happier if she had the gun. Even though she had never fired one before, she was sure she would be better than Bryce.

"Yeah, don't," Griff said. He nudged Bryce back, grabbed Wilkes by the collar and shoved him against the wall. In a matter of seconds, he was expertly frisked. Bryce pointed his gun at Wilkes as Griff searched Boggs. He found the gun and the magazines. All three were bloody. He kicked them over to Maddy. "Use alcohol to clean those."

"No shit," Maddy said, rolling her eyes. "Did you think I was going to lick them clean?"

Griff growled, "Just clean them."

Wilkes was watching them, his head kinked far around on his neck. "I have cars coming. I'm supposed to escort the geek and the woman back to Magnus Plaza. We have room for one more."

"Geek?" Bryce waggled the gun at him. "I think you should be a little more careful who you're calling a geek. And Maddy and I aren't going anywhere with you." Bryce glanced over at Maddy, who was at the nurses' sink scrubbing the gun. She nodded defiantly.

"It's the only way you'll be safe," Wilkes explained. "We have a pair of big-ass Yukon Denalis on their way, and you'll have an eight-man security team. Seven, now. You need any help, Boggs?"

Boggs was red-faced, rocking back and forth, clutching his wounded hand. "I need a fucking doctor who can stitch my damned thumb back on."

Griff shook his head. "First, tell me where the others are? Where's the rest of your crew?"

Wilkes held up a finger and cocked his head. There was gunfire below them. "That's them. They're keeping a lane open for us. I think the shit's coming unglued faster than Magnus thought it would."

"What shit is that?" Griff asked.

"Dunno." Wilkes' eyes dropped. He suddenly seemed lost and uncertain. "Whatever it is, I'm starting to wonder if we're a part of his big picture." He and Boggs shared a look. "Magnus is way over-paying us. We're getting a million each for this. At first, I was jacked, because, you know, it's a million fucking dollars. That's like a hundred times what we should get, but now I wonder if it's worth it."

Bryce lowered the gun. "A million dollars? It really is like money's no longer worth anything to him." He glanced over at Maddy, who had stopped in the middle of cleaning one of the magazines. "He said soon, I just didn't think it would be this soon. God."

"How can money not mean anything?" Boggs demanded. "I better get paid for fuck's sake." He was no longer as fearsome as he had been. Bryce saw that he had crooked teeth and a lazy eye. He was sweating in fear.

Maddy put the magazine down and stared at her hands. "He has a different vision for the future of humanity," she mumbled, echoing Magnus' words. "He's creating a utopia. That's what he said. No more money. No more murder. No more war."

"Then he's fucked up," Wilkes spat. "Because if you look out the fucking window, all you got is murder and war."

"He's making it the last war," Bryce said. His lips were pursed as if he found the words sour. "He's done something to… to make us kill each other, and all that'll be left is his little group of cultists."

Groaning, Boggs sat up, putting his back to the upended desk. "We're not killing each other. He made zombies. Christ, look at them." The pile of corpses at his feet barely appeared human. Even in death they looked like monsters, twisted into human shapes.

Maddy went back to scrubbing. "There's no such thing as zombies. Those poor people were clearly subjected to some sort of chemical compound that affected the limbic system."

Wilkes turned and dropped his hands to his sides. They seemed suddenly heavy. Either that, or he was suddenly weak. "What's the fucking difference? If it walks like a fish and talks like a fish, it's probably a fish. Either way, this is all the more reason to get back to Magnus' compound. If he knew this was coming; if he planned it, then he's probably got it all worked out how to survive. Right?"

Griff shook his head. "No. We're going to head down to the Federal Plaza. There's an FBI station there. We'll be safe there until we can get word to Washington about what's going on."

"The Federal Plaza!" Wilkes cried. "That's like thirty or forty blocks. It's all the way downtown. Jeeze. You'll never make it."

Bryce held up a hand. "We can if we take one of those Yukon SUV things, right?"

Wilkes sneered, "That ain't happening. You ain't touching my ride. You see, we only get paid if we deliver you to Magnus, not to the FBI. But hey, if you got the cash, I'll sell one to you."

"Weren't you listening?" Maddy said, looking up from the gun again. She'd been trying to figure out how to get the bullet out of the gun's chamber so she could clean the barrel without blowing her hand off. "Money is worthless."

"Not yet it isn't." He grinned, which turned his eyes to dark slivers. "Money is still money, at least for a little while. A million fucking dollars might get me a boat, and I can see myself living the pirate life if this all goes down like you think." The grin slowly faded; with his gun sitting in Bryce's hands, the million dollars seemed to be slipping away. "How about this: I come with you."

Maddy snorted and Griff scoffed, saying, "That ain't happening."

"Unarmed," Wilkes said. "You guys are an investment. I need you alive and let's face it, officer, with these two backing you up, you probably won't make it five blocks without my help."

Bryce thought there was safety in numbers, but as Griff and Maddy refused to hear it, so he kept silent. Griff handcuffed the two men together, linking their arms before he barricaded them in a supply closet. When they began to whine, he said, "Stop your crying, one of your men will come for you."

"If this fire gets worse, they'll be here any minute," Maddy noted.

"More like any second, " Griff said and took off down the hall, racing for the stairwell door with Maddy and Bryce hobbling after, grimacing and groaning from the pain. Along the way, they passed room after room of infected people. They screamed and screeched, and if they hadn't been tied to their beds, they would've chased the three down with ease. No one asked what was going to happen to them if the fire grew worse. Some things were best left unasked.

The stairwell was grey with smoke. People—normal people —were going in both directions, gagging and coughing. Others were huddled in the smoke, covering their faces and crying. Some were sprawled, unmoving. Even with the little blue masks, the trio sucked down smoke. It shriveled their lungs. Bryce went light-headed and fell into Maddy, who fell into Griff.

He shouldered them off of him and squinted through teary eyes downwards where the smoke was thicker. There were more limp bodies. He wanted to go to them. He had a duty to go to them and save them if he could. But he also had a duty to the city.

"Has anyone tried the north stairwell?" he asked an older man with a graying military-style brush cut.

"Check it yourself, shit-breath."

Griff couldn't tell if he was in the initial angry stages of the infection or if he was just a bitter old man. He glared but said nothing as Brush-cut pushed ahead of the others.

"Anyone else? The north stairwell?" No one around them had tried it yet, so Griff turned and ran back onto the floor, followed by Bryce, Maddy, and a half dozen others. They kept to the middle of the hallway, assaulted by furious screams on every side. Bryce and Maddy were the last to make it to the north stairs. Even a man on crutches passed them by.

Bryce was nearly crippled with pain. On top of that, he was famished beyond the point of simply being hungry. He felt weak as if he hadn't eaten anything in days. Maddy was even worse off. Sweat trickled from her pores in tiny rivers and her heart thudded a million miles an hour. When they stopped, she dropped and lay gasping.

This had Griff muttering into his blue mask in disgust.

"It's the drugs," Bryce said, his eyes going in and out of focus. "We need a car or…or…a taxi."

"You need to walk it off," Griff shot back. "Get up. Come on, Maddy." He helped her up and then opened the door to the sound of screams echoing up through a grey haze. Again, people were pushing up towards them.

One man saw the guns in their hands. He pointed down and hissed, "It's *them*. The ones from the TV."

Someone else saw their masks and grew excited. "Do the masks work? Do they keep you safe?"

Griff had no idea. "Maybe, I don't know. Look out. Stand aside, please. Grandma, you too." He started down and was at the next landing when he realized Maddy and Bryce weren't with him. "Get your asses down here!"

Reluctantly they followed. The screams bouncing off the walls were terrible. They went on and on, drilling into their ears. They had to endure two stories of it before they found the screamer.

Chapter 8

Janine O'Neil was a big woman, standing over six foot, with thick, tree-trunk thighs. At thirty, she was in her prime. On the rare occasions that someone tested her patience, they discovered, to their dismay, that she could swing her hands like meaty sledgehammers. At nine o'clock on that Thanksgiving night, those big fists had proven useless. The people attacking her were fast and she was no sprinter. They had caught her as she ran into the stairwell, where she turned and fought, but they were jackals and she was the wildebeest. In a frontal attack she held every advantage and she pounded each to the floor with mighty swings of her sledgehammer fists.

But, like a bad dream, they kept getting up.

It didn't seem to matter that she was breaking noses and crushing eye sockets. It slowly dawned on her that these weren't people high on some strange drug compound. She didn't want to admit what they were, but she knew deep down what the greying skin, the dank red mouths, and the black eyes meant. These weren't people anymore.

This realization sapped her strength and quickly she began to flag, her breath growing ragged and harsh in her throat. She tried to flee up the stairs, but prey is always weakest when they run. They caught her from behind and dragged her down. From then on, she fought to save her face and throat, but she did so at the expense of her legs and belly. They tore into her and she bled.

Twice, Janine was able to push to her feet and scramble a few stairs higher. Twice they caught her. By the time Griff reached her, the fight in her was gone. Blood loss and exhaustion made her lethargic and like an animal, her eyes rolled in their sockets. She was now only waiting to die.

Griff took aim at the closest of the creatures—center mass, like he'd been taught. Then the word *zombies* ghosted through his head and he lifted his sights. When he fired in the narrow concrete stairwell, the gunshot was like a canon.

Both Bryce and Maddy flinched in pain as it felt like spikes had been driven into their ears.

The other two zombies, teenage girls with bits of flesh in their braces and blood dripping from their chins, turned mad eyes to Griff. He shot one of them before she could move. She toppled backwards and went tumbling down the stairs, her head making a sickening knocking sound each time it struck cement. The second girl charged up at him, leading with her red mouth. Griff fired from a range of three feet. Her black brains exploded out the back of her head and covered the wall.

Bryce, his hands over his ears, moaned in disgust at the sight. Maddy's stomach flipped and she felt her gorge rising. Clamping a hand over her mouth, she turned and hid her face behind Bryce.

Griff stared down, wishing he wasn't seeing this. He had witnessed some serious shit in his time, but nothing compared to what lay before him. Janine was the fountainhead of a red river. Great, insane amounts of blood, seemed to flow from her. It cascaded down the stairs with each of the creatures adding to it until it was too much; until it was impossible to look at and remain sane.

But pulling his eyes away from the red river, meant that he had to mentally deal with Janine. She lay mewling and gasping with one of the creatures draped across her legs. Its mouth was stuffed with a link of her intestine.

"Kill me," she whispered.

Griff drew back at the request; his gun hand dropping to his side. He wanted to hide the 9mm. Her demand was insane. It would be murder. There'd be an investigation, and at best he'd be arrested and stripped of his badge. At worst, he'd fry, or rot in prison for the rest of his life. It went against everything he had been working the last ten years for.

And what about their ammo situation? They probably had only sixty rounds between them and there was no telling how many more zombies they'd run into before they made it to the Federal Building.

But how could he say no? The woman was clearly in terrible pain and with the hospital on fire, her chances were slim. Slim didn't mean zero, however.

"Let me see if I can find a doctor," he told her, clinging desperately to the idea. "Just…just hold on."

"Don't leave me." She reached out for his leg, but he quickly stepped around her. Without looking at her, Maddy, then Bryce followed after. There were other people on the stairs, however they stayed back, some even retreating back the way they had come. Most were too afraid of catching the "zombie virus" as everyone instinctively thought of it. Some were too disgusted by Janine. They couldn't handle seeing her stomach torn open, turned into a sickening bowl of soup and gnawed intestines.

Griff really meant to find a doctor or a nurse, one who wasn't infected, that is. Sure, the ER and the ICU were hotbeds for the inflicted, but what about oncology or radiology? Hell, even an obgyn doc would work.

On the next floor down was a sign for pediatrics, in-patient surgery, and the cafeteria. All this could be found behind a door that was venting plumes of dark smoke around its edges. The fire was worse than he thought. He had figured it was a small thing, more smoke than flames.

It had begun in the third floor kitchens as a half-dozen infected had stormed through the cafeteria, chasing an unarmed hospital guard. When Pappy Martinez, a line cook with thick tattooed arms and more scars than he could count, heard the commotion, he had picked up a knife in one hand and a hot skillet in the other, and charged out into the fray. Almost gleefully, he had laid about with his makeshift weapons.

But the weirdos causing all the ruckus wouldn't stop no matter how many times he stabbed them or smacked them with the skillet. Pappy was strong, but he had the endurance of a line cook not a boxer, and within a minute he was winded. After two minutes, he was gasping. He fled into his kitchen where a second cook waited, holding knives in both hands.

Everyone else had run off.

"Those won't work!" Pappy cried, meaning the knives. They both looked around and came to the same conclusion: if there was one thing that killed everything, it was fire. And it did. They grabbed mops, dunked them into the grease pit and set them ablaze using the stove burners. A quick smack in the face with the heavy mops was all it took.

It took much more to witness the death they had created and both men were sickened seeing humans coated in old bacon grease burning like torches.

Not only were the deaths sickening, they were also stupid. The human torches didn't die right away. They set the kitchen on fire first as they blundered about with their eyes burned out of their sockets. The other cook ran off, leaving Pappy alone to deal with the fire. He grabbed an extinguisher and did what he could; however his mop had left a trail of grease drippings that wound back to the grease pit, and when that caught fire there was nothing he could do. The heat was so fantastic that the hair on Pappy's arm curled and turned to ash before he could get close.

Even the automatic fire suppression sprinklers couldn't tame the fire. Not that it mattered. One of the human torches had wandered into the dining room and had fallen against a wall, setting the carpet on fire. Soon the entire room was ablaze.

Pappy called 911—along with over thirteen hundred other people in Manhattan alone. There were a hundred fires and a thousand murders, and the city was coming apart at the seams. It wouldn't have mattered if any of the calls had gotten through. The streets were packed solid with traffic and what cops that were left were already up to their throats in undead.

The fire went unconfined and although it had started slowly, it was now eating the building from the inside out. The heat was so intense, it radiated through the cinderblock walls, making Griff cringe and he threw up an arm to shield his eyes which felt like they were shrivling. As bad as it was, he would rather face it than having to deal with Janine. "I'll get help," he yelled back to her… It was a lie and he knew it was a lie the second the words slipped from his mouth. No help was coming. Not the fire department and not the police. Even if there were doctors left in the building, they would be working on the patients who actually had a chance.

Janine was not one of these.

Maddy, who was thinking the same thing, couldn't look at her. She was a pacifist at heart and the idea of hurting an innocent person, even in mercy, was too much. She kept her eyes hard away from the big woman as she tiptoed by her.

This left Bryce, and he knew it. He could sense Maddy's weakness, and he could see how Griff's adherence to the law was stopping him. The only thing stopping Bryce from doing the right thing was his natural squeamishness, something he realized he could no longer fall back on to hide from difficult choices.

He didn't want to look at Janine, but his eyes were drawn to her and caught her staring at him. There were great fat tears building in her eyes. Her jaw was quivering. Her hands were shaking as they fought to keep her innards from slithering out onto the stairs. Bryce took all this in and his resolve weakened to the point that he took another step down.

"Please," she whispered.

Her pain was like the heat sweeping up the stairs. It was a force that could only be denied by running away. But there was no running left in Bryce just then. Below him the heat was a wall he would have to burst through and above was a slow death from smoke inhalation. He hesitated long enough for his guilt to overcome his squeamishness.

"Close your eyes," he said. She looked away, which was even better. He tried to aim the gun from where he was, but his hands were shaking so badly he knew he would only end up blowing her face off, if he hit her at all. He had to get closer. Those three steps were the hardest of his life, and when he got close, he had to use two hands to hold the gun still.

Bryce wasn't strong enough to watch as he pulled the trigger. This time the sound of the gun was strangely muffled in his ears. *Had it worked right?* he wondered. Chancing a peek at Janine, he saw brains, pink and grey, spattered across the stairs. "God," he said, shuddering. Maddy looked him in the eye for all of a second before turning back to the heat and the smoke— these were easier to deal with.

"There's no use turning back," Griff said over his shoulder; he didn't want to look back at what was essentially a murder scene. None of them did. "We just have to get past the door. It'll be better below this floor."

"I think we understand thermodynamics, thank you very much," Maddy snipped. "But what if you're wrong? What if the fire started further down?"

Griff shrugged. "Then we deal. This is the third floor. It can't go too much further." When it came to fire, this wasn't logical. They had no idea where the fire had started. As far as they knew, the basement could be on fire and they could be rushing down into a veritable oven. Griff swallowed thick spittle. "I'll go first." He pulled his jacket in front of his face and, without another word, sped down the stairs, taking them three at a time. He disappeared into the thick haze.

Maddy and Bryce waited, their faces, stretched in fear, were a perfect match. Maddy wanted to cling to Bryce, but it was *Bryce* and her dignity wouldn't let her. "You okay?" she called out to Griff after a few seconds.

"Yeah… It's okay… down here," Griff said between coughing fits.

The two PhDs looked at each other. "After you," Bryce said. "Ladies first." Maddy wanted to shove his faux gallantry down his throat. She knew that he just didn't want to go first…at the same time, she didn't want to go last. If something happened to her, who would come back for her?

She took a deep breath and went jiggling down the stairs. After five steps, the heat was too much. The skin of her face felt like it was stretching and peeling back from the bone. But it was her bare feet that had her screaming, "Fuck me!" The concrete was, literally, blistering hot. She stumbled and her arm came down on the metal railing, which was even hotter.

The swinging flesh of her arm sizzled when it hit the railing. She screamed again and then sucked in a great lungful of black smoke. Even with the blue mask, her head went instantly light and the next thing she knew, she was falling.

Then Bryce was there, straining against her weight, his eyes at slits, his useless hospital gown sliding open. The pain in his feet was so intense that it leant him strength. He *had* to get away from it. Taking as fierce a grip as he could on Maddy's gown, he hauled her to her feet and together they stumbled past the door.

With every step down the heat dropped away and in seconds, Griff was there, helping to take some of Maddy's weight. The three of them lurched down and down, each slowly regaining their senses as the air cleared.

Finally, they were at a door marked: Ground Floor.

Griff reached for the handle but Bryce stopped him. "Just a second, please. Please. I just need a second." Huffing and feeling like he could faint at any second, he collapsed back down onto the stairs and looked at the soles of his feet which were vibrantly red and covered in blisters . Maddy did as well, gingerly touching the bubbles that were forming and making a whining noise deep in her throat.

"Shit. Your feet," Griff whispered. He hadn't considered their lack of clothing. All they had on were the flimsiest of sheer blue hospital gowns. Griff yanked off his suit coat and gave it to Maddy, who had to struggle her fleshy arms into it.

She snugged it across her heavy chest. "Thanks, but I don't know how far I can get like this. Maybe we should wait here until things calm down a bit."

"Maybe," Griff said. They were safe, at least for a little while and he really didn't know how they'd be able to go on. "Maybe for a little while."

Bryce surprised him, saying, "No. This, whatever this is, was done by Daniel Magnus. It's not going to end until he decides to end it. It's only going to get worse and our feet aren't going to get any better any time soon. We need to push on."

"What about you?" Griff asked, looking at Maddy. He was sure she would say no, but she surprised him as well, agreeing with a quick nod. "Okay, we'll go on. It may not be that bad if we can commandeer a taxi or some other vehicle. And there's still the subway." He put out a hand and helped Maddy to her feet. "The FDR is two blocks east. We'll snatch a cab and…" He shoved the door open as he spoke, but his words stumbled at what he saw.

The gates of Hell had opened and its demons were swarming over New York City.

Chapter 9

The dead littered the lobby. They were flung about like trash. What once had been stark white marble tile covering the floor was now splashed with red from one end of the spacious area to the other. Benches were overthrown and chairs knocked about so that their legs stuck upwards like feeble, dying roaches.

Many bodies, torn and bleeding, were heaped in piles by the elevators. Picking over them like vultures were the undead. They rooted among the corpses like pigs at a trough and when something moved or moaned they went into a frenzy, ripping and tearing until the sound stopped.

As Griff stared in horror, an elevator let out a pleasant chime and its doors slid open. The undead immediately swarmed in. A woman screamed and a man bellowed a curse. The two tried to rip themselves free of the zombies but they were like clawed leaches and they dragged the pair down. Griff shut the door cutting off their screams.

"What's happening?" Maddy asked in a whisper.

Griff found himself staring past her. The wall was white and blank, and on it was a replay of what he'd just scene.

Bryce pushed past him and cracked the door. What he saw was a continuous, repeating nightmare. Zombies with wet red faces worried over the corpses, blood up to their elbows. When the elevator chime sang out, their reaction was a pavlovian horror. Greedily they would charge the doors, glee on their dripping smiles.

Sometimes the people coming out would try to make a break for the street, thinking they could outrun their fate, but some of the zombies were shockingly fast and the people were pulled down and devoured just shy of the doors.

Mostly, however, the victims saw what awaited them when the elevator doors opened and foolishly tried to shut the doors before the zombies could get in. Every once in a while, the doors shut in time and the people would ride back upstairs where the smoke was growing denser by the minute. It was an easier death.

Usually, the cars were flooded with the beasts the moment the door opened. People were crushed against the wall, half suffocated, unable to move, unable to defend themselves. They died slow, horrible deaths, one bite at a time.

Four of the six elevators were still operating. The other two had bodies keeping the doors from closing. These rang shrill alarms, which only added to the din that shivered the air. What had been muffled eight floors up, was an explosion of sound that assaulted Bryce when he faced it in person. Ten thousand screams filled the air, hundreds of guns were firing at once, and what seemed like every car in the city was honking its horn for all it was worth.

When he had woken a few hours earlier, New York had been in what could be described as a "curiously nervous" setting, since what was happening in the city seemed minor compared to the devastation in L.A. That mental setting had quickly slipped into a worried "wait-and-see approach" as the local news grew darker, and frightening stories began to swirl.

Sometime in the last hour, the city had switched into panic mode. A television wasn't needed to see the fires or hear the sirens and gunshots. And it didn't take genius-level thinking to realize that their concrete jungle was surrounded by water and that it would take very little to trap them there among the creatures. The creatures that were multiplying at an alarming rate.

No one knew the exact rate of contagion because it depended on the situation. In the first few hours, when the city was unaware and people were going about their business normally, the initial four thousand people infected on the subways had gone on to infect an average of seventeen others before they were killed or confined to a bed in one of the now disintegrating hospitals.

Those sixty-eight thousand which constituted the second wave had a much harder time of it since the city was on alert. Each of them had only managed to infect six people on average. Still, at seven that evening, there were close to four-hundred thousand zombies in the greater New York area.

At that point it was already a virtually unstoppable army, but when Griff opened that stairwell door at a little after ten that night, the numbers had doubled, with another eight hundred thousand in the early stages of the infection. That was roughly ten percent of the population of the city.

Panic was the only appropriate response.

Unfortunately, people who panicked did stupid things. All at once, millions of people made a mad rush to escape the city before it was too late. Those with cars filled them to capacity with what they considered their most precious items and tried to flee. Heading east to Long Island didn't seem all that smart since they'd just be stuck on another island, so a quarter of a million cars tried to go west to New Jersey.

Other than a few ferries that had stopped running, there were only three ways to cross the Hudson River by car from Manhattan: a pair of tunnels and the George Washington Bridge.

The traffic literally inched forward, then stopped altogether as the governor of New Jersey closed its borders. By then the demons were running rampant, attacking people in their cars. Traffic became completely fused, but that didn't stop people from honking their horns endlessly.

Bryce stared out from the stairwell door in complete shock. Maddy stared out in despair. There would be no taxi. She would have almost no choice but to run out into the madness on blistered feet, covered in nothing but a gown; she felt like throwing up. With one hand clutching her stomach, she reached around Bryce and pulled the door closed. "Try calling the FBI again," she said to Griff, speaking so quickly her words tumbled over themselves. "Or the police. Try the police. Tell them we're important and we need help. Tell them we're the only ones who know what's going on. Please."

"Sure. I can try, I guess." Griff pulled his mask down so that it hung on his chin like a blue beard. He dialed 911, not realizing that, for the most part, the police force had been absorbed into the army of undead. They had been the first to come in contact with the initial waves and thus some of the first infected. There were tens of thousands of men in blue shambling around the city.

The phone went right to the recorded message: "All circuits are busy. Please try again…"

"It'll be okay," Griff said. He had a tick working under his left eye. It wasn't going to be okay. Somehow, in the middle of an apocalypse, he'd become saddled with a twerp and a chubby feminist. They were anchors around his neck. That was his reality.

Leave them, a voice whispered from deep inside. *Your only chance is to go on your own.*

But they were important—potentially—and he had an obligation to get them somewhere safe. "Shit," he muttered. Louder, he added a second time: "It'll be okay. We keep moving. Shoot only when you have to. Keep the chatter to a minimum. And keep up. Your feet are going to hurt, but it'll be worse if *they* get you."

He turned to the door, but Maddy grabbed his arm. "But…" She began to hyperventilate and couldn't finish what was going to be an incomplete whine, anyway.

Griff pulled her hands off him, saying, "We don't have a choice. I'll go first. You two stay together." Then he just walked out into the lobby. He didn't run. He didn't even hurry. Griff acted like he belonged there, and somehow he was ignored. The undead had become predators and were more likely to attack someone running.

Maddy and Bryce clung to each other as they walked so close to Griff that they kept kicking the back of his shoes. By a miracle, the three of them made it to the jam-packed street. There were bodies here, too. Some were sprawled across the sidewalk, some were draped across the hoods of cars, some moved in the shadows. In the dark, it was impossible to know which was human and which wasn't.

"This way," Griff whispered.

He scooted between an ambulance and an empty car, ducked low and started south. Maddy and Bryce followed, hobbling as best they could. This wasn't very fast or very quiet. Maddy, whose feet stung like she was walking on coals, kept up a constant, "Uhhhhh. Uhhh. Uhhhh."

Griff had to stop and plead with her to be quiet. "We'll find you something to wear soon. New York is filled with shops." This was generally true, it just wasn't true of that part of New York. They passed a doughnut shop, a Starbucks, a Staples, a car rental place that was on fire, and a liquor store that was shuttered and had men with guns on the roof.

Maddy stopped making the sound for a few minutes, but started up again after stepping on some glass. Bryce had stepped on the same glass and now the bottom of his right foot felt wet. He hissed with each step and was just thinking that they would never make it thirty blocks when he heard something behind them.

It was a dark being of great size and even greater malice. The creature reached out with a clawed hand with fingers eight inches long and nails almost half that. From it arose a stench like Bryce had never known. It filled his nostrils and drained the strength from his already weak legs so that he stumbled into Maddy. When she looked back and saw the thing, she instinctively shoved Bryce away from her and towards *it*.

Now there was barely a foot of empty air separating him from death. He was seized with sudden panic and without thinking, he lifted his pistol. He might have fired if something midnight black hadn't suddenly appeared an inch from his face. It was Maddy. She had her gun aimed as well.

Griff turned just in time. "What the hell? What did I tell you two?" One of the cars they were passing had its door flung open. He grabbed a suitcase from inside, pulled it out, and heaved it over their heads. It struck the creature with a muffled thump, knocking it to the pavement. "Only shoot if you have to."

Bryce was about to make an excuse, but now that his fear had subsided a little, he was able to visualize the creature in a way that he hadn't before. It wasn't nearly as big as he had thought. The black blood it was covered in had allowed it to merge with the shadows, making it appear larger than life.

In reality, it wasn't large at all—or rather, she wasn't large at all. The zombie had been a sixty-year-old adverting executive who just happened to get on the wrong train that day. She wasn't big and she wasn't all that strong, and she certainly wasn't fast, seeing as she limped, dragging the remains of her left foot.

As they hurried away, she struggled to her one foot and came after them. When she came out of the deeper darkness and into a circle of light thrown down by a streetlamp, Bryce saw that she was also missing a hand and most of her face.

"Shoot only if we have to," Bryce repeated as he hurried to catch up with Griff. "I thought she was bigger. Sorry."

"It was a she?" Griff looked back at the stumbling thing. To him it was only a shape and a small one at that. "I hadn't noticed. But it doesn't matter…"

A much larger shape suddenly shifted in a minivan off to their right. This was definitely a big one. Griff ducked down and scurried around a yellow cab. Maddy and Bryce followed. As Griff stalked forward, he pointed down at a soda can. Maddy stepped over it and pointed as well. Bryce was craning his head back as the creature pulled itself from the minivan. This one was large and completely intact. In fact, it wore a blue uniform, complete with bullet-proof vest.

Bryce didn't see the can and his bare foot gave it a kick. The can went bouncing, end over end, and as it did, all the other sounds in the city seemed to take that exact moment to pause. Bryce froze as time stood still for a dozen beats of his heart. Of course, it was racing so fast that the moment lasted only three seconds.

Then the creature charged. It leapt onto the hood of the cab and then dropped down in front of Bryce—now, he had to shoot. His gun came up, pointed at the thing's head. He fired, aiming for the forehead. The pull on the trigger was greater than he had imagined and his hand as weak as ever. The barrel lifted as he strained against the trigger and when it went off, the bullet blasted a beautiful part through its hair.

He had missed.

"Shit!" Bryce hissed as it jumped at him. He fell back, firing his gun as fast as he could pull the trigger. His eyes were at squints and his face was twisted in a rictus of fear. Two bullets struck: one in its chin and another on the side of its neck. It felt neither.

Maddy fired at the same time, hitting its shoulder with the first bullet, and the building across the street with her second. Neither of these hurt it, either. It was up to Griff. Calmly, he fired once and blasted out its brain.

All six shots came in a two-second spread and once the creature fell at Bryce's feet with an awful thud, there were only the echoes of their guns bouncing from building to building. The three stood stock-still.

Then, all at once, all hell broke loose.

Chapter 10

Suddenly, the dark street was filled with people. People and zombies. They came charging out of cars and buildings, and from every nook and cranny that might hold a person.

The humans knew only that there were three people with guns, and guns meant safety, or at least they'd be safer than before. That was the assumption. It didn't matter if the three were cops or drug dealers. And it didn't matter that there were other people who had been hiding nearby, either. To them, that was a bonus. There was safety in numbers…or so they assumed.

The zombies didn't make assumptions. All they cared about was ripping the trio into pieces. Single-mindedly, they charged only to be distracted by the other humans.

A wild, swirling fight seemed to erupt out of the blue. In the darkness, it was nearly impossible to tell who was a zombie and who wasn't. People attacked other people or ran from other people. Only the zombies seemed to know who was human for certain.

Griff was taken by surprise by the suddenness of the attack. He waved his gun in the faces of the closest people. "Back off!" The first woman did, throwing her hands up and darting behind a car. The next woman ignored the gun entirely and came blazing in with her teeth barred. Griff shot her, blasting those teeth out the back of her head.

Bryce and Maddy were shooting, too. Out of fear of hitting a human, they had to wait until almost the last second before pulling the trigger. Even with their targets so close, they wasted round after round. In a blink, Bryce's gun was empty. The gun he had taken from Wilkes was a Sig Sauer 320 Legion with a 10-round magazine. The bullets went faster than he could've imagined.

"My gun…it's empty!" he cried, holding up his gun. He had no idea what to do. Yes, he had another magazine, but he had no clue how to replace it. "What do I do?"

Maddy, who had a seventeen-round magazine and was spraying bullets everywhere, demanded, "How are you out? What're you doing?"

"Nothing," he answered, coming to stand very close to her —almost, but not quite hiding behind her. "It just ran out. How do I get the other one in?" The little button that ejected the magazine was black on black and looked like a decoration to him. He tried pulling the magazine out of the bottom of the grip, but it remained firm.

"The button on the side, you idiot!" Maddy shouted and fired again, missing her target and hitting the back window of a Prius.

Before Bryce could do anything, Griff had him by the neck of his gown and was yanking him along. They stepped around a woman being eaten by an extremely fat zombie. The woman was screeching loud enough to be heard ten blocks away. Maddy aimed her gun at the zombie, but Griff grabbed her arm. "Stop shooting. Both of you. We have to get out of here." The fight seemed to be growing around them as more undead streamed towards the sound of their guns and the dreadful screams.

In front of them, the doors of a gleaming Lexus burst open and a family of four leapt out. A woman, blonde and leggy, had been in the driver's seat. Her name was Victoria Deitch and up until that afternoon, she had been almost violently anti-gun. Now she was desperate for one. She attacked Bryce, and clung to him, pleading, "Take us with you." Up close he saw that she had a narrow face with a high forehead and frightened grey eyes that couldn't seem to see that Bryce was wearing a hospital gown and that he was as scared as she was.

Next to her and clinging as much as the woman was a golden-haired child of maybe six. With her button nose, pointy chin, and her puffy sky-blue coat that matched her eyes, she was a precious little thing who would be dead soon. Her mother had only a fireplace poker as a weapon, while her dad had an old softball bat. He swung it Babe Ruth style at an onrushing zombie.

The girl's brother screamed as the bat whipped past his face, nearly hitting him. He ducked away, crawling beneath another car.

Victoria tried to go to him while still yanking on Bryce's arm. At the same time, Griff pulled him in the opposite direction, growling, "Come on."

"Help me," Victoria begged. "We have to get to him."

As much as Bryce wanted to help to save her husband, he was more worried about himself—zombies were charging from every direction. Her husband at least had a bat. Bryce's gun was still uselessly empty. There was a moment when he was stretched between them and then Griff began shooting, his gun flashing and barking thunder. Maddy was pushing him forward and shooting as well. The little girl was screaming. So much was happening at once that Bryce's head began to spin.

Then the five of them were moving forward in a weird scramble with the woman looking back as her husband jumped up on a car. He was surrounded and was laying about with the bat, knocking heads.

"My son!" Victoria shrieked. "We have to get him."

Desperation gave her strength and she swung Bryce around. Now Griff was accidentally choking him as he pulled on his collar, and Maddy was stepping on his toes as she bulled him out of the trap. Still Victoria wouldn't stop trying to get him to go back. Couldn't she see the pain he was in? Or the fact that his feet were bare and blistered?

"Jordan! Jordan, run!" Victoria screamed.

But Jordan didn't run. He was terrified.

The woman was torn between saving her daughter and going back for her son. Before she could make up her mind, their little group was overwhelmed by the dead. The magazine in Maddy's gun ran out of bullets a second after Griff's did, and for a short time, the only weapon between them was the woman's fireplace poker.

She let go of Bryce long enough to wave it around like a fencer might. This form of defense was utterly useless. With courage that even she didn't know she possessed, she pushed her daughter towards Bryce and took an actual swing at one of the undead. The poker tore a furrow in its cheek. It didn't even blink.

It reached out to grab her and once she was in its claws it would've sunk its teeth into her beautiful face, however, Bryce tripped it as it passed. It fell face-first and Bryce stepped down on its neck with all his weight.

"Give me that!" He held out the gun and reached for the poker. Not realizing it was empty, she made the trade eagerly.

Bryce drove the poker down with all his might, stabbing the creature in the top of its head. In a sickening display, its body went into spasms. Bryce watched for a second too long and when he looked up, he saw Victoria aiming the empty gun at an onrushing zombie.

In a move that might have been instinctual, if Bryce had possessed *any* fighting instincts, he leapt forward with his left knee cocked up to his chin. As if he had practiced the move a hundred times, his left foot shot out and crashed into the zombie's chest. Something crunched like dry kindling inside it and it went flying back.

"Holy crap!" Bryce was wide-eyed in amazement. "Maddy, did you see that?"

She had and for some reason, she felt a stab of jealousy. It took her a moment to realize why. Bryce might've been in pain from whatever they had been given, but he wasn't like her: A jiggling sweaty freak, who thought her heart was about to explode.

"I saw it," she muttered. "You kicked one of them. Great. If you had…"

"I need bullets!" Victoria cried, holding up the gun. "This thing's empty. You gave me a fucking empty gun!"

Griff came up behind her and snatched it out of her hands. "We don't have time for this," he snarled. He was just barely holding off the dead and he knew his ammo wouldn't hold out much longer. He tucked the pistol away. "Listen lady, either stay and help your husband, or shut up and keep up. We aren't slowing down for nothing."

As he said this, his eyes inadvertently slipped to Victoria's daughter. Victoria put a protective arm around the girl. "Where are you going? Are you just running away or…"

"The Federal Plaza," Griff said. "It's downtown."

She knew where it was—how *far* it was. The distance scared her. On a normal sunny fall day, it would be over an hour-long walk. Out here, with monsters running around and the world gone crazy, she didn't know if she could make it. But what was her other choice? Her husband was leaping from car to car, drawing some of the creatures away, but where was Jordan?

There he was! His eight-year-old legs were speeding him away from her on a parallel course that her husband was taking. "The Federal Plaza!" she screamed at the top of her lungs. "We're going to the Fed…"

Griff slammed his hand over her mouth, crushing her lips into her teeth. "They heard you. The entire fucking city heard you." The dead certainly heard her. The five of them had been in a small, zombie-free zone. It was now closing in on them fast. "This way."

The FBI agent took off at a run, heading west along 31st Street. Normally, it was a pretty street: tree-lined with brownstone condos rising five-stories on either side. There were three lanes between the sidewalks, and each had a line of cars that went as far as they could see. Although the sidewalks were virtually empty, Griff didn't trust them. There was no telling what lurked in the dark shadows next to the stairs running up to the buildings.

It was better to keep to the middle of the quiet street.

The five ran and limped along the narrow lanes with Griff in front, his pistol at the ready, and Bryce taking up the rear, armed with only the three-foot poker. At first, Bryce was able to keep up, buoyed by the *kick*. Nothing in his life had ever felt so natural. As a kid he had been bookish and geeky, and had never considered playing a sport, but if he'd been forced to choose one, it would've been baseball. It was the only sport that required a calculating mind. There were just so many numbers involved. Angles had to be calculated, velocities determined, averages were constantly reworked.

That part of the game he understood. Hitting a rock-hard ball being thrown at his face at ninety miles an hour, was where he and the game diverged. Still, he had to wonder if baseball players who hit homeruns felt something similar to what he felt when he had kicked that zombie. The thrill of his action ran constantly through his mind: the leap, the perfect body position, the explosive thrust of his leg at the exact moment, the crunch of bone.

He couldn't deny the rush that went through him when he felt the creature's bones breaking. It was somewhat barbaric and at the same time, wholly natural.

As great a feeling as it was, the high from it couldn't last. He began to lag. Maddy was as well. She was gasping. Her lungs burned. All of her burned. But they couldn't stop. A small group of the dead were shambling after them, while from either side, zombies would suddenly appear out of the shadows and charge.

Thankfully, the cars were bumper to bumper, making a wall of metal on both sides of them. This slowed the zombies down. They had to climb over the hoods. Climbing was not something they were particularly good at. It's the only reason Bryce was still alive, and he knew it, just like he knew he wouldn't be able to go on much longer.

Frantically, he looked left and right as he ran, hoping to find someplace they could hide in and rest for a bit. At the corner, he stopped and looked in four directions. A rib place on their right was shuttered. Across from it a bank looked blank and impenetrable. To their left was a parking garage that was frightfully dark and finally there was a Trader Joe's that had a delivery truck half through its front window—it had been looted down to its last bag of chips.

They kept running.

"Is there a subway around here?" Griff asked. He had a slight sheen of sweat at his hairline but otherwise looked like he could go for miles.

Victoria, in her loosest jeans and white sneakers, was also barely winded. She pointed ahead of them. "The Six Train is just another few blocks away, on Park Ave. But I don't think we should try it. Even if we get in a car, we'll be trapped. And what happens if we get to the next stop and there's some of them on the platform? The doors open, no matter what."

"I like the idea of being out of sight," Griff said. He looked up uneasily at the buildings. There was no telling who or what was staring down at them. The *what* was answered when they passed the next stoop. Glass broke three stories above them. It rained down on the sidewalk just before a zombie splatted down. They all jumped, then made the same horrified look as it started to crawl towards them, leaving a trail of oily-looking blood behind.

Victoria's little girl started to choke, though on what no one knew. Still, she was being loud and the shadows began to swing towards them. With the creatures coming up from behind, they were once again on the verge of being trapped.

"I say we try for the train," Griff said. Another five hundred yards was nothing to him. Without waiting for a reply, he started for an intersection, which resembled a cross between a parking lot and an obstacle course. The cars were so jammed together that it was easier to leap from car to car.

Unfortunately, this also made them *obvious*. The car hoods clunked with each step and where many streets were dark, the lights here gave off a pretty amber hue. To make matters worse, some fool had abandoned his Mercedes, but not before turning on the alarm. When Griff stepped across to it, it began shriek and whoop, and its lights flashed and blinked. Every zombie within sight turned and charged.

Chapter 11

It was nearing midnight and the trap had closed on them.

Thirty or forty zombies converged on the little group, coming from all directions. In the shadows, they looked like normal people; drunk maybe, but still normal. There were housewives and bankers, plumbers and toll-takers. Most were still dressed as if just coming back from a long day at work. Two of them were in suits. One was torn up, its face completely gone, all except for its teeth, which were gaping wide. The other was still buttoned up. His shoes gleamed; the crease in his pants was as sharp as it had been that morning; his tie was even cinched around the grey flesh of neck. He had blood on his chin and all down the front of his shirt.

The creatures clambered over the cars, sometimes falling in between them and getting stuck, and sometimes going headfirst making a sound like a coconut splitting open. This only slowed them down for a few seconds.

Griff stood on the Mercedes and looked for openings. There weren't any, which meant he would have to make one. "This way," he commanded, heading west as they had been. Eventually they needed to go south, but just then there were more of the beasts in that direction.

He was like a mountain goat going from car to car, while Victoria and her daughter, whose name turned out to be Tessa, were like gazelles—not as nimble, but quick, lithe and beautiful as their golden hair streamed behind with each jump. Maddy and Bryce resembled senior escapees from a nursing home. Gingerly and with a great deal of groaning, they tried to keep up.

Some of the creatures were fast, but even the fastest couldn't judge angles, and instead of rushing to cut them off, they went directly for them, and lost whatever advantage they had in the process. Most were slow, however. They were missing chunks of muscles, fingers, feet and even entire limbs.

But they were tireless. Even as Griff blasted a hole through the onrushing creatures, the ones coming up behind grew closer and closer. Bryce even had to stop and stab one through the eye with his poker. It went deep enough to tear through the underside of its brain. Sadly, the hooked part of the poker got caught on the thing's eye socket and when the zombie fell, it yanked the poker from his hands.

Now he was completely defenseless.

"Wait up!" he hissed. Everyone seemed so far ahead, except for Maddy. She had just jumped to the next car, Griff's dark coat flapping around her like a crow's wing. The car's hood dented under her weight. Like an infant first learning to walk, she toddled to the back of the car, paused to take a shaky breath and jumped to the next, barely clearing the gap.

"Can't…go…on," she gasped, pulling her mask down.

Bryce put one of her arms over his shoulder, and together they went up and over the truck. After two more cars and a van, they made it out of the intersection and found Griff, Victoria and Tessa waiting, crouched low.

"You got to keep up," Victoria snapped, a little too loudly. "We may not be able to wait next time."

"Hold on. They were drugged by the same people we think started all this," Griff muttered, hoping that by speaking softly, Victoria would get the message and speak quietly as well. "They're important."

This was nice to hear, only just then, neither of them felt important at all. They felt like useless baggage.

"Still, we can't stop. You hear them, right?" Griff cocked his head to listen. Behind them was the sounds of the zombies getting closer. "Besides, it's not that much further to the train station." He stood, ready to go.

Maddy waved her hand. She was too winded to speak and needed more than fifteen seconds to recuperate. Pushing herself up, she squeezed between a pair of cars that had a foot of space between them. Beyond the cars was the dirty, gum-dotted sidewalk and an old Italian deli. Although it was dark and clearly closed, the deli was one of the few places they had passed that didn't have its metal gate pulled down.

"Get back here," Griff hissed. The first of the dead had fallen from the top of the van. Griff ran over and slammed his foot down on the back of its neck as hard as he could. The creature had been a programmer in life and its pencil neck snapped under the blow. As if it had just licked an electrical socket, its body spazzed wildly then went limp.

Even with a broken neck, it still tried to turn and bite Griff's shoe. "We have to go!"

Ignoring him, Maddy cast about for something to smash the front window with. Nearby, lying in the gutter, was an oblong rock that the owner used to prop the door open on nice days.

Although her legs were jello, she bent, picked up the rock, and heaved it at the front window. As it sailed at the glass, she feared the rock would bounce right off, and she didn't think she had the strength left to pick it up again. She didn't know what she would do then.

You'll die. The words whispered through her mind just as the rock struck. The glass shattered and cascaded down and seemed to explode, covering everything in nasty crystalline shards.

Too late, she remembered she was barefoot. "Fuck! We're going to cut our feet to ribbons."

Bryce didn't dare move from where he was. He was surrounded by the glass. Bending, he peered into the deli. "There's some to-go boxes. We'll make a path. Hey, Lady."

"It's Victoria."

"Sure, Victoria. Could you run in there and…"

She was already striding past him. "I'm not deaf and neither are those things. Why are we trapping ourselves here?" The idea of being trapped was large in her mind. To her the entire city was a trap. It was this way of thinking that had led her into talking her husband out of staying locked in their apartment. It didn't matter that their front door was stout oak and had a reinforced frame and multiple locks. In her mind, no door would hold if things got worse, and they had definitely gotten worse.

Grumbling curses, she stepped through the destroyed window, leaned over the counter and grabbed the closer stack of boxes. She made a trail of them back to where Bryce stood. Her daughter began to hurry forward. "Tessa, no. Let them go first."

Bryce and Maddy looked at each other, neither wanting to be the first inside. Grumbling, Griff stomped by, his leather shoes crunching glass. Now it was a race not to be last. The zombies were climbing the cars, drawing nearer. Victoria grabbed her daughter's hand and jogged for the door. Maddy was closer and followed her inside.

"Shit," Bryce said, limping in last.

It was an old deli, with grime along the edges of the worn linoleum. The glass counter, smudged with layers of fingerprints, ran lengthwise down the narrow room. Judging by the rows of meats and the artfully arranged cheeses still on display, the owner had closed his business in a tearing hurry.

The fantastic smell of the place struck Bryce like a hammer and his stomach immediately rumbled. Pastrami, roast beef, maple turkey, rotisserie chicken. He caught the scent of each. They were irresistible and, as everyone else was hurrying through to the back, he leapt over the counter and yanked off his gloves.

A spiral, honey-glazed ham was right in front of his face, and no force on earth could've stopped him from ripping off a great hunk of it and stuffing it in his mouth. A soft groan escaped him. He tore off another hunk.

Despite the dark, his eyes picked out the plastic bags under the register. He snatched one and began grabbing fistfuls of meat, then cheese, then the scent of bread caught his attention and he threw four or five baguettes in as well.

"Gotta have mayo," he said around a mouthful of salami. He was chewing and swallowing as fast as he could. By the time he had tossed mustard in on top of the mayonnaise there were zombies on the sidewalk outside the deli. He ducked down and duck-waddled down to the end of the case where he could sneak around the counter.

There was a door to the back rooms being held open a crack by Maddy. She glared daggers at him but didn't dare say anything. As quietly as possible, Bryce slipped through the door and followed Maddy into a narrow hall that was made even more narrow by the stacks of boxes stored along one wall. Maddy had to walk sideways, and even then had to suck in her stomach. They passed a vile-smelling bathroom, a storeroom and an employee lounge that doubled as a second storeroom. It was only a "lounge" because of the taped-over leather couch of ancient origin that sat across from an old twenty-inch Sony TV.

Then they were at the backdoor. Griff was about to lead them out when he saw the bag in Bryce's hand. He looked inside. "Did you...did you steal that?"

With the world falling down around them and the owners having fled to who knew where, it was hard to call what he had done stealing. "I wouldn't call it stealing, I'd call it survival."

"Now's not the time," Maddy whispered. The sound of glass crunching in the front of the store was making her crazy with fear. "Just go for God's sake."

"What if there's an alarm on the door?" Victoria asked.

"Then we're screwed," Griff answered. He pulled out Bryce's gun. Victoria tried to snag it, but he held it out of reach. "Stop. Bryce, where's your other magazine? You had two."

Sheepishly, Bryce handed it over and watched Griff deftly switch out the magazines. He made it look easy. "How'd you get that thingy forward?"

"Right here. This little button next to the slide." Griff gave him back the pistol. He looked over Bryce's head at the door at the end of the hall, afraid that it would burst open any second. "If there's any of them in the alley, we're going to have fight our way out. Stay in single file and stay close."

He took a deep breath and opened the door a crack. He expected to find himself looking out onto a slimy, trash-filled alley that ran the length of the block, instead he was shocked to see a tree not ten feet away. It was spindly and barely fifteen-feet in height, but it was still a tree. And the alley wasn't any sort of alley he'd ever been in.

For one, it wasn't straight. It jogged left and right depending on how far back the buildings extended. And there were more trees than just the one. He counted eleven. He found this mystifying, especially as they grew up out of little circles cut out of the cement flooring.

Down the alley was a little patio of sorts. Strings of bare bulbs hung over a dusty card table and a couple of folding chairs. Next to one of the chairs was a rusty coffee can filled with cigarette butts.

There were no zombies or people anywhere in sight. It was refreshing.

Maddy hurried to the table and groaned down into one of the chairs which groaned back at her in its own way.

Throwing manners to the wind, Bryce didn't wait for Victoria to sit before he collapsed in another of the chairs. He immediately began making a sandwich of immense proportions.

"You could be eating the germs that did this, you know," Victoria remarked. She sounded as if she really didn't care. He only shrugged and crushed down the sandwich with the palm of his hand. It was still so big, he looked like he'd have to dislocate his jaw to take a proper a bite. He gave it his best shot and Victoria turned away to look at her daughter.

Tessa was pale, the color of the moon. She was quiet, staring at a hopscotch grid that ran half the length of the alley. There were forty-two boxes, numbered in a childish scrawl. It was something she understood. Nothing else about that day made any sense to her.

"Call daddy," she said. "You gotta tell him about this place. 'Member he was talkin' about finding somewhere safe? This is safe, right?" Why else would the skinny man grown-up be eating? Or the fat woman grown-up be sleeping?

Maddy hadn't expected to fall asleep. She had sat, closed her aching eyes for all of one second, and now she was snoring.

Victoria checked her phone and got the same pre-recorded message. Then she checked the internet and found it wasn't working either. "He knows where to meet us." She glanced over to Griff who was standing next to the back door of the deli. He had found a length of wood, taller than himself, and was wondering how he could use it to block the door. "Hey, mister. I think I should have one of the guns. This guy didn't even know how to load it."

"I knowb dow," Bryce shot back around a mouthful of sandwich; it was the last mouthful. He had wolfed down the rest. He pulled out the gun and pointed to the little knob. "See this?" He was clueless when it came to gun safety—his finger was on the trigger and the muzzle of the gun was pointed directly at Tessa. It was at that moment that the door to the deli banged open.

Bryce jerked and the gun roared.

Chapter 12

Bryce had jerked just enough so that when the gun went off, the bullet singed the air a fraction of an inch from Tessa's head. In shock, the six-year-old wet herself, but didn't feel it. She couldn't feel anything. Adrenaline shot through her and it felt like every nerve ending in her body was on fire.

As tears sprung into her eyes, her mother snatched her into her arms, Maddy snorted in her sleep, and Bryce dropped the gun. He stared at it as if it had gone rogue and had tried to kill the girl on its own.

"I'm sorry. I thought it was… you know…" He trailed off, not knowing what to say. He couldn't exactly say that he thought the safety was on since he had never put it on safe. And he couldn't pretend he didn't know it was loaded since they had just watched Griff load it. Bryce had screwed up. He's been stupidly careless and nearly killed a little girl—he thought he was going to throw up.

"Stop shooting!" Griff snapped. He had no idea what was going on and assumed Bryce was shooting at the zombie that had just pushed open the back door of the deli. How he could miss the creature framed there was beyond comprehension. That morning, the zombie had been a bus driver named Tamara Ripperdal. As a human, Tamara had been unable to control her eating and had gone up two sizes every year since high school.

As a zombie, she filled the doorway. When Griff saw her, his first reaction was to try and shove her back inside using the board. The gunshot had the other zombies charging and there wasn't time. He went for his own pistol, a Glock-17. It slid from its holster as smoothly as if he were drawing an oiled dagger from its sheath. His arm unfurled and he fired in one motion.

At a range of six feet with a target the size of a small pumpkin, Griff couldn't miss. The gun banged and Tamara collapsed in the doorway.

"Come on!" Griff was already running down the alley.

Victoria glanced once at the fallen Sig Sauer lying on the cement and all her fears of guns came roaring back. She grabbed her daughter and chased after Griff.

Bryce picked up the gun and spent a second he didn't have flicking the safety on. He then snatched up his bag of sandwich fixings and was about to run as well, only just then he realized Maddy was still asleep.

"God! Maddy! Wake up." He shook her roughly until her eyes blinked. They were still out of focus when he heaved her out of the chair. "Get your gun. Maddy! Pick up your damned gun." He shoved it into her hands and began pulling her along by Griff's black coat.

"What's going on?" she muttered. "Zombies?"

Bryce looked back over his shoulder at the deli. Something huge was shoving other zombies out of the way to get through the partially blocked door. From its clothes, to its skin, to its eyes, it was midnight black. It was huge and stronger than the others. Nothing had bitten it. It was whole. At the sight of the thing, Bryce was suddenly struck by a nearly paralyzing fear. It was a fear that made no sense. Yes, he was afraid of the zombies, of getting eaten or being left behind by the others. His fears up to this point had been right and natural.

This fear was different. It was otherworldly, as if he were seeing something alien from another world or... "From Hell," he whispered. He was looking at a demon, he realized.

"Bryce?" Maddy had felt the fear as well, but didn't know what was causing it. "What is it?"

He couldn't say the word *demon*. He was a scientist for God's sake and was sure there was a reason his soul felt like it was shriveling inside him as if it were trying to hide.

"J-Just, zombies. Hurry. Please." He pushed Maddy ahead of him and ran, looking back over his shoulder.

The sight of the demon filled him with dread and he forgot his aches and the fire in his joints, and he ran faster than he had ever in his life. This wasn't saying much. Tessa was outdistancing him and Maddy was able to keep up. Still it was a personal best.

The alley had a large opening to the west, one that a car could drive through. It also had a narrow one to the south. It was barely a foot and a half wide. Much to Maddy's dismay, Griff chose the narrow one. He slid in sideways, gun at the ready. Victoria went next and then Tessa, her puffy blue coat making a whistling sound as it scraped across the filthy wall.

"Jesus," Maddy whispered at the sight of the gap. Without another choice, she pushed in and got stuck right off. "Oh shit. Bryce! Shit. Help me."

Bryce's heart began to hammer. She was being too loud! The urge to leave her filled him and he looked back. The demon was at the table they had just abandoned. It was turned away, which settled Bryce for a moment. He shushed her, as he pulled her out. "Try it without the coat on." She ripped it off and tried again. This time she just managed to slip in. Her gown, front and back, scraped heavily along the wall and snagged on every imperfection along the walls. She was moving so slowly that Bryce began to go from foot to foot in his rising fear.

The demon had turned towards them. Behind it, the alley was filling with the dead.

"Hurry for God's sake," Bryce whispered. He could feel his bladder wanting to let go on the spot.

Maddy tried. She pushed sideways as hard as she could. Her gown tore as it caught on a jagged bit of cement. She tried to keep going but after ten feet she realized that she would be naked by the time she reached the other side.

Bryce watched her from the opening of the gap. He had only progressed a foot into it, afraid that Maddy would get stuck and that he would be trapped. The weaker Bryce inside him wanted to run away. He could slip into the shadows and sneak off…and Maddy would be killed. The demon would get her and devour her, chunk by chunk.

It was drifting towards them, sniffing the air. Bryce was torn between doing the right thing—helping Maddy—and running away. *It can smell my fear*, Bryce realized. *Or is it the pastrami?*

The aroma coming from the bag of meat and cheese was heady and strong. Was it luring the creatures on? Coming to an instant, but painful decision, he swung the bag in a full circle and sent it flying off towards the wider entrance to the alley. It fluttered as it sailed through the air and then landed with a louder than expected thud. The demon turned in that direction and ran with a strangely stiff gait towards it.

Bryce immediately slipped into the gap and began pushing hard against Maddy, forcing her deeper into the narrow chasm. She whimpered as the gown tore completely and hung from her like a death shroud. Now it was her flesh going red and raw. Somehow, she managed to hold in the pain.

Unfortunately, she kicked a pipe that clanked loudly into another. It was only then that Bryce realized that underfoot were lengths of old rusting rebar and wrist-thick iron pipes. The metallic clank brought the zombies hurrying to the narrow crevasse. The first one to the entrance was a chubby, middle-aged waiter who had been still living with his harpy of a mother that morning. The zombie virus had freed him of that particular horror.

He was slightly rounder than Maddy; regardless, he threw himself into the opening. His once white shirt tore off him in seconds. Then his skin began to peel back. Bryce felt the sandwich twist in his belly as the zombie kept coming unaware that he was flaying himself alive. His hideous black blood acted as a lubricant and he slid onward, leaving a sickening trail along both walls. Behind him, the other creatures fought to get into the crevasse. They roared and gibbered and laughed maniacally.

Weren't these zombies? Shouldn't they simply moan?

"Hurry, Maddy. Please." Bryce was so afraid that he had to clench his cheeks to keep from shitting himself. He begged Maddy to hurry, but she could only go so fast, and the bloody creature was closing rapidly. Bryce twisted around so that he had the gun pointed. Not wanting to waste ammo, he waited until the creature was five feet away before he pulled the trigger.

Nothing happened.

He had forgotten he had put it on safe. "Fuck!" He backed up as quickly as he could and nearly ended up tripping over more of the rebar.

The zombie slid closer, while behind it the others teemed. Most of them were smaller, skinnier, faster. They weren't really bothered by the narrowness of the crevasse and it dawned on Bryce that killing the first zombie would only make things worse for him.

He knew what to do. Sticking the gun in the gown's only pocket, he knelt and grabbed a long hunk of rebar. Planting one end against a crack in the cement, he leveled the other end at the zombie. It didn't blink as it pushed itself against the rebar. The metal dented his skin, deeper and deeper, making it look like its flesh was made of white rubber.

Then the rebar broke through with a sickening *pop*. Not only did Bryce hear it, he felt it vibrate along the metal and up into his hands. And still the creature kept coming. There were more pops as it pushed the metal through its diaphragm, its stomach and then out its back. And it kept coming.

Bryce *almost* panicked. He could feel the fear just below the surface, but he had it under control, barely. For him, *almost* panicking was a moral victory and it buoyed his sinking spirits

—then he dropped the pistol he'd been desperately trying to pull from his pocket. Just like that, his moral victory became a losing battle. He could feel his fear like a physical force inside him. It shook the core of his being and he would've run away only Maddy was still mostly lodged in place and was only slowly retreating.

Bryce turned back to the creature and up close, he saw that the thing was grinning. It had a steel bar right through its abdomen and the thing was happy!

"Fuuuck!" Bryce cried as he dug for the gun among the pipes and poles. Most were long, ten feet or more, but one pipe was only four foot in length. He picked it up and had the same odd sensation he'd had earlier with the "kick."

The pipe, two inches in diameter and about twenty pounds in weight, felt wonderfully right in his hand. He hefted it and just holding it calmed his frayed nerves. The gun became an afterthought. In the narrow confines, attacking with the pipe was relegated to the overhead bash, which was perfect since he was facing zombies.

He lifted the pipe, paused, gritted his teeth and swung it in a sharp, fast arc. The happy look on the thing's face disappeared as the top of its head cracked like an egg and blood shot out its ears. It fell forward, but because there was still three feet of rebar sticking out of his chest, it couldn't fall completely. It sort of slumped to the side, half blocking the lane.

Behind it were the others. These ones moaned properly. It was an eerie, terrible sound, but at least it made some sense.

They climbed over each other to get at Bryce. They also climbed over the once grinning zombie, only to be met by the pole he wielded. He lifted it high once again and began hammering the creatures as they came on. In the narrow space, he had a distinct advantage. There was no room for maneuver. They came on completely without fear and didn't even throw up an arm to ward off the blows he rained down on them.

Bryce killed them, one after another. They piled up as high as his head, and still they came on, crawling over the top of the pile. His arm began to ache and quickly, the pole lost whatever magic it might've had. He swung and swung, and with each crack of the pipe, vibrations shot up the metal and into his hands. Blisters formed along the delicate skin of his palms; evidence that he hadn't done a day's worth of manual labor in his life.

Sweat was dripping into his eyes when he heard, "Hey!" It was Tessa hissing from the end of the alley. Maddy was finally through. Bryce swayed for a moment before he reached down and grabbed his pistol. He then slid along the gap between the buildings. Just as he came out, he was greeted with a mostly naked Maddy. She was holding the scraps of her gown around her.

"Where's the coat?" she asked.

Bryce looked back. He had dropped it and now it was being trampled by the dead as they pushed slowly along the lane. "Back there," he said. "Sorry, but there were so many of them. We'll get you something. There's stores every…"

"Enough!" Griff barked as quietly as a man could bark anything. "We'll worry about clothes when we're safe, and that's not now." They had emerged onto another street blocked with cars. Most were abandoned. One had a terrier in it that was going out of its mustached mind. It was barking and growling, looking like it would tear them to pieces if it could only get out.

The sound was drawing the dead from the surrounding buildings. Victoria was already pulling Tessa up the block. Soon, they were all running again, as behind them the street filled with the dead. The little group had been terrified a block over when there had been forty of the creatures after them.

Now there were hundreds.

Chapter 13

Bryce ran doggedly, his bare feet slapping the pavement. Pain shot from his soles, up his legs and along his spine with every jolting stride. His shoulders ached and his hands were numb…except for the pain from the blisters. He wanted to toss aside the pipe. It was heavy and, compared to the Sig Sauer, it was a primitive weapon. And yet, he only had ten rounds in the gun. They would go in seconds; he had learned that the hard way.

Behind them were howling, moaning, gibbering beasts— some were also laughing in a mad, over-the-top cackle. The laughter was insane, even more so than all the rest, and the sound of it made him want to puke in fear.

Just ahead of him he could see Maddy; in fact, he could see way too much of her. She was starting to lose even the shreds of her gown and now her jiggling rolls were visible.

As much pain as he was in, he felt bad for her. Not only was she being tortured by the drugs running about inside her body, she was also being humiliated. It didn't seem right.

To add salt to her wounds, they were passing rows of boutiques. She was a brick throw away from being dressed in thousand-dollar jeans and tailor-made jackets. For the first time in her life, she stared longingly at the designer clothes. She stared for a second too long and hit an open car door. It was a glancing blow but it still took flesh off her right arm.

Bryce darted around the same door, but then saw that the driver had left behind a blanket. It was snowy white and seemed to glow in the dark. He grabbed it and picked up the pace and after a few seconds came abreast of Maddy, who was huffing and puffing. She was too tired to say thank you, but he read it in her eyes as she pulled it around her shoulders.

A shuffling grunting coming from behind them had Bryce looking back over his shoulder. It was one of *them*. The creature was tall with a runner's lanky body. It put out a long, long arm to grab him. It seemed to stretch and stretch until it was inches from his neck.

Then Bryce had yet another moment he couldn't explain. Without even knowing he was going to do it, he stopped, pivoted to the side and ducked under the grasping hands. The creature couldn't control its momentum nearly as well and it shot past, but not before Bryce swung the pipe around in a blur.

Crack!

It struck the thing's right knee and shattered the kneecap into a dozen fragments. The joint became unhinged and the zombie collapsed in a rolling ball of arms and legs.

A second zombie had been on the tail of the first. It too couldn't stop on a dime and it tripped over its lanky friend. Bryce smashed it in the back of the head and ran on. He was too tired to be amazed that he was doing actual manly things. He was too tired for anything, really. The last time he had run this far was never. Although he wasn't fat, he had no endurance and little strength.

Still, on a normal night and in proper shoes and shorts, he figured he could've run twice as far without feeling like his legs were about to give out from underneath him.

It was the fear; it sapped his strength. And it was his feet; every step was an agony. In the dark he kept landing on rocks and cracks and who knew what.

Sheer determination kept him running with his head down. They were going south now, block after block. Their way west had been stopped by hordes even larger than the one following them.

"Behind you," someone hissed from above.

Instead of looking back right away, Bryce glanced up at the dark building. There were people poking their heads from windows watching them run. There were at least a dozen of them and more were peeking out from behind dark curtains or heavy blankets. It made him realize that the numbers of people fleeing or infected were just the tip of the iceberg.

Millions more were hiding, waiting to see what was going to happen, perhaps waiting to see if someone would rescue them. But who would? They had already passed scores of abandoned police cars and fire trucks of all sizes. And the army was notorious for moving slowly, at least at the beginning of any emergency, and from what Bryce could tell, every minute counted.

The city had been turned on its head in a matter of hours. In a week there'd be nothing left but ruins. It meant Bryce would have to protect himself.

Three times he stopped to fight zombies. By necessity these were short battles. When the dead got too close, he would climb up on a car and, with his advantage in height and reach, he clubbed them to the ground. Then he would run on before the main horde caught up.

The third time there were just too many zombies all at once. He barely got onto the car before a hand ripped down his back. A high, girlish scream tore from his throat as he teetered on the verge of falling back into the grasping diseased hands of the zombies. He would've fallen; however, his gown ripped and he tumbled forward off the car.

His left arm took the brunt. Shrieking pain shot from his elbow and up his arm bone.

"Shiiit!" he cried. His first reaction was to curl into a ball and make whimpering noises until the pain became bearable, but there was no time. Zombies were swarming over the line of cars to get at him. With a hiss, he forced himself to his feet and began to run again. With his arm paralyzed from the pain, he couldn't stop and fight—and the dead were getting closer.

"Griff! Agent uh, Meyers?"

The agent turned just as he was about to jog down into a subway station. Bryce was lagging fifty yards back and was just ahead of seven or eight of the faster zombies. Maddy was ten feet in front of him, running slowly, meandering back and forth in her exhaustion.

"Get down there," Griff ordered Victoria, pushing her towards the stairs. "If a train comes, keep it from leaving the station. Tell them there are FBI agents on route. Go."

Victoria looked down the steps and pulled back; the lights along the wall gave off a yellow hue that made everything seem, not just odd, but evil. Some station lights were like this, their glass coverings were old and covered in layers of pollution, and normally, she would've swallowed her fear and trotted on down the stairs, knowing there would be people down there and that everything was the way it was supposed to be, despite the odd light.

This wasn't a normal night. She took one look down and balked. There weren't going to be people down there, only monsters, and nothing was the way it was supposed to be.

There has to be a better alternative, she thought. Desperately, she looked around, hoping to see a free traffic lane and a taxi, or a police precinct brimming with officers.

Griff shoved her from behind. "Go! Tessa, go with your mom." He shoved the girl, too. There was no time for fear. The moment they were headed down, he settled in behind a car, his forearms resting on the hood, his Glock aimed at the shadow creatures just behind Bryce. He couldn't look at the mass of them further back; the street was filled with crazed creatures that were hell bent on tearing him limb from limb. He had to force his mind to ignore the screams and moans and the sickening laughter.

His entire focus had to be on his sights, his target and his breathing. He had to aim low. A head shot from this distance was chancy and with so few rounds left, he couldn't justify taking the shot. Slowly, he squeezed the trigger until the gun went off: *BANG!* It seemed extra loud and the echoes raced around the buildings and ghosted up the street.

The zombie behind Bryce didn't feel the bullet shatter its femur. It simply couldn't run anymore and it fell. The one behind it tripped over the first and fell in a tangle of arms and legs. This set off a chain reaction among the leading pack of creatures and five of them sprawled over the sidewalk, giving Bryce an extra ten second lead. It was all Griff could afford. He waved Maddy on, hissing for her to hurry. He then turned and went down the stairs, taking them three at a time.

The 23rd Street station was no frills compared to some. To the left was a bank of machines where MTA cards could be filled. Beyond that were the turnstiles, then another short set of stairs that ran down to the platform. Victoria and Tessa were on those stairs, hunched and peeking around the corner.

Griff vaulted the turnstiles and went down the stairs. "What do we have?"

"More zombies," whispered Victoria. Griff's face fell. He pictured another horde, but when he looked around the corner, he saw that there were only three of them. Two on the tracks closest to their platform and another across the way, standing on the northbound platform staring at the tile walls with blank eyes.

There were also bodies splayed out in sickening poses and surrounded by drying blood. In the ugly yellow light, they didn't look real.

Griff went to the edge of the platform and looked both ways. "You think the train's still running?"

Before she could answer, Maddy plowed her girth into the turnstile, her mouth hanging open, her hot breath huffing in and out. She couldn't speak and she definitely couldn't get over the turnstile. She could only lean on it, sweat dripping from her chin. Bryce came down a second later. He stumbled right up to her, unceremoniously planted both hands on her backside, and began to push.

Even with his help, she couldn't make it over. Griff had to hurry back up the stairs and drag her across in the least graceful manner possible.

"Thanks," she gasped, drawing her blanket around her shoulders.

Bryce leaned against the turnstiles much as Maddy had a second before. His legs were shaking and his stomach was growling. He was hungry again, which didn't make any sense. Behind him, zombies began tumbling down the stairs, their heads cracking against the cement. More bodies fell on these in an avalanche of horror. Hundreds of them spilled down the stairs. So many that they blotted out the ugly yellow light.

"Fuck," Bryce muttered before he heaved himself over the turnstile. He teetered down the final flight of stairs and saw the empty station. After the frantic commotion above, it seemed abandoned, as though a train hadn't passed that way for years. "What are we going to do?" The turnstiles wouldn't stop so many zombies for long and it appeared like their only choice was to run endlessly onward.

For Maddy, "endlessly" meant only another few hundred yards at the most. Bryce had maybe twice that left in him.

Victoria glared at Bryce. The heat of it was a force. "You can start by giving me your gun." She turned her glare towards Griff. "He almost shot Tessa! He's a menace and I have a right to protect myself, too."

"I don't know what rights any of us have anymore," Griff said, checking his magazine. He started to thumb bullets from his spare to fill his main. "If you want, you can take off. No one's stopping you." He jutted his chin down the length of the platform. There was an exit at the far end of it and no zombies between her and it.

"No. I don't think so." She eyed Maddy, who was too tired to shift the remnants of her gown beneath the blanket. It was a coldly calculating look that Bryce read as: *I don't have to outrun the zombies. I just have to outrun her.* Victoria went on, "But we need a plan one way or the other."

Griff walked out onto the platform. The two closer zombies immediately started to shamble towards him, while the third was still enthralled by the tiles across the station. Squatting, he looked along the tracks as they disappeared into the darkness. There was a bit of a walkway three feet above the tracks; it was black with tar, grease and muck. There was also trash strewn across it, as well as across the tracks.

"We'll head down there," he said.

Tessa went green at the idea. Victoria's lips turned downward like a grouper's. "And just hope a train doesn't come by and crush us?"

"Yup."

Victoria saw Griff was implacable, so she looked back and forth from Bryce to Maddy. Both wore expressions that suggested that being hit by a train wasn't a bad plan at the moment. "What about them?" She meant the zombies that were even then stumbling towards the turnstiles. When they were crowded in a mass like that, they took on a grey sameness. They were no longer individuals; they were just zombies. "They aren't going to be slowed by some stupid train tracks."

"Yeah they will," Maddy replied. She gestured to the two zombies on the tracks that were scrabbling uselessly, trying to climb up to eat them. "Can you kill them for us, Bryce?"

He was surprised she had asked him and not Griff. The FBI agent was the superior physical being in all regards. But he didn't have the pipe. Bryce went to the edge, hefted the pipe and slammed it down on the first. *Tank!*

Tessa turned away and Victoria's lips pulled down even further; they were practically at her jawline now.

Bryce killed the next one with equal ease. He turned exhausted eyes to Maddy. She plopped down on the platform, swung around and wiggled until her feet touched the closest railing on the tracks. "Come on. This is the only way to keep them from coming after us."

"You want us to go down there?" Victoria was close to running away. It was the smart move. The zombies would go after the nerd and the cow, while she and Tessa ran to the end of the platform. They could make it—but they would be all alone. Being alone was bad. She hesitated, not wanting to be the next down.

"Is this the *third rail* we have to watch out for?" Maddy asked, pointing at a separate and thicker line of metal that ran parallel to the two normal tracks.

Bryce grinned and climbed down next to her. "I get it. Smart. Come on guys. Hop down. It'll be okay."

Griff actually chuckled. "I hope this works." He turned and put his hands out for Tessa.

"What works," the little girl asked. "What are we going to do?"

Maddy answered. "We're going to fry some zombies."

Chapter 14

As the five of them began to climb, slowly and with great care, over that dreaded third rail, the zombies hit the turnstiles. Some of them seemed to remember how to go through and pressed their hips against the metal poles. Other than the blood, the torn clothes, and the evil black eyes, they looked like they were hurrying off to work. However, none remembered the cards that had to be passed through a slot to activate the turnstiles.

One or two climbed over without a problem. The rest hesitated just long enough to be crashed into from behind and then trampled underfoot. A pile up ensued, but not a large one, and the turnstiles acted like nothing more than a large speed bump. In seconds, the dead were pouring over them.

They rushed at the five, dropping down onto the tracks without regard to safety. Legs were broken and skulls cracked. Those that fell first became a cushion for the hundreds that came next. They raced at Griff and Bryce who were trying their best to lift Maddy over the third rail. Had it just been a normal piece of metal, she could've gotten over it without a problem. But with 1500 volts coursing down its length, it was death to touch.

With a steadying hand and a light boost, both Victoria and Tessa had gotten over easily enough. They were light and athletic. Maddy was neither.

Victoria saw the speed of some of the zombies and cried, "Throw her over! Just throw her!"

Two-hundred pound women did not come with hand-holds and throwing one was out of the question. Griff did the next best thing. He cupped his hands and bent his knees. "Put your foot here. Bryce, get her from behind. One, two…three!" He heaved upward while Bryce, with a hand on each soft cheek, shoved as hard as he could.

With their adrenaline pumping, she felt lighter than expected and together they sent her flying. She landed hard and groaned in pain. There was no time to ask if she was alright. Griff cupped his hands again and nodded at Bryce. Bryce hadn't needed a boost like this since he was six and he hesitated as if it was part of an Olympic event.

"Come on!" Griff shouted.

"One second." He grabbed the pipe he had dropped and tossed it over to the next set of tracks. Then he made the mistake of looking back at the zombies racing towards him. There were so many. And they were so close. "God," he whispered, before he practically jumped on Griff. Thankfully, Griff caught his foot in his cupped hands and pushed him up and over.

It was Griff's turn to come across; however, there wasn't any time. He ran from the grey mob. Beneath his once shiny shoes, were imperfectly placed wooden railroad ties. Some had six-inch gaps, some had eight. Some were raised half an inch, some were raised an inch and a half. To make the run even more challenging, the tracks were also strewn with trash; old yellowing newspapers, dented cans and broken bottles. There were even soggy diapers flung here and there.

One misstep and he would be done.

The dead had to overcome the same obstacles, and they were less vigilant as well as less agile. Many fell and were trampled. Some fell into the third rail and seemed to get stuck to it as they twitched and jerked.

The fastest wouldn't fall. A hideous, faceless woman dogged him for half the length of the station. It didn't matter that she was wearing a single high-heeled shoe, she still kept up... and even began to catch up! The long night was finally wearing on Griff. He was tiring and his legs were beginning to feel like lead. He considered turning and ripping off some 9mm rounds, only he knew that if a single bullet failed to hit perfectly, she would be on him in a second.

And there were others behind her, desperate to get at him, desperate for blood or flesh or simply to kill. Griff didn't know what made them so insane, and just then, with the woman's foul breath on the back of his neck, he didn't care.

He flung himself in a desperate dive through the metal columns that ran along the inner edge of the tracks. Unlike Bryce, Griff was a true athlete and he shot through without hitting one. He landed with a thud, his shin whacking hard on the closer rail. Ignoring the pain, he jumped up, ready to run again. There was no need.

The faceless woman was jitterbugging on the rail, her limbs contorted, her teeth clamped down on her tongue so hard that she was spitting blood. She was just one of many. Griff's race down the tracks had thinned out the horde so that when they hit the third rail, there weren't enough of them in one spot to create an insulated barrier. They tried to cross, and they cooked. Some fried in their own fat, popping and sizzling. Some were flame-broiled as their clothes caught on fire. Some slow-roasted. The stench of burning hair was sickening.

Maddy gagged, while Tessa hid her face in her coat. Griff was gasping in the vile air as he came back to the little group. He didn't need to tell them to get moving. They stumbled south to get out of the foul haze. Bryce was the only one not effected by the odor. He kept it to himself, but the smell had only made him hungrier—there were implications to this that he didn't want to think about.

They popped into his head, regardless. How could he find the putrid stench of roasted human flesh appealing? Was he turning into one of them? Was this how it started?

Bryce stumbled after the group to the end of the station. They stopped where the real light ended. Ahead of them was *the* tunnel; a great black mouth ready to swallow them. Every fifty yards down it's length was a dim bulb that shed a tired yellow light that only truly illuminated a little half circle of wall. The tracks were dark and in that dark things scurried and squeaked.

Involuntarily, Bryce curled his toes inward which saved them from being crushed as Victoria spun and stepped right up to him. "Give me the gun." He hesitated for half a second and she poked him in the chest. "Look, I'm sick of this shit. You aren't using it anyways and I have a child to protect. And you have that bar."

Realizing she was being harsh, she tried to smile as she gestured at the pole, but one end of it was tacky with black blood, and the smile sagged back into the grouper look. "Please, for Tessa."

Griff opened his mouth to say something, then shut it. Now that things had calmed down somewhat, he realized he didn't want to be the man who denied a mother the ability to protect her child. He would let Bryce be that man.

But Bryce wasn't that man, at least not right at that moment. He knew he was something of a coward. Bravery was for the big and the strong, not for the scrawny, and yet, he felt he had handled himself fairly well so far.

"Here." He reached into the gown pocket and took out the gun. Naturally, his finger fell on the trigger.

"Hold on," Griff said, stepping forward. Gingerly, he took the gun from Bryce. "Let's get some ground rules in place before someone gets killed. Number one: keep your finger off the trigger until you're ready to fire. Number two: keep the gun pointed down until you have a target. Number three: wait until they're right on top of you to shoot. This is it for the bullets until we get downtown."

Griff then spent a minute showing them how to load their weapons, how to aim, and how to fire.

While he did, Bryce sat on one of the rails, picking glass from his feet. He was surprised they didn't hurt more.

Tessa watched him. She was remarkably composed for a kid standing on the edge of a dark tunnel filled with rats. Her hands were stuffed deep into her pockets. "Aren't you cold? All you got on is that dress."

Bryce looked down at himself and realized that the hospital gown, when worn outside a hospital, was very feminine. "Cold?" He hadn't given it much thought, but it couldn't be more than forty-five degrees out. He touched his cheek and found it cool, but not cold. "No. I guess all the running around has kept me warm. Look at Maddy, she still's sweating." She looked like a glazed ham, but he wasn't about to mention it.

Griff was cold. He had his hands tucked up under his armpits and he was hunched in on himself as Victoria worked the slide of the pistol back and forth. He gave Bryce's feet a quick glance. "You gonna be okay?"

Bryce shrugged. If he stepped on a shard that would be it. They would have to leave him behind...alone. The thought sent a shiver up his spine. Griff caught it and told him, "You're doing great. You and Maddy. I thought we were screwed a few times back there. Nerd power, right?"

"Yeah." Bryce didn't know what he meant by that, but gave him a grin, nonetheless. "What are going to do when..." A scrape of a shoe on the stairs stopped his lips. It was a small, sly sound and it froze him.

"What?" Griff asked, his voice not quite a whisper.

Bryce held a finger in the air, his head cocked. The step came again, quieter now. Griff shrugged and Bryce put the finger to his lips, before holding out a hand. Griff obliged, and pulled Bryce to his feet. Maddy had heard the sound as well and had her neck twisted so she could peer around one of the supports. She saw the demon first.

Black on black, huge and strong. It was staring across the turnstiles at the tracks where the bodies smoldered.

"Kill it," Bryce said, his voice a high squeak.

Griff stepped to his right and saw the demon, though in his eyes, it looked only like a man. Sure he was big and the ugly yellow light didn't help, but it seemed so much like a man that he hesitated. It wasn't until the demon turned and he saw the bloody arm it carried, that he realized he was wrong. No person would carry the remains of an arm around with them.

The demon saw Griff just as the agent raised his Glock and fired. The demon was quick and dodged to its left as the bullet took off its ear.

"Did you guys see that?" Griff muttered, moving to his right to get a bead on the thing. It ducked down before he could fire again. In a black blur, it raced away up the stairs. "I don't think it's turned all the way into one of them. It knew I was aiming for it."

Victoria was edging into the tunnel, pulling her daughter along. "Who cares? There's probably a million just like him, and weren't you the one saying not to waste bullets?"

"Yeah. You're right." Something about the demon didn't seem right to Griff, and it made the hair on the back of Bryce's neck stand up.

Maddy hadn't seen it. She'd been doing her best not to throw up from the fumes rising from the bodies. "Can we get out of here?" she begged.

Griff pulled his eyes from the yellow-lit stairs. "Of course. That's probably smart. Maddy you stick right on my tail. Then Tessa and Victoria. Bryce'll have our back."

This did not sit well with Bryce. Although the demon had fled, there was no telling if it would come stalking back. The others shuffled forward a few feet, but he paused at the edge of the tunnel. The darkness seemed to have deepened. "How far is it until the next station?" By this, he meant how far was it until he could feel even the least bit safe again.

As she counted the stops in her mind, Victoria's eyes flicked to the ceiling where decades' old paint was peeling. In the dark it looked like dead skin. "Uh, nine blocks about. Union Square is the next station and then Astor Place. The Six is almost a straight shot downtown. We can be at the Fed Building in two hours, if we don't run into any more of those things. What happened to them? You guys said you knew something?"

"They might know something," Griff corrected. And even what they knew was pretty thin. It amounted to: Daniel Magnus could be behind this, but they don't know what he did or how he did it, or how to fix it, or if it can be fixed. Still, it was a start. With that, he plunged into the darkness, completely unafraid of the huge black rats. Somehow, he ignored the squeaking and the quick darting movements of the vile creatures.

Maddy could not ignore the vermin. She drew her limbs in and spent more time watching her mincing toes than where she was going. Twice she ran into Griff and both times she clung to him. What scared her more than the rats was the dank, wet darkness of the tunnel. Light down in the tunnel felt unwanted, like a trespasser who didn't belong. Whenever they edged away from one of the dim lights, the darkness swallowed them whole and brought to life hideous creatures that lurked in the primitive portion of her brain.

I have a PhD, she told herself. *I'm a grown woman. There's nothing in the darkness but darkness*.

Except that was not entirely true.

Chapter 15

They were not alone in the tunnel.

On the raised walkway was a mound that looked like a pile of crumpled clothing sitting in the dark. Griff passed it by without even raising his weapon. Maddy saw it move and could smell the death hovering around it like a cloud. She had her gun pointed but not aimed. Her hand was shaking too badly to actually aim.

If it attacked her in the darkness, she didn't know how she'd be able to kill it before it got close. All it took was one bite and that would be it for her. She'd change into one of *them*. Unless she was already changing. Was there any other explanation for her fever and the pain etched throughout her body? At the thought, her stomach turned over again and a rumbling sour burp escaped her throat.

The thing raised its head as they passed and sniffed at them but didn't attack.

A mile or so later, somewhere south of 18th Street, they came upon a group of slow shamblers groping blindly. They were between the dim lights where the darkness was deepest, where it was a force that could almost be felt. They snuffed and shuffled towards the group—there was no way to know how many there were. Three? Ten?

Griff stopped so quickly that Maddy stepped on his shoe, nearly letting out a scream. It came out as a gasp. The sound was strangely loud, magnified by the intense quiet. Maddy slapped her free hand over her mouth as the creatures came closer. Victoria's quivering hand on her back almost brought out another scream.

The little group crouched, bunched together, clinging to one another as the dead came on. Maddy felt trapped. There were flesh-eating creatures in front, a killer currently off to her right, people crowded in from behind, and the darkness surrounding her, crushing inward. She began to hyperventilate and her panting was loud, despite the hand over her mouth.

It drew the creatures ever closer.

Victoria edged back away from Maddy and might've run if Bryce hadn't been right behind her. He seemed to be standing steady, but he was really frozen in fear.

Then one of the dead hit the third rail with a sudden shower of sparks. In the brief light, they could see the ragged line of beasts. The hideous creatures seemed to go on and on down the tunnel. There were more than enough to swallow every bullet they had and keep coming. Luckily, they were on the next track over.

The third rail was saving the little group once again. Still, they clung to each other as the dead passed by. Their pace was that of a languid stroll on a hot July evening and it was a long hour before Griff felt it was safe enough to inch their way south. Gradually, as their fears subsided, they picked up the pace. Even Maddy was able to relax. Her fear was replaced by bone-aching weariness. By then it was late, or rather early, sometime after two in the morning. Victoria and Tessa walked, leaning in on each other. Bryce kept close, his shoulders slumped from carrying his pipe, his mouth hanging open, his head hanging.

Griff felt the wear of the journey as well. His dress shoes, bought specifically for the trip to New York, bit into his toes with each step. The shoes had been Plinkett's idea. The senior agent didn't want to be seen arresting Daniel Magnus in shoes, worn at the heel and scuffed at the toe. Griff was wearing the remains of his finest suit as well. Now, the jacket was gone and his pants were stained and torn along one thigh.

But I'm alive, he told himself. Alive and carrying on with his mission. He would get Maddy and Bryce to the FBI field office at any cost and then hope to God they would be choppered out of the city, and that he would be with them. Him and Plinkett, if he was still alive.

This was going through his mind when he saw a soft grey light ahead. They had finally reached the Union Square station.

Instead of relief, their fears began to flower again. The utter darkness, which had been terrifying only minutes before, was now the shield that had kept them safe. No one wanted to leave its protective arms and venture out into the light where the dead could see them. Even worse than leaving the darkness, the tracks suddenly diverged robbing them of the protection of the electrified rails on either side.

Griff, who was the least familiar with the subway system, stayed in the middle, express lane. It was a mistake that became apparent as the tunnel opened onto the station. Now, there were chest-high platforms on either side of them. Brightly lit platforms, with haggard, twisted creatures roaming around on them. Griff pulled them low and had them duck-walk through the filth along the edge of the closest platform.

In no time, Maddy's legs were cramping and she had to stop. Despite the danger, no one complained. The suddenness of the apocalypse had left them all exhausted and they needed the break.

With the dead wandering around almost right above them, they rested on the tracks with their feet pulled in to keep from being seen. Griff only gave them ten minutes before he was pushing them on again. While the others crab-walked, Maddy had to crawl; she was too tired to be embarrassed. Crawling had one advantage; she couldn't see the hideous faces of the dead. She kept her chin down and kept moving.

They crossed beneath a walkway that ran to another set of tracks. The undead were there as well. Not many, but then it didn't take many to change their fate.

In fact, it took only one. Thirty feet above them, a woman with long, straggly black hair leaned on the rail. Half her face was a scabbed-over ruin, but her eyes were still intact. They were bleary and unfocussed, like a drunk who'd just stumbled from a bar at closing time. She sniffed the cold air and caught their scent.

It didn't take a bloodhound. Bryce could smell his own fear, and the acrid whiff of Maddy's sweat. Griff had his own male aroma just as Victoria had her female one. Tessa smelled of mud and something worse. She had stepped in a pile of undead excrement not long before and it clung to her hundred-dollar boots, rendering them almost worthless. *Almost.* Just then, both Maddy and Bryce would've given anything for a pair of shoes.

The woman with the oozing scab for a face had on only one shoe. She'd lost the other hours before in a desperate race against a howling doctor with mad eyes and blood coating him from chin to belt. She never had a chance. The shoe was long gone, which was neither here nor there as she pulled herself over the railing and dropped down onto the tracks, hitting with bone crushing force within arm's reach of Tessa's shit-covered boots.

Tessa, her eyes shocked into wide circles in her pale face, drew in a long breath to let out a scream that would be heard from one end of Manhattan to the other. She kept sucking air in as every muscle in her body went taut. Just before she exploded, Victoria spun her daughter part way around so they were face to face.

"Don't," Victoria begged. She'd nearly screamed as well, but there was no rush of feet, no chorus of the dead moaning, no mob pouring down onto the tracks. It was just the one woman. She had red, stick-like bones poking up out of her sweater.

None of them expected her to move and they all jumped when her hand shot out. Somehow, without even looking, she managed to grab Tessa by the ankle. Tessa freaked. Fear was a mountain inside her skinny, six-year-old chest. It was so enormous that for the moment she was unable to scream, unable to even kick. The fear seared through her, making her spasm and jerk as if having a seizure.

Victoria kicked for them both, shoving backward uselessly, her feet pushing on the wooden ties as though she were backing up a ladder. There was no getting away. The zombie's grip was iron and Victoria simply dragged it along. "Get it off of her! Get it off!" she begged in a hissing voice.

Maddy was closest, but she had set her gun down and had scrambled away from it when the woman splatted down between her and Tessa.

Although Griff was tired, his reflexes hadn't yet slowed, and he had his gun out and aimed in the blink of an eye. But didn't shoot. Situational awareness kept him from pulling the trigger. There were a dozen zombies all around them, and if he fired, they would be on them in snap; and who knew how many more were lurking along the overpass or just up the stairs out of sight.

"Bryce, the pipe." Griff pointed at the pipe sitting uselessly in Bryce's right hand.

He had been shocked into inaction. Now he reacted quickly, acting more like a warrior than a thinking scientist. The thing's grip on Tessa's ankle was the problem and the solution was obvious. He brought the heavy pipe up and around, and smashed it down on the thing's wrist, breaking both the ulna and radius. This freed Tessa, who crawled onto and over her mother, desperate to get away from the zombie. Victoria scrambled away, too, though she wasn't in any danger. The scabbed-over zombie couldn't move, it could only flail uselessly.

The commotion, brief as it was, had gone unnoticed, and for the moment, the group was apparently safe as they scurried away. But they weren't out of danger, yet. The creature held out her good hand to them as though she were begging for them to come back to be eaten. When they didn't, she opened her drooling scabby mouth and screeched at the top of her lungs.

"Christ!" Bryce cried, flinching back from the scream. It was only when Maddy shoved him from behind that he realized it was up to him to end the scream before it brought every zombie in the station rushing down on them.

Darting forward, he smashed the pipe down on its skull like he should've done in the first place. The top of its head dented inward with a revolting *squish* sound. After that there was a pause as everyone in the group sat unmoving, listening for the sound of zombies coming for them. It was a short pause. The damage was done, and zombies were flooding onto the platform. Griff hopped up and raced forward only to have two of the beasts fall from the walkway thirty feet above and land directly in front of him. Like the athlete he was, he hurdled them without breaking stride.

Maddy, who couldn't jump a curb, tried to skirt around them and almost stepped onto the third rail. She pulled her foot back just in time and as she did, Victoria knocked into her from behind, and had Maddy not been so heavy, she would've been thrown onto the rail. A curse ripped from her lips; however it was drowned out as Victoria started shooting at the two creatures, neither of which were capable of moving anything more than their arms.

Too late, Griff yelled, "No!"

The creature's scream had been bad. The gunshots brought a legion of undead on them.

Victoria emptied half her magazine into the two, blasting hunks of flesh and hair from them and knocking them onto their backs. She and Tessa danced through the carnage and then raced past Griff. He was taking aim at one of the faster zombies that was cutting across the platform and had a bead on Bryce, who was pushing Maddy ahead of him.

Griff fired, snapping the bullet an inch from Bryce's ear. The near miss turned his frightened expression into something comical, making him look as though he'd just taken a bite out of a lemon.

With the zombie down, Griff turned and charged after Victoria and Tessa. There were more zombies near the far end of the platform, and Victoria had her gun aimed.

"Wait!"

Again, he was too late. Victoria began blasting away. Amazingly, she managed to kill two of them before she ran out of bullets. This left two more. One was lame and slow, and looked as though it had been half-eaten. The other was a child, no bigger than Tessa. She had a grinning black mouth and quick bare feet. Victoria took one look at it, turned and ran, dragging Tessa along with her.

They rushed to Griff and hid behind him. Victoria was screaming about bullets; Tessa was hyperventilating again. At least one of them had their hand on Griff's arm. His hand was too steady for this to spoil his aim, and yet, he still missed. Unbelievably, the creature had anticipated the shot and dodged just as he pulled the trigger.

For Agent Griffin Meyers, this was his demon.

He fired again and just like before, it juked to the side. It was closer this time, and he didn't miss his target by much. The bullet ran a furrow across the side of her head and a cloud of red mist hung in the air behind her, as he lined up what he could only hope was his last shot. If he missed, she would be on him before he could properly aim. She'd be on him, and he'd be missing a chunk of flesh…and he'd be infected.

In a blink, it was four feet away, three, two…she darted to his left as he pulled the trigger and the bullet whined off one of the tracks.

Chapter 16

The demon girl had been too quick and he had missed. The bullet skipped off the track, sending up a spark. This spark seemed to explode into a thousand, which flashed over Griff as he threw himself to the side. His gun was still tracking the creature as he cringed from the sudden light.

The demon girl had juked too far and had stepped on the third rail. She jitterbugged as Griff climbed to his feet. The scene was both horrible and enthralling, and he had to pull his eyes from it or die.

More zombies were coming at them. A glance down the tracks showed him that the demon girl might have saved their little group. Zombies were spilling from the darkness at the end of the platform. They would've been halfway into their arms if it wasn't for the girl. Still, they were only saved for the moment.

"Onto the platform!" Griff cried. His voice was embarrassingly high.

He grabbed Tessa and practically threw her onto the platform. Victoria was fit and didn't need help. Maddy needed all the help she could get.

While Griff helped to heave her up, Bryce was in back, facing down a small horde. He swung the pipe back and forth, whacking at the outstretched hands. Going for a head shot seemed far too risky. The zombies were three and four across; a miss could overbalance him and leave him vulnerable. It was scary close as it was.

A look over his shoulder saw that Maddy had finally made it up. It was his turn, but there was no one to help him. The zombies were closing in on them in a semi-circle, and Griff was rushing to keep a lane open to escape, which left Bryce stuck on the tracks with zombies in front and behind.

He ran from the closer group and towards the end of the tunnel, but as he did, his eyes strayed to the third rail. He would jump on it if he had to. It would be quicker. *Like being struck by lightning,* he thought. *A zap, some sparks and then…*

"Hey! Up here." It was Maddy, waving her arms at the zombies chasing Bryce. She was trying to distract them and was nearly losing the white blanket in the process. "Look at me!" At the invitation, some turned and the sudden change in forward momentum caused a pile up.

Bryce took advantage of the moment. As he ran, he tossed the pipe up onto the platform and then leapt after it. He hit the edge and began to squirm and claw his way onto the cement. It was true he looked like someone with a serious handicap, but it did the trick and he managed to get away from the greedy hands.

Maddy tried to help him; he shoved her away. "Go. I'll catch up." As bad as he felt, he didn't feel as bad as Maddy looked. She seemed to have aged twenty years since their helicopter ride. She left him lying on the platform staring up at a grungy ceiling. The beasts were fighting each other to get to him, but he had time to take a couple of ragged breaths before pushing himself up. It was all the rest he could expect to get for some time.

His bare feet padded back to where he had left his pipe and as he bent to retrieve it, he saw something among the dead that made his heart skip a beat. *His* demon was back. It came loping up the tracks, dodging the shamblers, and with ease, it vaulted onto the platform. Bryce couldn't be sure, but it looked as though it had grown.

The pipe in Bryce's hands suddenly felt like nothing more than a stick and his arms like twigs. The demon certainly wasn't afraid of him or the pipe. It came for him wearing a grin, showing black gums and white teeth. Bryce quailed before it and wanted to run, shrieking, but he dared not. This was no jackal. This was a lion and it knew it.

It stalked forward, unafraid.

Then Griff was shooting his gun, making it thunder in the tiled confines of the station. This stopped the demon and it slunk low. It was still without fear; however, it was cautious. It respected the gun and perhaps Griff as well. The demon looked past the shaking Bryce Carter at its true foe.

And that was fine with Bryce. With its attention elsewhere, he turned and ran, chasing after the group, which was even then heading for the stairs. Only Maddy was waiting for him. She stood four steps up, waving him to hurry. For Bryce, he was flying. He had never been a sprinter, but his fear had him speeding so fast that he caught up in seconds. Only when he was on the stairs did he chance a look back.

The demon was nowhere in sight, which was almost as unnerving as if it had been two steps behind him.

Bryce backed up a few of the stairs before Maddy smacked him on the top of the head. "Come on!"

Once again, they were being left behind. They trudged up the stairs to an open area where tens of thousands traversed every day. It was strangely dark and mostly empty. The dead were there, some immobile, lying in congealed blood, and some marching towards them. There were too many coming at once for Bryce and his pipe.

Griff cleared the way with his Glock.

The sound was outrageous and both he and Maddy flinched every time he fired. She wasn't about to complain. Maddy knew full well the direness of their ammo situation, and as much as she wanted to blast the zombies out of their way, she knew she would only be wasting nine bullets out of ten. She stuck close to Bryce. His pipe made sense, even if he didn't. He had always been a dweeb, a weakling, a loser, now he was…different.

She glanced at him, thinking that he was discovering some new brave aspect of himself. Jealousy reared its head inside her. Here she was, a burden unable to defend herself. Sure, she could blame Magnus for drugging her, but the truth was, she wouldn't have been much better off if she had never met him. *And here's Bryce guarding our backs.*

This was only partially true. Bryce wasn't guarding their backs so much as he was too afraid to turn around. The demon haunted him. Zombies were one thing. He had seen enough movies to know what he was dealing with when it came to them, but the demon was different.

He was still spun around when a door they were passing banged open; he might've screamed, though if asked he would've called it a "yelp."

No one noticed since Tessa shrieked as though she were being tortured. The poor girl was a mess. Her nerves were frayed and she couldn't seem to stop shivering like an inbred poodle.

It wasn't zombies that charged from the door, it was people: a black man of thirty or so in a stained, green uniform, and an elderly white couple who wore matching Statue of Liberty t-shirts under snug woolen coats. The three gave off an eye-watering bleach smell as they rushed out.

"Don't shoot!" the younger man cried. He held a broom in one hand and had the other hand raised. His name was Jayson Lantz, and he knew a cop when he saw one.

Griff lowered the gun, slipping his finger from the trigger. It wasn't something he'd admit, but he had nearly plugged Jayson square in the forehead. He didn't know what to make of the three. It was dark and he couldn't make out their eyes but he didn't think they were infected.

That was the only good thing he could say about them. Jayson appeared to be exactly what he was: a custodian with a bit of a growing pudge and nerves that were already shot, even though he'd done nothing but hide for the last eight hours. The old couple: Mr. and Mrs. Harriman were worse. They were newly retired tourists from middle America who had lived a soft but frugal life, and had picked the wrong time to crack open their piggy bank for a trip they'd been dreaming of for thirty years.

"Take us with you," Mrs. Harriman begged.

Griff hesitated, wanting to suggest they get back in the closet and that he'd send help when he could. Then he remembered Janine, wallowing in her own blood a fruit bowl sized hole in her guts. No one was going to come back for the old couple.

Victoria surprised Griff. "Let them come. The more the merrier. There's safety in numbers, right?" She even reached a hand to Mrs. Harriman and pulled her from the closet. Victoria had her reasons for inviting them along and they weren't altruistic. It was clear, someone was going to die, and soon. They'd had near miss after near miss and their luck couldn't hold out forever.

She had figured the cow would be the first to die, of a heart attack if nothing else, and she hadn't cared. But the FBI agent cared. He was the real deal, and if he thought Maddy was worth risking his life for, maybe others would as well. Victoria had the image of a black helicopter landing on a building downtown burned into her mind—she and her family were going to be on it.

Griff darted into the closet where there were more mops and brooms. The city bought new ones on a weekly basis, but after a single pass around the station, they were too disgusting for words.

Victoria accepted hers with a grimace. Maddy leaned on her mop like an unlikely fantasy wizard. Mr. Harriman brandished his like a spear; his knuckles stood up like white peaks on a spotted plain.

"These are just for the moment," Griff said, speaking over his shoulder. He was already on the move, heading for the glowing exit sign. As much as he wanted to drill them in the use of their makeshift weapons, there was no time. They would have to deal.

When the group emerged into a pre-dawn twilight, the city was being swept by yet another wave of newly turned zombies. At midnight there had been eight-hundred thousand zombies roaming the streets. The number was up over 1.2 million now. Another two million were straight up dead, and a like number had "escaped."

Escaping didn't mean they were safe, not by a long shot. Across the Hudson, Hoboken was a giant bonfire, and the highways west through New Jersey were even more jam-packed than the streets of New York. To the east, Long Island had become a death trap for its seven and half million people. Ferries had stopped running hours before and marinas were being overrun by the richest refugees in the history of mankind. The 1% proved just as feral as the rest of humanity.

Even with zombies crawling up the stairs after the group, Griff paused at the entrance to the subway station. They were on the corner of 14th Street and Broadway. Across the packed street was an open park of sorts. People and probably zombies were running. There were screams nearby; some loud and fresh, some muffled. There were gunshots, but no car horns. As a city, the time for honking was over.

"Which way's south?"

It took Victoria a second to orient herself, but before she could answer, Jayson pushed past her and pointed. "This here's Broadway. It goes all the way to the Staten Island Ferry, which it ain't runnin' no how. You ain't from New York?" It was disappointing. Some nobody cop from some nowhere state wasn't going to be of much use.

"*We're* with the FBI," Victoria said.

Jayson cast a sidelong look at Maddy with her dirty white blanket. She had it knotted around her throat like it was a cape. *Nut job*, he thought, *or retard*. Bryce, twitchy and fearful, didn't look much better. But they had guns and all he had was a mop.

"Sure, FBI, right." He didn't care as long as they got him out of there. "Where are we going? Huh? We gotta get outta Manhattan, you know what I'm saying? And south ain't…"

He jumped as the sky suddenly roared. Six F15 fighter/bombers shot overhead, invisible despite being just a little over a thousand feet up. Their pilots had their guidance receivers up and running, and had for the last ten minutes. They should've dropped their payload before they crossed above the island, but what was being asked of the flight leader cut against everything he had joined the Air Force for.

Thirty years old and he was being asked to kill who knew how many innocent men, women and children.

"Target is cleared hot," the young captain said into his radio. He received five reluctant "Affirmatives."

The captain let out a long breath before finally saying, "Release. Release." He had never rippled off munitions with less enthusiasm.

His Eagle suddenly felt light and nimble as the 2,000-pound laser-guided bombs dropped away. Keeping his target designator fixed, he banked his flight of jets in a gentle arc. None of the pilots took their eyes from the target. The George Washington Bridge looked ghostly grey. The cars packed across it were barely visible.

How many thousands of people were stranded on it, desperate to get across? How many innocent people were about to die all for a mission that seemed hours too late? The very eastern part of New Jersey was already swarming with the dead, and yet it was cut off from the rest of the country by the broad Hackensack River.

Already fifteen bridges across it were being targeted. To keep the northern part of Jersey from being flooded with the dead, the George Washington Bridge was next on the list.

The captain's chest began to tighten. "It could be worse," he muttered, trying to reassure himself. The governor of California had ordered what amounted to carpet bombing every street, road, highway, and driveway that led to or from L.A. The footage was sickening. In the captain's eyes, it was straight-up murder.

A blinding flash of light made him jerk and his Eagle bucked. His bird was spirited that way…or he was just a poor pilot. He felt like a terrible one as he watched the bombs striking the center of the bridge in quick succession; *wham, wham, wham!* The tons of high-explosives hit within seconds of each other, creating a multiplying effect that shivered the entire structure.

The top deck of the bridge absorbed the first eight Paveway bunker-busting bombs and was in the process of disintegrating when the following four passed through the upheaval in the blink of an eye. They buried themselves five feet deep into the surface of the bridge before detonating, causing the reinforced concrete to ripple like water.

Although the upper deck of the bridge had a gaping hole taking up most of its width, the second deck was not wholly destroyed by the explosions.

As the young captain watched, the entire thing shook and twisted as the ripple washed completely down its length. Like a wave in still water, the ripple rebounded and came back, smaller, weaker.

When the dust settled, the bridge still stood. And the dead streamed across.

Chapter 17

Seconds after the jets roared overhead there were brilliant flashes of light from the northwest. These were followed up a second later by the echoing thunder of the explosions. It was like a great hammer the size of a building was striking the earth's crust. The echoes were still bouncing back and forth when a hot gust of wind blew down the street and washed over them.

Jayson, who had lived most of his life in Harlem, knew what had been hit by the jets. And he knew the repercussions.

"They're trapping us," he whispered.

"Us?" Bryce asked. "Like us, us? Why would they do that?"

Griff was staring toward the glow. He remembered seeing the bridge across the Hudson on the flight in from Boston. He thought it strange that there was only the one for such a large city. And now it was gone. They *were* being trapped. A shiver ran up his spine at the idea, and he turned to look at Bryce and Maddy.

It occurred to him that the two were now his only real hope of getting off the island, but would anyone really believe that these two knew anything of importance? Not looking like that. They looked mad.

"We need to get you two dressed," he said. As if they had forgotten that they were in the filthy remains of hospital gowns, they looked down at themselves.

"We don't have time for that," Victoria said. Amazingly, she punctuated the sentence with the snap of her fingers in his face. "We need to get downtown before the sun rises. Think about what this is going to be like when they can see us. You ever think about that?"

A check of his watch showed it was after five. They weren't going to make it before the sun was up, especially if the two remained shoeless. "Clothes first. If you're worried about the sun, you are free to leave."

"What kind of FBI officer would leave a mom and daughter?" Victoria replied in a huff.

Griff rolled his eyes but before he could say anything, Jayson pointed east. "There's a shop you can get some clothes at right down here. You never did say what's downtown."

"An FBI field office," he answered as he started down along 14th Street, mop in one hand, his Glock in the other. There was no reason to tell them to keep together. They were bunched like sheep, stepping on each other's toes. "We should be safe there."

Ahead was something of a mega boutique, but they had to pass a combination pharmacy and grocery store before reaching it. The building's windows were smashed in, showing the place had been ransacked, looted and partially burned. It was larger than it appeared from the outside, large enough to have its own deli section.

Bryce stared in, and at the sight of the food thrown about, he felt a change come over him. It wasn't a normal human feeling, but at the same time, he didn't think it was zombie either. He went weak, weaker than before. His thin muscles began to quiver and he found himself heading through the glass, stumbling, barely able to hold himself up.

Most of the shelves were empty. It didn't matter. There was a pre-made sandwich that someone had kicked down an aisle. He could smell the ham through the cellophane. In seconds, he was tearing into it, while his name was called behind him—the voice sounded as if it was coming from down the block.

He had it half gobbled down before Griff had him by the elbow and turned him sharply about. "What the hell?" the agent grumbled. "We really don't have time for this."

"Starving," Bryce said around a mouthful. "What about her?"

Maddy had followed them inside and was guzzling water from a clear plastic bottle. In a blink she'd downed a quart and was reaching for more. She had sweated out a gallon of water, maybe more. She didn't know she'd been that thirsty until she caught sight of the bottles.

Behind her, the others were creeping into the store. They were all in stages of thirst and hunger, and that included Griff, who realized there was no use fighting all of them, and went to find something to eat as well.

Bryce grabbed a handcart and hurried for the deli where he ate as he shopped. He craved meat and the sandwich he made himself was of heroic proportions. When he went to wash it down, he didn't want water, he wanted straight milk. "I've always hated milk," he remarked to Mr. Harriman, who was picking over the remains of the store with an eye to survival. In his cart were vitamins, medicine, a first aid kit, canned goods, and a large knife.

This was smart and Bryce wondered why he hadn't thought about doing the same thing. He went in search of a backpack. He found one covered with Spiderman images of various sizes. Next to the rack was an entire display of soft, fuzzy socks in bright neon colors. All thoughts of prepping for survival went out the window.

"Oh yeah! Maddy! Maddy, get over here."

By the time she hobbled over, he was already slipping on a pair. "Oh my God," he moaned, sounding like he was starring in his own erotic video.

Maddy tried to hold back, but made the same bedroom noises when she put on the socks. Griff watched with a tired, depressed look. The two were regressing. "They'll have shoes in the other store. And socks. We can be there in a minute."

There was no use talking to them. They wouldn't stand until they had fit pair after pair over their feet.

With his stomach full, a pack filled with food and an inch of soft padding on his feet, Bryce felt like a new man. He looked like an idiot, but he was sure that would be fixed quickly.

Everyone had grabbed backpacks. The Harrimans' were heavy and rattled with pills. Jayson's clanked with bottles; he had discovered the small wine stock. Victoria and Maddy's were light, holding just enough food and water to see them through the day.

Only Griff didn't have one. He didn't see the point. Food wasn't their immediate problem and nor was it really a secondary one just yet. Stopping Daniel Magnus was paramount. Everything else took a backseat to that goal.

"Can we please get moving!" he hissed when Maddy started pawing through the remains of the pharmacy for pain pills that were more potent than Tylenol. "In case you forgot, we have a mission." It was hard for him to believe he had to beg them to keep the looting to a minimum.

"Just a minute," she said without looking up as she scanned the bottles. "You don't know what it's like. The pain is gnawing. It's endless. Right Bryce?"

Bryce was making himself another sandwich, this one bigger than the first. "It's worse when you think about it," he said, spreading mayo with his fingers. "You got to focus on something else. Man, I could use some spicy mustard."

Griff's lips pressed together into an angry frustrated smile. Victoria caught the look. "We could leave *them* here and come back for them. Or send help for them. Or not. Maybe they're not important."

"No. They're important." More important than some pretentious, privileged housewife, he didn't add. He held a great deal back as he gazed about at his group. Jayson was sipping away at a bottle of pinot grigio. Mr. Harriman was fussing with a buckle on his wife's backpack and complaining about his arthritis. Tessa was standing off to the side, looking tiny. The little girl was still in a state of shock. Her eyes slipped in and out of focus.

"They better be important," he said under his breath as he went to the front. A zombie was across the street. Even with thirty cars between them and a gun in his hand, Griff felt a stab of fear.

The zombie slowly moved on. By the time it was out of sight, the group was ready to go. After a quick peek up and down the street, Griff stepped out, glass crunching under foot. Victoria jostled to go next. In case they had to run, she didn't want to get stuck behind the cow or the geezers. She pulled Tessa through next.

Maddy was about to follow Tessa but stopped half in the store.

"Wait a sec," Maddy whispered. On the air was a soft, distant rumble. It was the sound of engines large but new. There was also a hum that made her nervous, though she couldn't tell why. "Agent Meyers. Hey! Something's wrong."

There was. They weren't following him. Otherwise everything seemed about as good as could be expected. In the predawn light there were only a few zombies in sight and they seemed to be so ripped up that they were hardly a real threat. "Whatever it is we'll be better once we're inside the store. We can talk about it then. Look, it's right here."

Maddy poked her head out and saw the boutique. It was the next store, forty feet away. Its window was already shattered, as well. They'd be back inside in seconds…if it weren't for the glass. Three layers of socks weren't going to protect her feet from the shards sprayed across the sidewalk.

Mr. Harriman nudged her from behind. "Go or get out of the way," he grumped in a low voice.

"Just hold on for a moment." She thrust out her mop and with a few swishes of it she was able to follow the others outside, where she felt vulnerable and exposed. They were being

117

watched. It was more than just a feeling to her. Meekly, she stared around, and although she couldn't see the watcher, she knew there were eyes on them.

She tried to tell herself that it was nothing. There were still millions of people in the city. How many thousands were lurking in the tall buildings that loomed around them? How many were cutting through the park across the street where the shadows were still as deep as midnight, or hiding in the bumper to bumper cars?

Of course, they were being watched. It would've been a surprise if they weren't. So why was she unnerved? She couldn't say, which made her hesitation pointless. Almost as if the eyes were chasing her, she scurried up the street and slipped through the broken window.

It was dark inside the store, and quiet. The looting here had been on a much smaller scale. The people who had broken in had come for very specific items, none of them related to survival.

"We have ten minutes," Griff said. "You hear me? This is not going to be a shopping spree. Victoria will help Maddy and I will help Bryce. The rest of you; if you're not here when we're done, we will leave you behind. Victoria, do you know where the men's section is?"

The women's department was clearly marked, and all around them. Victoria gestured deeper into the store. "Upstairs."

An odd look passed across Bryce's features. Victoria was dragging Maddy away before she realized what it was. Bryce was embarrassed—he didn't shop in the men's section. He had the build of a fourteen-year-old boy. Maddy couldn't spare much in the way of sympathy.

"What size are you?" Victoria asked.

And there was the reason why. Maddy was a petite-plus, plus, plus which made shopping something of an ego nightmare. "If you can get me some shoes, I'm a size eight. Something soft, okay? Like Uggs?" Maddy was partial to Uggs since they were roomy.

Victoria had something to say about Uggs, Maddy could tell, but the woman kept it to herself.

The moment Victoria was gone, Maddy hurried to the Plus-sized section and began working her way through the pants. They were always the hardest to find in her size. She didn't bother looking for jeans; they'd have to be tailored to fit right.

As her circumference was greater than her height, most of her pants had to be tailored. Tops were easier; she could roll up the sleeves.

Maddy had three outfits picked out in minutes and rushed to the changing rooms just ahead of Victoria.

"I got you two pairs. Eight and Eight and a half. What about uh, you know, undergarments?" Victoria was glad the curtain hid her face. She was a petty woman and was sure she wouldn't be able to hide her revulsion if Maddy asked her to go hunt down g-strings.

Maddy's ears went red. She had heard the hesitation in Victoria's question. "Agent Meyers said we only had ten minutes so I think I better pick some up later. Maybe see if they have a coat? Just in case it gets cold."

"It's already cold," Victoria muttered. Maddy heard but said nothing. She was too stunned at her appearance to reply. The outfit she had tried on first: a grey sweater and a pair of soft joggers were draped on her as if she had picked out clothes two sizes too large.

"Are these tagged wrong?" She pulled off the top and inspected the size. It was a 24. She tossed it aside and grabbed a woven V-neck blouse in black. And it too hung on her like a sheet. "No way." With eyes grown wide, she stared at her reflection. There was no denying it, she was smaller, by a lot.

In growing excitement, she rushed out of the dressing room and grabbed an armful of clothes in various sizes. She chose a new dressing room and began throwing clothes on and pulling them off until she found her new size.

"I'm an 18."

"Is that a good thing?" By her tone, it was obvious Victoria didn't think so.

Maddy stepped out of the dressing room wearing black leggings and a navy-blue blouse that was long on her wrists. "Yeah, maybe. I don't know. I was a 24 yesterday."

Victoria stepped back, eyeing Maddy. She did look slimmer, though it was hard to tell since she had been wearing a blanket for most of the night. "Six sizes in a day? That's not possible. Unless there's something wrong with you. You and that guy were in a hospital, weren't you?"

"Yeah but that was…"

"Was what?" Victoria took another step back. "What was wrong with you?"

Maddy could only shake her head. She had no idea what had happened to her and Bryce. The only thing she knew for certain was that she hadn't been given LSD. "I don't know."

"Are you going to become one of them?"

"I don't know that either."

Chapter 18

Victoria dropped the coats and backed away.

"I'm not contagious," Maddy told her, though in truth she had no idea. The only thing she knew for certain was that Agent Meyers hadn't changed one way or another and Bryce had been skinny to begin with. It wasn't exactly a scientific study. "Maybe it was all the sweating. How much water weight can a person lose?"

Neither knew and neither made a guess. In an odd silence and with something like an accusation in her eyes, Victoria skirted around Maddy and hurried back to the front.

Maddy collected her gun, sighed once at the remnants of her gown, and followed after, though not as quickly. She couldn't pass a mirror without pausing. This wasn't vanity, it was amazement. She even attempted a smile, something she rarely did when looking in a mirror. For most of her life, mirrors were something to avoid.

At the front of the store, she found an equally stunned Bryce Carter. He hadn't lost weight, in fact he looked oddly bigger now that he was wearing actual clothes: blue jeans and a soft grey sweater. At the corner of his mouth was a bit of mayonnaise, all that remained of the sandwich he had made himself. Maddy pointed at his lip.

Absently, he wiped it away. "I got taller," he told her.

"I got skinnier," she answered. "A little bit."

Griff stared back and forth. It was more than a little bit. She wasn't exactly skinny, but she was noticeably smaller. And Bryce looked less like a runt. He walked up to the scientist, remembering the first time they had met in the elevator back in Boston.

Yes, he was taller.

"Magnus did this," he stated. "I just can't see why. For fun? Because he could?"

Victoria stood well back, holding Tessa close. "Maybe he gave them a different form of the zombie virus. A subtle one so no one notices. Then when they get in with the FBI or whatever, they turn."

"We should get masks," Mrs. Harriman said. "Why don't we have any masks?"

Her husband ignored her. "Did you say Magnus was behind this? All of it? I knew it! I knew it was one of them rich pukes."

"Did they have any masks back in the pharmacy?" Mrs. Harriman said, ignoring her husband in return. "I bet they did. Dear, run back and get us some masks. Oh, and some Lysol, the spray stuff. You know, for the germs."

Mr. Harriman had picked up on one word: "Outside?" He said it like *outside* was a foreign country and definitely a shit hole of a country. "We can make masks. We wrap our faces with scarves and…"

Something out the window caught his eye. It was one of the dead. It had been a skinny Puerto Rican kid, barely a teen with a mustache that was so thin it looked drawn on. One of his arms was missing; there was a ragged length of skin hanging from its shoulder, black and crusty on one side, pale and marred by teeth marks on the other.

It was missing an ear as well. In its place was a wet, black hole. Its nose was fine. The creature was sniffing the air as it came closer to the break in the glass. Then it stuck its head inside and the sound of its snuffling grew. No one moved. Other than Jayson, who sat on the counter, the nearly empty wine bottle on his lap, they all stood like manikins, frozen in odd poses.

"Hunaahhh," the creature said. "Hunnnnahh." It nodded and turned to look out across the crowded street. "Hunnnnahh!" It was loud now.

"It's like it's calling someone," Maddy whispered. She pointed at Bryce, and then to the pole he'd been carrying around.

"You want me to kill it?"

"Duh."

It was turned away, and it was small, and it only had the one arm—these were the deciding factors that allowed Bryce to grab his pole. His boots were so new that the treads squeaked on the still polished floor. He had to tiptoe through the displays until he was at the last counter. From there, he had a good view of the street. Although it was not yet sunrise, the dark was not so deep and he saw the dead were filling the park.

"Hunnnnahh!" It was something of a moose call, but it did the trick. The dead turned to the one-armed Puerto Rican zombie. A few began to crawl across the cars. One hopped up easily and began to leap from hood to hood.

It was Bryce's demon.

Bryce ducked down behind the glass counter as it dropped from the last car. It shoved the Puerto Rican zombie away and stuck its dark head through the gaping opening in the glass. It sniffed as the other one had. Then it grinned as it turned its fearsome gaze on Bryce.

Taking hold of the pipe in both hands, Bryce stood. He couldn't feel his feet. His legs just seemed to end somewhere beneath his shaking knees. Fighting the skinny, one-armed teen was one thing, the demon was too much. It was still too human, and at the same time it was too much of a monster.

It started to step through the hole when Griff suddenly appeared. The thing darted back as Griff went for his holstered gun. His hand was slow. He had found a black leather jacket to ward off the cold and the zipper got caught on the tag. The demon stood back from the glass, shaking its head.

"What the hell?" Griff muttered, keeping his voice low. "It just gave you a look. How the hell do these things give anyone a look?"

Bryce had seen the look. It was contempt. *He thinks I'm afraid*, Bryce thought. *He thinks I'd hide behind Griff...and he's right on both counts*. "Maybe some of them can still think."

The demon could do more than give looks. It put its head back and screamed into the sky. It was part battle cry, part summons. The scream sent a shiver up Bryce's back and he jumped when Griff slammed a hand down on his shoulder.

"We gotta get out of here," the agent said, pulling Bryce away. The street was flooding with the dead. The two raced back to the group who were gearing up, throwing their backpacks on, and grabbing their mops. In the face of so many zombies, these "weapons" were pathetic and their wielders even more so.

They didn't need to be told to run. In a near panic, they were darting in and around the clothing displays, heading for dead escalators. Griff was the youngest and strongest; he went down first, followed closely by Victoria and Tessa. Jayson, the bottles in his backpack clanking loudly pushed down next. He was a nightly drinker, but a full bottle on an empty stomach had him lightheaded and he stumbled down.

By then zombies were pouring through the hole in the glass and racing after them. Mr. Harriman had his wife go in front of him, and then, in a fit of foolish chivalry, he insisted that Maddy go next. Bryce was last. He waited at the top of the escalator, holding the pole as the dead came on. Both the Harrimans were having trouble on the odd escalator stairs. At the top and bottom the steps were uneven, while in the middle they were high and sharp.

Bryce looked back and saw Mr. Harriman only halfway down and moving with a gimp, favoring his left leg. "Hurry, God damn it!" he yelled. There was no reason to be quiet now. The zombies had spotted him and were tearing through the aisles of clothing, crashing into the displays and the racks without care. Feeding was their one desire; nothing else mattered.

The one-armed zombie had been trampled, as had any that failed to get out of the way of the bigger faster beasts. Bryce edged to the stairs, desperate to run. He was close to panicking, close to racing down the stairs two at a time and trampling Mr. Harriman who was taking forever, mincing his way down.

"Oh God," he whispered, glancing at the pole in his hands. Against so many, it was next to useless. He dropped it and darted to one of the circular racks that was hung with a swirl of jolly green and red Christmas sweaters. With his adrenaline pumping, the rack was surprisingly light and he drove it forward at the onrushing creatures.

Amazingly, he was able to knock the first one down as he smashed the rack into its chest. Then two more went down, flailing and snarling, tearing at the sweaters. This was the high point of Bryce's battle. His momentum was checked by the creatures crowding in.

A second later a firefighter with dead eyes and no fingers left on either hand struck the rack with its beefy shoulder and hurled Bryce backward. The firefighter fell over one of the zombies, but two more took his place and pushed Bryce to the edge of the metal stairs. He was just thinking about his pipe when the heel of his new boots kicked it and it went skipping down the stairs.

Now the only thing between him and death were a rash of ugly Christmas sweaters. He strove against the rack with all his strength, and held out against the might of a dozen zombies…for three seconds. Then he was smashed backwards, but only for a few feet, then the legs of the rack hit the sides of the escalator.

This gave him a breather and he looked back to see Mr. Harriman was nearly down. When he turned back, he saw that one of the smarter zombies was lifting one end of the rack.

Bryce fled down the stairs screaming, "Go! Go!"

The rack was heaved up and thrown to the side, then a river of grey flesh poured down the escalator. In the narrow confines of the stairs they fell over each other, and fell over each other some more, and kept falling. But they were so mindless that this barely slowed them down.

With hands grasping at his heels, Bryce made it down with Mr. Harriman only steps ahead of him. For some insane reason, Mrs. Harriman had waited for him while everyone else was racing away. They were going to die and die horribly.

"Get the hell outta here!" Bryce screamed as he shoved Mr. Harriman. He reached for his pipe, thinking he would give them a ten-second head start...if he could. The dead on the escalator were in no position to fight. They were piled five deep in places and any of them that managed to get to their feet remained upright for only a few seconds.

Bryce began beating at the pile with his pipe, crushing heads with each blow. And still they came on, body after body, too many for one man to stop even a fraction of them.

He had given the Harrimans thirty seconds; however when the first beast managed to get to its feet, Bryce knew he was out of time. With the zombie hot after him, Bryce turned and ran. It was a fast one and in a straight sprint would've run Bryce down.

There was nothing straight about their sprint. They wound in and out of the racks of clothes. When he could, Bryce pulled down displays to slow his pursuers.

"Bryce!"

It was Maddy, waving an arm. She was holding open a door off to his right. With every step, he was heading away from her and likely towards a corner where he'd be trapped. He juked hard to his right and it looked like a tidal wave of clothes sweeping towards him as the zombies broke in a long line, crashing through the racks and upending tables.

It was a terrifying sight and Bryce couldn't take his eyes from it as he ran. The store was far too crowded for that and he blundered into a display of high-end purses. In the dark, they felt alive, their gold chains seemed to attack him, wrapping themselves around his neck, his arms and the pipe. He fell, but hopped up quickly and ran on, flinging aside the purses.

The door beckoned so close. A zombie was closer and cutting at him faster than he thought possible. The creature, Phil Biggerstaff, who'd been a middle school gym teacher the day before, was whole with a mouthful of white teeth and long arms. He looked like he was running downhill at Bryce.

Bryce tried to swat at him with the pipe, a backhanded, weak attempt that did nothing to slow the creature and those white teeth grew closer, and the mouth opened wide. Its lower jaw looked like a castle's drawbridge coming down. Its gaping maw appeared to stretch wider than humanly possible. Then again, it was no longer human.

Phil's fingers were clawing at Bryce's new sweater when a gun fired, making a hole within a hole. Maddy had shot it through the mouth and the bullet blasted out the back of its neck, taking chunks of Phil's spinal column with it. Phil collapsed, but his momentum carried him into Bryce and the two crashed down.

The door was so close.

Maddy was shooting over him, screaming words that were chopped up by the sound of the gun. She wanted him to hurry and he was doing the best he could on his hands and knees, scrambling for the door and into a long narrow hall.

After the vibrancy of the boutique, the hall was ugly. It had cement flooring and cinderblock walls painted in industrial grey, making Bryce feel as though he had just stumbled into a prison.

He pushed to his feet just as Maddy slammed the door shut. Not a second later, it shook as something smashed into it. She stared down at the door's handle. There was a matching one on the other side. If these were true zombies, they'd only get the door open by accident.

It began to pivot down.

Bryce grabbed it and pulled up. The metal bit into the soft flesh of his palm as he and some creature on the other side struggled for mastery. Strength against strength. Although Bryce had gotten a little larger, he was still only an ounce or so over a buck-fifty and no one would call him strong.

"Run," he hissed, sweat dripping down from his thick hair. The others were fleeing down the hall, running at various speeds. Maddy was gasping as much from fear as the sixty-yard dash she had just ran. She would need time to get away. Probably more time than he could give her. "Go. Before it's too late."

But it was already too late.

There was a click as the handle went all the way down.

Chapter 19

Maddy threw her weight against the door, and for just a second wished she had the extra weight back so she could just sit there as a human door stop. Although it had been a short sprint, she was too spent to run anywhere just yet. Their escape had turned into an endless slog of running and fighting and screaming.

And their breaks always seemed so short.

She couldn't tell if straining against the door constituted a break or not, but at least it didn't involve running.

"Thought they got you on the stairs," she said. Their faces were inches apart. His breath smelled of ham; there were worse smells. "The old lady. So slow." The door behind them was thrumming as more and more zombies plowed into it and smashed it with their fists.

"Yeah. You should go. I got this." Bryce's entire body was trembling from the effort of holding the door closed. She jerked her head down the hall to where Mrs. Harriman was practically being carried by Griff, while Mr. Harriman limped after. The other three were congregated by the far door, fifty yards away. It would be another race to an uncertain fate.

Maddy didn't want to know what was beyond that door. Another alley, long and narrow? Or a street filled with cars and dead humans with wicked smiles and skin in their teeth? Or maybe it ended onto a bricked-in courtyard where the smokers went on sunny days. Maybe they would die horrible deaths.

"Sorry," Maddy said in a breathy whisper. "All this. My fault."

"No. It was Magnus. He did this. Kinda wished we said yes to his offer." They'd be safely locked away in one of Magnus' steel towers. He'd be Bryce-1 and have his own lab. Sure, he'd have to jump through hoops and make actual progress, but that was science in the real world. Of course, in the real world if he didn't perform up to standards, he'd just get fired.

What would happen if he didn't perform up to Magnus' standards? Would he be kicked out among the dead? Weaponless? Shoeless? Left to fend for himself with nothing but a scrap of thin cloth on his back.

"Woulda…said…yes…now," Maddy gasped.

The door was beginning to slide open bit by bit. Bryce nodded for Maddy to leave. He'd be lucky to give her a ten-second head start now.

She thrust away from the door and ran down the hall. It was a dream-like sprint. Her feet felt like they weighed twenty pounds apiece and the concrete floor took on a quality that made it feel like she was running through mud. Although she was a poor sprinter, she did one thing right, she refused to look back. Her eyes stayed focused on the far door.

She didn't want to see or even know what was going to happen to Bryce as the door came open with a bang and three dozen zombies filled the hall. They roared and screamed with one voice. It was like static filled with hate.

"I can make it," Maddy whispered beneath the sound. "Can make it. Make it." At thirty yards, she was losing steam quickly. Ahead, Jayson was waving her on. He looked past her, his eyes growing with every second. They were right behind her. Their horrid moans and screams were so close she could smell their putrid breath on her neck. She could smell feces and old blood and...*Polo*?

"Behind you!" Jayson screamed, but not to her. "Behind you!"

At the door she turned and saw Bryce five steps behind. He spun, winging his pipe around and leveling a creature that had once been the owner of an Asian bodega in Queens. As a zombie, he had been small, quick and vicious. Now he was dead, his brain crushed into pink jelly by the pipe.

Another zombie fell over the dead Asian. A third leapt over both only to get Bryce's backhand blow across the chin. His jaw snapped in half and was dislocated by the force of the blow, which also sent him face first into the wall, breaking his nose. It glared daggers. Bryce turned and sped for the door where he was nearly cut in half. In his zeal to slam the door shut in the face of the howling mass, Jayson would've trapped Bryce in with them if Maddy hadn't grabbed the handle.

Bryce didn't notice one way or another. He was outside with a metal door between him and a frightening death and that was all that mattered just then.

They found themselves on a back-alley loading dock. It was a cramped, awkwardly narrow alley, with a dogleg that made seeing down the street on either side impossible. With its jutting ramps, it was not suited for a bigrig; instead, there were seven or eight smaller trucks in sight. And no zombies.

The Harrimans were standing off to the side, breathing in great gasps, staring around in shock. They seemed surprised by the grey light eating away at the last of the night. Griff was running for a hand truck, hoping to block the door with it. Victoria was dragging Tessa away from the door which Maddy and Jayson were bracing with their bodies.

In the new light, Bryce saw that their escape wasn't going well. If they couldn't get the door barricaded that would be it, some of them would die. The Harrimans for sure, Maddy too and maybe Tessa.

Deep down, Bryce felt the urge to run, to leave the others to their fates. It was a primal feeling. It was survival of the fittest. Sure, he wasn't very fit, but he was better off than some of them. *Run and don't look back*, a soft voice whispered. *Aren't you a scientist? Isn't this how evolution works?*

"Bryce!" Maddy was straining back against the door. "What're you doing?" There was something like shock and accusation in her eyes, as if she had heard his thoughts.

Ashamed, he smashed his shoulder against the door, which banged and bucked behind him as the dead piled against it. There were so many of them; and his new boots kept sliding on the dirty cement; and if he slipped…fear gave his saliva an iron flavor.

"Maddy, move," Griff barked as he rolled up with the hand truck. The five-foot tall metal device was designed to carry boxes. It had two wheels and a thin metal plate at the bottom. Griff rolled it to the door and began kicking the back of it. Slowly the metal plate slid beneath the door.

Bryce stepped back for a moment, hoping the hand truck would hold the door. It didn't. There was a screech as metal tore across cement. Griff plowed his shoulder against the door while Bryce kicked the truck back into place. This worked for a moment, but then the door began to slide open again.

"Move!" It was Maddy. She grabbed the top of the truck with both hands and leaned back. The extra friction stopped the door but would it last? Bryce doubted it. He spun, looking for something else to brace the door with. His eyes fell on a wheeled dumpster that was squat and ugly, coated with hardened slime and what looked like puke.

He took one step towards it when he saw someone step from around it. No, it was some *thing*.

The demon was there.

Goosebumps burst across Bryce's flesh by the thousands and he took a step back. *Run!* a voice screamed in his head. It was the voice of panic, not of reason. The demon was whole and strong. It wanted Bryce to run. It wanted to chase him down and corner him in some dark basement where it could feed alone.

Bryce had dropped his pipe. When he reached for it, the demon grinned and started forward. It wasn't afraid. Bryce couldn't say the same thing. His hands were slick on the metal. Would his grip hold? Would it matter? The beast wasn't like the rest. It could think. It wouldn't wait for a blow to fall. It would block the blow with one arm and dart in with its mouth open wide…or it would dance back and let the pipe uselessly kick up sparks.

Either way, Bryce knew he was no match for the thing.

"Griff!" he cried in a high, strangled voice. He had just blared out his fear for all to hear.

"Get that dumpster over…" Agent Meyers saw the demon in mid-command. The sight of the creature shook him. How was it there? How had it known to come around the building? Impossibly, it had cut them off. It had set a trap. "What the fuck is this thing? Bryce, take my place."

He had his back to the door but still had his hands free. Reaching under his leather jacket, he pulled his Glock. The demon needed to die and quickly.

Bryce backed from the demon. Its grin dropped away as its features twisted once more into that look of disgust and disdain. It had nothing but contempt for the gun and scorn for anyone who was weak enough to use it. It growled out a roar and beat its chest with one hand. Its meaning was clear: it was challenging Griff to fight it man versus demon.

"Don't do it," Maddy hissed. "Just kill it."

Despite the roaring and screaming permeating the door, the demon heard this and it bared white teeth. It reached down and picked up its own ace in the hole: it was the one-armed Puerto Rican teen. Having been trampled by a battalion of zombies, he was significantly worse for wear and bled dark blood from dozens of cuts.

The demon gave it a shake. It put its head back, opened its mouth and let out a scream that echoed down the alley. When the echoes reverberated back at them, they brought with them a low sound that gradually grew in volume. It was the moans of a hundred zombies.

They came stumping up the alley, filling it, their grey bodies shoulder to shoulder. At first they didn't see the group up on the platform, but when they did, they rushed at it and began to claw their way up.

Jayson and Maddy abandoned the door and ran, chasing after Victoria and her daughter, who were already tearing away. The Harrimans couldn't keep up. Griff and Bryce caught up to them after forty yards. Mrs. Harriman was blubbering in fear as she ran.

"Go on," Mr. Harriman said, giving his wife a shove. He turned to face the horde with nothing but his mop. His life expectancy had been reduced to half a minute.

Griff groaned as he exchanged a look with Bryce. The two stopped as well. "Go be with your wife. Hiding's your only chance."

Mr. Harriman turned and was about to run but he jerked as if stung. "I think the time for hiding is over."

Victoria was pulling her daughter back, pointing over her shoulder, her face screwed up in terror. There were more zombies coming at them from the other end of the alley. Griff guessed there were forty or fifty strung out along the alley. And he had only twelve bullets left.

"Try the doors!"

There were four other doors; all were locked. Griff stepped back from one and fired three times at the lock. One missed by a hair, the others were dead on, but did nothing but chip metal and gouge the keyhole. Then the first of the zombies were on them.

Chapter 20

Bryce saw that they were lost. They were trapped without enough guns and ammo to shoot their way out. Filled with regret, he hefted his pipe, hoping to get to the demon and kill it before he died.

"I should've fought him when I had the chance," he muttered just before he swung the pipe, catching some black-eyed housewife in the head and denting her skull two-inches deep. It wasn't passing up his opportunity to kill the demon that he regretted. No. Killing it would've been good though he doubted he could have. But he didn't regret passing up the chance.

What he regretted was passing up the opportunity to stay with Magnus and his cult of crazies. If he had the chance to replay that day…yesterday—it felt much longer ago than just yesterday—he would've jumped at the opportunity. He'd probably still be sleeping. What kind of utopia got a person up before seven? None that he would want to be a part of.

Another zombie. This one was ridiculously small. It had been a child of eight or nine though boy or girl he couldn't tell. It was shirtless and mostly skinless as well. A great hunk of its scalp had been torn from its head and what was left dangled like a combover in a crosswind.

Bryce pitied the creature and swung the pipe like a hammer. There was an unpleasant squish sensation, as if the child's brain had been rotting long before it turned into a zombie. He went to hack at another when there was a roar above him. A pair of green helicopters, their rotors slashing the air, swept overhead just above rooftop level.

Everyone stared upwards, including the dead.

"Down here!" Victoria screamed, waving her mop back and forth in the air, as if it were a flag. The scream went unheard and the mop unseen. Three seconds later the copters were gone and the upside down world went back to being upside down.

Bryce cracked the skull of a big one and felt the metal zing into his palms in a way that was both disgusting and comforting. Of course beating someone's brains in was horrible, but on the flip side, he wasn't mewling in the corner, tears wetting his cheeks, piss staining his pants. He was going to go down fighting.

"Yaaarrrg!" he screamed as he swung the pipe again. It was a battle cry of sorts, that was more impressive in his own ears than in anyone else's.

The others looked over to see what was wrong. When they saw that Bryce was still holding his own, they went back to defending themselves as best they could, which was little more than thrusting the dead back with their mops. They were in a quickly shrinking perimeter as the dead clambered over each other to get up onto the platform.

"Shoot the door again!" Victoria begged.

Griff turned to the door—a different one with a clean, unmarred lock—and was about to shoot when it rattled. He stepped back just as it came open. He raised the gun and found himself staring down the barrel of another pistol. It was Wilkes, wide-eyed and nervous. Griff blinked in surprise as a strange, childish hope surged through him.

"You!" It was impossible that Wilkes was there in front of him. Impossible and fantastic. Griff had been looking at a terrible death and now, in a blink, here was his salvation.

Wilkes looked past him as if he wasn't there; he only cared about Bryce and Maddy.

"We gotta go," Wilkes called out. "Come on." The bald mercenary turned and raced up an ill-lit hall. His sudden appearance was so shockingly unexpected that no one moved right away.

"Come on!" shouted Griff. He started to sprint after Wilkes, his feet flying. Then he remembered he was an FBI agent, not some spineless civilian. He stopped and let the others pass.

Bryce was last, rushing in just ahead of a faceless, bloody horror. Griff hurried back and slammed his mop into the thing's chest, driving it back. He had hoped to get the door shut but there were too many of them. Grey filthy hands reached through the doorway in greedy hunger.

The two ran, chasing after the others. Only Maddy was visible, once more holding a door open. It was reassuring to both men seeing her there. She was not going to allow them to be left behind.

"Is that popcorn?" Bryce asked. As he stepped past her, his stomach let out a great rumble of hunger. The smell hung in the air of the hundred-seat theater they had entered. The only light in the room came from a couple of exit signs. Huffing and puffing up a center aisle were the dark figures of the Harrimans. Bryce didn't need to see their features to know it was them.

At the top of the aisle were Victoria, Tessa and Jayson who stood gasping next to Wilkes.

"We all good?" Wilkes asked, looking past the Harrimans and to Bryce. "Anyone bit or scratched?"

Bryce looked down at himself. He had blood all over him. In the dark it looked black. "Fuck me. I don't know, maybe. I need a bathroom." The others stepped aside as Bryce hurried up the aisle. Wilkes went through the door first and held it open with a foot as he trained a semi-automatic pistol outward.

The hall was only slightly better lit. Ahead, was the soft glow of a bathroom sign. Bryce jogged to it, whispering over his shoulder, "Someone find some bleach. Please." He was in a panic by the time he got into the bathroom. He tore off his backpack and then his shirt before scrubbing his hands, arms, face and hair with the hottest water he could stand.

Someone gave him bleach and he happily doused himself with it. When he looked up, he saw that everyone was in the bathroom with him.

"I found this," Maddy said, handing him a zippered warm-up jacket. It smelled of stale sweat and weed.

Wilkes' lips were curled as he looked at the ragged group in the harsh light. "Okay. I got room for these three." He pointed at Bryce, Maddy and Griff. "The rest of you may want to hole up here for the duration."

"Hold on!" Victoria cried. "Who is this guy? Is he FBI, too?"

"Who I am is none of your business, ma'am," Wilkes told her. "I'd barricade the doors and keep away from the windows. I'll send help when I can."

This left the group speechless. Victoria looked back and forth from Bryce to Griff and then to Maddy, before she darted to the door and threw her body against it. "No. Nope. No way. You are taking me and my daughter with you. Tell him Agent Meyers."

Wilkes began to bluster. Griff cut across him. "You'll take us all. I don't care if we have to sit on each other's laps, we're all going. And we're going to the Federal Building."

"I have my orders," Wilkes stated, "and they don't involve any extras or any side trips. I'll drive you to Magnus Plaza or you can walk wherever. It's your choice."

"I choose Magnus Plaza!" Victoria cried, clutching at Wilkes. "We're small. Put us in the fucking trunk. I don't care. Just take us with you."

Jayson also was not above begging. In a fog of wine-breath, he said, "You gotta take me too. I can fight. Ask these guys. And I know the subways like the back of my hand. Come on, Jack. You gotta…"

"Enough!" Griff snapped. "We're not going to Magnus Plaza. We're going to the Federal Building and that's final."

"Maybe we should ask these two," Wilkes said, indicating Bryce and Maddy. "Maybe after all this they might want to take Magnus up on his offer."

Maddy refused to look at Bryce, or anyone really. She went to the closest sink, ran water and watched the stream. She wanted to be safe. That took precedent over everything. But "safe" was a fluid concept with varying degrees. Magnus might be able to offer her immediate safety, but how could she trust a man who had started the apocalypse on purpose?

What would someone like that do to her the moment she outlived her usefulness? "Of course, I have to live long enough to outlive my usefulness before I worry about that," she muttered under her breath. She was torn in indecision and decided not to decide. She'd let Bryce decide, and knew that she wouldn't be happy whichever way he went.

But he couldn't decide either, mainly because he didn't know which way Maddy would go. He decided to stall. "How'd you find us?"

Wilkes wasn't expecting the question, and by the way his eyes shifted, Bryce guessed that his answer would be a lie.

"Easy. You told me where you were going. It wasn't hard to follow you…and we have a drone. It was a piece of cake."

This seemed logical, so where was the lie? Maybe there wasn't one. He stared hard at Wilkes. The mercenary stared just as hard back—hiding something. Griff broke the staring contest. "The FBI can protect you. Wilkes is proof that you're important to Magnus, just as we thought."

"You are important," Wilkes agreed, heatedly. "And yes, I am the proof. Me, and the two Yukons, and my seven men! What is the FBI giving you except one kiddie agent? Nothing. You won't make it four blocks let alone four miles. You need me. How many rounds do you guys got between you? A dozen?"

Griff decided this was as good a time as any to check. "I have nine. Maddy?"

"Four." Maddy glanced at Victoria who gave a little embarrassed shrug. She had dropped the empty gun ages ago and couldn't remember where.

13 bullets? The number was a shock.

"We need to go with this guy," Victoria stated, unequivocally as if hers was the only vote. "He's the only one making any sense."

"What about your husband?" Bryce asked.

She went pale and her eyes shifted away as she answered, "It's what he would want. He'd want his wife and daughter safe. Besides, we probably have half the zombies in the city after us. I bet he's already there." She looked down at Tessa. "Him and Jordan. They are fast and strong."

Bryce heard the lies as she spoke them. Deep down she guessed they were already dead.

"Maybe we should go to Magnus Plaza for their sakes," Maddy said. "I don't think all of us will make it if we keep going south." This included herself but it felt more like charity when she added the others.

"Listen to her, Bryce," Wilkes insisted. "We'll let them pile in. We can be uptown in an hour, safe and sound."

This smelled of more lies. Bryce's eyes turned flinty as he gazed hard at the merc. Where were the lies? Sure, Wilkes might drive them all uptown, but would any of them be allowed into the compound? Or would it just be Maddy and Bryce? Griff had made it pretty clear that Magnus was only recruiting the very best and brightest. That wasn't this group. It wasn't even Wilkes.

"You still after that million?" Bryce asked softly. "You still think it's worth it?" Wilkes didn't need to answer for Bryce to know he had hit the mark. "Yeah, that's what I thought. There are banks all over the city. All empty. All waiting for someone to pop in and take what they want. So…if it's not money you're risking your life for, what is it?"

He grunted out a laugh. "You're my ticket inside. They said it was fascinating that you were still alive. That was the word the egg-head used. *Fascinating*. I thought it was a fucking miracle, but it's a miracle that's gonna work in my favor. I worked out a deal. If I get you two back, me and the boys get to go in."

"What a great deal, for you," Griff said. "But they aren't going to let the rest of us inside, are they?"

Wilkes' face went sour. "I don't know. Maybe. It's worth a shot isn't it?"

Maddy shook her head. "No. Not even a little." She couldn't imagine pushing the Harrimans out into a street filled with the dead. "How about this. You get us down to the FBI headquarters and we'll see if they let you in. If you behave honorably, I'll put in a good word for you." It's strange she used the word: honorably. She used to chide people for supporting colonialism when they used the word.

It felt weird but correct this time.

"Me too," Griff said. "You know the boys in Virginia will want to know everything there is to know about Magnus. It could mean a trip out of the city."

Mrs. Harriman raised a hand. "For all of us? I don't know if I can keep going and Walt's knees are all swollen, and…" Her husband squeezed her hand and shook his head. No one wanted to hear about his knees.

"I hope so," Griff told her, "but I don't know for certain. What I do know is that you'll have a better chance with us than with this guy and Magnus."

Jayson put his hand out and touched Griff's sleeve. "What about my family? My pops is up in Queens and…"

Wilkes slapped his hands together in anger. "We don't have time for this! I have two vehicles outside and they aren't going to wait around forever." He stormed out of the bathroom and into the dark hall with its colorful movie posters and red velvet ropes.

No one followed.

He was back in seconds. "Fine. We'll go to the FBI first."

Chapter 21

The group ran to the front of the theater where the smell of the popcorn became almost dizzying to Bryce, who was once again starving. It had the opposite effect on Maddy, who went green and began to pant in an effort not to puke.

Wilkes barely noticed the smell as he tromped to the doors and stared out at a street clogged with cars and a sky filled with dark smoke. A smattering of zombies trailed down the street. There were no Yukons in sight. "Son of a bitch!" Wilkes hissed. He dug out a radio. "Where the fuck are you guys?"

His radio crackled: "It got too hot and we had to vacate. Coming around in five."

"Okay, roger that. We're going to need to make some room." He glanced back at the group, with a curled lip. "We're picking up a total of eight. It'll be four per vehicle." There was silence from the radio which had Wilkes shaking his head in anger. "We have the fucking room. They'll go in the back. Four and four."

The other radio operator took half a minute to respond with a bland, "Roger that."

Like a bull, Wilkes blew hot air from both nostrils as he turned. He stared at the pathetic group. "Okay. The grandparents and mom and daughter go in car two. The others will be with me in the lead vehicle."

They looked back and forth at each other. Jayson had a new bottle of wine in hand, a red this time. He drank it like it was water. Tessa was blank-eyed and held her mother's hand in a fierce grip. Victoria wasn't happy with the seating assignments and started in on Wilkes as if he were the manager of the local Waffle House who had just told her they were fresh out of blueberry syrup.

Bryce wasn't about to let five-minutes go to waste. Beneath the smell of popcorn was the familiar scent of hotdogs. He leapt over the concession stand counter and went for the frankfurters that had been left out by employees who'd had a front row seat to the beginning of the apocalypse. It was a wonder they turned off the lights before fleeing.

The frankfurters were cold and that was fine with Bryce. He grabbed one and stuffed it into his mouth like a stogie. With his hands free, he snatched up another five and dropped them into a popcorn bag. A sampling of candy bars also went into the bag, as well as some gummy-worms.

"Tessa?" he called to the girl. Her mom was still giving Wilkes an earful. "You want anything? They got mega-Snickers. Or I can get the slushy machine going. Ooh, Dippin' Dots!"

Like a nervous stray, she eased forward, stopping just shy of the counter as if Bryce was one of those strangers who offered kids candy her mom was always going on about. "I like Dippin' Dots." She took the plastic bowl and spoon from Bryce. She jerked her head in a quick bow as way of thanks, something Bryce found oddly proper.

"And what about you, Maddy?"

Although the sight of the candy only added to her discomfort, the idea of the frankfurters burned through her nausea. She needed meat. "Just a hotdog. No bun or anything." Her stomach tried to rebel at the first bite. After that she inhaled the rest and asked for seconds. She had just ripped off a hunk of her second frankfurter when the big black SUVs pulled up on the sidewalk right out front.

Wilkes screamed for them to move as the doors opened and armed men leapt out guns blazing. It had been relatively peaceful out front for the previous couple of minutes. Now there were zombies everywhere, almost as if they had been lying in wait.

Victoria led the way, yanking Tessa outside and right into the first vehicle. Griff followed them inside. Then Jayson, and finally, the Harrimans. Now there wasn't room for the mercenaries who were shooting down the dead. Wilkes yelled curses as he shoved Maddy and Bryce towards the second vehicle.

Maddy slid in and then crawled into the backseat and Bryce was about to follow when something caught his eye and he stopped.

The demon was there. It and the skinny one-armed Puerto Rican. It had been waiting to trap Bryce and the others. Now, it was in a fury, pushing the dead faster at the two vehicles. It stopped only to glare at Bryce. Their eye-contact was broken moments later as Wilkes pushed him into the vehicle, forcing him into the far back with Maddy. Then they were speeding away, bouncing over the dead and clipping cars.

"Change of plans," Wilkes said into his radio. "We're going south. The FBI is going to get us out of the city."

In the seat next to him, the driver stared at Wilkes in shock. "The FBI? What the fuck? Since when?"

"Since…" Wilkes blinked, realizing that he had the two people he needed to get into Magnus' steel fortress. "Never mind. Continue as planned." He looked back at Maddy and Bryce's shocked faces. "Sorry but I got a sure thing with Magnus. All you guys can offer…"

Unseen, Maddy slid her gun from her pocket. She grabbed the hair of the man in front of her and stuck the gun an inch from his ear as she aimed at Wilkes. Her finger on the trigger. "You'll go south or you won't go anywhere," Maddy said. Wilkes smirked and the mercenary with the gun next to his ear only gave it a casual glance, as if unafraid.

"You won't shoot," Wilkes said. His eyes flicked to the other man in the middle seat. He hadn't put his gun away yet; he brought it up and aimed it at the side of Maddy's head. She could smell the acrid propellant drifting from the bore and she felt the heat from it on her ear.

"You think that'll keep me from killing you? After everything I've seen, getting shot in the head doesn't scare me at all."

Wilkes grinned. He had cold, uncaring eyes. "Looks like we're in a pickle that only you can fix. You see, we're going to keep on driving back north, so either get shooting or get your fucking finger off the trigger." As if she were holding nothing but an empty squirt gun, he turned from her and looked down at a map of the city.

They were currently heading east on 12th. Really, they were on the sidewalk. Ahead of them, the lead SUV gunned its engines and roared into a Mercedes that was halfway up on the sidewalk blocking their way.

"Raptor 1, what are you doing?" Wilkes yelled into his radio. "This route is not clear. I repeat…" The Yukon bucked as they ran over a body. "It is not clear."

"I have you in sight," the radio crackled. "Hang a right. Your next right."

"I think you meant impasse, not pickle," Maddy said around a grin. "You know to the right is south?"

Wilkes was thrown against his door as the driver heaved the car into a hard turn. They couldn't afford to slow down. The dead were streaming in from all over the place, including from above. Bodies fell from rooftops to thud unpleasantly all around them.

"Now a right," Raptor 1 said, speaking through the radio. "Right, and another right. There you are. I got you in sight." The lead Yukon was plowing through trash and the occasional zombie. Both SUVs turned right once more and were now heading north.

"There's too many!" someone with a radio in the lead vehicle screamed.

Raptor 1 cried, "Speed up! You're going to have to ram through."

Bryce, who had slid into the middle of the bench, had a good view of what was coming. He leaned back, bracing himself as the first SUV blasted into a crowd of dead creatures. Grey, half-clothed bodies went flying. Blood rained down on the second SUV. Blood and a head. It thudded onto the windshield and clung there, a ghastly ornament.

The driver was smart enough not to attempt to use his windshield wipers. This was not true of the lead driver. In a sweep of the wipers, he blinded himself. His windshield became a red-grey mess and, instinctively, he slowed. Their only chance had been momentum and when they lost it, there was no getting it back.

"Reverse!" Wilkes screamed.

Maddy and Bryce ducked to the sides as the driver flung an arm back, torqued around in his seat and began driving the big machine in reverse at full speed. The engine whined as they shot backwards. Now the dead were smacking inches from where Maddy and Bryce were sitting. Bryce turned around, holding his pole at the ready and it wasn't long before the glass cracked. Then it shattered as they hit a big flabby beast of a woman.

She had to be near on four-hundred pounds and by then their backward momentum was too weak to overcome such resistance. She and four others went down under the SUV's wheels and the vehicle high-centered over the pile of wiggling bodies. The driver reacted poorly; he yanked the gear down to drive and tried to drive forward off the bodies only to be smashed into by the other SUV.

That was it for the vehicles. They were swarmed from front and back. Wilkes began barking orders and everyone piled out the left side of the vehicle closest to the buildings and found themselves outside something called The Bean. The rich scent of coffee came to Bryce as did the stench of urine and feces dripping from the pants of some of the zombies.

He also caught a whiff of…popcorn?

A quick look through the mayhem confirmed they were only half a block from the theater they had just abandoned.

BAM! BAM! BAM!

The mercs were clearing a path through the zombies. With the sidewalks flooding with creatures, the lead mercs ran between the two Yukons, stepping on bodies that weren't just still warm, but still moving. They went up and over the cars in the street, while above them, a small drone buzzed.

Bryce hated being out in the open. It was wrong. The dead were completely focused on them, and now they were surging from alleys and beneath cars. Some threw themselves out windows and more fell from rooftops.

Maddy grabbed his arm as they crossed front to back over a station wagon. "Look!" The demon was there, moving to cut them off. "We can't be out here." She was right. The demon was too fast and the zombies were unrelenting. A foot chase out in the open would always be in their favor. She pulled him off the car and then, before he even had his feet completely under him, she pushed him towards a lurching zombie. He still had the pipe and he leveled the creature with one swing.

"Get back here!" Wilkes bellowed over the sound of guns firing. Their group was already spread out in a ragged jumble across the width of the street.

Griff was in the back with one of the mercs, a barrel-chested man named Nick Withers. They were trying desperately to protect the Harrimans who were slow going up and down the cars. Victoria was shoving Tessa along; with so much danger all around, the little girl was unraveling fast. Jayson was running with his thumb corked in his bottle to keep the last of it from spilling.

Wilkes wanted to turn north, he was pointing up the street, unaware how dangerous the demon was.

Maddy pushed Bryce over the zombie he had felled and together they ran south between the narrow, zigzagging lane between the stopped cars. "This way!" she screamed.

Bryce did his best to avoid the zombies as they ran. When he could, he scrambled over the back of a car to get into a different lane. All too often he had to fight. The pipe gave him an advantage, but it was no guarantee. He had really only perfected the overhead two-handed chop. Any other swing felt odd or weak. And his footing was all over the place. He was like a kid trying to teach himself tennis.

When two came at him, he crushed the one's skull with a hacking attack that was a beauty to behold, however against the second, he gave it a backhand blow that was more of a swat than a strike. It was made ineffectual by the cars crowding in and by his own ineptness. Two more joined the fight and he found himself swinging the pipe as if it were a fencer's foil.

He was able to knock their reaching hands away but was driven back. More of the creatures came from their left. They were screeching in rage and frothing at the mouth. Their nails scraped paint from the cars as they came on. Then one of the mercenaries charged up and began firing into the creatures while at the same time a second merc grabbed Bryce's hood. He pulled back, choking Bryce. Then Maddy had him by his free hand.

It was madness spun into chaos by the exploding guns and the screeches. The second merc released the hood and began firing as well.

"Shit! Fuck!" one of the mercs screamed, though why Bryce didn't know.

He didn't look back as he followed Maddy over more cars and towards a frozen yogurt shop that had its cage pulled down over its front window. He started to pull back. The cage had a heavy padlock holding it down and they had already seen how ineffective guns were against locks.

"Help me up," Maddy said.

"Up?" It was only then that he noticed the scaffolding jutting over the sidewalk. There had been construction going on. He set aside the pipe long enough to cup his hands as Griff had done down in the subways. Although she was down a few dress sizes, she still outweighed him by fifty pounds and he grunted and swayed as she stepped up onto his hands.

She seemed to take forever getting a handhold and then a foothold on what was essentially a big ladder.

The zombies roared in and Bryce was forced to let go. Now he had Maddy screaming and zombies tearing at his clothes, and guns going off all over the place. He jumped for his pipe. The metal felt good in his hands as he swung it like a bat, back and forth. As much as he wanted to cave in skulls, he had to get the hands away from him before they got a hold of him.

Bones broke; fingers, wrists and elbows. He held them off long enough for Maddy to claw her way to safety. By then he was surrounded and his arms growing weak. Maddy leaned through the metal bars and fired down. She killed two of them and blinded a fourth before she was out of bullets. It was barely enough. Bryce bulled his way past the blind one and ran down the covered sidewalk. In a sprint, he was much faster than the dead and by the time he made it to the end of the block, he had enough of a lead to climb the metal bars himself.

Maddy came puffing up just as he got to the next level. Side by side boards allowed them to walk back. They were both too out of breath to say a word. They stared out through the crisscrossing bars at the street. It was filled with the dead. Maddy and Bryce's sudden departure from the group had created an opening in the wall of besieging zombies and Wilkes had wisely retreated through it.

They had smashed their way into a camera shop and were racing through it. Their drone went with them. Other than the masses of creatures just below them, the two were all alone.

Chapter 22

"We better get inside," Bryce said as the scaffolding began to shake and shimmy around them. The dead wanted up and when they realized that they couldn't climb, they'd pull it down.

Just within arm's reach were the windows of the apartments above the store. The first three had their blinds down; from behind one someone hissed a warning, "Get away. I have a gun."

Bryce smelled old sesame oil and dirty socks coming around the cracks, he didn't smell a gun. Still, he wasn't going to fight anyone just to get inside. There were a dozen windows to try. He peered into one four down from where he'd been threatened and saw a darkened apartment. It had a lived-in feel and was neat but empty. He tried the window and found it locked.

A tap with his trusty pipe fixed that. Skinny as he was, he slipped in easily enough. Maddy twisted and turned trying to get inside with some grace. In this, she failed miserably and Bryce had to half-drag her across a sink full of dishes. They collapsed on the floor and paused to listen.

There were sounds within the building: a whispered conversation in the apartment next door, a thumping from somewhere above them, a child bawling far down the hall, and the clank of the scaffolding as the dead attacked it.

"I need a moment," Maddy said. She was sweating again—if she had ever stopped—and her heart was racing at over a hundred beats a minute. Her hand was on his arm and she could feel his heartbeat. It was slow and steady despite the dash across the street, and the fighting, and the climb. "Why are you like this? How come you're not like me? It feels like I'm on the verge of dying."

"Like what?" Bryce got up and looked around at what he supposed was a typical New York apartment: tiny, minimalist, roaches scurrying under the sink. Hoping that Maddy couldn't hear them, he went to a cupboard and took down a glass.

She had heard the roaches but as Bryce washed out the glass, she took the water he handed her. "I don't know. You look pretty good. And you can fight and climb. And I'm just a big blobby mess."

"I don't think you're too bad. You've made it this far, which is more than a lot of people can say." And that included two of Wilkes' mercenaries. Their bleeding bodies were visible from

Bryce's vantage point. They had been savaged by the horde. Not only had their clothes been ripped from their bodies, but most of their skin had been as well. The red mess should've put Bryce off his appetite; however, he still had his sandwich fixings and his bag of frankfurters. He started chowing down on the hotdogs as if he were in a contest.

When he glanced back at Maddy, he saw that she had fallen asleep. "I'll give her fifteen minutes." He went to the window and peeked out through the scaffolding, looking for the demon. The good news: it wasn't climbing up to get them. The bad news was that it was nowhere in sight.

Could it get into the building? Probably. "Even if it could, how would it find us? There's got to be a hundred apartments in this place." And there were others making a lot more noise than Maddy's soft snoring. Doors were opening and frightened people were hissing back and forth across the hall. Somewhere on the floors above them, someone was rolling a suitcase around. Someone else was finally getting around to filling a bag with canned goods. The clunk of tin on tin was loud in Bryce's ears.

"The demon will go after them." Probably. Maybe. "It's a zombie and they're food, so it makes sense." Nothing about this really made sense, especially the zombies. Magnus had created them to destroy humanity, but who would destroy them once all the people were gone? "Maybe he thinks they'll starve. Or maybe they eat each other."

With that fresh in his mind, Bryce chomped down on his last hotdog. Rubbing his hands on his hoodie, he glanced at his pipe. New blood was drying over old and none of it smelled good. Turning his nose up at the business end of it, he took it to the sink and began to clean it. When it was back to grey, he inspected himself and scrubbed away any bloody spots he found.

By then the scaffolding sat calmly against the building. The dead had found climbing too great a puzzle, and as their food had disappeared, they lost interest. They hadn't lost interest in the two dead mercenaries. The smell kept them coming back time and again to stare down at the bodies.

Where were the others? Bryce wondered. Gunshots had continued for half a minute after they had disappeared, and then there had been nothing, not a sound. Bryce scanned the windows across the street, hoping to see Griff or Victoria looking out, looking for them. "They could be a mile away by now. Maybe the demon is after them."

A door slammed out in the hall and then two more. There was a flurry of activity; feet running, the scrape of something heavy being moved. *A dresser*, Bryce guessed. He could picture it being shoved in front of a door. Someone was barricading themselves inside their apartment. But they weren't hiding from a zombie. The dead made noise. They moaned and stomped about.

It was this sudden lack of sound that raised goosebumps over his body. Bryce went to the door and listened. There were frightened whispers. The scrape of steel as a knife was pulled from a drawer, the creak of flooring out in the hall. It was close.

Suddenly Bryce knew the demon was there. He darted to where Maddy lay and shook her. "It's here," he whispered.

Her blue eyes went from unfocused to sharp in an instant. He helped her up and then pointed to the window, but before either could take a step towards it there was another creak from the hallway, and a second later there was a soft snuffling sound. The demon had their scent.

Foolishly, the two froze in place, waiting with their breath held. They should've raced for the window, or blocked the door, or searched for better weapons. Instead they stood there until the demon launched itself at the door. Two-hundred and twenty pounds of muscle, bone and hate shook the door and bent the striker plate and the lock.

Maddy let out a garbled yelp and ran for the window. She went out much quicker than she had coming in, which wasn't saying much. The demon hit the door twice more before she made it through with Bryce right behind her.

Just as Bryce crawled out onto the wobbling planks, the demon broke the door in. It was at the window in a flash.

"Up! Up!" Bryce cried.

Maddy had been looking down at the street where the zombies had thinned out some. Currently, there were only forty of the creatures; plenty to chomp her down to the bone. But going up wasn't exactly a simple thing to do. Ten feet above their heads was another walkway and it looked as though they would have to climb up the outside of the structure to get to it. Maddy wasn't exactly nimble.

To give her time, Bryce smashed his pipe at the window the demon was trying to crawl through. A normal zombie would've gotten its head caved in; however this one darted back.

"Come on out," Bryce told the demon, "and see what you get." The demon slipped back into the kitchen and Bryce almost cheered, and might have if the scaffolding hadn't started shaking violently again. The dead down below had spotted them and were redoubling their efforts to get them. "Hurry, Maddy. There's more…"

A knife came flying from the kitchen window. He caught sight of it in mid-air tumbling end over end heading right for his soft belly. His eyes were quick, his reflexes weren't just slow, they were non-existent. The shock of seeing the knife froze him for just that split second. Then it struck with a meaty thud, and he jumped back, tripped and nearly fell from the scaffolding.

Looking down he saw he wasn't on the verge of death as he had expected. The knife had not been designed for throwing and had struck him handle first.

And now the demon was climbing through the window, or at least it was trying to. In life, it had been a steroidal behemoth with tremendous shoulders and a chiseled chest. The window was only so big and with the sink just before it, it was an awkward climb.

Bryce leapt up and went to smash the demon's head in. It was right there, bald as a stone and the size of an immature watermelon. However, just as he heaved the pipe back to attack, something grabbed his jacket from behind. It was a hideous thing seemingly composed of nothing but layers of blackened scabs with two dark eyes poking through.

It and the other zombies were going crazy to get at him and Maddy. The larger ones had trampled the smaller ones and were using their bodies as stepping stools. The scab zombie had been the first to climb to the top of the corpse pyramid. Bryce backhanded it with his pipe. It was a hardy swat and the thing rolled back down.

Two more fought to take its place.

"Hurry Maddy!"

He ran down the trembling walkway, and began climbing after Maddy. His climb was slowed by the pipe, but there was no way he was going to give it up, especially as the demon was now on the narrow platform.

Up and up they climbed with the demon keeping pace and the entire structure rocking and swaying as more zombies streamed in. The demon was ten feet to the side, five feet down and catching up quick. It was so close that Bryce didn't think there'd be time to attempt to break into any of the windows and climb through.

His only hope was to get to the top first and kill it as it tried to scramble up. It was Maddy's only chance as well. They were climbing seven stories worth of scaffolding and she was falling behind. He developed a pattern and a little chant to go with it. "Hook bar. Foot, foot, hand, hand. Hook bar…"

At the top, the metal was vibrating and making rickety sounds as if the entire thing was on the verge of collapse. But he couldn't worry about that.

He hadn't beaten the demon to the top. It clawed its way onto the rock and pebble-covered roof a second before Bryce. It grinned as it stood. Ten feet away, Bryce stood as well, his heart hammering in his chest, his breath coming in gusts. He hefted the bar and the demon nodded, before looking away towards the city. It wanted this, a fight between the two of them out in the open, where the entire world could see it kill Bryce and drink his blood straight from his neck.

A chill that had nothing to do with the cold struck Bryce. The demon was even more intelligent than he could've guessed.

It's making a statement, Bryce thought. *It's asserting its dominance.* This came to him as a fact, but a confusing fact. Bryce was a scrawny little man. Asserting dominance over him was not exactly difficult.

"Who are you?" Bryce asked. By that he meant: *How do you fit in with Daniel Magnus, and what did he do to you?*

The demon spread its arms as if to announce in a pseudo-godly manner: I am who I am.

It was not always this creature. The day before he had been Louis Brennan, a model and personal trainer. A good man with a genial, open smile. A driven, capable man who had been constructing his life like a mason constructing a tower. Each brick lifted him higher. Each made him more than he had been.

Louis Brennan was dead now and this thing was in its place.

The demon slid its dark eyes away from Bryce as Maddy finally got to the top. It still didn't attack.

Maddy was gasping and lightheaded. She edged behind Bryce, not at all understanding the situation, but knowing she was in even more danger than when she'd been climbing the scaffolding.

"Go," Bryce whispered. She saw that he was terrified. His knuckles were white ridges, his lower lip shook. He had every right to be frightened. The demon was strong and powerful and Bryce was just Bryce. He wouldn't last more than ten seconds unless the demon wanted to play with his food before it ate it.

Maddy turned and ran, her eyes sweeping back and forth, looking for some way off the roof. At the far end was a little brick structure with a door that had to lead down into the building. She knew it was going to be locked even before she reached it. The knob didn't budge. To her right was another building, butting right up against the one she was on. It was shorter by twenty feet. The only way down to it was to jump or trust her weight to a rusty downspout.

She turned to her left where a taller building was just as close. This one had a ladder that went up three stories. The ladder was shockingly narrow and went up and up. The building seemed to be leaning over her. Under any other circumstances she wouldn't dare set one foot on it. Even with the demon right there and a horde of zombies fighting to get up to eat her, she hesitated.

What would she find if she made it to the top? Another locked door? Was she going to risk her life just to find herself trapped once again? Her instinct for survival drove her up the rungs. The moment her hands grasped the ladder, the demon grunted.

Bryce saw that it would fight him now. Man to man. It would fight him and win.

Chapter 23

The demon stalked forward, its black eyes glittering evil. It was a foot taller than Bryce and eighty pounds heavier. Even with his pipe, Bryce knew he didn't stand a chance.

"Hey, maybe I can help you," he said, his begging voice high and reedy. "I know who did this to you. His name…"

In a shockingly quick move, the demon darted to Bryce's right. Bryce reacted with more speed than smarts. He swung the pipe and missed by three feet as the demon danced back, and then in again swinging a whistling punch at Bryce's head. He ducked and was just clipped by the blow. It made his eyes cross.

The demon was a blur of darkness as it followed up the first swing with another. Again, Bryce tried to duck away and again, he was just quick enough not to take the full brunt. Rock-hard knuckles glanced off his cheek, spinning him around.

Now his vision was a blur. Even still, he saw the darkness coming for him, and he threw himself back to avoid the blow. His feet tangled and he fell. With his momentum going back, he balled and rolled with it, something he hadn't done since he was four years old. It was a smooth move and seemed to take the demon by surprise.

It hesitated, allowing Bryce to get to his feet. The world around him teetered as he hefted the pipe. The demon didn't fear the pipe in the least. In fact, the creature unfurled a new grin and nodded encouragement. It wanted Bryce to attack. *So it can jump aside at the last second*, Bryce thought. *I'll be over-balanced and unable to defend myself. Or if I'm too slow, it'll slide into the swing where the force will be blunted and weak. Its teeth would be so close, perhaps too close to keep it from resisting the urge to open me up.*

The only thing keeping the demon from killing Bryce was the demon. Bryce had one chance to stop it. If he could get in the perfect swing. It would have to be fast and hard. He couldn't take half-measures. A tepid swing would be useless against such a creature.

The perfect swing would require the perfect position and to that end, he began back-peddling towards the edge of the roof with the demon coming on eagerly, hoping to pin Bryce in a position where he couldn't retreat, but before it could, Bryce dodged to his right. He backed some more, making it seem like he was going to keep retreating, then he suddenly dodged right again.

Now, it was the demon with its back to the teetering scaffolding and the seven-story fall.

It was unafraid. In fact, it looked like it was enjoying itself. *Overconfident*, Bryce thought. *Good*. In pretty much every movie he had ever seen the powerful but over-confident foeman always lost. This would be no different. His retreat had allowed him to clear his head.

Bryce took a deep breath, cocked his left elbow, pointed it at his target and charged. The move seemed to take the demon by surprise. It only stood there waiting for Bryce's powerful overhand attack. It didn't even step forward to lessen the blow.

A surge of elation swept through him as he brought the pipe down in a picture perfect swing. It came so fast that the demon was even slow in trying to block it. All it could do was raise a hand.

WHAP!

The pipe, twenty pounds of skull-shattering death, was caught by the demon square in the palm of its hand. It had to have hurt, maybe even broke some bones, but it didn't flinch. Bryce stared in shock even as the demon grabbed the bar with its other hand. Only then did he come to his senses. He needed the pipe. Without it, he was nothing.

He tried to pull back against a creature with four or five times his strength. The demon withstood this with one hand. Its other hand hung limply by its side and Bryce could only hope that he had broken bones. Not that it mattered too much. Even one-handed, he was no match for the thing's strength.

But he was smarter…he hoped.

The weakness of the single grip was in its inability to overcome torque. Bryce stopped trying to pull and instead tried to spin the pipe out of the thing's grip. He pitted the strength in both arms against the thing's grip strength. Against a normal man, he would've been able to break his grip in seconds. Against the demon half a minute of straining went by before he made any headway.

Feeling its advantage slip away, the creature took one step back, pivoted and heaved its body around, slinging Bryce towards the edge.

The motion was so powerful that his feet left the rooftop. His only hope was to hold onto the pipe for dear life. He was spun in a half-circle before coming down scattering rocks as his feet dug in.

"Huragh!" the demon grunted, through its beaming smile. It was laughing. It took another step back, and as it began to pivot, Bryce had sudden insight: the demon was going to simply let go of the pipe this time and he would go flying. Would a seven-story fall kill him? Or would he be still alive when the dead got to him and began to eat?

Bryce was stuck between two fires. If he held onto the pipe, he'd be street meat. If he let go, he'd be beaten to a pulp with it. His answer to this problem was to hold on for two seconds and let go mid-spin just before his feet left the rooftop.

It was an ugly solution to an ugly problem and he did not stick the landing. He hit the rooftop on his side and rolled out of control right off the roof. He expected to hit the scaffolding; however, it was being pulled back from the building by the seventy or eighty beasts attacking it from below. There was a three-foot gap, and he fell right down it, letting out a less than manly yelp.

His hands flung out and he caught metal and somehow managed to hold on. Above him, the demon made that ugly laugh sound again before it dropped down after him. It fell only seven feet before it spread its legs, landing with one foot on the metal of the scaffolding and the other on a window ledge.

It swung the pipe, one-handed.

To avoid it, Bryce let go of the metal, dropped another couple of feet and found another handhold. He swung himself through the bars and landed on one of the little walkways. Against the demon, it was one of the most unsafe places to be and he immediately ducked through the bars to the other side of the scaffolding…the side that leaned out over an eighty-foot drop, with a mob of crazed zombies raging to get at him.

"God!" he cried as a foot slipped. For a brief moment, he dangled, and for that brief moment his bladder was tested. It was touch and go.

Then he got a foothold just as the demon climbed through to the walkway; though it did with less agility than it had shown previously. It had to hook an elbow to get through—the pipe had broken bones in its hand when it caught it.

Bryce saw that the maimed hand was his only chance and he started climbing up as fast as he could, forcing the demon to climb after him. One handed, the creature was awkward and slow. Like Bryce had, it refused to let go of the pipe, almost as if it had some sort of spiritual value beyond its capacity to crush heads.

It slowed the demon down and Bryce took advantage, going on the offensive. With the demon on the outside of the structure using its crooked arm to hold itself as it climbed, Bryce saw an opening and darted back inside the scaffolding to deliver a swift kick to the thing's chest. It was like kicking a slab of beef.

The demon didn't even grunt. Its return strike, delivered just as Bryce went to kick it again, was a sharp jab with the pole straight to Bryce's sternum. He felt something crack as his breath shot out of him. The blow sent him stumbling back, fighting to draw in air. He grabbed the scaffolding to hold himself up and was shocked at how badly it was shaking.

And only then did he hear the scream of metal as it bent. The entire structure was now at an angle that it would never recover from. It was going to fall one way or another.

The demon realized this as well. It cast aside the pipe and started to climb up. Bryce had been thinking about climbing down and kicking in a window, only he just remembered Maddy. There was a good chance she was stuck on the higher roof. She'd be cornered and killed.

Bryce went after the demon.

It was already higher than him, though not much higher. In fact, its crotch was at head height. Bryce crossed the scaffolding, balled a fist, and drove it home in an epic nut-shot that would've been the death of a lesser man.

Not only did the demon shrug it off, it lashed out with a kick that split Bryce's lip and sent him back again. Bryce was up in a flash, spitting blood. He went for the demon again, this time a little smarter. He aimed his blow for the thing's left knee.

The haymaker connected and didn't just dislocate the thing's kneecap, it also knocked it from its perch. The demon slipped and fell, yet managed to catch a bar on the way down. It was three feet below Bryce and hanging by only the one hand. He might have been able to clamber down and kick its knuckles until it let go, only the metallic scream from the scaffolding was reaching a frightening new height.

Bryce jumped to the building side of the scaffolding and started climbing up as fast as he could.

Across from him, the demon was moving even faster. It caught up in seconds and Bryce saw that it would reach the top first. Then it would be a hop across to his side of the scaffolding and then a skip to the roof, and Bryce would be toast. He tried to go faster, but his head was still spinning and his lungs felt like crumpled socks inside his chest.

Then the demon was over him, looking down, grinning. It was still on the scaffolding, the fingers of one hand hanging over the edge, its left leg limp behind it. There was now a gap of four feet from the edge of the roof to the scaffolding. Even with only one leg, it could leap across.

Unless it was a larger gap.

The thought hit Bryce like a slap to the face, while the repercussions of what he envisioned was a punch to the gut.

It had to be done.

He launched himself at the edge of the roof, pushing off with his shoulders and driving with his legs, widening the gap. The structure was coming down, one way or another and he was the final straw. Too late, the demon saw what he was doing. It scrambled up and tried to jump across, its legs pistoning out, which only added to the streetward momentum of the tilting scaffolding.

At the last second, Bryce grabbed for the lip of the roof and held tight as the demon fell past. It flung out a hand, looking to hook Bryce's hoodie, but missed. Still, its diseased nails scraped down the side of Bryce's neck, peeling back the flesh and nearly pulling him from his hold.

Bryce barely felt the deadly wound. He had his head twisted around, watching the demon hit the side of the building and bounce towards the scaffolding as it toppled over. Part of structure hit a light post slowing the fall enough for the demon to land flat across the bars and ride it down to the ground where it smashed into the parked cars, crushing dozens of zombies in the process.

Bryce pulled himself onto the roof, thinking he had won. When he looked back down, he saw the demon. It was still alive. Furious, one arm dangling uselessly at its side, and its knee crooked and perhaps broken, it stared up at Bryce, murder in its black eyes.

Chapter 24

Gingerly, feeling new and very sharp pains all over his body, Bryce stood. His head swam and breathing was difficult. His face hurt where he'd been punched, his back hurt from where he'd been flung, his hands hurt from the splinters and popped blisters. He was in such a state that it was a few seconds before he felt the burning scratches on his neck.

Groaning, he pulled off his pack and dug out a bottle of water. Dousing the scratches helped the pain but not the fear.

He had no idea what was causing people to turn into zombies. Was it an airborne pathogen? Blood-borne? Something in the water? He had no idea, but if it was viral in nature, being scratched wasn't good.

"Neither is breathing the pathogens in," he muttered, feeling his stomach flutter. He had lost the little blue mask Griff had given him ages before.

It was surprising how little he knew about the zombie virus. He'd been in such a running state of panic that he hadn't given it much thought. Being eaten alive had been a far more pressing issue and the virus had taken a backseat in his mind as "Something Magnus had cooked up." But that wasn't good enough now that he had been scratched and had spent far too much time in close proximity with the demon.

What sort of viral load had the creature been carrying? Was every breath that left its lungs a whisper of death? Or did it have to spit in someone's mouth to infect them? And what was the incubation rate of the pathogen? From his point of view, it seemed to be impossibly high. Even the quickest replicating pathogens took at least a day before symptoms showed themselves.

This disease seemed to be turning normal people into monsters in hours. It didn't seem possible.

"Unless there's a latency period," he muttered. This was an unnerving idea—in some diseases people were infectious before showing any symptoms. Perhaps these asymptomatic spreaders had been roaming around the city for days and that the disease had already been spread far and wide. In which case, Bryce was worrying for nothing; he was already a dead man.

He felt as if he were already more than half-gone as he walked over to the narrow ladder and stared up.

It was a long way up.

"Just don't look down," he told himself. The rungs left his palms rusty orange and the height left his stomach a wreck, though once safely at the top, he was hungry again, and exhausted, ready to collapse. He forced himself on.

There was no sign of Maddy. Just like on the lower roof, there was a stairwell access door, though this one was built into the side of an elevator machine room. A brass knob hung from a kink of metal. Maddy had taken a brick to it.

Bryce went to the door and glanced in at a dark set of stairs. "Maddy? Hello?" The stairwell was quiet in a deserted way, and yet, there were plenty of soft noises running along its concrete walls. There were people whispering in the building, someone was frying an egg, a toddler was being shushed, someone was praying.

But no sound from Maddy.

He slipped down the stairs, his ears pricked for the slightest sounds. Down he went, his fingers trailing on the wall, feeling strange vibrations that he couldn't place. When he reached the ninth floor, he went to the door and touched the knob. In a flash, he knew she had touched it as well.

Except, he couldn't have known. There was no way. He wasn't a psychic or a palm-reader. Still, he knew.

The ninth floor was dark and quiet in the same way as the rest of the building. Bryce stared around, looking for clues, while at the same time ignoring his reality. Maddy had run down the hall a minute before. He knew it because he could smell her fear. That wasn't right. He wasn't a psychic and he wasn't a bloodhound. Still, he knew. The smell of fear had a tang to it—another thing he shouldn't know.

Hours-old fear hung in the air, acting as a backdrop to Maddy's sharper scent. He followed her scent down one end of the hall to another staircase. Again, he knew she had touched the knob when he shouldn't have. Turning it, he tried to open it only to find resistance and to hear a sob.

"Hey, it's me. Maddy? It's okay."

"Bryce?" Maddy heard his familiar voice, and yet she refused to believe it. Bryce Carter was a lot of things: usually smarmy, an infrequent genius, and a full-time dweeb. What he wasn't was a real fighter. Yes, he'd been able to kill a few of the smaller, slower, weaker zombies, but he couldn't have beaten the demon.

No way that had happened.

Maybe it tripped and fell off the building by itself, she mused. She cracked the door and saw the swollen lip, the bruise on his temple, the torn clothes. "What happened? Is it dead?"

"No. It's injured, though."

Her face fell. With the undead, injured didn't mean much. "What about Griff and the others?"

He shrugged. They might be holed up across the street, but without a weapon and with a hundred zombies between them, they might just as well be on the dark side of the moon.

"I don't know. We should…we should move on. The demon's still out there but won't be for long. It'll get in here and…" He shrugged again and showed her his empty hands. "I won't be able to stop it now."

Moving on meant leaving the safety of the stairwell. Even though Maddy knew that safety was more illusion than reality, her heart began to hammer at the idea of going out into the open. Bryce took her by the hand and led her downward. By the time they reached the bottom floor, they were clinging to each other.

The west-side entrance to the building consisted of a glassed-in vestibule. It had a fine view of 10th Street with its dozens of abandoned cars and its walking corpses. There were only four in sight and none were paying any attention to the door. Across the street they saw a parking garage, more apartment buildings and something called the Digital Daydream.

Only the garage was open. It looked like a gaping black mouth spewing a metal tongue—there was a traffic jam even in the garage.

"We go through the garage. What do you think? It'll go on through to the next street?"

Maddy didn't know and didn't want to find out. She didn't want to leave the building. When Bryce opened the door and crept out into the crisp New York sunshine, she hesitated for only a second before following after him. As frightening as going out was, being alone was far worse.

The two duck-waddled between the cars without being seen. Then they crept down into the black entrance of the garage.

Bryce had assumed that the lane into the garage would circle upwards; however, it circled downward instead. They both stared into the void. It was bereft of light. Maddy wasn't going down there. The smell of her fear was sharp now.

"It's okay," Bryce told her. "There's an elevator." The elevator doors wouldn't open without a keycard. Luckily, there was a staircase. Not so lucky, it smelled strongly of piss. Both turned up their noses and took to the stairs. They found the first-floor door locked and neither gave it another look. They were still too close to street level to think about knocking. The second floor was locked as well; however, the third-floor door was held open by a stick.

Bryce kicked it away.

Just like the last place, there were people in this building, too. They huddled in the dark, their furniture piled against the door. Bryce and Maddy could smell them and each other, though neither mentioned this. Neither wanted to be a freak. Neither wanted to admit that they were turning into something else... something like the demon.

They paused at each door, pretending to listen to whispers that were loud in their ears. With each pause they sniffed around the edges of the door. They quickly found an apartment that was empty.

"Do you think it'll be safe to rest?" she asked. They'd been going all night and she was dog-tired.

He nodded, lying. There was nowhere safe in the city anymore. "For a little while. I think the third floor is good if we can find an open apartment."

"You don't think we should break down the door?" she asked, tapping the door. It was fairly solid. "I don't want to be trapped anywhere if they come." That was a good point. Bryce bunched his shoulder, prepared to bash in the door, something he wasn't looking forward to. Maddy stopped him. "Maybe look for a key, first?"

Most of the doors had little welcome mats and all had the little ledge above the frame. Bryce looked askance at the idea but cherished his shoulder too much not to at least try. They went down the hall sniffing and poking under the mats. Only about six apartments in ten were occupied. The rest were mute and abandoned. All save one. Inside that apartment was a corpse with its wrists slit. The rich iron aroma of blood was nauseating to Maddy.

They had nearly walked the length of the floor when they finally found a place that wasn't just unlocked, the door was open a crack.

There was no doubt it was empty, and yet, Bryce knocked and called out softly, "Hello?"

159

Maddy pushed past him. "I need to sit," she said and plopped onto a white leather couch. Her exhaustion was suddenly a piano on her back and she didn't think she could lift it for another second.

The couch was a trim little thing that matched the exactness of the apartment perfectly. Other than a few open cabinets, the six-hundred square foot apartment was bright, airy, perfect and looked like it was ready to be photographed for a magazine spread.

Bryce didn't notice the decor. To him it was all a blur of white and silver as he pulled off his backpack and started to make yet another sandwich.

"Maybe you should wash your hands first," Maddy suggested. The smell of fear on him had already faded. Now the predominant smell about him was that of the demon.

He caught a whiff of it too. "Or maybe a shower." Getting up seemed like a chore, so he put it off for a few more minutes by asking, "Do you want to go first?"

Her eyes were drooping already. All she wanted was to sleep and yet, following after Bryce in the shower seemed less than ideal. With a groan, she pushed herself up and, after teetering for a second, went to the bathroom, which was just as neat as the rest of the place.

As the hot water streamed over her, she had to wonder how many more showers she could expect to get in the next few weeks. With the city in chaos, the power wasn't going to last much longer. *Had Magnus thought of that?* she wondered. She was sure he had. It didn't take a genius to chart a path once a zombie apocalypse was unleashed.

First the law would crumble, looting would become widespread, the power grid would fail, water would stop running, then morality would be replaced by animalistic survival of the fittest.

But Magnus and his cult of robotic followers would be safe in his steel towers. She pictured his plaza; the seven great skyscrapers set in something of a ring, towering over a little park. It wasn't hard to imagine his seven-thousand followers toiling like ants, bricking over the first-floor windows and doors.

"I bet they have tunnels," she muttered as she soaped up.

The smell of frying meat struck her, making her stomach growl and heave simultaneously. She stopped the shower seconds later and hurried to find Bryce cooking on all four burners.

"We don't want the meat to go bad," he told her. He was eating a sandwich at the same time as making six others and frying a steak he had found in the nearly empty fridge. "Hungry?"

She finally was, but only for the steak and some green beans that had been forgotten in the corner of a lower cabinet. They ate in silence, Maddy nibbling slowly, too tired to be enthusiastic about an under seasoned steak. Bryce gorged himself until he couldn't hold his eyes open a second longer. It could be their death to fall asleep, but they were both too done in to keep going; they had to take the chance.

Without asking, she took the bed and, after a quick shower, he slept on the couch. He slept deeply as the sun ran its paces overhead. Maddy dreamed of screams and gunfire. She ran endlessly in her dreams afraid that something was coming for her. Something bigger than herself or the demon, or all of them. Something even bigger than the city. Something that could destroy it in the blink of an eye.

Chapter 25

They moved slowly in a crouch, their eyes always out. It was mid-morning and yet the sky was dark. The air was filled with dust and ash. Bombs had been raining from one end of New Jersey to the other for the better part of the night. Even miles away, they could feel the explosions coursing up through the ground.

Although Maddy had the better nose, she was fourth in line. Bryce led the way. He was taller now. Tall and thick with muscle. Everything he ate seemed to either go to building muscle or bone. In his right hand, he carried a sledgehammer. It was a fearsome weapon.

Maddy carried her climbing axe in her right hand and the garbage can lid in the other. The lid was dented and stained. It was an ugly shield, but it was still a shield.

"We have to hurry," she hissed. Time was squeezing in on them. She could feel it in her bones. Death was coming. Death from above. She cast a fearful look up and just then the sky was lit in an unholy radiance. The air screamed in agony and the earth melted under the…

Maddy's eyes came open and she found herself staring into a golden death…no. It was the setting sun. And the sound of screaming…those were fighter jets tearing across the sky. And the earth shaking that was really…the earth *was* shaking. The thunder of explosions rippled in the west and for a moment Maddy felt the same fear of time spinning away that she'd had in her dream.

"Bryce," she whispered, climbing from the bed. She found him sitting on the couch, yawning and stretching his arms out. He was smaller than he had been in her dream and yet as he stretched, the arms of his hoodie showed most of his wrists. And it was tight across his chest. He was still growing.

She looked down at herself. After her shower, she'd thrown on the navy blue blouse and had been too tired to even glance at a mirror. Now she saw it hung on her like a sail. Suddenly, her dream and the explosions became meaningless. She went back to the bedroom and stared at herself in the full-length mirror.

"It's still happening," she mumbled in shock. Her heart was still racing at frightening speeds and the fever was still raging. Her body was burning through its fat reserves in a way that was simply not possible.

Bryce stood in the doorway, practically filling it. His shoulders had broadened and his chest had become thick. He was obviously taller now. "You look...great. How much weight have you lost?"

Maddy despised scales even more than mirrors. They screamed the truth about how fat she was. She hadn't been on a scale since her last doctor's appointment two years before. The scale had read 226 and she had only gotten bigger since then. Now she couldn't be more than a hundred and forty pounds.

"A hundred pounds." She couldn't stop staring at herself. As great as the weight loss was, a nagging voice kept whispering, *What if it doesn't stop?* She didn't want to think about that. "You've grown."

He looked down at himself. His feet stuck out like he was growing scuba fins. And they seemed strangely far away, like his legs had been stretched. He went to the mirror and stood next to Maddy. His jeans were high up on his ankle and felt like they were strangling his crotch. Still, it was hard to tell how much he'd grown, especially with Maddy next to him. She hadn't just slimmed down, she had grown taller as well.

Absently, Bryce licked his lip only to realize that the cut on it was gone. The same was true of the bruise on his temple. His hands were unmarked as well; no blisters, splinters, cuts or scrapes. He pulled a sock off and found his strangely large foot to be equally healed. How long had it been since he'd been hobbling around barefoot and bleeding?

Then he remembered the demon scratches and twisted around to see them. They had healed as well.

"Whatever Magnus did to us, has its upside," he remarked, still staring at himself. "I don't even feel the glass feeling. You know, in the joints?"

She bent her elbow and realized that there was barely even a ghost of pain where before she would've cried scratching her nose.

"That demon might've started out like this," she cautioned.

"I don't feel very demony," he said. He had to resist the urge to flex for the mirror. He'd never had anything to flex before. His arms had always been soft pale tubes that would "plump up" slightly if he attempted to make a muscle. Now he could feel the weight of muscle that hadn't been there two days before.

They both stared at the mirror until Bryce's stomach rumbled. He went for more food. As he did, Maddy cast one last look at herself and then went to the dresser. The woman who lived there was a size eight. Everything was too small for Maddy still, but not by much. She decided to take a pair of jeans and a t-shirt. These went into her pack just in case she continued to shrink.

By the time she was done, Bryce was onto his second sandwich. She watched him tear through his food while a tingle of fear crept over her. The idea that time was running down was in the back of her mind. It was smart to heed the fear. Nukes were a distinct possibility, and so was being left behind by the FBI. The city was quickly becoming a lost cause.

"We should get going," she said.

"Yeah. South still?" He went to a window and looked out. The view was to the south, that was true; however as they were on the third floor they saw next to nothing except yet another street filled with cars. "Do you know if there's a subway station nearby? I hate the idea of being out in the open."

She could only shrug. "The last time I was in New York, they seemed to be everywhere, always a block away."

They didn't seem so prevalent now. Bryce turned and gazed around at the darkening apartment. "We need weapons."

Weapons were not to be found, at least not suitable weapons. The best he could find was a big knife that had a good edge on it. She picked up a thin one and pictured shoving it in a zombie's eye. They also grabbed a few cans of food, just in case, before slinking out of the apartment.

Bryce went first, moving slowly, afraid to find the demon lurking around every corner or behind every door. If he had healed quickly, it suggested that the demon would've as well.

A back entrance to the building opened onto yet another alley, this one wet and dim. The sun, a pale disk, was mostly hidden behind mountainous clouds of black smoke, and the shadows were deep. Maddy expected to smell more piss in the alley, but was pleasantly surprised to breathe in the aroma of pumpkin.

Just down the alley were long wooden boxes set against a brick wall. It was an old urban garden that hadn't been tended in a year. Two of the boxes were broken and knocked on their sides. The last was filled with worn brown dirt, trash and leaves.

Somehow a single pumpkin was growing among the cigarette butts which constituted the only form of fertilizer in the box.

Right next to it were two old trashcans. One had a bashed-in lid. Maddy picked up the lid and stared at it in awe, her mind going to her dream. There was a handle on top. It was a small loop of metal that fit her hand nicely.

"A shield," she said, in something of a daze. Had the dream been prophetic? Or had the idea of being protected spawned the dream, and finding the garbage can lid only happenstance? She hoped to God she couldn't see the future. As much as she liked the idea, she didn't want to be around when a nuke went off.

Bryce grinned as Maddy hefted the trashcan lid. For a moment, she struck him as "cute." It was disconcerting since they had hated each other since the moment they had met. "It's nice. We should get some tape or…"

His words were drowned out as green helicopters flew by. They were spaced out, one per street, heading south. Bryce and Maddy took one look at each other and then ran west down the alley until they came out on Broadway. They had their hands in the air, desperate to wave the copters back. They were about to yell their throats out to be rescued. The yells died on their lips.

There were zombies among the cars. A lot of them.

The two ducked back into the alley. "What do we do?" Maddy asked.

"We should, uh…" Bryce had no idea what they should do. "We should, uh…I don't know. What do you think we should do?"

"I don't know. Are the streets worse? They look worse."

It was hard to tell. "They're not better." He wanted to scamper back up to the apartment and hide like all the sane people seemed to be doing. The streets belonged to the dead.

A muffled shriek came to them. It came from somewhere in a building across the street. It wasn't just their heightened senses that allowed them to hear the cry. The city had become eerily quiet. The constant horns were no more. The sporadic gunfire had trickled away to short bursts. The screams of frightened people had become whispers.

Accompanying this lone shriek was a thumping and a low growling that grew more intense with each passing second. Then the shriek came again, high and shrill. The zombies on the street turned to the sound and began to congregate against the building. They stared upwards in eagerness, which was rewarded moments later when a third floor window was smashed outward.

Maddy and Bryce should've been using the distraction to hurry off down the road, instead they watched in horror as a woman tried to scramble out onto a tiny ledge.

"Oh God," Maddy whispered, pressing her hand to her mouth.

"We should go," Bryce muttered, and yet he made no move to go. There was a crack of wood and a shout. Inside a man was fighting and cursing. Then he began to grunt and scream. Sobbing, the woman climbed further out onto the ledge, holding onto the window frame with just one hand. Below her the horde groaned in pleasure waiting for her to fall.

She did not fall. Smartly, she kept her body plastered to the wall. In seconds, the man went silent, and not long after the first of the dead came to the window snuffling. It was inevitable. Even from down on the street, Bryce smelled lavender shampoo beneath the stench of the zombies and the bitterness of the smoke. The zombies smelled her, too. They had no fear of heights and the first one didn't just reach for her, it tried to walk out onto the ledge after her.

It fell head first, crashing down on the dead below. The next dead creature didn't get a chance to climb out. It was pushed from behind and fell soundlessly down onto the horde. The next creature took Bryce's breath away. It was the demon. At the sight of it, Bryce pulled Maddy down behind a car. She had seen it as well.

On the ledge, the girl started screaming. Bryce chanced a look and saw the demon reaching for her, stretching out a long arm. She inched further away, doing everything she could to keep her body pressed to the wall. But its arm was very long. It grabbed her by the wrist. Had she been thinking straight she would've hurled herself from the ledge in the hope of either breaking free or pulling it down with her. Instead, she tried to hold onto her perch and fight the grip at the same time.

It was a losing battle. Eventually, her right foot slipped and she fell, but only for a few feet. Then she dangled, her wrist crushed in its grip. As he pulled her into a room filled with starving zombies she screamed into its grinning face.

Chapter 26

The woman's screams sent the zombies on the streets into a frenzy. Some tried to climb up the building to get at her. Others ran around, screaming in unison with her screams. They pounded the cars and slapped the sidewalk. Most of them, however, surged to the closest door and bashed their way inside.

Maddy was the first moving. She hurried down the street, doing her best not to look at the building where the screams were lasting longer than possible. It sounded like she was being tortured rather than eaten. *Or it's both*, Maddy thought.

Just as they reached the end of the block, a new scream came from the building. The zombies had found another person hiding. How many more were in that building? How many were unarmed except for a steak knife and a frying pan? Their only chance was to come out fighting. Some would die, but the rest might get away.

Bryce hesitated, one foot on the sidewalk and one in the street. "Someone has to…" he choked out, but couldn't go on. The only chance those people had was if a leader took charge and rallied them, but it wasn't him. It couldn't be. He was too afraid. He was too weak.

Maddy guessed the reason for his hesitation. "No. We have a duty. Magnus did something to us, remember? We have a duty to the rest of the country…"

"I know," he hissed, angry at himself for even hesitating. A real man would've simply done the right thing. Griff would've. He had already proven his heroism time and again, while Bryce had done little that didn't involve saving himself. He stomped away, crossing the street without looking left or right. It was impulsive and stupid, and he paid for it a second later as a creature lunged at him.

The undead thing had been a high school volleyball player and still had her blonde hair neatly done up in a ponytail. The flesh had been eaten off her face and Bryce could see her gumline and all her teeth. He grimaced in revulsion as he brandished the knife. Even before the big girl came flying at him, he knew it was a poor weapon. But it was worse than poor.

She practically threw herself onto it and didn't bat an eye as it ripped into her guts. All she cared about was tearing his face off. Her hands were as large as a man's and her grip left bruises on his arms as she pinned them against his sides and came flashing in with her lipless mouth stretched wide. Barely, he was able to hold her off. But she was too close to pull the knife and he had to let go of it to save his face.

Heaving with all his strength, he pushed off the car and thrust her back. He had grown over the last day and a half, and could now be called average.

Average wasn't going to cut it against six-feet of blonde fury. She heaved him over a car and he landed with a hard thud. His fighting instincts were those of a toddler's and he was still rubbing his elbow when she stalked around the car. The blonde woman might have done more damage except Maddy stepped over and stabbed her in the neck with her knife.

Maddy had the fighting instincts of a fetus. Her stab was more of a poke and drew less blood than the average nosebleed. The blonde zombie spun on her faster than she expected and she only barely got her shield up in time. The zombie grabbed it with both hands. Maddy held on for dear life as she was slung back and forth, slammed into the cars on either side. It didn't take long before the zombie wrestled the lid from Maddy's grip, and flung it aside, nearly hitting Bryce who had just gotten to his feet.

Maddy let out a frightened yelp and ran, dodging open car doors, and the stiff glass-eyed corpses that were strewn about. She found herself running back the way they had come, directly towards the crowd of zombies.

Without thinking, she dropped down and squirmed beneath a minivan, scratching for the other side before the zombie could reach under and pull her out. It tried and even caught hold of one of her Uggs. Her feet had become narrower with her weight loss and the boot slid right off.

"Son of a bitch!" she barked. The last thing she wanted was to find herself running around the city barefoot once again. But there was no getting the boot back. She rolled to the other side of the minivan and took off back towards Bryce, Except Bryce seemed to have disappeared. *He left me?* This was astounding and frightening…and not true.

Bryce was crouched down behind a grey Volvo. He was hiding! "What're you doing?"

He waved her on angrily. "Just go!"

"Fine!" If asked, she wouldn't lie: just then, she hoped the zombie jumped on him and took a bite out of his chicken-ass. But the zombie had her black eyes focused only on Maddy. She didn't see Bryce or the trashcan lid he held, not until he jumped up as she came abreast of him and smacked her in the face with it. *Clank!* The sound was tinny and would've been comical if the zombie actually had a face and they were on a TV sitcom.

By definition, zombies shouldn't be able to affect a look of surprise, and that was infinitely true of a zombie without a face, and yet, the blow was so jarring that her brain, low-functioning as it was, short circuited.

The zombie jerked to a halt and stood there long enough for Bryce to line up another shot with the lid. He went for its temple and used the edge of the lid, hoping to crack the thin bone and send splinters into its brain. That didn't happen, but he managed to knock the thing down. It fell to the pavement, its dark eyes going in different directions.

Up went the trashcan lid for the killing shot. Bryce sucked in his breath, ready to crash the lid down, but stopped when he saw something out of the corner of his eye. It was another zombie; a thin one with one arm and a thin little mustache. It was the Puerto Rican zombie that had sniffed them out that morning.

It raised its one arm, pointed at Bryce, and let out a shriek loud enough to call every zombie in the city. "Run!" Bryce cried as he gave up on the blonde zombie and fled down the street. Maddy had already been running, though her shoeless stride was herky-jerky and slow. He caught up with her quickly and begged her to hurry. Behind them, the late afternoon shadows swarmed with the dead.

She did her best. They raced past more parking garages, two banks, four restaurants and numerous clothing stores—all of which were caged and locked. Ahead on the left, steps banked down to a subway station. Bryce aimed for it, only to stop short as three zombies lurched onto the street from the stairs. They ran on with Maddy flagging badly. A three-hundred yard sprint had her racing heart close to bursting.

"I…can't," she wheezed.

Bryce understood. Desperately, he looked for a safe place to hide or climb to, but there was nothing, and the crowd of zombies continued to grow larger. Maddy had slowed to a dragging jog before he saw a door where the cage across it had been partially pulled back. There was a gap just wide enough to slip through one at a time. A foot beyond it was a heavy wooden door that once had a glass middle. The glass was broken.

"It'll slow them down," Bryce told her as he shoved her through the gap. He squeezed through after her and found himself staring down a long narrow hall. They were in another apartment building. This one was dark but not abandoned. Bryce slammed the door shut, grabbed Maddy and dragged her down the hall as behind them, the dead were already tearing at the cage, trying to rip it from its frame.

"Just a few more steps. We'll be out the back and halfway to Kansas before they get in."

If there was a backdoor. He had no idea. They hobbled along, passing a dozen doors; at the thirteenth they heard a child ask, "Can I get some milk?" His voice was high and clear, with not a hint of fear in it.

Bryce gave Maddy a shove in the back and then pounded on the door. "Shut that kid up, damn it!" he hissed. "*They're coming!*" Like a switch had been thrown, all sounds ceased on the other side of the door. Bryce took a step away but was struck by a thought: *Would them sitting in the dark holding their breath be enough?* The one-armed zombie had sniffed them out. Would it smell the kid? Would it call the other beasts to bash down their door?

He turned back and whispered at the door, "You guys should run."

They would have to hurry. The first of the zombies had gotten through the gate by then and was climbing through the opening in the door where the glass had been. Bryce ran, catching up to Maddy who was at the back door and peeking out.

"They're out there, too," she gasped.

"How many?"

Her eyes dropped away. "Four." For her it was a shameful number. Had she been like Bryce they would have a good chance to get away from only four. As it was, she would die. She had just sprinted three-hundred yards, a feat that wasn't possible even the day before. As great as it was, it was all she had in her until she could rest for a few minutes.

Bryce looked out. The four were large and whole. They smelled of fresh blood and shit. Without a weapon, four was too many for him. He shut the door. To their right was the base of a staircase. Bryce pulled Maddy to it. She stumbled on the first step and lay panting. He pulled her by the arm. "You can do this. Up. Up. Come on." Someone or some thing was running down the hall. The stairs were open, meaning there weren't doors leading to each floor. It made the two feel vulnerable and neither paused when they got to the second floor. Below them a zombie was snuffling. It smelled them. It smelled their sweat and the shampoo they had used, and the meat slowly spoiling in Bryce's pack.

Another zombie joined the first and then two more. Soon the first floor hall was filled with the dead. By then, Maddy and Bryce were on the third floor checking doors. All the doors were locked and most of the apartments had people hiding in them. They decided to go up another floor and were halfway down the hall when they heard the first crash.

The zombies were attacking one of the apartments, smashing at the door! Was it the one with the child? Maddy dropped her head, stunned by sudden guilt. This was her fault. She had been too weak to go on and now someone was going to die because of her. She stood there uselessly until the first scream rang out. It was like a punch in her gut. "We should do something."

"It's too late," Bryce told her. Besides being too late, he was weaponless and she only had one shoe. They began to check the other doors, doing their best to ignore the screams. They hadn't progressed far when another door began to be hammered on. The beasts had found another family.

"If they go door to door," Maddy said, "They'll eat their way through this entire building."

Bryce was already picturing exactly that. "We have to rouse everyone in the building. If we can get them together and rush the zombies in one big group, we might be able to save a lot of people."

"Or we lead them to the slaughter," Maddy said. "The zombies are too strong."

"We don't have to kill them, we just hold them back until the upper floors are clear." But what would they use to hold them back? Brooms? Couch cushions? None of that would work for more than a few minutes, maybe even only a few seconds. They needed something that would kill the creatures, something any person could use. Baseball bats would be great, but how many people owned one? A few, which wasn't good enough. They would have kitchen knives and small household hammers. *Maybe* someone would have a gun, but would they be good shots? Not likely. What they needed was… "Fire," he whispered.

Chapter 27

"Fire?" Maddy felt queasy at the thought. "What if it gets out of control? There's old people in the building. You can smell them." There was a granny somewhere on the floor. Maddy took a deep breath and, based on the smell alone, she pictured an eighty-year-old woman who regularly doused herself in Chanel No. 5. She also powdered her drooping breasts and had half a carton of Virginia Slims in her bed stand.

Then people die, Bryce didn't say out loud. People were going to die one way or another. He could only hope to save more than he'd lose…and it was his only hope to save himself. He bit that back as well. "Give me a better idea and I'll use it."

Maddy was surprised at how forceful he was being. The ghost of old Maddy felt her feathers getting ruffled. The new reality-based Maddy only shrugged. She didn't have a better idea and didn't want to die, so why put up a fuss?

"Okay. Fire. We can use anything with aerosol. Hairspray and a lighter will make a flamethrower. There's also cooking oil…"

More screams from below. The two pretended that they weren't scared out of their wits.

"G-Good," Bryce told her. "Start knocking on doors. We don't have a lot of time." He turned and pounded on the closest. "Hello! Hey, listen, the zombies are downstairs. They're going door to door, and we need…"

"Go away!"

Bryce stared at the door for a moment then pounded harder, his fear coming out as anger. "If you want to save your family get your ass out here!" He didn't wait for an answer but went to the next door and thumped the meaty part of his fist into it. "Zombies are pulling people out of their apartments and eating them. Everyone out."

Doors started to open and frightened people began peeking out into the darkened hall. "Grab what weapons you have," Bryce told them. "We have to break out or we'll be trapped. Who's alone? You?" He pointed at a thirty-three-year-old woman; she smelled of cats. "Go up to the top floor and start alerting them."

"But…" She pointed into her apartment where a grey tabby was peering out.

"But nothing," Bryce barked. "The only way we're getting out of this building alive is if we have the numbers. You want to live, right?"

The woman nodded, but couldn't commit more than that. Maddy took her by the arm. "It'll be okay. They won't leave without us." This helped calm the woman. She cast a last look back at her tabby as Maddy moved her to the stairs. They went up three flights to the top floor. The people here were more relaxed about light and noise. They figured they had a buffer of people between them and the undead.

Fewer of them opened their doors—until Maddy started talking about using fire to stop the zombies. Then they began to scramble for gear and weapons. Almost all of them had their bug-out bags ready. Unfortunately, half were using suitcases and many of these had multiple suitcases and looked as if they were heading out on vacation.

By the time Maddy had alerted the floor, the cat-lady had disappeared. Maddy grabbed another unsuspecting volunteer. This one had a ferret in a cage, a hiker's pack on his back, complete with sleeping bag, and a composite bow. His arms, scrawled with blue-green tattoos, were thick, which was good. His eyes were bleary and his breath smelled of whiskey, which wasn't. Still, he had a twisted but pleasant smile for her, even with the screams coming from below.

"You're with me," she told him.

He didn't argue; another plus in his favor. "You only got one shoe on," he said, a light twang to his voice.

"Yeah, a zombie took the other one." She pushed through the dazed throng to the stairs which were dark and empty. The people were acting as if the stairs led to hell, and there was no saying they didn't. "We're going to alert the next floor. The more the merrier."

He matched her step for step, looking at her out of the corner of his eye. "I'm Sid. Sid Pits. You ain't living in this building."

She glanced at him. His dark hair stuck up in chaotic angles, his lips were thick and twisted, his knuckles were scarred. His name fit. "Nope. I'm from Boston. I shouldn't even be here." They came to the first door. "Start knocking. Make sure everyone has a weapon. If they don't have one, see if they have anything that'll…" A harrowing scream came from the first floor. It sent a shiver down Maddy's back. "See if they have something that'll burn."

"Like a torch?"

"I was thinking something like hairspray or that non-stick spray stuff for cooking."

He grinned at this, showing crooked teeth that were in need of a brushing. "Flamethrowers. Right on." Excitedly, Sid began banging on doors. Everyone knew Sid and they followed his directions exactly. On the other side of the hall, Maddy struggled to get the people to understand the danger they were in. She found herself begging through cracked doors for the people inside to save themselves. Some refused to listen, while others waited until they saw the hall filling with their neighbors before they finally crept from their apartments.

She was still banging on doors when Sid came rushing up. "I got you this stuff." He had slung his bow and had his ferret cage set on top of a cardboard box. Inside the box were a pair of boots, two cans of hairspray and a lighter. "Them grey boots are a seven. You a seven, right?" She had been a six, but that was before. Plopping down, she slipped on one of the grey boots and, happily, it fit and was even a little on the small side. There was no time to kick off her other Ugg and put on the second boot as a roar erupted from the front staircase.

There were screams and a single gunshot. The zombies had spotted Bryce and the others.

Like panicked sheep, everyone around Maddy ran for the back stairs. She was very nearly trampled and had to duck into someone's cluttered apartment to keep from being trampled down by the stampede. The apartment was crammed with boxes and over-sized furniture that sucked up empty space. There were a dozen fine places to hide and the urge to squirrel away into one of them was strong. She knew it would be death to hide.

"Ooh, this is Rhonda's place," Sid said. "Never been in here. It's nice."

In Maddy's view it was cramped and smelled of sex. A lot of men had been in the apartment. Too many for Maddy to feel it was safe to touch anything. She turned back to the door.

When the surge of people had swept by, Maddy whispered, "We can go," and hurried down the hall, dodging the frightened people who were running up out of the dark staircase. They were running away from the battle—if it could be called such. Bryce had envisioned a concerted charge and a violent clash in which desperation would lend the people strength, and weapons would give them the edge.

Instead, his front line had disintegrated out of fear and had turned and fought their way up the stairs, knocking down anyone who got in their way. Bryce and a few others yelled for them to come back, then they yelled for help, then they simply yelled in a frenzy as they fought to hold back the flood of zombies.

It was an ugly battle fought by people who knew little about fighting with weapons that were barely weapons.

Bryce had the garbage can lid and a golf club. The man next to him had taken a leg from his kitchen table and was using it as a heavy club. A third was flailing about with twin meat cleavers like he was in a Saturday afternoon kung fu movie; fingers were flying like grey french fries.

The person with the gun was a vocal supporter of the second amendment, but thought it only pertained to muskets. He was so enamored with his position that he had put his money where his mouth was and had purchased a .50 caliber muzzle-loading rifle. It was a gorgeous weapon: four-feet in length, blued metal barrel, hardwood stock and a vintage coiled spring lock. He had even fired it a handful of times.

His first shot, with its fiery blast and huge sound, was so much like a bomb going off that it nearly gave Bryce a heart attack. The bullet, a huge hunk of lead, snapped past his ear, and exploded the throat out of one the beasts, dropping it on the spot. The musketeer then spent two minutes, fiddling with his fancy powder horn, poking his greased patch into place, dropping ammo like they were marbles, and tapping a bullet down into place with his short starter and then poking it all the way down with his ramrod.

He aimed, closed his eyes and fired. The gun made a *click* noise; he had forgotten the percussion cap. He stared at the gun in confusion as the man with the cleaver let out a scream.

A zombie had fallen into him, knocking him back. He tried to squirm away hacking at the thing's grasping hand with his cleavers, but zombies didn't need fingers to kill. The creature crooked an arm around the man's leg and bit down into his calf. The zombie's teeth couldn't cut through the man's denim. Still, the pain was ferocious and it ratcheted up his fear. He hacked one of his cleavers down as hard as he could, embedding it in the zombie's skull, killing it.

This didn't do much to help him. His legs were trapped under the zombie and a second later another creature crawled over its dead comrade to get at him. The man started freaking out, screaming and hacking around with his lone cleaver. Maddy came down the stairs, just as Bryce tried to pull him up.

Another man in the second row also tried to help. He was a squat little guy in a puffy jacket who had snapped off the working end of a broom and was using it as a spear. Spears were not the most effective tool against the undead, and this was doubly true of homemade spears. The spear only seemed to enrage the zombies more and they came on screaming and wailing loud enough to shiver the soul.

Very soon the cleaver man was buried by bodies and now his dying screams, muffled by the weight of the bodies on him, grew pitiful but there was nothing that could be done. Bryce and the others were forced back, one stair at a time.

It wasn't long before they lost the spear man as well. He stabbed one of the creatures through the chest; a feat of strength given that the zombie had been a bosomy woman. As a human, she had liked to keep things held in tight and her bra had been industrial strength. When the spear snagged on it, there was no getting it back. She advanced up the hunk of wood protruding from her chest, clawing her way up it, stomping over the dead to get at the spearman. His nerve broke. He let go of his end of the spear and tried to run.

But it was too late for him.

He had let the chesty zombie get too close and she tripped him up as he turned. More diseased hands grabbed him and he screamed in mortal fear. Bryce tried to get him back, wading into the mess, hacking left and right with his 1-iron; however the creatures had too good of a hold on the guy and he was pulled down into a torrent of grey clawed hands and flashing teeth.

The jeans and the puffy coat the man wore made sure that his death would be a slow one. Tiny feathers flew as the coat was shredded.

Bryce felt the man's dying in his own chest and he cried along with the man as he hacked about with his club. As desperate as he was to save the man, the more heads he crushed the further the man was buried and it wasn't long before he disappeared completely beneath the foul, hateful mass.

Eventually, Bryce had to step back, his lungs billowing and his hands numb. Two stout men took his place and started beating the dead, one with a tennis racket and the other with a softball bat. The bat was aluminum and when it struck it rang out *Tank! Tank! Tank!* like the man was taking batting practice.

For half a minute they held the dead back. But they were skittish, afraid to be touched. They were extra fearful of blood and when the bat got red and wet the batsman's swing grew short and ineffective. The Musketeer finally stepped up again and set off another semi-explosion in the dark stairwell.

He killed one of the beasts, blowing its head near in two. As fine as that was, it undermined their cause. In the light of the blast the wriggling mass of zombies was more frightening than ever and the man with the racket turned and pushed his way back up the stairs, slamming into Maddy and knocking her down. She didn't blame him for running. There were simply too many of them. They were a stinking grey mass of evil. In the semi-dark they looked like they had formed one terrible being with a hundred arms and a thousand hungry mouths. The sight made her want to puke.

Bryce tried to fill the hole left by the man. He grabbed a fellow who was dual wielding golf clubs and pulled him down beside him. "We only have to ho-old them back for a li-ittle longer!" he bellowed over the noise. In mid-bellow, his voice broke twice, although whether it was out of fear or because of his inhuman growth was hard to tell.

One way or another, there was no hiding his fear. The trashcan lid rattled and he held the golf club with a white knuckled grip.

His less-than manly bellow had the opposite effect as intended. People started to back up the stairs. Maddy counted seven men and two women failing in their duty to stop the press of zombies.

"There's nowhere to run!" Maddy shouted. She was on the landing and could see down the hall where people were pushing to get to the back set of stairs. There were screams from that direction but they were wordless. People were forcing their way down from the upper floors, inadvertently shoving those at the very front right at the zombies. There was no room to fight. It was a scrum and anyone who fell was trampled almost immediately.

Maddy and Bryce had been too slow. The trap had closed on them and now two hundred people were going to pay the price.

Chapter 28

"There's nowhere to run! We have to hold until the way's clear!" Maddy shouted. This was hardly a pep-talk and for one of the women it triggered a panic attack. She tried to bolt past Maddy. She carried a dust mop and Maddy grabbed it with both hands. "No! We can't run. We have…"

Words were beyond the woman just then. Maddy might as well have been screaming at her in Russian. She yanked back on her mop for only a second before she simply let it go and ran.

"Or maybe you can run," Maddy muttered. She looked down into the dark stairwell and saw Bryce and two others hacking with their odd weapons. "We have to hold for a few more minutes!" she cried to him.

Bryce aimed a blow at a grey balding head and struck it with a meaty *thunk!* "Don't know if we can. Getting tired." They were barely keeping the dead back as it was and with each swing, Bryce's arms grew more heavy.

"Just hold on!" Maddy yelled over the men and the raging zombies. She turned her mop sideways and pushed the hesitating men closer to the fight, knowing that their only hope was to bottle up the zombies as far down in the stairwell as they could. "We just have to keep them back for a few more minutes."

The second of the women tried to slip around the mop. "I can't," she begged. In one hand she clutched a broom and in the other she had a big jug of old bacon grease.

Maddy jabbed her with the mop, pinning her to the wall. "Yes, you can. You have to." Maddy grabbed the jug. "Fire'll stop them. Just don't burn anyone." Maddy poured the grease over the woman's broom and her own mop. Then she paused to find her lighter, slapping at her pockets.

"Use mine." It was Sid Pits. He flicked his lighter and the mop went right up. The flames were huge. The fire looked as though it was going to consume the mop in seconds so Maddy pushed down the stairs with it held aloft. Everyone ducked away and she had an open shot at the front rank of zombies who were all staring, captivated by the fire. She shoved it squarely into the face of the largest of the creatures. It was already bleeding from bat and golf club wounds, neither of which had done anything to slow it.

The fire did the trick. The grease was still wet and when the mop slapped the thing's face it left a slick of burning fat behind. The flames shriveled the zombie's eyes and burned out its nasal cavity. Its hair went up so that it looked like it was wearing a burning crown. The fire seemed to douse its hate and demonic hunger and it only stood there filling the stairwell with the sickening stench of roasted human flesh.

Maddy stared in disgust, her face twisted and her throat working up and down. It was so horrible that she almost waited too long to use the flaming mop a second time. Another of the creatures charged up the stairs getting too close for her to jam the mop in its face without setting her own hair on fire.

Bryce was suddenly by her side. He lashed out with a front kick to the thing's face, knocking it back just far enough for her to set it alight.

They both had to duck away as one of the men came forward with the broom. It was a roaring torch that he jabbed repeatedly at the zombies. His first few strikes were horrific but, the straw of the broom was burning away too quickly. In no time the end of the broom was nothing but a blackened husk. "Gimme more oil!" he cried.

The woman who'd been holding it had disappeared into the grey smoke never to be seen again. Near the landing was the man who'd been fighting with the tennis racket. He grabbed the jug and poured the grease over the broom and then onto Maddy's mop as she held it out to him. It was still on fire and adding more grease caused it to explode in flames.

Maddy swung the burning mop away just as the man with the jug flinched back as the jug caught fire. Blue flame flickered around the sides a second before it flashed into a roaring fireball. Under any other circumstances the man would've dropped it and ran. Trapped and with so many zombies fighting to get up at them, he took the extra seconds needed to throw the jug down into the mass where it seemed to detonate. Fire coated the dead, burning out their eyes and setting their clothes alight.

The heat and the stench grew too great and everyone flailed back up the stairs. For the moment, the zombies were stymied by the fire. They cared nothing about flame, and pain was only a nuisance if they felt it at all, but the thick smoke hid the fleeing humans and the horrid smell masked their scent.

Bryce stood gasping on the third floor landing, his golf club bent and useless, still in one hand. Around him the others were retching or staggering away down the hall. The crowd at that end of the building were panicked by the nauseating stench and were pushing even harder on those in front of them, either not realizing or not caring that they were pushing people to their death.

"What do we do?" a man next to Bryce screeched. It was the musketeer. His gun was only half-loaded. The ram-rod was still stuck down into the barrel.

"We, uh…" Bryce began. He looked over at Maddy who shook her head, clueless. Bryce began to get a shaky desperate feeling deep in his gut. "I don't know. Is there a way to climb down? Like a fire-escape?"

The musketeer had the fingers of his left hand in his mouth. Around them he mumbled a "no."

Bryce needed time to think, to come up with a real plan to escape. "Okay, we have to slow them down. I say we block the stairwell. Check to see if any of the apartments are open." The musketeer ran down the hall shaking doorknobs until he found one a few doors down. Bryce ordered the bigger men to take the living room couch while he and the others grabbed the kitchen table and chairs.

Maddy, with an armful of comforters, ran ahead. The fire was smothering itself and the zombies were already groping forward through the thick haze. She heaved the blankets at them. As she pulled the can of hairspray from a side pocket in her pack, ghostly grey figures appeared next to her in the smoke and threw down chairs and cushions. A side table went next.

By then Maddy had her can and lighter out. The hairspray blew bright flame. She aimed it at the face of the closest zombie and turned it into a human torch. Confused, it took a step back and fell into the others. This gave her a few more seconds and she dropped to one knee and relit the hairspray, this time aiming for the edge of the closest comforter. For some reason, it refused to catch fire.

A crocheted blanket laying on top of it did, however. It went right up, nearly taking Maddy's bangs with it.

"Look out." It was Bryce. He and the musketeer threw the kitchen table down the stairs. It hit with a crack before bounding into the zombies, knocking two down. "More stuff!" Bryce cried, grabbing Maddy's shoulder. She saw that Bryce was in the moment and thinking only of the next minute. They needed a plan for the next five minutes, and the next ten, and the next two hours.

She shrugged off his hand and watched him race away. The few people left on this side of the building were all running around grabbing whatever they could. More oil was found, as was a mattress, and white curtains. It was all thrown down into the well of the staircase. The fire was going strong and the smoke from it was deadly. She wobbled up the stairs, lightheaded.

"You're gonna burn down the building around yourselves," mused Sid Pits, his breath perfumed with fresh whiskey. He seemed unconcerned by the prospect. He had found a silken silver scarf and had it wrapped around his neck in a fashionable loop. It clashed with his composite bow.

Maddy caught the pronouns that excluded himself. "How are you going to get out of the building? You have a way. I can tell." And she could. It was more than just the pronouns. Somehow, she knew.

"I do but it's not for everyone."

"What's that mean?"

He grimaced, his thick lips twisting. "It means certain people…certain small people won't make it." He wanted to stop at this, but she glared up at him. If there was a way to escape, she *needed* to know. "I'm going to jump over to the next building across the alley. It's a good fifteen feet."

This deflated Maddy. She couldn't jump fifteen feet, not even with a running start. The new and improved Bryce probably could. She glanced over at him as he dragged a dresser down the hall by himself. He was even bigger than ever. The jeans he had on had split, showing plaid boxers, and the hoodie was stretched even tighter across his chest and shoulders.

She looked down at herself and thought she might have lost a pound or two since she had gazed at her reflection in the mirror, but that hour hadn't imbued her with the abilities of a gazelle.

But was there any other option?

"Show me," she ordered.

His look for her was a sad one, telling her that he didn't think she had a chance in hell of making the jump. Still, he tromped up the stairs, his silken scarf swaying gently. He was empty-handed which reminded her.

"Where's your ferret?"

Sid looked back, confused. "My what? Oh that. I thought it was a weasel. Either way, I let it go. No big loss. It weren't mine. It just looked cool."

Let it go? she wondered, *Where?*

This begged even more questions, which she didn't have time for, since she was sure the answers would be as confusing as Sid was. She held back until they reached the roof. Right away she saw that she was screwed. On two sides of the building were taller buildings. Their windows were barred. Another side looked out over the street, which was crowded with the undead smashing their way inside. This left only the alley.

The next building looked much further than fifteen feet away. It had to be twenty, easy. And the fall…

"Oh God," Maddy gasped and turned away. "No. That's insane."

"You ain't wrong," Sid agreed. There was a lip to the roof; he had his foot up on it as he looked down. He spat. "Getting all eated up is more so, dontcha think?" She refused to entertain either idea. He grinned his crooked grin, shrugged off his pack and bow, and went to sit on an old folding chair that had once belonged to a patio set. Next to the chair, sitting like an obedient dog, was a coffee can filled with cigarette butts.

Sid fished out a box of brown cigarettes and lit up. "If you guys figger a better way out, you come and get me, alright?"

Maddy said she would, but there'd be no figgering anything. Smoke was billowing up out of the stairwell door and before she could get to it, the musketeer burst from it, wild-eyed.

"They're coming! Help me hold the door."

"Where's Bryce?"

"Who?"

Maddy shoved him away from the door. When she opened it, the screams coming up went right to her heart. They were echoing through the building and running along the walls. "What the hell happened?"

The musketeer tried to grab the edge of the door to close it but Maddy held on tight. "They came up the other stair…I think. I just know that one moment we were pushing this big hutch-like thing to the stairs and the next people were running everywhere. People and those things."

"They's zombies," Sid pointed out. He leaned back and blew a grey plume up into the dark sky, acting as though he had just proclaimed them to be daffodils instead of zombies.

"Either way, they came charging down the hall and I was this close to being trapped. There was fire in front and zombies coming up behind, and so I just ran."

The screams coming from the stairwell seemed to grow even louder. Maddy looked down into the haze and saw someone rushing up. At first, she thought it was Bryce, but it was the man who'd had the tennis racket. He was cradling burnt fingers.

"Where's Bryce? Did you see him down there?"

The man, handsome, clean-cut and tall, had a dazed look. "Who?"

"Never mind," she whispered. Their plan had failed. They hadn't saved anyone, and that included themselves. She looked back at the building across the alley. She would never make the jump. But Bryce might.

Turning to the musketeer she shocked him by snatching his gun right from his hands. "This thing loaded?"

"Yeah, but…"

She took his curved powder horn as well. He let out a squawk. She ignored it and headed down into the dark stairs. The vile smoke poured over her, and her ears were assaulted by the screams which were hitting a fever pitch. Down she went, deeper into hell.

Chapter 29

It was like walking into an oven. The heat dried up her face leaving it pinched and tight. With each breath, her lungs shriveled and her eyes grew squintier. A wind, hot and black, surged up the stairs at her.

The air was so intense she worried that her hair might go up in flames. Her hair or the powder horn she carried. Quickly, she hid the horn away and looked at the gun for the first time. Was it even ready to shoot?

Maddy cocked the gun before remembering that the ramrod had been stuck down its bore the last time she had seen it. It was still there, plugging the bore neatly. For a moment she wondered whether it was supposed to be there. As far as she knew, these sorts of guns fired a little ball that you poked down into the barrel. What was keeping it from rolling out?

Gravity, she supposed. Once she pulled the ramrod free, she made sure to keep the weapon pointed slightly up.

Two people passed her on the stairs, hacking and coughing. Both were heading for the roof, not realizing it was a dead end. Maddy didn't have the heart to tell them. She paused at the sixth floor which was filled with a dense grey haze. Halfway down the hall was the ghost of a woman running for her apartment door. In the smoke she was faceless. She fumbled with her keys and dropped them twice before getting one to fit into the lock. She disappeared, trapping herself in a burning building along with a hundred zombies.

She was not the only one. Almost everyone who could run from the back stairwell had fled to their apartments, sometimes with the dead right on their heels. Some made it, some didn't.

On the fifth floor three people were being eaten by a crowd of zombies. The smoke was even thicker here which was just as well since Maddy was already wallowing in guilt and seeing the faces of the newly dead would only add to her psychic burden.

Bryce was down the hall somewhere. She followed his scent and found him fighting a giant of a zombie with a great bulging beer belly and huge fleshy arms. In the smoke that swirled around them, it looked like an ogre. Bryce had found another golf club but it was only bouncing off the creature's great dome of a head.

She paused a few steps away from the fight to squint in at her gun, looking for… there it was, a safety catch. She released it and stepped forward until she was only a few feet away. With the big rifle snugged into the pocket of her shoulder, she calmly said, "Step to your right."

Bryce had heard her coming. The soft tha-dum of her mismatched boots let him know who it was. He jerked his head to the left to avoid a giant hand ripping at his face and then, almost casually, slid to his right. He had expected a blast from an aerosol can and jerked in surprise as the black powder rifle went off like a bomb.

The musketeer had over-charged it, adding almost ninety grains instead of the called for sixty. It was a well-crafted weapon and it held together, but the kick was fantastic and painful. Maddy's arm went instantly numb as her shoulder screamed and her feet went out from beneath her. She found herself on her ass staring up at the ceiling.

The zombie lost half its face and although its brain was still intact, its eyes had been flash roasted by the blast. All it saw was a grey misting blur. It certainly didn't see Bryce swing the club and it didn't feel the edge of the iron as it crashed through its skull and lodged there for all time.

It collapsed at Bryce's feet, a stinking grey mound. He tossed aside the headless golf club and helped Maddy to her feet, warning her, "The only way out is down the front stairs. It's going to be tough…and a little smoky."

"A little smoky?" She laughed and instantly regretted it. Her shoulder was still aching from the gunshot. Working her arm around in a circle, she asked, "And what about the fire? Are you going to call that little as well?" He growled and was about to make an excuse when she pointed up. "The only way out of here is from the roof. We're going to have to jump to another building."

She started pulling him along to the stairs, but he balked. "Hold on. A jump? What sort of jump?" He could feel her pulse through her damp hand. It was revved more than usual. She was afraid…more than usual.

"A big one across the back alley." She wouldn't look up at him.

"Yeah? Can we make it?"

Her shrug brought about a wince. "Maybe. Probably." *There's no way*, she thought. Still, they had less chance going through the smoke and the fire…and the zombies. There were too many zombies and they scared Maddy more than any fall would. Even then a dozen people were screaming, dying slowly.

Bryce heard the lie in her voice and it scared him. "O-Okay. Let's see this jump."

They abandoned the screamers and the people hiding in their closets, doing their best not to think about how this was their fault. But it was in the back of their minds, nonetheless. They had brought death to the people in the building. Death seemed to follow them, or it was in the air around them. Maybe it was in their touch. Neither knew, but it felt as though the two instigated all of this by turning down Magnus.

Of course, this was absurd, and yet guilt was frequently an absurd beast and that was especially true in this new world. It had no place there.

At the stairs they both stared down in shock. The fire could be seen as a hellish red glow and the heat from it seared into their faces. It was out of control and soon it would force everyone and everything up to the roof. Their time was running out. They raced upward and found that the rooftop door was closed against them. It could not be locked from the outside, though it could be held. On the other side was the musketeer. He smelled of blackpowder.

"It's us, open up," Bryce said, tapping on the door.

"How do I know you're not one of them? Or that you don't have one of…"

Bryce slammed his shoulder into the door, knocking the man back. There was no time for useless fear. There were plenty of real fears in front and behind. Bryce strode out into a cold night. Right away he felt the cold in the split of his pants. Embarrassed, he cast a look back at Maddy. Split pants were the furthest thing from her mind. She only had eyes for the little ledge and the gravel-covered roof across the canyon of brick. It was a long way.

There were seven of them up in the cold and none were more afraid than Maddy. She was the smallest, the chubbiest, the least athletic. The man with the burned hands held them in front of him; they were shaking. Next to him was a soft and balding of forty. He stood a few feet from the edge, muttering and shaking his head. Behind him and using him as a shield against any stray wind that might blow him over the side, was the musketeer. He was stark white and kept looking back and forth from the door to the edge, trying to decide which was worse.

The decision was going to be made for him soon enough. Someone was racing up the stairs, trying to outrun a pack of zombies.

Only Bryce and Maddy heard the person coming. They looked into each other's eyes and saw that each was thinking the same thing: if they held the door shut, the person's death would give them an extra couple of minutes to come up with an idea. Ashamed, Bryce turned away.

"Someone get the door," Maddy ordered. "Someone's coming."

The musketeer felt a surge of crazy hope. A moment before he hadn't wanted to let the people knocking through the door, now he latched onto the idea that maybe this "someone" would be able to help them. It was a childish thought.

The person who came up was a shrieking woman. She ran up out of the stairs and then ran in a circle around the roof, her eyes wide and crazy. "How do we get down," she cried, clutching at the man with the burned hands.

"Get that door shut!" one of the men barked. The disappointed musketeer slammed it shut and for a few seconds it was silent on the roof. All eyes went to Bryce. Somehow he had ended up in the middle of the group and they were all looking at him for answers.

Which doesn't make any sense, he thought. *I'm just me. I'm no one.* This was true, but they didn't seem to understand. With every eye on him, he went to the edge of the roof and looked across the alley. It was frightfully far, but it was fast becoming their only hope. The zombies were just on the other side of the door. "Who wants to go first?" He certainly didn't. Yes, he might have been in the middle of a curious physical change, but mentally he was still the same slightly built, easily frightened little man he had always been.

Sid flicked his cigarette away and pushed out of his chair. "That'll be me."

There was a thud as something smashed into the door. "Hold on!" the musketeer shouted. He had his back to the door while the balding man was trying to block it using the folding chair. "We need a real plan. One that doesn't involve jumping. What about climbing?"

Again, everyone looked at Bryce. He glanced down again and then up at the surrounding buildings. Without ladders and rope, climbing up was impossible and climbing down meant falling. There were just too many places where there weren't holds of any sorts. And anyone who actually made the climb down would have to deal with zombies falling from up top and likely, more waiting below.

Had it not been for the fire they had set, they might've been able to pile themselves against the door, but that bridge was burned along with half the building.

"Jumping is it. It's our only choice." His eyes flicked to Maddy. She wouldn't look up.

"If you even call it a choice," the musketeer snarled. "You did this to us. You set that fire. You should be the one who goes first."

"No," Sid said, quickly. "I'm going first." He looked down at the drop and spat. Reaching into his jacket, he pulled out a flask and took a swig. He then held it out to Bryce. It was pewter and engraved: *William, The Best Man is also my Best Friend*.

Bryce took a slug of very expensive whiskey—it still burned going down. "I can go first if…"

Sid shook his head. "If you don't make it, I might lose my nerve." He unslung his pack and heaved it across. The bow went next, then his coat. The Hawaiian shirt he had on made no sense. "Wish me luck," he said, backing up. There was no preamble, no short speech, and no hesitation on his part. He took off at a run for the edge and threw himself across the chasm.

Breathless, everyone watched as Sid sailed through the air. His arc did not end with him landing on the roof, but rather against the wall of the building with a heavy grunt. He was high enough that his chest hit the lip. Like a desperate cat, he scrambled to hold himself up. He kicked and clawed his way onto the other roof. Then he lay there, gasping.

"I want to go next." It was the forty-ish balding man who was holding the door shut along with the musketeer. His name was George Rawlins and although suicide had been much on his mind the last couple of months, he didn't want to go out kicking and screaming with some grey-faced punk eating his pecker off.

The musketeer looked panicked, as if he would have to go third simply by being next to George. "No. Someone's got to hold the door with me."

"I'll do it," Maddy said, her voice a harsh whisper. Her fear was a raging monster inside of her. As bad as the zombies were the jump was insane. She didn't want to be anywhere near the edge of the roof. She couldn't even think about it.

Bryce pulled her away from the door. "She's too small. One of you other guys will have…" One of the men rushed to the door; he was supposed to hold it closed but it looked like he was holding onto it for dear life. It was an unsettling display of cowardice which made George hesitate. He had been working himself up to attempt the jump; now he turned away.

Bryce found he couldn't look in their direction. "You'll be fine," Bryce told Maddy. "I'll go before you and, and, and I'll catch you." It was a ridiculous thing to say and they both knew it. She wouldn't get close to the wall and if she did, how was he supposed to catch her? Even if he managed to grab one of her hands, simple physics would suggest that she would pull him right off the roof.

"Maybe," she whispered. *Or maybe it'll simply be easier to stay up here and get eaten.* The thought was cowardly and she hung her head in shame.

"Get out of the way," George cried in a high warbling voice. "Step back. Get the fuck back!" There was already a clear lane through which he could run. Nonetheless, everyone stepped back. It was to George's credit that he didn't pause. He sucked in a huge breath and ran for the edge of the roof

He had been an athlete once, and his eighteen-year-old self would've landed feet first on the other side. Even his thirty-year-old self would've hit much like Sid had. This version of George was years past his prime. His thighs were soft and marbled with fat. His calves were thin and grew quickly tired. When he couldn't lounge, he liked to sit. His jump was poorly timed and poorly executed. He had wanted to take off from the lip, thinking the extra ten-inches in height could make the difference. But his stride was off.

At the last second, he saw that his jumping foot was going to come down two inches too short, so he stretched his leg slightly. This, in turn, made his bunched muscle slightly longer, giving him less spring.

"Shit," Bryce whispered while the man was in mid-flight. He wasn't going to make it. Even stretching out his long arms did nothing. When his body slapped against the wall, his fingertips were three inches from the top. In vain, he scratched at the wall like a cat trying to climb a tree. Even claws wouldn't have helped. His nails ripped from their beds and he fell, screaming.

Chapter 30

George hit with an appalling splatting thud. There was silence on the roof for only a few seconds before the woman who had come charging up last let out a long wail. Her legs buckled and she collapsed on the roof, covering her face with her hands. She was still howling in misery when the door banged again. She was exciting the zombies.

"Someone shoot me," she said. When no one said anything, she pointed at Maddy. "Shoot me."

Maddy had forgotten she was even holding the musket. She let it fall from her hands. "I can't." It wasn't as if she was against the idea. Far from it. Going out in a blink was smart. She was just against the idea of becoming a murderer in her last few minutes left on earth.

"No one's shooting anyone," Bryce said, forcefully. "We can figure this out."

"What's there to figure out?" the woman said. "I can't jump across and there's too many zombies to fight. The only thing that makes sense is to kill ourselves as painlessly as possible. But if you got some big idea, let's hear it."

She waited patiently until it was clear Bryce had no big idea. She then got up and went to the gun. It was a big piece, long and unwieldy. Sitting down, she pulled off one shoe and stuck one toe in the trigger guard. Twisting slightly, she was able to put the bore to her forehead. "I'll do it myself," she declared.

Maddy held out the powder horn to her. "I'll go next," she said.

"You won't," Bryce snapped, grabbing her arm and dragging her away. "You're going to make this jump." He tore off his backpack and held up the shoulder straps. "You see these? I'll have a hold of this side; you just have to jump and grab the other. I'll stick it out as far as I can and that guy will hold my legs."

As though he was viewing the live performance of some sort of bizarre theater, Sid had been watching the others and sipping from his flask. "I can do that." He pointed the lip of the flask at Bryce. "You just got to make the jump first."

The frightened energy racing through Bryce evaporated, leaving behind only fear. "Yeah," he said. "Yeah. Okay. I-I can do it. *We* can do it." He leaned in close to Maddy. "Magnus changed us. We're stronger now. You and I can both do this."

"I can't."

"Yes, you can. All you have to do is get close…If you don't trust me, trust Magnus. Come on. Don't you want to see where this goes? Don't you want to see what you'll become?"

A part of her did. More and more she knew she wasn't going to turn into a zombie. Instead, she was turning into someone much greater than she had been. Yes, her heart was tripping and the sweating was unnerving, but every time she was able to rest, she came back that much stronger.

The words: *I think we should give you a chance*, floated through her mind. Magnus had said that. Was this her chance? This thing he did to her? Looking out at the chasm it didn't feel like much of a chance.

"I'll catch you," Bryce repeated. "Just promise me you'll jump if I make it."

Maddy glanced over at the woman who was getting step by step instructions from the musketeer on how to load the weapon. The moment was surreal. Zombies were banging on the door. Black smoke was billowing up the side of the building. The city was black and full of death. Sid raised his flask to her.

"Okay," she whispered.

Bryce gave her a false grin. He was scared to death. "Don't look down," he told himself. "Look at the lip and then…yeah. Then jump." After throwing his pack across, he took a couple of steps back, scraped out a mark and then came forward, taking large, exaggerated steps to the edge of the roof. There would be only one shot at making the jump and he wanted it perfect.

At the edge he told himself not to look down. But he did and it was a mistake. George was not dead. He had broken over fifty bones and was bleeding both internally and externally, and yet, for the moment, he was still alive. A zombie was trying to suck the marrow from his shattered femur. George was making a gurgling sound and beating his hand lightly on the creature.

"Shit," Bryce whispered. He backed away and went through the steps again. He was ready, and so was the woman with the gun. "I'll catch you, too," he promised her. She said nothing; she only looked down at the gun and ran her hands along the beautiful stock. She would wait and see. They all would. Everyone stared in silence.

Bryce went to his mark and began to take large breaths as he bounced up and down. This was it. Putting it off for even a minute might doom them all. He took a great gulp of air and took off for the edge of the roof with one goal in mind: he'd make the takeoff perfect and everything else would fall into place.

The jump was very much like that first front kick had been. It felt *right*. His foot came down on the lip exactly on the ball, and his momentum added to his leap, and out he sailed over the sickening drop. Now his eyes were on the other roof.

He was not going to make the jump; he was coming in short. The question was how short and could he throw out his hands far enough to make any difference? George had done nothing to change his trajectory. Bryce kicked like he was still running in the air and stretched out a single arm as far as he could. Unlike George, he didn't slap hard against the brick. His one grasping hand was hooked into a claw, while he used the other to protect his face and absorb the impact.

That hooked claw held tight to the edge of the roof.

"Gimme your udder hand," Sid said, suddenly appearing above him.

Bryce swung his hand up and Sid grabbed his jacket. Looking into his face, Sid said, "If I pull you up, you gonna owe me a life debt. You cool with that?"

"Yeah, Christ! Just pull me up."

"Christ, huh? It's good you a Bible man cuz you can't go back on a life debt," Sid said, and began pulling as hard as he could. Hauling one's self up in this way was not like it was in the movies. It was much like the last couple of days: a desperate clawing fight to live.

Once he got one elbow up, he knew he was safe. Sid kept pulling until Bryce was lying, gasping on the roof. He rolled over and stared upwards and saw a few stars straining to shine through the smoke. Theirs wasn't the only building on fire. The view from this roof was more open to the west and he could see all the way into New Jersey. There had to be a hundred fires scattered across his view.

Just like Bryce, people were discovering that fire was a double-edged sword. "It's still a sword," he muttered, justifying his actions under his breath.

"You wants a sword?" Sid asked, grinning. He was becoming softly drunk. There was a nice phlegmy purr to his voice and warmth behind his eyes. It was the perfect state, he thought. He could still function but not give a rip about the screams and the people trapped on the other roof. They were all going to die, one way or another. The thought soured his buzz and he took another swig.

The woman with the gun had the right of it. Best to go out quick and easy.

But she was hesitating now that Bryce made it across. In the back of her mind was a murmur of hope. She looked up at Maddy, thinking if that girl could make it then she might have a chance too. "Go," the woman said to Maddy.

Maddy had been staring across the alley. She had said she would try, but all the strength had drained from her legs. Bryce had barely made it. His approach, his launch, his form in the air had been perfect. The word *Olympic* danced through her mind. She couldn't equal it and she would fall.

"I can't," she said, her words barely audible.

"Yeah. That's what I thought." The woman pulled the bore of the gun up under her chin. As she worked her toe into position to press down on the trigger, she said, "There's no shame in this. I always said I wasn't built for an apocalypse. I thought it would be the food. You know? I can't eat canned food over and over. It would make me crazy." She laughed and although it was soft, it still wasn't sane. "Do me a favor?"

Maddy pulled her eyes from the chasm. "Maybe."

"If this, you know, doesn't do the whole job, can you finish it? You know, quick?"

"You want me to kill you?"

She shrugged. "Only if it doesn't work all the way."

The roof began to tilt under Maddy's feet. She put a hand on her forehead, saying, "I don't know if I can."

"I can," said one of the other men. In the dark he was somewhat featureless, but Maddy could see that he wasn't particularly big and that his shoulders were rounded and sloped. He wasn't going to be able to make the jump either. "I'll do it, but I get next dibs on the gun."

"That's *my* gun!" cried the musketeer from the door. "I say who shoots it and who doesn't. And I say I get it next. After that…" He shrugged. He'd be dead, it wouldn't matter to him who shot it.

"Are you gonna kill her?" the sloped-shouldered man demanded.

The musketeer abandoned the door, leaving only a single frightened man to hold it against the zombies. He screamed for help, but no one came to his rescue. Instead, the man with the burnt hands pushed between the others. "You're all idiots."

Drawing in a hot breath, the musketeer was about to give a snippy reply when the man ran for the edge of the roof. He never had a chance. Much like Bryce had, he was able to hook the far building with one hand, which was covered in blisters and weeping fluids. It slipped right off the brick, leaving behind a wet print and some blackened flesh.

He screamed all the way down and hit with a thud/splat that was, if possible, even worse than the first one.

Just like before, there was a moment of drawn silence. Then the musketeer poked the other man in the chest and was poked back. This turned into a scuffle as the zombies battered at the door even harder, and the man there cried out in fear. Bryce hissed for Maddy to jump and Sid laughed, staring into the mouth of his stolen flask.

In the midst of this, the woman with the gun said a prayer and jerked the trigger with her toe.

Of course, the bullet did not kill the woman right away. The world was no longer that easy. The huge lead ball blasted upward passed between her jawbone and her tongue, exploded out her upper teeth and her right eye, before sizzling right up the side of her cranium.

She was stunned, half-blind and bleeding, but she was still conscious. Everyone stared in horror and that included the man at the door who should've been fighting back against the zombies. They bowled him over seconds later and charged onto the roof. It was pandemonium.

Maddy's first thought was to go to the woman. She didn't deserve to die like this. There was no telling what her fate would've been if Maddy had been able to keep up with Bryce when they'd be down on the street running from the horde, or if she had just said yes to Magnus in the first place, or if she hadn't denied the woman a quick death out of weakness, confusing mercy for murder. Everyone else was motivated by fear, but Maddy's guilt came first. She went for the gun lying off to the side.

With the creatures surging up onto the roof, there was no time to load the thing. Grabbing it by the bore, she raised it over her head, barely feeling the heat of the searing hot metal.

"Sorry," Maddy whispered and brought the gun crashing down, aiming for the woman's head.

Chapter 31

The musket was rugged and heavy, the perfect club. Maddy brought it up and around as if she was chopping wood, and she would've ended the woman's life except the musketeer put a hand out. The stock slapped into his palm a foot from the woman's head.

"Mine!" he cried, yanking it from her grasp and nearly toppling her. She stumbled into him and he shoved her away.

Before Maddy could get her feet under her, a mostly naked, grayish man rushed down on her. It was not a small zombie by any measure and should have been able to throw her to the ground and tear her neck out with ease, only it did not possess the full complement of fingers that a normal person was born with.

It had just three, none of which was a thumb. It tried to grab her and bite her, but it was like bobbing for a very large apple. Maddy wasn't about to stand there and have a chunk taken out of her. She still had fingers and she grabbed the nearest outstretched wrist, pushing it to the side, and in the process, turned the creature halfway around.

Again, it turned for her, swinging its other arm like it was a bat and her head was a ball. It was an obvious move and not particularly fast, giving her plenty of time to duck under it. The zombie had put too much into the swing and now it spun around. She darted to her right along with it so that its back was in front of her.

For Maddy Whitmore it was a shockingly elegant move. She didn't think she could've repeated it even if she practiced for a week. The move was out of the blue and for some reason, it empowered her, taking away her fear and replacing it with bravado she had never in her life experienced. This allowed her to attack when she might've run away. Taking it by the hair she ran forward and tossed it straight off the roof. There was no reason to watch it splat.

"Behind…" Bryce started to say.

He was too late. She was already spinning, taking in another of the creatures. It was charging in at her, leading with its open mouth. She dove to the side and rolled. The thing stretched out a hand as it went flying by; its fingers missed hooking her V-neck by an inch.

"Jump!" Bryce shouted over the sudden din.

It had become her only option. There were two zombies for every person on the roof and more crawling up out of the choking smoke. Since she was off to the side alone, she was the only one who stood a ghost of a chance.

And still she hesitated.

She backed up from the edge, took three big breaths and then froze. The air seemed to freeze around her as well; she could see Bryce's mouth moving and his hand slapping the brick, begging her to get moving. Next to him, Sid was pointing and yelling soundlessly. Gone were the screams, and the shouts, and the animalistic growls.

One thing cut through the soundless haze that surrounded her: laughter. A mad cackling was cawing up from the stairwell. It made the hair on her arms stand straight up. In her mind, she pictured a scabby zombie, coming up the stairs, chicken-like, its arms wrapped around itself, held in by a filthy blood-streaked straight jacket.

The laughter and the image filled her with such a mortal dread that it weighed her down, physically. Standing there, she felt like the Maddy from a week before, dumpy and slow, easily winded and with the jumping skills of a tortoise. And she knew that if she started running, it would be like she was running through a nightmare. Her strides would be torpid as if the roof was covered in a foot of thick grasping mud.

Her head creaked around in slow motion until her eyes fixed on the door. Out came a stumbling, one-legged zombie. She was small with pink ribbons in her hair. Instead of laughing, she let out a howl from a lipless mouth and rushed to join the others feasting on the musketeer. The shadows in the doorway were cast around the glow of the fire, giving them a semblance of evil, however the next shadow exuded such menace that Maddy's legs trembled.

It was the laugher and it was coming from a demon. A great behemoth of a woman strode from the smoke. Her head, covered in a mass of wild magenta-colored hair, came within inches of the door frame and her arms, hanging on monstrous hips, scraped the sides. She wore pants that were spitting along the seams and high up on her ankles. Obviously, she had been a big woman to begin with, but like Bryce, she had grown in the last day.

Tilting back her pale face, she sniffed the air and immediately caught Maddy's scent. New laughter broke from her red, red lips. She charged.

It seemed to Maddy that each new terror dwarfed the one before and this was no different. Her fear spiked to an overwhelming level, making the jump and likely fall seem not so bad. Maddy's body took over and suddenly she was sprinting for the edge of the roof. If asked, she wouldn't have been able to say which foot was her dominant one; her body knew.

Her right foot hit the lip in stride and she hurled herself through the air as behind her, the behemoth slid to a halt, sending rocks skittering down into the alley eighty feet below.

Maddy's arc was not high and her forward momentum seemed to seize up midway across the chasm. She started to fall, the earth sucking her downward. Then Bryce was at the edge on his hands and knees. In his right hand was one strap of his pack. He flung it outward and there, floating in front of her face was the other strap.

She clawed the air like a drowning man would claw at the water. Her left hand swished an inch from the strap and now she was falling for real. It felt like an invisible hand was yanking her down as she pinwheeled her other arm around, again like a swimmer.

The strap zipped into her palm and her hand closed around it. Although the rest of her was something of a loose bundle in a skin bag, her hand was a rock, fused around the strap. A fraction of a second later, it felt as if her arm was pulled from its socket, but that pain was nothing compared to smacking into the side of the building. Her eyes crossed and the air shot from her body, but by God her grip on the strap was like iron. She wasn't letting go for nothing.

Looking down between her dangling feet was the body strewn alley. It would've been a terrifying view had it not been for the behemoth. Maddy jerked around, afraid that the demon was already flying through the air at her.

Although the demon's laughter had been insane, she wasn't crazy enough to attempt the jump herself. Yes, she was strong, but she was also somewhere well north of three-hundred pounds.

Maddy was still staring in fright when she felt herself being hoisted into the air. Bryce was pulling her up, one-handed. She was impressed and at the same time her fear of falling abruptly doubled and she clung to the strap like a cat out at the end of a branch. The moment she was up, she found herself clinging with equal ferocity to Bryce.

"Man, that's all sorts of fucked up," Sid said. Across the way, the behemoth had thrown aside the zombie with the pink ribbon and was on her hands and knees feasting on the musketeer, looking very much like a pig at a trough. Sid went to suck from the flask. When it only dribbled whiskey into his mouth, he leaned over the edge and whipped it down at the milling zombies.

"The fire'll take her," Bryce said, meaning the behemoth. "I hope." Having a second demon on their trail would be too much. "We should go."

Maddy only just seemed to wake up to the fact that she was still holding Bryce. She stepped back. "Yeah, we should go, but how do we get down?" The building didn't have a door leading down into its belly like the others.

"Over here," Sid said and jogged to one end of the roof where a ladder ran down to a fire escape, which was old and rickety, shaking with every step. Sid had the unsettling habit of dropping down the last few feet of each ladder with a shimmying *chang!* Too late, Maddy asked him to knock it off, but the damage was done. The noise had attracted a pair of zombies.

Thankfully, they weren't the frightening demonic types or the weird bloodhound ones, like the one-armed Puerto Rican had been. They stared upwards, their mouths hanging open.

"Either of you's don't got a gun or nothing, right?" Sid asked.

"If we had guns don't you think we would've used them by now?" Maddy groused. They had come down three stories, and had passed six different apartments; each had been occupied. The last thing she wanted was a repeat of the last shit-show they had endured.

"Okay, yeah, whatever. Ain't no harm'n askin'. We's gonna need weapons right?"

Bryce looked down at the pair of zombies. One had been a maid in a swanky hotel and still had on part of her uniform. The other was an old man who had misplaced his dentures when he had turned. *They're stronger than they look*, Bryce had to remind himself. Whoever went down first would have them both waiting to attack with suicidal fury. And he would be that person. Sid was already easing to the side to let him and Maddy past.

Sid's foot thunked against a ceramic pot. From it came the somewhat unpleasant scent of marigolds.

"Let me have that will you?" Bryce asked, pointing at the pot. Sid grinned and hefted the pot. He didn't hand it to Bryce, but instead leaned over the rail and lined up the pot with the maid zombie.

"Bombs away," he said and released the pot. He whistled a long note until the pot crashed off the shoulder of the maid. Her arm hung limp, but otherwise she was unfazed. "Crap!" Sid went up a flight and grabbed another pot. "We used to do this to rats, 'cept we used bricks."

Maddy thought it an evil practice even when it came to rats. She said nothing about zombies. Sid whistled again as the pot fell. This time the pot scored a direct hit on the maid. Four pounds of dirt and clay dropped from forty-four feet was enough to drop the creature in her tracks.

"Shazam!" Sid hissed, clapping his hands.

"Quiet down!" Maddy snapped at him. "You want more of them to come? You only have two pots left."

Sid made a face, muttering, "Whatever," as he turned away. He was sure that only one pot would be needed and he was wrong. He missed both times and grandpa zombie was still there waiting to feed.

"It's just the one," Bryce said, mostly to himself. After facing the demon and leaping across the chasm, the old zombie didn't seem terribly frightening. "I can do this." He worked his way down the zigzagging ladders until he came to the final one. This was a dropdown ladder. He unhooked it and found the creature directly under the bottom rung. The ladder was solid iron and weighed ninety pounds. The drop wasn't far, but it didn't need to be.

He let it fall. The ladder rattled down straight at the beast and struck it on the bridge of the nose and drove it into the ground, pinning it there. It wasn't dead. Not that Bryce had expected it to be. The creatures were like cockroaches. He slid down the ladder as if he were a kid again, landing squarely on its throat and crushing the zombie's larynx.

For good measure, he raised his boot and slammed it down as hard as he could. Although it couldn't breathe, it still tried to get up. Bryce held it down.

"Let's go!" he whispered.

Now that the immediate danger was over, Maddy came down the ladder like a geriatric while Sid came down like a fireman on his day off. He stared down at the weakly struggling zombie. "I think, grandpa shit hisself."

Maddy ignored this. "Where are we? Which way's south?" Even in the dark, the street didn't look like a lot of the other streets they had passed. It was narrow and paved with cobblestone. There were no storefronts and almost no trash.

"This is Greene Street and south is right down here." Sid pointed the way but didn't start south himself, content with letting them lead. His fear was ungrounded. The moans and cries of the dead were all behind them. Up ahead, the street was empty, except for the cars, that is. There were always more cars and more dead bodies. Some were on the sidewalk; however most were in the street, or half dragged from their cars.

The trio didn't so much as walk down the street as much as they slunk. They were virtually defenseless. Bryce scanned each car they passed, hoping to find something he could use: a bat, more golf clubs, a shotgun.

Sid also looked into the cars. He seemed almost desperate as he mumbled to himself, "No. No. What's that? Soda? Fuck that."

"What are you looking for?" Maddy demanded of him. "Bryce looked in those cars already."

"Bryce?" Sid laughed. "That guy's name is Bryce? His parents hate him or something?"

Maddy remembered saying something very similar and she felt a stab of shame. "No more than yours did, *Sid*."

"Looks like you don't know jack sh...Oh, here we go." He pulled a bottle of *Fireball* from a car. It was unopened. He cracked the seal and drank right from the mouth. After a second, he made a face and coughed. "Ugh. I hate Fireball. Cinnamon whiskey, so stupid." He took another swig and made the same face. He then held the bottle out to Maddy.

She had never been much of a drinker and she hesitated, making him laugh. "Look, we gotta face this shit, but there's no saying we gotta do it sober. Besides, it's Thanksgiving. It's a fucking holiday and this shit kinda tastes like someone mixed gasoline and Christmas in a bottle."

Maddy wanted to argue with him. It was simply her combative way; however in this case she couldn't think of any real reason why she shouldn't be at least a little bit tipsy. After wiping off the lip and then laughing at herself for worrying about germs while surrounded by a city filled with living corpses, she knocked back the bottle.

Chapter 32

Bryce turned when Maddy began spluttering and coughing as if she had just sucked down poison.

"Went... down...wrong pipe." She had gone a brilliant red, all save her eyes, which were like glittering sapphires.

For just a flash, Bryce was struck by her. She was...pretty. Somewhere along the way she had lost another ten pounds and where once her face was round as a pie, she had cheekbones again and her chin—singular, she only had one now—was pointed with the tiniest cleft.

He found himself staring as she thrust the bottle at him. It smelled sickeningly sweet. Bryce shrugged and took a swig, making sure to modulate the amount so he didn't end up like Maddy. The whiskey wasn't bad. It also wasn't good and he had no problem giving the bottle back to Sid when he held a hand out for it.

"Get drunk if you want," Bryce told him, "but if you can't go on, we'll leave you. And if you can't fight, you'll die. We have a long way to go still." He turned on his heel and marched on.

Sid caught up and watched Bryce walk for half a block before asking, "You got somewhere to be? Trust me, Jack, your appointment's been canceled. Your flight's been delayed and the road is fuckin' closed. All of 'em. You see the fuckin' news? The whole world's been bent over and is gettin' a poundin' right up the ass."

"Yeah," Bryce agreed.

"Yeah? That's all you got to say? Don'tcha fuckin' get it? This is the end of times. God has spoken. He's given up on us and is burning this bitch down. The only question is how you wanna go out?" He grabbed Bryce and spun him around. "You saw how them other guys died. Screamin', pissin' their pants. Is that how you wanna die?"

Bryce licked his lips. It was a question he didn't want to think about. He had seen a lot of death over the last few days; none of it good, none of it right. "I don't want to die. It's why we have to keep going. If we stop..." His mind flashed to the demon. The last they'd seen of it, it was pulling a woman into an apartment. What were the chances it had gorged itself into a stupor? When it came to the demon, it was best not to count on anything. He had to assume it was on their trail. "If we stop, we die."

"We's gonna die any how," Sid said, swigging from the bottle. "Them zombie freaks are everywhere. Chi-town. L. A. Boston. They even got 'em at Washington. At least they'll be safe from the nukes." He glanced up as if expecting to see in-bound rockets streaking across the sky. There was only smoke. Maddy glanced up as well, remembering her dream and feeling the fear of it creep over her.

Sid went on, not noticing how Maddy's pink cheeks had gone the color of milk, "I was gonna go live it up in one them fancy Park Ave hotels, but up town seems out of the question. It seemed like there's a shit-ton of them up there. So, I don't know. I think I might go to one them down by the river. The Hudson, not the East River. There's some big ones. Big and fancy is how I want to go out."

He sighed and took another sip.

"We're going to the Federal Plaza," Maddy told him. "The FBI has a field office. We think they might get us away to somewhere safe. Who knows, they might take you too."

"I wouldn't get his hopes up," Bryce said. "Without Griff, they may not even take us." She had forgotten about that. Her mouth closed with a little click of her teeth. "Our best hope is if Plinkett made it through."

Neither of them held out much hope of that. More than likely he was dead, but if he had made it through the city on foot in the middle of all the chaos, why hadn't he returned with help? Had he been denied? Maybe the FBI didn't think they were worth it. Or they were already gone. Maybe they felt New York was lost.

Bryce hadn't had a dream about nukes but didn't need one for him to fear that eventuality. It soured him. Jutting his chin at Sid, he said, "They're not going to take him. Why would they?"

Sid sneered, his hackles rising. Maddy put a hand on his arm, answering, "Because he's been in close proximity to us. We don't know how the pathogen is transferred. I'm beginning to wonder if it even can be transferred from person to person. Don't give me that look. It could be something in the water supply for all we know."

This brought a laugh from Sid. He was feeling the warmth of a good buzz again. "I'll drink to that." Nervously, they watched him take a mouthful and wipe his lips with the back of his coat.

Bryce feared they had found an anchor in the form of Sid, and that sooner or later, he was going to drag them down. Maddy kept giving him the side eye which Bryce took to mean she was thinking the same thing. That was good, at least. She wasn't deluding herself as she did all through college, taking on one lost cause after another.

He led them south through what felt like a ghost town. The buildings were mute and dark, like great windowed tombstones, and other than the endless cars and the mutilated corpses, the streets were empty.

The darkness echoed with forlorn screams and the occasional gunshot. Each of these reminded Bryce just how defenseless they were. He came across a brick and carried that. Maddy found a stout little cane next to the body of an old man. Sid had his bottle, which he held by the neck and brandished at a collie-mix that growled at them. These were all terrible weapons and Bryce knew they should stop and search one of the buildings for something better, and yet they were on a streak—they hadn't run across one of the demons since they leapt across that chasm.

They had to duck and hide from gangs of zombies. These forced them on detour after detour. And there were plenty of lone zombies as well; these fell into two categories: those that had a destination in their wormy minds and tromped towards it without looking left or right, and those that had gotten to their destination and stood there, staring blankly at a wall or a door, or maybe a crack in the sidewalk. As long as the three of them were quiet and kept cars between them and the zombies, they were easily avoided.

Despite all the back and forth, Sid, sauced as he was, managed to keep them heading slowly south.

After an hour, they came on a higher-end fashion store. It stretched for half the block and took up two floors. Bryce knew he had a dreadful split in his pants and his boots felt like they were shrinking around his feet. He needed new clothes, but he needed to get to safety more. He planned on marching right past it.

Maddy had the same idea. She barely gave the Thanksgiving Day specials a glance. Orange and brown weren't really her colors anyway. Then she caught sight of a display positioned just in front of a second-floor window. The manikins were dressed in winter flair: blue, silver, and white. Two stood with ski-poles in their plastic hands. Another leaned jauntily on a kid's sled.

The last one had an arm raised and despite its perfectly drawn smile, it looked strangely aggressive, almost like it was about to attack the other manikins with the tool it had poised over its head.

It was an ice axe.

She stopped in her tracks and Sid knocked blearily into her. Half his bottle was gone and he couldn't seem to keep his eyes fully opened or his mouth completely closed.

Maddy barely noticed. Her mind went to her dream—*They moved slowly in a crouch, their eyes always out. It was mid-morning and yet the sky was dark. The air was filled with dust and ash. Bombs had been raining from one end of New Jersey to the other for the better part of the night. Even miles away, they could feel the explosions coursing up through the ground.*

Maddy carried her climbing axe in her right hand and the garbage can lid in the other. The lid was dented and stained. It was an ugly shield, but it was still a shield.

"We have to hurry," she hissed. Time was squeezing in on them. She could feel it in her bones. Death was coming. Death from above. She cast a fearful look up and just then the sky was lit in an unholy radiance. The air screamed in agony and the earth melted under the…

She was shaken by a sudden and violent tremor. It started in her shoulders before it coursed down her entire body. The ice axe looked like the very same one from her dream.

"Climbing axe," she whispered. That's how she had thought of it in her dream. She had never seen one in real life, only in documentaries. And she had never seen one with a blue handle and a shining aluminum head, like the one in her dream *and* like the one the manikin held.

"We need to go in there." She pointed.

Bryce saw the climbing axe right away; two feet long, slightly curved with a narrow pick-like head. It was better than carrying a brick, though he didn't think it would be the best weapon against something as horrible as the demon.

"No. We keep going. The FBI will have weapons for us." Maybe. If anyone was even still there.

"I dreamt of that axe," Maddy said. "That axe. Not an axe like it, but that axe right there."

Bryce did not believe in ESP or precognition or any of what his father called "happy horse-shit." His first impulse was to discard the idea completely out of hand until he realized that up until the day before he hadn't believed in zombies either. Still, a dream prophecy about an ordinary axe seemed both farfetched and sort of useless. If she had dreamed about a machine gun, that would've been handy.

"Let's say that's true; you dreamed about an ice axe…"

"That axe."

"Sure. That axe. In the dream, was it magical? Did it play some important role in our lives? Or did you just have it?" When her eyes darted away, he knew. "So you just had it, or one like it. It doesn't do anything for us right here, right now." He pointed down the street. It was empty for blocks. "Look at that. We got a free shot downtown. After everything we've been through. After all the obstacles we've had to…"

"I'm going to get the axe," she said, speaking over him. "It's important. I know it. You guys can stay here if you want."

Bryce grabbed her as she turned. "If you get the axe, it becomes a self-fulling prophecy, making it meaningless. If I dream of purple socks and I go out and buy purple socks does that make me a prophet? Does it make the socks important? No. This is a coincidence."

She paused. A part of her knew he was right. Another part of her knew there was more to the axe than it being just an axe.

"I'm getting it."

Bryce groaned and rolled his eyes. When Sid handed him the bottle, he took a healthy swig. They followed her to the front doors, which were protected by the usual roll down metal gate. She gave the window a glance.

"It's pretty lucky you have that brick," she noted, putting her hand out for it.

Bryce pulled it back. "Are you kidding me? You know how much noise you'll make? If there's no way in, then that's that."

"There's gotta be one them side entrances," Sid said in that odd way of his. "Or an alley entrance."

Maddy beamed at him. She marched down the block and found an odd little door that didn't seem to belong to either the clothing store or the copy place next to it. She tried it and found it unlocked. It opened on a dark alley. Sid, who couldn't see more than five feet into the shadows balked. Maddy and Bryce gave him a queer look.

207

For them the shadows were not so deep. They noted the half-filled dumpsters, the accumulated years of gunk along the edges of the bricks, the partially frozen puddles that smelled of fermenting piss. The only thing that moved in the darkness was a frightened house cat. After years of demanding to get out of its apartment, it had been released into the wilds of the city by a frightened couple who knew they'd never get out of the city hauling a cat-carrier around.

The cat slunk beneath one of the dumpsters and shook in abject fear.

Maddy felt a moment of sympathy for the creature, but knew that with all the death surrounding them, that it was misplaced. Just a few steps down from the cat was a side door just as Sid said there'd be, and it was held canted open by a broom.

"What are the chances?" Maddy asked, an eyebrow cocked.

After his experiences over the last few days, Bryce guessed the chances of finding an open door like this in an otherwise locked building were probably one in two-hundred. They were steep, but not astronomical. "What are the chances the streets will be empty when we get going again?"

She said nothing to this, knowing that even if it was fifty-fifty, the side trip for the axe wouldn't be worth it.

"We'll be out in no time." She pushed aside the door and found herself in a dim corridor. She smelled cardboard, leather, and a partially eaten tuna sandwich that was going from bad to worse in a garbage can four doors down. They were in the "Employees Only" section.

Behind them was a stunted and fantastically crowded warehouse. Ahead were bathrooms, human resources and the office with the tuna sandwich. She hurried past all this to swinging double doors which led out onto the floor. Her eyes swept past the clothes until she saw the escalators.

"I'll be right back."

"You have one minute," Bryce said. He was already kicking off the toe-crushing boots he'd been wearing. Just to their left was a shoe section and he figured he'd be able to find replacements for the boots in seconds, especially since style meant little to him at the moment. "Sid, can you find me a pair of pants?"

Not far away was a table with neatly arranged hundred-dollar joggers. He pointed distractedly in its direction as he put his foot down onto the metal device used to measure shoe sizes. For most of his life, he had been a size seven and took great pains to keep that fact to himself. Just then, the device measured him at a ten.

"Whoa," he whispered.

Sid was not so quiet. First, he dropped his bottle and cursed flamboyantly about the inequities of life. Then he asked in a slurry voice, "What you wear? A medium or sometin?"

"Better make it a large and in something dark."

Maddy heard all of this as she mounted the escalator stairs with her mismatched boots. She would need to change them out sooner rather than later. The singular Ugg had gone from warm and comfy to tight and damp. Her feet were sweating as much as the rest of her.

"Let's hope that stops soon." She reached to her side where she could normally grab handfuls of flesh. Now she had an inch or so, and it was mostly skin. "Don't complain. It could be worse." Her mind blinked to the woman who hadn't been able to kill herself with the musket. That was a hundred times worse. She was just thinking that things could always be worse when she reached the front window and the winter display.

It was the climbing axe from the dream. *Her* axe.

She slid it out of the manikin's formed fingers and as she did, she saw movement down below her on the street. Like grey water, zombies were flooding the street, pouring around the stranded cars.

"No," she hissed and ducked away out of sight. They had to get out the back before it was too late.

It's already too late, a voice whispered in her mind.

And it was.

Chapter 33

The voice whispering its insanity was certain, but Maddy wouldn't believe that it was too late until she saw it with her own two eyes. Precognition was junk science; she knew that. Even after the axe and her dream she knew it.

It was a fact.

And yet she ran full out as fast as she could for the far end of the store to a window that faced the next east-west street. She pushed through manikins that were dressed for a high-powered corporate meeting. At first, the street seemed deserted. Then she saw slinking shadows and there was Bryce's dark demon. Even from fifty yards, it struck a chill into her heart.

It was moving among the cars, shoving smaller zombies down, hiding them. Maddy's mouth fell open as she realized they had been about to walk into a trap. She found herself staring at the axe. It had been important...or it still was. She didn't know.

The voice again: *It's too late.*

Maybe it wasn't. The axe and the dream had saved them from the ambush. They just had to get out of there before the trap closed all the way. "The alley," she whispered to herself. It was the only way in and maybe their only way out as well. She spun on the spot and sped for the escalators. "Bryce! It's them." She took the odd metal stairs three at a time, the axe in her hand all but forgotten.

Bryce didn't have to ask who they were. He was tying a pair of red and gold sneakers that looked like clown shoes in his mind, but fit him nonetheless. His hands worked in a blur.

"Hurry!" Maddy was about out of her mind with fear. She inched towards the double door and the moment he stood, she and Sid ran for them. Bryce quickly caught up.

"Did you close the door behind us?" he asked Sid.

Sid hesitated, making anything he answered suspect. What came out of him was a cinnamon smelling string of syllables that were essentially meaningless. They found out soon enough that he had been sober enough to do the right thing; the door to the alley was shut. He grinned. "What'd I tell ya?"

He went for the door. Bryce was a second too slow, recognizing the coming danger. Maddy felt it, but was behind him and too far from Sid.

"No," was all she had time to say before Sid bashed open the door with his shoulder in his eagerness to flee. Unlike Maddy and, to a lesser extent, Bryce he could not smell the zombies on the other side of the metal door.

Luckily for Sid, the zombies were just as surprised as he was. A small crowd of the grey-skinned creatures turned dull eyes towards him. They and Sid stared at each other for a full second, which was enough time for Bryce to haul Sid back inside. Bryce went to yank the door shut, but by then grey hands had a hold of the edge. There was a short tussle, pull against pull. It was a tug of war that Bryce had no chance of winning… unless he changed the dynamics.

Without warning, he reversed himself and threw his weight against the door, which went flying open. The dead fell back in a convoluted pile as if they were pins in a bowling alley and for a moment they stared up at the clouds of smoke with dull confused eyes. Too late, one tried to grab the door again. It lost three fingers when Bryce slammed it shut.

He turned to glare at Maddy.

"Don't start," she snapped. "Your demon is out there and the only reason the road was clear before was because it was setting a trap."

This killed his anger. If what she said was true—and he knew that it was— the implications were…too much for him at the moment. He couldn't deal with precognition on top of everything else. He could deal with cold facts. "Does it know we're in here?"

"It shouldn't, but yeah, I think so." There was no "think" about it. She knew that it knew—both were impossibilities in the face of science.

Bryce felt that his hold on what was real and what wasn't, was slipping. Except, that is, for the certainty of a terrible death that seemed to hang in the air around them. That was a reality that he didn't want to face anytime soon if he could help it. "There's got to be another backdoor. The warehouse!"

He sped past Maddy, heading to the left to where the smell of cardboard wafted down the hall. The double doors here were similar to the ones that entered onto the floor, except they were painted and they had two small windows set at head height. Bryce glanced inside and saw a narrow, two story warehouse. It was so cramped that the shelves seemed to lean outward under their burdens.

There were no zombies in sight and nor did he smell any. Still, he was careful when he stepped through the doors. A dozen metal push-brooms and three wooden mops hung on a board next to the door. Bryce chose one of the mops and snapped off its head with his foot. Now it had something of a point. It was not exactly fearsome, and yet it was better than the brick he had left back in among the shoes.

At the far end of the warehouse were a pair of rolling metal doors. Both Maddy and Bryce went to each and sniffed as Sid watched, his thick lips twisted by confusion. They looked like dogs working over a hydrant. It was off-putting and he took another swig.

The sharp cinnamon smell was distracting to Bryce. It almost overpowered the smell of gasoline and sewage coming from the other side of the door. Maddy closed her eyes and let the different scents gently breeze through her. Yes, there was gasoline dripping from a nearby truck and a sewage line was backed up, but there was also a whiff of someone frying with sesame oil and someone else had their nasty bong sitting outside their window. She also smelled zombies, but they weren't close.

She nodded to Bryce and he went to the chains that raised and lowered the doors. They would be loud going up, but there was no other way to leave the building that wasn't being guarded by zombies. He took a chain in hand and gently pulled down. The chain rattled through the pulley and there was a dreadful squeak that had probably gone unnoticed for years. In the dead quiet, it was almost a scream.

Bryce could only stand it for two seconds. By then there was a foot-high gap. Good enough to slip under. They dropped down and scrambled beneath the door and found themselves in a two-lane street that, in the emergency, had been turned into four lanes; there was barely room to walk.

There wasn't a zombie in sight. Neither Bryce or Maddy trusted their eyes, however. They sniffed out the zombies—none were very close. But there was something on the air that made them both edgy.

"What is that?" Bryce asked. There was a tiny mechanical sound coming from somewhere nearby, but with the brick walls rising so close on either side, they couldn't pinpoint the direction. It made no difference. They were heading south, sound or no sound.

Bryce led the way, his spear held out in front as he slipped between the cars. They slinked low to keep themselves hidden as much as possible and then inched south. With every step the stench of zombies grew. Soon even Sid could smell them and hear their moaning. He tugged on Bryce's hoody and jerked his head, hoping they'd take a side street. To him, west was just as good as any other direction, if it didn't have zombies.

He was ignored and they kept going, slowly, car by car. It was excruciating for Sid. His legs ached and his head had begun to pound, which was no wonder since he'd been more or less drunk for the last day and a half.

Then they were through the trap.

With every step, the ugly fecal smell grew less and the moans became softer. Sid grew weak with relief. After a block and a half, he decided a little self-medication was in order and he unscrewed the top of the Fireball.

"Close fucking call," he said as way of a toast, and tilted the bottle back. He then offered some to the others.

Bryce grunted a, "No," and shook his head. Maddy shook her head, feeling her stomach roll slightly. The smell was pungent and it got worse as he looked up and let out a cinnamon burp that went on and on. Maddy had to turn away, waving a hand in front of her face.

Sid snorted laughter and even Bryce grinned, but the light moment lasted for all of a second, then they heard something snuffling behind them.

Goosebumps flared across Maddy's arms as she caught an ugly but familiar scent. It was the one-armed Puerto-Rican. He was seventy feet back at an intersection, his nose in the air, tracking them by smell alone. It was fifty-fifty that he had them dead on; they'd know depending on if it turned or kept coming.

It kept coming, slowly, not yet certain. When it had them zeroed in, it would let out a scream and then it would be another race for their lives.

"We have to kill that thing," Bryce whispered. Maddy nodded at this, while Sid only chewed on the ragged nail of one thumb. "You two keep going and leave the whiskey bottle open. If it's following that scent, I might be able to kill it before it can alert the others." He touched the edge of his broom-spear. It was jagged and pointy enough to kill a person; there was no telling how effective it would be against a zombie.

"Might?" Sid asked, turning up a lip at the spear. "I don't like no might. You should use the axe thingy. That'll do the trick for sure."

Maddy's hand gripped the handle tighter, though only for a brief moment. With a guilty grin, she held it out to him. "No thanks," he said, pushing it away. As much as he wanted the climbing axe, it was her weapon. She had dreamed it. That made it personal in a way that he felt, but couldn't fully understand.

"Go," he told them.

They squat-walked away, their shoes scraping loudly in his ears. He was suddenly hypersensitive; he could hear their breathing plain as day, and the smell of the whiskey was foul and heady. As their impressions on the world faded, he caught the first expressions of the zombie. Its snuffling was the most obvious. Its smell hit him next. Yes, it had the shit-stink of a zombie, but it also had a subtle ammonia scent, like its clothes or shoes had been regularly in contact with a cleaning agent.

Bryce, his heart rate picking up, ducked down at the front of a car and watched the zombie's stumbling feet come closer. It would pass within two feet of him and if it had its nose in the air, he planned on driving the tip of the spear up into the soft flesh of its neck and into its brain. One quick, hard jab should do the…

The creature stopped suddenly and now its snuffling became a soft sniffing. It had discovered a new scent, one that was closer. Bryce could almost…no, he could definitely feel the Puerto Rican's eyes shift toward the front of the car.

"Shit," Bryce muttered and stood. Twenty feet away, the zombie grinned, showing bloody teeth. "Yeah, keep smiling and see what you…" In mid-sentence, Bryce leapt over the edge of the car and charged, catching the creature by surprise. Still, twenty feet was a lot of distance to cover when all it had to do was let out a howl.

It was unafraid of both Bryce and his spear. A scream ripped from its black hole of a mouth as it sprung forward. It was a cagey creature and seemed to know the spear's strength and its own weakness. It came at Bryce hunched, protecting its throat and holding its one hand out to catch the spear's point.

Bryce had to pull the tip of the spear back as the creature seemed to be inviting him to stab it in the hand, chest or shoulders, places that would do little harm to it. He had only one shot at ending the scream and killing it quickly, so he edged the tip of the spear to the side and, as the zombie followed it with his dark eyes and one hand, it left itself *slightly* open to a second attack. His sneakered foot flashed up in a hard front kick that Bryce hoped would crush the thing's larynx. Precision and timing were absolute keys to landing such a strike on a moving target.

He missed by the smallest margin. Still, his foot crashed upward under the thing's chin and hammered its head back. It was a heavy blow that staggered the zombie and cut the scream off.

Now, Bryce tried to tear out its throat with the spear but again his lack of training showed. He was just a touch slow and the tip tore into the grey flesh an inch off target. Worse, the beast grabbed the spear before Bryce could pull it back. Its grip was shocking in its strength and it was all Bryce could do to get the spear back.

By the time he did, he saw the demon leading a horde of zombies down the street. It was leaping from car to car, completely healed, and moving fast.

Bryce turned and sprinted away. In no time, he came to an intersection. Fifty yards ahead of him, Maddy and Sid were running down the line of cars. Amazingly, Maddy was in the lead by ten feet. Sid was reeling and stumbling. He was drunk and had no chance; he would die quickly if Bryce fought the demon and lost…no. That was wrong. The demon wouldn't kill Sid out of hand. It would come up behind and blind him or give him a quick blow to the back of the head. Maiming him would be that much more fun. That way his screams would echo throughout the city.

Then the demon would go on to Maddy who'd be breathless and reeling and in no position to fight. The axe she had bet their future on would be useless.

They would die if Bryce didn't do something. He turned and looked back at the demon and then amazed himself by flipping it off before running west on a side street. His plan was simple: he would draw the demon away and, if it was possible, try to escape. Bryce was fifty yards down the street before he realized that the demon and its horde wasn't following him. It was going after Maddy and Sid.

They didn't stand a chance.

"No, no, no," he whispered as he jogged back a few steps. He wanted to go back for them, but it was too late. There were dozens of mindless beasts between them.

Chapter 34

Bryce turned away, his mind spinning quickly. It spun and spun, uselessly. He was alone, cut off from anyone he could call a friend and he only had the vaguest of notions where the Federal Building was: south.

The truth was that for first time in his life he needed people. And they needed him.

With no plan whatsoever, Bryce found himself sprinting. He ran back the way he came, dodging the zombies. When he got to the street they'd been on, he tore south, sprinting on a parallel course with the zombies. It didn't matter that some of them saw him in the dark; he was already past them when they did, his new longer legs stretching out going faster and faster. They were a blur.

A hundred yards went by in ten and a half seconds. He came racing up and found the head of the mob attacking a dry cleaner. The shadows and the night made it seem as though there were countless numbers of them, howling and swinging fists, trying their best to break down a metal gate that had been pulled down over the front.

Maddy and Sid were nowhere in sight and since they weren't screaming under a pile of the undead, he could only guess that they had gotten away!

It was Bryce's turn to disappear, a trick that was growing more difficult by the second as the dead realized that he was not one of them. He spun his spear as the first of the dead came rushing up. The whirling hunk of wood distracted it long enough for Bryce to pick his target: the thing's right eye.

The spinning stopped with a slap as the wood came to rest in his palm, and in one quick lunge, he drove the point four inches deep. Blood poured down the shaft as the monster's body jerked. Bryce had learned his lesson and snapped the spear back out again in a blink before grey fingers could grab it. This time there was no need. The zombie was already dead and Bryce was gone within the same second, racing down the remainder of the block to the next cross street.

He went west, loping easily, feeling strangely young for the first time in many years. He *was* young. Twenty-eight was plenty young, and yet he had always felt he had gotten old before his time. It was too many days spent in a classroom and not enough time spent out doors. It was too many hours in front of a computer. Too much of his life had been wasted, trapped in his own mind.

Now he was suddenly filled with energy and life. He was also hungry. But a sandwich would have to wait. The living dead were after him. Glancing back he saw that the moaning crowd numbered no more than fifteen, which suddenly seemed like a small number.

"Don't be stupid," he muttered to himself. Fifteen was way too many for him to handle. He also knew that fifteen could turn into fifty in a blink. "And Maddy still needs me." Sid, too. The thought of Sid with his bottle was aggravating, and he decided on the spot that he would smash it when he tracked them down. "Which I better get doing."

He was far enough away from the pursuing zombies that they were mere shadows, so he ducked down behind the cars, crossed to the other side of the street and crept back the way he had come.

At the corner, he saw that there were zombies everywhere up and down the street.

In the light of a neon sign, he could see that the gate protecting the dry cleaners had been torn down, but with no humans in sight, the mob was slowly dispersing, following whims or stray scents. Bryce was just thinking that the only way to get through the loose crowd was to sprint through it. However, just as he was about to take off, something came whirring down at him from above.

It sounded like a flying fan, and in a sense, it was. He found himself staring at a four-propeller drone. With its camera lens shining like a black eye, it had an alien feel to it.

"Wilkes?" he asked it in an excited whisper, his heart bounding. Just then, it didn't matter that Wilkes had been hired to drag him back to Magnus' plaza, kicking and screaming if necessary. If Wilkes was alive then maybe Griff was as well, which made the chance of being sheltered by the FBI that much greater.

The drone bobbed up and down. Was that a yes? "Can you hear me" It bobbed again. "Listen, I'm good. You need to find Maddy." It bobbed again. He pointed towards the street they had been on before the Puerto Rican had found them. "She was right down there. She and another man went through a…"

It buzzed a little further away, rising and dipping, wanting him to follow it west. "No. I'm okay. You need to find Maddy." In answer, it jerked a few feet further away. "We don't have time for this. Go." He pointed with his spear, but the thing's movements only became more frenzied. "No. You need to find Mad…" He stopped in midsentence as the volume of zombie moans began to grow.

He turned and saw that the mob had spotted either him or the drone and was heading in his direction, fast. The same was true of the zombies he had fooled into running up the block. They were coming back on the double. So much for saving Maddy. With the creatures coming from both directions, he was going to have trouble just saving himself.

The drone buzzed to a fire escape that had been drilled into the front of the building he had stopped across from. The fire escape was black and ugly, and why it was in front, he didn't know; it was just one of those things that were routine in New York City.

The drone flew up to the metal retractable ladder clearly trying to tell him he should jump for the lower rung. That had been obvious from the start. A brand new jaguar, bottle green and sleek, was parked halfway onto the sidewalk, and with his new found athleticism it was nothing for Bryce to leap from the hood of the car to the ladder. Unfortunately the ladder hadn't been hooked properly and it came rattling down with Bryce hanging on like a frightened cat.

With a crash, both the ladder and Bryce landed square on the hood of the car, denting it.

Bryce was stunned by the impact and rolled right off just as one of the zombies came charging up. It went directly for him which meant crawling across the car. It slid off the hood just as Bryce had, plowing face first into the curb. It sat up, leaving most of its front teeth behind.

By then Bryce was on his feet and jabbing with his spear. The tip tore through an eye of another beast. It was slow to realize it was dead and stood for a few seconds, giving Bryce time to sling it from the shaft and towards the closer of the onrushing zombies. That was all the time he had for fighting. Dozens of zombies were closing from all sides—all except skyward. Up the ladder he went, nearly losing his spear at the first platform as the zombies raged around the base; in that short span, the car had been buried beneath a swarm of grey bodies.

Some of the creatures mindlessly attacked the ladder, while others attempted to follow him up. Those that fell became the base of an ugly, squirming pile that mounted steadily higher. It was half as tall as the ladder by the time Bryce reached the second floor of the building.

From there the stairs zigzagged their way upwards and when the zombies reached these, they would come on even faster. Bryce wasn't worried for himself. He knew he was already out of danger from them, but what of the people in the buildings? Had he just doomed another hundred people to a horrible death?

He squatted outside a shaded window and could smell a woman on the other side of the thin glass. She gave off alluring scents that told him she was young, dressed in leather, had recently painted her nails and liked vanilla scented candles. She was afraid, but not panicked.

The zombies would smell her as well and, when they couldn't get to Bryce, they would go for her, and a single pane of glass was not going to stop them.

"Hey!" He tapped the glass. She went still. "I know you're in there. You're in danger. There's a mob of them right below me and if I don't get out of sight soon they'll keep coming."

"Then leave."

"It's too late for that. They're going to get up here." She still didn't move and so he tried a modified version of the truth. "I'm with the government. The FBI."

The curtain was suddenly swished aside and there was a girl. For a moment, she was only a shadow. She was black and dressed in black, standing in a darkened apartment. Then Bryce's night eyes kicked in and her outline formed itself into a person: leggy, narrow-waisted, black hair coiled in a single braid. She had a broad face with frightened doe-eyes and full lips that were pressed into lines. She had youthful good looks that were a year or two from maturing from pretty and into beautiful.

She unlocked the window and stood back. Her name was Nichola Lines and she regretted opening the window almost immediately. In his grey joggers, his red and gold tennis shoes and his ill-fitting hoodie, Bryce looked nothing like an FBI agent. The broom-spear didn't help either. At least she had a baseball bat, which seemed a much more appropriate weapon.

Nichola hefted the bat as he clambered through the window. "No need for that," he said as he eased over the back of her couch.

Bryce found himself standing in the middle of her apartment and feeling strangely huge. Excluding Nichola, everything around him seemed so small. The walls were close. The ceiling low. The kitchen looked like it had been built with midgets in mind, while the bed was a massive thing that took up a third of the room. But what was it doing in the living room? Slowly, it dawned on him that the twenty by twenty foot room was the entire apartment. All of the girl's possessions fit in this one tiny space and for some reason this struck him as weird.

"I'm Bryce," he told her, his eyes still flicking around. A stack of textbooks with a plant sitting on top of it told him she had recently been a student. Her coffee maker was new and large, while the TV was small and old; combine those with the double lamps around her bed told him she was a reader and a dreamer.

A packing crate sized suitcase sitting by the door suggested she read romance and never anything to do with the apocalypse. He was sure that inside would be more clothing than she needed, some canned food, and the things she felt were treasures. She would have to leave it all behind.

"I'm Nichola," she said, without lowering the bat. She did not like how his eyes were flicking around her dark apartment. Was he going to rob her? He certainly wouldn't rape her. Not with zombies piling up outside her… "What the hell is that?" she asked, pointing at the drone, which was bopping up and down a few feet from the fire escape. It was trying to get a clear shot of the inside of her apartment with its camera.

"It's a drone." He turned around and whispered to the machine, "We're going out the other side of the building. See if the coast is clear." The drone bobbed again and disappeared.

"A drone? And you can talk to it? Have it call the police. Or some of you guys and…hold on. You want to go out the other side of the building? No way. It's just like what's out there. It's all the same. What we need is for your guys to come here and get us."

He grimaced. "It's not that easy. Nothing ever is." A glance out the window showed him that the dead were still piling up in a great mound. It was insane. But they still had a minute or two. He turned and went to her suitcase. "You can only take a backpack. Grab some food, a lighter, some water. The rest stays. We have to travel light."

She darted in front of her suitcase, cutting him off. "We? I don't even know you. I'm not going anywhere."

"Then you'll die. They can smell you. Hiding won't help and neither will your bat. Not for long." The moans were drawing closer. One of the creatures was gibbering like a monkey. The sound made his skin crawl. "You don't have to come with me, but you can't stay here."

Nichola was having trouble processing all of this. The idea that they could smell her had caused her mind to short circuit. Her dark eyes flicked to the window and out at the night. "I think you need to go. Out the way you came. Go on."

"It won't matter if I leave," he insisted. "They're going to get in here one way or another."

"But…"

He shook his head. "If you stay you die, it's as simple as that! So make a damned choice."

"Where are you going? Somewhere safe?"

"I hope so. We're heading to the Federal Plaza, downtown. Hey, do you know where it is? All I know is that it's south."

She knew; she walked past it every day to get to work. The question for her was why he didn't know. "Yeah, sure. I know where it is. You really FBI?"

The lie had made him feel strangely *wrong*. "No, but we have one with us and we're hoping to either find a safe place with them or a way out of the city. Like I said, you don't have to come with me, but you can't stay here. It's the truth; they will get in."

Nichola was struck hard by indecision. Over the last few days, she had constructed a lie. It was iron-clad and simple: her apartment was her safe zone. She told herself that she couldn't be hurt as long as she kept her door locked and stayed inside. But that had never been true. And yet how could she go outside? The screams…there were so many screams out there.

Half a minute went by without her saying a word. Finally, the drone came back. Bryce went to the window where the sickening pile of zombies was growing. One was hanging on the ladder and had a grey arm hooked over the bars. It stretched its other hand up at Bryce.

"Up for yes," Bryce said to the drone. "Is it clear on the other side?" It went up and then jiggled slightly. "It's somewhat

221

clear?" This time it went up a couple of feet. "Alright. We'll be right out."

It jiggled again.

"I'm bringing a woman with me." It jiggled some more which he ignored. So what if they didn't want him to bring her along. He had endangered her life. It didn't matter that he had done so simply by climbing the ladder.

Bryce and Nichola looked at each other in the dark, her tiny apartment the only thing between them. A week before there would have been a true gulf between them, one that might never be bridged. They were two very different people, but with the dead outside, history, culture, and ingrained mental attitudes were suddenly replaced by nothing more than ten feet of carpet.

"Are you coming?" he asked.

She answered, "Yeah."

She looked down at her suitcase. That morning she had packed it until it was bursting at the seams, then repacked twice more, careful to place in it only those things that really mattered. It weighed sixty pounds and just then, it seemed like sixty pounds of nothing.

Hanging in her closet was a backpack she hadn't used since school. She darted for it and was back scrambling in the suitcase in seconds. Taking his advice to heart, she took only some canned goods and a couple of water bottles. At the last second, when Bryce's was at the door listening, she threw in some clean underwear.

"Ready," she said, throwing the pack across her back. "Can we tell some of the others?"

"Others?"

"Some of the people I know in the building. Mrs. Fran across the hall. She's a little old but she doesn't know anyone other than…"

He shook his head. Mrs. Fran would have to make it on her own. "Sorry. We'll be lucky to make it ourselves."

She hesitated at this, but when he went into the hall, she followed, directing him to, "Take the stairs down the hall and on our right. They open onto a lobby." Although the hall and the stairs were dark, the lobby still had its lights on. It felt like they were suddenly thrust on stage.

Nichola tried to back into the staircase, but Bryce grabbed her hand. There weren't that many zombies out on the street and only a few had seen them. "We'll be fast. Aim for the head, just don't overcommit."

"What's that mean?"

But he was already out the doors. Instead of running from the dead, he held his spear out at the closest of them. With the shreds of its flesh hanging around it like an old kimono, it was a ghastly thing and Nichola wanted to run screaming from it. It was insanity itself.

Her hand was on the door to the lobby when Bryce's closed on her wrist. "If we go back, we doom everyone in the building, including your Mrs. Fran. We can fight through. Trust me."

It was an odd thing for Bryce to say. For good reason, he had never asked anyone to put their trust in him. That was the old Bryce. That man had been small and weak.

"Okay," Nichola whispered. "Just don't let me die. You owe me that."

She might as well as asked for the moon. Bryce nodded, regardless.

Chapter 35

The ragged creature smelled of blood and reeked of shit. Its lower intestines had been torn open and the contents were still dripping out.

Nichola gagged and backed away.

Bryce saw it as disgusting but weak. It was missing a great deal of flesh and muscle. It was still dangerous, but only if it was part of a mob. His spear flashed up and out; the jagged point going straight into the thing's gaping mouth and through the roof. The wood pierced its brain and it dropped on the spot. Bryce was already onto the next one; this one was large and strong.

Strong, but slow and stupid. After facing the demon, squaring off against a single zombie didn't frighten him as it had...in fact, it didn't frighten him at all. That struck him as strange and oddly satisfying. *I'm no longer a complete coward*, he thought as he darted to his left around a fire hydrant. The creature banged its knee right off it without blinking, something that would've had the average person rolling on the ground with tears in their eyes.

Hitting the hydrant did cause it to lose its balance slightly. Its right hand came down and in a flash, Bryce took advantage and jabbed with the spear, sending the point into the thing's eye socket. The zombie did not die. The spear's angle was wrong. It grabbed the shaft and tore half its face off pulling it free.

It held onto its end of the spear with a grip that Bryce wasn't going to be able to break. If he couldn't break the grip, Bryce decided to break the thing's leg instead. He lashed out with a low front kick, aiming for the same knee that had hit the hydrant. The blow made a crunching sound and the zombie collapsed into the street, still holding onto the spear as it fell.

Rather than risk breaking his only weapon, Bryce gave it up and danced back like a boxer...a trained boxer. The move was again, weirdly natural. It flowed, as did his reactions.

A beast was charging from his left. It almost seemed as though it was moving in slow motion as it stretched long arms out to Bryce. He saw it perfectly; the torn plaid shirt, the untied All-star Converse sneaker, the old blood that ran up its arms, the torpid look in its dark eyes. He saw all this with amazing hyper-awareness, just as he saw in his periphery eight of the beasts break towards them.

Eight was too many.

"On your left," he said, casually, as he took hold of one blood-covered arm and pushed outward, redirecting the charging zombie and using its momentum to plow it face-first into the side of the building with crushing force. Its frontal bone shattered like an egg and it fell.

"On your left!" This time Bryce barked the words. The creature was only steps away.

Nichola turned and had it been an actual person coming at her she would've brained it with her bat, but it was a nasty faceless woman who smelled of raw sewage. It was a horror and Nichola could only thrust her bat out uselessly. With strength that was a shock to Nichola, the thing grabbed the bat and yanked it from her hands.

She turned to run, but Bryce was there, flying in with a kick that leveled the ghastly woman.

"What are…" she began, but he was already moving. In a blur, he snatched up the bat, whirled and smashed it down on the head of the big beast with the broken knee. He then thrust the bat at Nichola and stooped to pick up his spear.

"This way."

To her dismay, he started running *at* the zombies that were converging on them. "No," she said in a whisper. There were too many of them and they were too strong. Her only choices were following him or running back inside. Her hand went to the door, but she stopped herself from fleeing. She had a moment of perfect clarity as she envisioned herself sitting in her dark apartment with her bed and refrigerator pushed in front of the door. In her vision, she had been there for a week; her food was gone and the kitchen faucet only burped at her as it spat out dribbles of brown water. Outside, the world was cold and grey, and empty.

"God," she said and raced after Bryce and into the middle of the crowded street. He was just leaping down from the hood of a car, his spear tearing into the upturned face of one of the dead. They crashed down, the zombie's head splitting open as it struck the pavement.

"Take that one!" he ordered, pointing at another zombie, one pushing between two cars.

"Take it?" The moment of clarity passed and now her mind was on the fritz. There was only static between her ears. He wanted her to kill the zombie. "Right. Right." She cocked the bat and let it fly right across the thing's face, turning it halfway around with the force of the blow. But it was not dead, and now another slid over a car's hood at her.

It fell at her feet and she gave it a tepid whack with the bat because it suddenly struck her that she didn't know how the monsters became monsters. Was it blood? Was it an alien parasite that filled the air with invisible spores? Were there tiny zombie worms that were even then crawling into her ears so they could burrow into her brain?

She jumped back and wiggled a finger in an ear, a scream of fear and frustration caught in her throat.

"Come on!" Bryce yelled. The zombies were multiplying. For every one he killed, two more would pop up out of the blue. Not far up the block, the drone was hovering over the stairs that led down into a subway station. Between it and them was a narrow zombie-free lane, but it wouldn't last.

They had seconds and Nichola was wasting them trying to climb over a pick-up truck instead of killing a rather weak and mutilated child zombie that stood in her way. Although Nichola was young and nimble, the truck sat on four jacked up wheels and by the time she dropped down on the other side, the lane had closed.

"We'll fight through," Bryce said, hoping he sounded confident because he certainly didn't feel it. The zombies in their way were large and whole, which made them doubly dangerous. He grabbed her leather jacket and shook her, saying, "But you have to fight. Got it?"

He charged with his spear out before him while Nichola came behind, hoisting her bat. She had nothing that could be mistaken for an actual fighting style and it showed. To get in a proper swing, she had to set herself like a batter at home plate, but her feet wouldn't listen. They wanted to run her out of there as fast as they could. Her body tried to accommodate both the attack and the retreat and she did something akin to a dance. She'd dart forward a few steps, hurry back a couple of steps, while juking to her right, and swinging the bat somewhere in the middle of this.

Her first swing was too weak and she only knocked away a grey hand reaching for her. Her next was too strong. It had been less than a minute and already she had forgotten Bryce's warning about over-committing. The bat clipped off the head of a lurching zombie and before she knew it, she was spinning around, her body playing catch-up with the bat.

She turned three-fourths of a circle and before she could spin back, the zombie was on her. Its teeth latched onto her shoulder. The pain was intense and her fear spiked right to the edge of panic. Her body spasmed in a wild cat-like twist, which tore teeth from the zombie's mouth.

They fell from her leather jacket, which had held up against the bite. The zombie tried to bite her again, but now that she knew her leather was proof against the creatures, her fear dropped away. Taking the bat in both hands, she smashed the zombie square in the mouth, knocking out more teeth and sending it reeling back. Another came lunging in at her, but she ducked under its hand and ran, only to smack into Bryce.

He had waited for her and in those lost seconds they had become well and truly surrounded.

"What do we do?" Nichola cried.

Bryce had no answer to that. No real answer. "Fight," he said, and then tried to get through a sea of grey hands with his spear.

She found herself swatting at the hands, trying to drive them back. But the dead couldn't be driven back. They came on relentlessly forcing the pair into an ever-shrinking perimeter. Bryce's spear became a blur, stabbing and jabbing, fast and faster, but it was not a good weapon for the situation. It didn't have stopping power and any strike that wasn't perfectly precise was, more or less, a waste.

Their backs were to a delivery van and Bryce was just thinking of dropping down beneath it and crawling away, leaving Nichola to be eaten, when a scream ripped the air.

You've done all you can, ghosted through his mind. It was a cowardly thing to think while at the same time, it was a perfectly human thing to think. Nichola was a stranger and her death wouldn't really be his fault. And besides it was unavoidable, and anyone else in his position would have thought the same…

The drone dropped down into the middle of the fight. Its presence managed to confuse a couple of the zombies allowing Bryce to kill one with an eye strike. Yanking the wood free, he turned and was just about to drop down and try to escape, when he heard a new scream…no it was a harsh yell. An angry yell.

Bryce's mouth fell open as Maddy Whitmore came charging out of the darkness, her climbing axe raised. Next to her was

Griff, looking tall and handsome, even though his thick dark hair was standing up in odd places. He carried a giant monkey wrench. It had to be almost three-feet long and when he swung it, he needed two hands. It did terrible damage, crushing in the head of one of the grey beasts.

And there was Wilkes with an axe. Bryce recognized him from his cold grey eyes alone. The rest of his thick, muscular body was covered in what looked like rags. On either side of him were his mercenaries, who were also covered in rags. Behind them were Jayson and Sid. Jayson had a two-by four, while Sid had two whiskey bottles; he held them by the neck, like hammers.

This group crashed into the dead, taking them from behind and wreaking a slaughter among the zombies. Their charge drove right through the undead in seconds.

"Bryce!" Maddy cried. She jerked towards him awkwardly and then stopped. She had been about to hug him, but the sight of Nichola stopped her. The younger woman was tall and gorgeous, while Maddy felt sticky and gross.

Next to her, Griff was staring at Bryce in an odd combination of nervous amazement and disgust, as if he were looking at some sort of carnival freak. "You barely look like yourself. You're so…" Words failed him. He had thought Maddy's transformation was stunning, but Bryce had gone from a pipsqueak to a "real" man practically overnight.

"We gotta move," Wilkes said in a stilted voice. He too was looking at Bryce in a strange manner. It was a calculating look. "More of them are coming." The night was loud with the moans and cries of the dead. They were being whipped into a frenzy.

The group ran for the closest subway where Victoria Dietch, her daughter Tessa and the Harrimans sat crouched with a few others who Bryce didn't recognize. "Twenty more blocks," Griff said, taking the lead. "We'll be there in no time."

Bryce made to follow him; only to falter on the first step as a cold feeling went down his back. It was the cold finger of death and it made no sense. He looked into the darkness, his blue eyes straining to see what was causing this absurd feeling to sweep over him.

"You feel it, too?" Maddy asked, her voice weak and hollow as if there was no breath in her lungs.

It's not just that he felt something, he *knew* something that he couldn't possibly know. Death waited for them down in the darkness.

Chapter 36

It was an insane thing to think and stupid as well. Of course, death waited for them down there. The specter of death was everywhere. There were bodies in the streets and blood in the gutters. Above them, buildings were on fire, and a jet screeched through the darkness having just passed over a river in which there were more corpses than fish.

So why the hesitation? Why the "feeling?"

It was a question he couldn't answer since he knew it wasn't a feeling. It was truth. Death lay down that tunnel. As a scientist, he instantly questioned the thought. Hadn't he tried to talk Maddy out of her "prophecy" regarding the ice axe not even a half hour before?

Somehow, this was different. It was so very different. "We should…" he started to say, only Wilkes grabbed him by the arm and began pulling him down the cement stairs. One of the mercs did the same to Maddy, only she jerked away, a look of revulsion on her face.

"Come on!" he growled and tried to grab her again.

He was sweating fiercely under his rags and his eyes were wide and wild. She could smell the disease in him.

"I can walk on my own," she shot back, sounding something like her old I-can-open-my-own-door self.

Two steps below, Bryce caught the same smell; it surrounded the man like a cloud. "Your guy," he said to Wilkes, "he smells like…" Wilkes jerked Bryce's arm and gave him a warning look. Quieter, Bryce asked, "Did he get bit?"

"And scratched. Two hours ago. This kid just popped out from under this bed and went fucking mad on him, and now I don't know what to do with him. Or any of these guys, either." They were at the bottom of the stairs and someone had flicked on a flashlight. The beam of light flicked around catching glints from the trash and a sign pointing the way, showing that they weren't in a subway station just yet, but only a long tiled tunnel.

In the light, Bryce picked out Victoria, disheveled and exhausted, staring at him with eyes grown baggy from lack of sleep. Crowded next to her were the new people: a softly gay man in his fifties and his much younger and far more rugged-appearing boyfriend. A quivering mother of fifty with two skinny teenage boys, one of whom held a sword of all things. The last was a single woman, dumpy and pale, with a panic in her dark eyes. She held the flashlight two handed, as if it were a sword as well.

"If this is them, does that mean we can go?" the mother asked. "Finally?"

"You coulda left anytime," Wilkes replied. He marched past her, heading down the corridor. "Flashlight girl, up here with me. Agent Griff take the rear. Bryce and Maddy, no more running off. We don't have the resources left to track you around the city. The rest of you fill in and keep quiet."

Nichola immediately disregarded the last order. "Why the hell are we going down there? He said we're going to the Fed plaza."

"From here on out" Wilkes groused, "forget what anyone says but me, and I said keep quiet."

"I'll talk if I want to," she shot back. "I don't know you. I know that guy and he doesn't look like he thinks this is the best idea."

Bryce didn't realize that he was wearing his emotions so openly. He shook his head and tried to affect a reassuring smile; he didn't quite pull it off. "Just a bad feeling. I'm sure I'm being foolish."

"You are," Wilkes told him, and began marching down the corridor, his shoes making a lonely clacking sound. Bryce took a deep uncertain breath and followed. The others hurried to catch up.

"It's safer to travel underground," Jayson told Nichola in a whisper of red wine. He'd been nursing a hangover even while the group slept in the back of a church. A new-found bottle was helping somewhat. "There's less zombies down here. And this here runs to the 4 and the 6 trains, which'll take us straight to where we need to go. You should stick with me." This last he said in a soft voice before raising his brows at the others.

"Why? Because you're black?" She rolled her eyes. She wasn't planning on sticking with anyone, except for maybe Bryce. He had been something else during the fight. Calm, precise, fearless. These were traits she could get on board with. Still, if it came down to it, she was going to run. There was nothing heroic about being eaten alive.

"You ain't thinkin' straight if you…" Jayson started to say, only just then there was a high shrieking scream from behind them.

They all jumped in fright and stared back where the stairs leading up to the city were not nearly as dark as the corridor. They were just gloomy enough to show a torrent of zombies pouring down them in a shadowy unending mass. There was no call to run and yet, in the next second, they were all running, pelting down the corridor at top speed.

The beam from the flashlight janked up and down making seeing anything difficult. Sid didn't see six-year-old Tessa and ran right over her. She went down, as did Sid, her mom, Jayson and both Harrimans. Bryce and Griff did what they could to untangle the clawing, scrapping people and get them moving again.

By the time they did, the zombies were closer, coming on in a howling mass. When one of them fell, it was trampled into grey goo and did little to stop the momentum of the mob.

Still, the humans were faster and a hundred yards went by under their feet before Maddy and Wilkes led them through a wide mezzanine that seemed to have dozens of branching corridors or stairs attached to it. The two hesitated and Nichola blew past them at full speed. She knew the way and didn't slow down even when she came to the metal turnstiles.

She had jumped enough of these in her time to fly over them, barely leaving palm prints behind. Maddy was slower. The Harrimans slower still and the slowest of all was Tessa, who was limping now, helped along by Griff and her mom.

In the very back was Bryce. He was barely winded from the run. Once over the turnstiles, he stopped with his spear at the ready, its point stained black. He hoped to slow them down long enough for everyone to make it to one of the middle tracks. There were four tracks all told, but there was no way to know if any of them had juice running through them.

While Mr. Harriman was still trying to ease his wife down off the platform, the first of the dead hit the turnstiles. Bryce worked methodically, going for the eyes with hard fast jabs. Three inches was as deep as he needed to go to hit grey matter.

A dozen of the creatures—the biggest dozen in reach—fell at his feet before the zombies flanked him. Then he was running for the tracks where Griff and Sid waited anxiously down in the filthy trough. On the next set of tracks, Maddy stood holding her climbing axe in one clenched fist. The others were strung out along the express tracks; Nichola was the furthest away, almost to the tunnel at the far end of the platform. Wilkes and his two remaining mercenaries were closer to Maddy, but backing away.

"Are the tracks hot?" Bryce asked as he dropped down.

"Ain't no one volunteered to lick 'em and find out," Sid said, wearing a curdled grin. Gingerly he took a giant step over the third rail. Bryce and Griff leapt over easily, then backed away as the dead reached the edge of the platform. The beasts didn't hesitate to judge depth or distance; they simply came on, falling down onto the first set of tracks.

There were so many of them.

The first couple of dozen didn't have time to get to their feet before more piled on top of them. More fell on this third wave, crushing everything beneath them. It was one from the fourth wave that finally tested the rail. It rolled from the mound, stuck out a hand, and froze. There was a great *Crack!* and the tunnel was briefly lit by a strange blue light.

Then the entire pile began to wiggle and squirm like worms thrown on a hotplate.

"It's working!" Griff cried. He grabbed Bryce by the shoulder and began backing away. "Come on spread them out." The three waved their hands and retreated with the dead following them and dying in ugly clumps. A sickening cloud filled the air, but the smell was not what had Bryce suddenly nervous. That feeling of coming death was growing in him again. He looked back at Maddy and saw that she alone wasn't giddy over the electrocution of the dead.

"It's here," she said.

They couldn't see the demon, but they both knew that it was somewhere in the dark.

"We have to go!" Bryce yelled over the noise. "Everyone down the tunnel, now." Griff heard the fear in his voice and started jogging with the rest, but Bryce stopped him. "Do you still have your gun?"

Griff gave him a partial shrug. "Yeah, but we're out of ammo. There was an ambush and we almost didn't make it."

"What about Wilkes? Do you think he's holding out on us?"

"No. He lost two men and that one guy got bit. I don't think he's going to make it. He's got that weird look in his eyes, like he's…" He stopped as he saw Bryce was no longer listening. Bryce was staring back down the tracks as a shadowy figure stepped over the third rail where the tracks entered the tunnel. It was so big that Griff thought his eyes were playing tricks on him.

Bryce saw it perfectly. "It's the demon," he said. "You should go."

"Is that the same one? The one from before?" Griff had seen a great deal of horror over the last two days, but nothing scared him like the demon. Its evil knifed through the stench and the darkness and sent a shiver down his spine. He gritted his teeth and said, "We'll take it together. All of us."

There was no "taking" the demon, and the idea of "all of us" was something of a joke. Jayson and Sid were too drunk to fight; they were stumbling down the tracks. Wilkes and his men were too selfish; they saw the demon and were shaking their heads, backing away. They couldn't be trusted. Victoria, the Harrimans, Nichola and the others were too weak or too afraid. They were clinging to each other, moving like frightened sheep in a clump behind the woman with the flashlight. She had become their leader and savior simply because of the light.

This left Griff and Maddy, and she was trembling at the sight of the creature. The best the three of them could do was slow it down.

All the spit in Bryce's mouth dried up, so when he spoke it came out in a whisper. "Take Maddy and get her to the FBI. I might be able to give you a minute, so hurry."

Griff wanted to protest, but *it* was coming closer. And Bryce was correct; it was too strong.

"You better run," Bryce said and turned from the agent. It felt strange that he was the one facing the demon. The day before it would've been Griff fighting it. Now, things were different. He had changed which was great and all, but the demon had changed as well. Not only had it healed itself, it too had gotten bigger and its nails were no longer nails, they were three-inch long claws, each coated with disease. And its canines were no longer perfectly lined up with the rest of its teeth. They were longer now and deadly sharp.

Against the claws, fangs and the rock-hard fists, Bryce had a stick.

The demon smiled, showing off its fangs and staring past Bryce at the gaggle of fleeing people. It was in no hurry, which was strangely worrisome. Didn't it want to eat them? Or make them suffer? Or did it think that Bryce would be easily killed and that it would have plenty of time to hunt them down?

"I won't be that easy," Bryce remarked, spinning his spear, praying the demon wasn't bright enough to spot his bluff.

This sparked a grunt of amusement from the demon. It came forward, slowly, its dark eyes centering on Bryce, who waited, hoping that his fear didn't show, hoping that he didn't stink of it. He hoped in vain. His hands were slick with sweat and the hoodie was damp and clung to his back—his bluff wasn't even fooling himself.

It took a good deal of willpower, but he managed to wait until the demon was within ten feet of him before taking his first frightened step back. Now, the demon grinned knowingly. It knew it was going to win.

"Like last time?" Bryce asked, trying to buy time for Maddy and the others. "You didn't win then and you won't win now." The boast was hollow and they both knew it.

The demon came forward, moving silently and with so little extraneous motion that it seemed to glide at Bryce, who flailed badly with his broom-spear, stabbing and hitting nothing but dark air as the demon dodged. Bryce tried again to run the creature through while stumbling backwards at the same time. The point shot through shadow and nothing else.

Bryce was off balance and the demon took advantage of his vulnerability, slashing with its new-grown claws. It dug three deep furrows across Bryce's neck, nearly opening up his jugular. As blood poured down the front of his hoodie, he threw himself back and felt the swish of claws just miss his eyes. A split-second later, the demon's foot crashed into his chest and sent him flying. In the near complete darkness, he found himself on his back, his spear uselessly pointed across the tracks.

His head had cracked against one of the railroad ties and a hundred stars blazed across his vision. They were gone in a blink, leaving behind strange purple lines in the darkness, which masked the approaching demon. It was attacking again. Bryce squirmed back, and more by instinct than anything else, he lashed outward with a kick and struck the demon's knee, stopping it just above him. Slightly stooped, it was perfectly positioned when Bryce brought the spear around like a baseball bat in a short, hard arc and connected with the thing's jaw. One more hit and it would be dislocated.

Bryce swung again, but this time the demon was ready and grabbed the spear and yanked it out of Bryce's hands.

Effortlessly, it broke the spear in half, tossed aside the blunt end and leapt on Bryce.

"Do it!" Bryce hissed as it raised the jagged hunk of wood. "I dare you."

Chapter 37

Bryce tilted his chin back, giving the demon a clear shot at his exposed throat. "Do it."

But the demon wouldn't. It could sense something was wrong. Bryce could as well. He could sense the shit out of it on the back of his neck where the tiny hairs were an inch from the electrified third rail and its fifteen hundred volts. The rail couldn't seem to hold in all that electricity; it reached out and stung him like dozens of fire ants, turning those tiny hairs to cinders.

"You're weak," Bryce goaded, ignoring the stings. They were nothing compared to what was coming. He was a dead man one way or another, but if the demon were to stab him right then, they would both fry and that would be a win in his book.

The demon was too cagey. It knew Bryce was up to something and when it figured it out, it immediately jerked back. Its horrid grin spreading once more over its black face as it stepped away. The grin was a compliment; an unsettling one. There was a certain dark intelligence behind it that was frightening. They both knew it was Bryce's master physically; the grin suggested that the demon was at least his mental equal as well.

It invited Bryce to get to his feet. Slowly, Bryce did, preparing for the attack that he was sure was coming. He was wary and the demon was as well and made no move until Bryce eased away from the electrified rail. It then lunged forward, eagerly, hungry to slay.

Without a weapon, the electrified rail was the only way for Bryce to defend himself and he quickly stepped back towards it. "Come on! Come get some!" The demon hissed, which made Bryce laugh. It felt good to laugh, even if it was just for a few moments. "Looks like we got a Mexican standoff, and with every second you hesitate, my friends get further and further away."

As much as that sounded like the truth, there was still the terrible feeling in the air that death was close. In fact, the feeling was growing. The demon seemed to feel it as well. Its grin was back, wider than ever, as if it was expecting something of its own. A trick or a trap or a...

Bryce chanced a look over his shoulder. The fight had only lasted seconds and he could see Maddy and the others quite clearly. With the drunks and the old folks and the injured child, they hadn't progress far down the tunnel and were nearing a place where the gloom wasn't nearly so deep. Some fifteen feet above them was a grate of some sort that led to the street. On his first day in the city, Bryce remembered walking over one of these and feeling nervous, picturing himself falling through. Even though people of much greater size tread them without hesitation, he had made sure to go around them.

Now, his eyes lingered on the grate. They were drawn to it and with his newly improved eyesight, he saw blackened fingers curl around the metal. There was a grunt like that of a wild boar, then a scream of metal as the grate was torn away.

Beneath the opening stood the woman with the flashlight. Her chest was heaving, as much from the run as from the horror that stood above her. She screamed and backed into Wilkes, who backed into the soft gay man. The woman should've run forward instead.

Down from the street dropped a hideous monstrosity. It was black, but unnaturally so. It wasn't dark skinned like the demon, it was burnt black. The flesh of its face was peeling in sheets and most of its hair had been broiled away. What was left was magenta colored, straight from a bottle.

"Holy shit," Bryce whispered. It was the female demon from the building he and Maddy had set on fire. It had tracked them down. Sid recognized the creature too and ran back the way he had come, a scream ripping from his throat.

"Stop!" Griff cried, putting his arms out to stop Sid. "We can fight it."

Wilkes had been backing away. "Fuck that shit," he said and then jumped over the rails and landed on the next set of tracks. The burnt demon jumped as well, laughter bubbling from her huge burnt lips. Wilkes turned and ran, and as he did, the woman with the flashlight tried to dart forward past the grate. Again, she made the mistake of stopping.

Down from the grate dropped a pair of zombies. One broke its leg on impact, while the other fell into the third rail and did a jitterbug death dance. More fell from the opening, filling the tunnel with their hideous shrieks. In front of Griff the group was disintegrating, running helter skelter back the way they had come. It looked as though they would run clean over Maddy and Griff. But what would they do when they got to the demon Bryce had been fighting?

It was now armed with a shard of Bryce's spear. This wasn't exactly a legendary weapon, but it would be enough to kill them all.

Griff thought it was better to fight the zombies in front. He grabbed Maddy's arm and over the shrieks of the dead and the screaming of the soon to be dead, yelled, "We can fight them and get past."

She pulled back, shaking her head. Her fear had spiked more than it should have and her nerves were jangling worse than they had been while on the roof of the burning building. The she-demon had come for her. It might play with Wilkes, killing him for fun, but maddy knew she was there with one true purpose.

"Maddy!" Griff yelled. "We have to fight them or…"

She tuned him out. The air had suddenly changed. There was building pressure as if something massive was coming right at them at great speed. Her mind pictured a missile hurtling towards them. "Not a missile," she whispered in sudden realization.

The trains had stopped running the night before. It had been the last order from the mayor before he had boarded a helicopter, never to be seen again.

Although the trains had stopped, it didn't mean they couldn't be started again, not when there was still power running through the lines. Not long before Bryce's group entered the tunnel, three conductors, their families and a hundred suddenly close friends had decided to escape the city in a desperate gamble. They had boarded an express train, removed the governor that restricted its speed, and were now hurtling along at breakneck velocity. It was conceded that they would have to maintain a certain momentum, a dangerous momentum to keep the train going if they hit a few stray zombies.

So far they hadn't and their speed had begun to creep up. With so many stations mere black caverns, it was a ride that had the bravest of them holding on tight. For the weakest, it was all they could do to keep their sphincters puckered. The man at the controls was in something of a religious fugue state, in which he was sweating freely and repeating the *Our Father* over and over again.

Still, he was smart and quick, knowledgeable and experienced. His eyesight had degraded, however, and in the dark he didn't see the people and monsters running along the express tracks. Not that it would've mattered. At eighty miles an hour, nothing short of a brick wall could've stopped that train in time.

Maddy caught the first hint of it as it dropped down a small slope a little less than a quarter mile away. Distance meant nothing, time meant everything. Eleven seconds was how long they had before the train reached them and in the middle of the chaos that was not much time. She wasted two seconds screaming a warning at the top of her lungs—it went unheard by almost everyone. She screamed again, "Traiiiin!" while yanking Griff around.

His eyes popped open and it took him a full second to react. By then, Maddy was already pushing people to the side, yelling the word, "Train! Train! Train!" over and over again. It was like a countdown.

With six seconds left, Nichola was the first to leap across to the west-side tracks. At five seconds, Sid flew through the metal columns, cradling his bottles. A few feet away, the soft gay man was trying to yank his much larger partner to the left, the big man had started going right instead.

At four seconds, everyone else was just realizing what the new emergency was. The Harrimans turned slowly towards the next set of tracks and eyed the rails; it would take a big step to get over all three without touching the electric one. A few feet down from them, little Tessa Deitch was in a full panic. Sickening fear had been growing in her since the day before. It had sat just below the surface ready to rise up and swallow her whole, and now it did. Her fear stopped her cold.

Victoria pushed her to the edge of the tracks. "Jump! Jump over the rails. Just don't touch that one." Her daughter wasn't listening. She was staring at the onrushing train.

Griff was suddenly there. He grabbed the six-year-old and threw her onto the next track before leaping over himself. There was no time to save anyone else.

Of the two mercs, one made it, the other was caught in mid-leap and sent flying into one of the columns where his head was torn from his body. The mom with the two teenage boys accidentally stepped on the third rail and went stiff as a board until the train crashed into her. Her younger son died a second later. He had been too indecisive and had looked first one way, then the other. Then he was creamed by the train.

Mr. Harriman lived. He was holding his wife's hands when the train took her. Her skin parted like wet tissue paper and what muscle she did have was soft as veal. He was left holding both of her hands by the stumps of her wrists.

Bryce and the demon played a game of chicken, each daring the other to jump first. They stared into each other's eyes until the last moment. Bryce jumped west and the demon went east.

Then the trained roared past, blood splashing onto the conductor's window. A broken face came halfway through the glass next. It was a human face, something he hadn't expected. He screamed and hit the brakes just as the train plowed through the pile of zombies. The sudden change in speed up front caused the third car to jump the tracks and from there things went to shit in a hurry. Forty-ton subway cars could not stop on a dime, especially traveling as fast as they were. They turned and tumbled and bent with a thunder that no storm could replicate.

The support columns separating the tracks could not take that kind of punishment and in a flash, they were blasted aside like a row of toothpicks.

Bryce felt the coming disaster and rolled as fast as he could, spinning over the local southbound tracks and under a cement lip where only rats scurried and nested. He rolled in, his head towards the terrifying chaos. He ducked away and looked back as Maddy found safety next to Griff under the lip. Victoria dragged her daughter to it as well, just as an 80,000 pound train car swept inches over them, people flying from it, scattering like broken dolls.

The next car was upside down as it whipped sideways across three sets of tracks. It swung by so low that the rails left grooves across what had once been its roof. The train car took Tessa with it as it ripped by. One second, she was there, being dragged to safety by her mother and the next she was gone without so much as leaving a drop of blood behind. Victoria screamed in anguish. It might as well have been a silent scream as nothing could be heard above the thundering.

Griff saw her pain clear as day. Strangely, after so much gloom, the tunnel was brighter now, lit by thousands of sparks. He could see, but what he could see was so terrible that he closed his eyes as the next car came on, bouncing and tumbling. The front of the car hammered Mr. Harriman into the wall of the tunnel, crushing every bone in his frail body and flattening him into a fresco of red and pink goo.

A moment later, the last car plowed into the tangle of metal in front of it. Then there were only the echoes of the crash, rolling endlessly down the tunnels beneath the city.

Shaking, Griff crawled from beneath the cement lip and stood staring about in shock. The tunnel, the tracks, the subway cars, were a conjoined, mutilated mess. Bodies and parts of bodies were everywhere, as were splashes of blood. The blood was like the city's graffiti: colorful but ugly; a testament to man's weakness. Dust and debris filled the dark air so that Bryce was only a ghost to him.

Bryce climbed up on the last train, hoping to see the broken body of the demon, hoping that his own personal nightmare was over. There was no sign of it.

A shiver went down his back. He saw Griff standing uselessly nearby. "Find out who's still alive. We have to get moving."

"What about the wounded?"

Bryce's eyes flicked away. "We have to get moving on," he repeated. "We'll do our best to protect those who can walk."

"And the ones who can't?"

It took Bryce a long time to answer, "They'll have to make a tough choice."

Chapter 38

When Wilkes had jumped to the next set of tracks over and ran from the burnt, magenta-headed beast, he had thought his fear had peaked. Then came the train, flying along in a silver blur. Like a fool he had stood there watching it come, thinking that everyone was going to die but him.

Then, when it crashed, Wilkes felt his heart seize up in his chest. It simply stopped out of sheer, overwhelming fear.

That fear kept him rooted in place, even as the third car turned sideways, taking out the metal columns like it was blowing out candles. The back of the train missed him by a hair. It came so close that the wind of its passing blew over him like the breath from a furious dragon.

He was in such a state that the wind alone toppled him over backwards. His knees, rigid as dandelion stalks, buckled and he fell with a warbling unheard cry.

After that, the next ten seconds passed in a rolling, crashing, oil-stinking fog where up and down changed position like Vegas dice thrown on green felt. His brain felt thrown, too and after it was all over, it was a few seconds before he realized that he was still alive. Alive, but buried beneath tons of metal.

Somehow he had ended up in a pocket that had been carved out of the floor of the tunnel by the impact of one of the trains. Around him were snapped-in-two railroad ties, twisted rails, broken hunks of cement, and most of a train car. He had only enough wiggle room to raise up a few inches and peer into the car through a gaping hole where a window had been.

The car was on its side. There were bodies strewn about. All were bleeding and broken, but not all of them were dead. One or two lifted an arm or rubbed their head, groaning as they did.

Wilkes went to rub his own head, which was aching and spinning. Only his jacket was caught on something.
Immediately, his mind screamed: *I'm trapped!* The panic which had been his one driving force not too many seconds before, bubbled up in his chest. The bubble went right to his throat and closed it so tight that he couldn't breathe. In terror, he started to jerk and twist, and with a gasp of despair, he ripped his arm up through his jacket and stared at it.

Blood leaked from a long cut beneath his elbow—and that was okay. His arm could move and he could feel his fingers...

they were all crushed and bruised, and the pain was akin to a shrieking numbness, but they still wiggled on command.

His other arm was just as perfect as it always was. His legs, on the other hand, ached and when he tried to move, he found they were well and truly trapped.

"Hey you," he whispered to a teenage girl. From what he could see of her, she was pretty. Beneath her heavy coat, she was something of a lump, but her lips were full and her eyes were dark and sad. She had the warm tan of a Puerto Rican who had just come back from a visit to the island. Sadness was not meant for a girl like her. Men would trip over themselves for a chance to see her smile.

"I need help," Wilkes said.

She shook her head and looked down at her lumpy coat where a dark stain was spreading.

"Ah crap," Wilkes whispered. "Hold on. Maybe I can…" He twisted and felt a sharp pain in one knee, but that wasn't what stopped his words in mid-sentence. His little carved-out pocket wasn't a perfect crater. One side went out for a bit like a trough and when he glanced down it through the gloom beneath the twisted metal and broken cars, he saw something move.

At first it was just a shadow and yet the shadow gave off an overwhelming feeling of dread. In his hard little heart he knew it was the magenta-haired demon.

Somehow the burnt creature had survived and now it was coming for the girl and anyone else it could find alive. Wilkes should've screamed for help, or warned the girl. He should have done anything besides cowering in fear.

"My stomach hurts," the girl said to him in a begging whisper.

Wilkes closed his eyes and gritted his teeth. The demon woman, burnt and horrible, was crawling closer, dragging her legs and leaving a bloody slime behind her like some monstrous evil slug. It slithered nearer, sniffing the air. Then it slid into the car and, it was so horrifying that Wilkes hid himself behind his hands.

"No," the girl said in a terrified whisper, her eyes jacked wide. "Don't please."

The demon crawled on, faster now. In a slick of shadow and blood it engulfed the girl and the sound of it chewing through her neck was enough to drive Wilkes mad. He crushed his hands into his ears, uncaring of the pain in his fingers.

There was another wounded person in the car; a boy of ten. His left leg was broken in two places; his ribs were stove in on one side; he had blood gushing from a wound in his head. Despite all this, he knew better than to try to hide. He tried to stagger from the wreckage, but the demon was greedy and gave up on the girl. It crawled after the boy and caught him as he fell from the car.

With his broken ribs, he could barely breathe, let alone call out or scream. He could only beg in a gurgling whisper. Somehow that horrible sound managed to sneak past Wilkes' hands. The whispers crawled between the cracks of his fingers, into his ears and straight to his soul. It was a rotted soul. He still did nothing.

Then Bryce was there, looking tall, his face fierce and angry. He was weaponless and yet his very presence was enough to send the demon scurrying beneath the subway car like a great burnt rat. Down there her claws and fangs would be an advantage, but Bryce followed her down regardless, stopping only when he saw Wilkes.

"I'm trapped," Wilkes said. He said it defensively, as an excuse.

"We'll get you out." Bryce paused unsure which way to go. He wanted to follow after the burnt demon—she was weak and it was smart to kill her now rather than have her spring up later healed and even stronger.

But the other demon was close. Bryce could feel its dark presence lurking out there. It was injured otherwise it would've attacked by now. The question was how injured? Bryce had already seen that it could take a terrific beating and still remain dangerous. And with its newly grown claws…

"I need a weapon," he muttered. Without a weapon, he felt naked and weak. That was the deciding factor. He had nothing to take down the demon with. It would have to wait, and hopefully they would be long gone before the thing healed. He was just thinking that it couldn't be that much further to the FBI headquarters when his eyes fell on the Puerto Rican girl. She was still alive, and because the world had become a sick place, he knew she would be alive hours from then, when the demons returned.

Their eyes locked. In hers was a spark of hope. In his was dread. He couldn't save her and he couldn't leave her, or the others, behind. Not alive, at least. He nodded and quickly glanced away to Wilkes. The mercenary was only half-visible and looked like he was being swallowed by the earth.

"Where's Griff," Bryce asked him, forcing his eyes away from the girl. Bryce had been growing as a man and a person, but he wasn't man enough yet to murder this girl in cold blood. He doubted he could even order someone else to do it. But he could push it all onto Griff.

"Dunno."

"I'll be right back," he told Wilkes, and started for the front of the car which had been torn clear off.

Wilkes saw right through him. "Get back here you coward. Don't you fucking leave me!"

Bryce hesitated at the door. "I said I'll be back." He returned quickly with Griff, Maddy and a shell-shocked Sid Pitts, who sipped from one of his bottles that had miraculously survived intact. Bryce said nothing of the scene in the subway car, and couldn't bring himself to look at the girl.

Maddy went to her and knelt. Her trembling hands opened the girl's coat and then uselessly traced her wounds. Maddy could feel her pain and fear. It came off her in waves. There was only one thing that could be done for her and she saw that Bryce was doing everything in his power to pretend not to know what that was. It was cowardly, but she wasn't going to blame him.

Griff's eyes bounded over the entire bloody, body-strewn car. His mind was still echoing from the crash and he was having trouble prioritizing what should be done from one second to the next. Wilkes helped focus him by demanding loudly to be saved. He used those exact words: "Save me!"

"Maybe we can just pull him out?" Bryce suggested. No one else had a better idea, so Bryce took one arm and Griff the other. With Wilkes cursing and shamelessly begging for them to be careful, they pulled him out. He lost a little flesh and most of his pants, but he could stand on his own and limp about, inventing new curses with each semi-hop. It was a successful extraction and yet Sid stumbled away, mumbling about how fucked-up the world was.

"What's wrong with him?" Wilkes asked, then he saw the pretty girl with the big eyes. They were big, unseeing eyes now. Wordlessly, Maddy tossed away a chunk of bloody cement, shut the girl's eyes and followed Sid out.

"Shit," Bryce whispered, embarrassed at his weakness. Maddy had done what he couldn't and his shame made him hang his head. It took an effort to leave the train car. There would be more wounded and they all would have to be dealt with, most in the same manner.

When the train crashed, there had been a hundred and eighteen people on board, most in the first few cars. These were demolished. The first car had been crushed like a soda can. The second was twisted and bent in two. The third and fourth had merged and from the front spewed an insane multicolored goo that had once been a dozen people.

Bryce stood on the car, feeling the strength leach out of him. It wasn't the dead that drained him, it was the living. They were beginning to moan and beg for help, but there was so little that could be done for them. There were no more hospitals or even doctors, for that matter. They had no equipment to pull them from the wreckage and even if they could get them out...

"We got to go," Wilkes said, breaking in on Bryce's misery.

"Now that you're safe, we have to go? Is that it, you worthless piece of..."

Wilkes hissed him quiet and pointed. Zombies were crawling over the wreckage. Some were broken and torn, barely able to move and some were perfectly intact. They were all hungry.

"Gather everyone who can walk," Bryce ordered. "I'll try to give you a few minutes."

"Hold on," Wilkes whispered before making the mistake of grabbing Bryce. He was still bigger and stronger than the scientist, but he was no longer faster.

Bryce knocked the hand away and darted in until they were nose-to-nose. "Gather everyone who can walk or you get left behind. We don't need you to find Magnus. Remember that."

"I remember that just yesterday you were a little shit." Wilkes wasn't the kind of guy that backed down from a fight, even in the middle of an apocalypse.

"That was yesterday," Bryce retorted, staring him in the eye. "Today you'll do what you're told." This was all the time either of them had. Bryce was unhurt and leapt across to another of the cars. He jogged down it and dropped to the tracks, landing next to Maddy. She had been trying to quiet Victoria who was attempting to dig beneath one of the subway cars with a broken hunk of wood.

A bare leg stuck out from beneath the metal. It might have been Tessa's and yet it was so torn and twisted that it could've been any child's.

Standing near them were the survivors of their group; it wasn't a large group: along with Griff was Sid—slow blinking and bleary-eyed. The infected mercenary, —wild-eyed and angry. Nichola—twitchy and skittish, ready to run; and the thirteen-year-old boy—he was so covered in dirt and dust that he defied description. He was nothing but a grey shape that blended into the background so perfectly, he would've been invisible if he wasn't still clutching the sword.

"We have to go," he told them.

"Bryce, no," Maddy said, softly. She shook her head, suggesting it wasn't a good time.

It would never be a good time, he realized. Good times for anything were gone. "The dead are coming. Maddy and Griff will do a quick scout for survivors. The rest of you cross the tracks to that far wall. Keep low, keep quiet and don't touch the electric rails."

"I'm not leaving without Tessa," Victoria stated and slammed the wood back down, losing another chunk of it.

"And what about my mom?" the thirteen-year-old asked. His name was Brian Addis and the sword in his hand belonged to his father, a deployed marine. "And my brother? He was right next to me." He stared with vacant eyes around the dust-filled tunnel. "They were right here."

Bryce didn't have time for this. "If I find them, I'll send them over. Does that sound fair?"

"If?"

"*When*," he replied quickly, lying with a fake reassuring smile. "They'll catch up. But first, I'm going to need your sword to hold back the dead." The makeshift group of weapons everyone had been carrying had mostly disappeared, buried under the rubble along with Tessa and the remains of Brian's family. Maddy had kept hold of her climbing axe and Nichola still had her bat and that was it.

Brian only hesitated a second before handing over the sword. He looked like he was going to be sick the moment he did.

Nichola pulled him close. "It'll be alright as long as we keep moving." She really wanted the boy to live, at the same time, the fugue state he was in would make him an excellent target if they were seen by the dead. He was a walking sacrifice, which was sad, but there was a lot of sadness in the world just then.

The group started to move out, all except Victoria. She continued to attack the crumbling cement with her broken board. Bryce grabbed it from her. "You still have a son and a husband. They're on their way to…"

"They're on their way to hell," she hissed, furiously, tears making her eyes look like clear blue pools of water. "They're dead! They're all dead. You know it. You *know* they are, right?" She had seen him and Maddy earlier. They had been afraid of the tunnel when it was clearly their safest route. They had *known* something bad was going to happen. And that hadn't been the first time, either. "What do you know of Jordan? Tell me what you know about my son."

He faltered, uncertain what he knew and what he could only guess at. "I don't know what's become of them. But…but your husband was strong and brave. There's a good chance they've been at the FBI field office since yester…"

"No!" she shrieked. "I want the truth, freak! Yeah, I know what you are. You and that girl, both of you are freaks. You aren't normal. You aren't…natural. I don't think you're even human anymore."

Chapter 39

The word freak struck home harder than Bryce had expected. All his life he had been a geek, a nerd, the little shit that the girls would look right through when they were drooling over the football players. And now that he was different…it was no different. He had exchanged one insulting title for another.

"I'm trying to tell you the truth," he told her. "I don't know what's happened to your son. I do know what happened to your daughter, Tessa is dead." The leg sticking from beneath the subway car was small, coltish with tiny blonde hairs. Only one toenail was left to the foot and a tiny bit of pink showed through the dirt. He knelt and touched the foot. It was still warm and he *knew* this was Tessa.

Victoria saw the truth on his face and more tears streaked through the grime on her face as she started to come apart inside. Her tendons and ligaments seemed to melt, and her muscles just pulled away from the bone. She collapsed, too weak to stand, too weak to live.

Bryce caught her. "Go with the others," he said, speaking straight into her ear. "You still have a son. He'll need you."

How could he need a mom like her? She had run from her husband and son. She had abandoned them. They were dead. That was the truth. That's what the freak wouldn't tell her. A scream of fury and despair built up inside her. She could feel it like a ball of fire, only just then a putrid, grey-faced monster appeared over the top of the train. The scream seemed to get trapped in her throat, and she realized that maybe she didn't want to scream.

Maybe it would be better if it just tore out her throat. "Yeah. I don't care anymore," she said to the zombie.

Bryce had been so focused on Victoria and the unnatural feeling of knowing, that he had disregarded his other senses.

The scraping he had attributed to a survivor. The scent of the creature was masked by the dust that filled the air. And the zombie, who was so covered in dirt and ash that it looked like a dumpling layered in grey flour, and it completely blended in with the filthy surroundings. The thing had been run over by a train and by some hellish miracle, it had come out of the collision unscratched.

And now it launched itself at Bryce. He was turned away, holding Victoria in one arm and the sword in his free hand.

To Victoria, Bryce moved in a violent blur, lifting her as he spun. His sword cut a silver arc through the air until it connected squarely with the zombie's neck. She expected the thing's head to go flying from its body...and so did Bryce. But the thing's head was still very much attached.

He set her on her feet before running his thumb over the edge of the sword. His lip curled. The sword had all the sharpness of a butter knife, which explained how the zombie was still moving. He went to it and saw that he had managed to cut halfway through its neck. Knowing that it would heal, he lifted the sword and finished the job.

Victoria turned away and dropped to her knees, her stomach flipping over.

"Get up," Bryce said, his voice both gruff and distracted by the disappointing sword. It would need an edge; of course the closest he'd come to sharpening a blade were those thousands of times he'd put a wicked point on a number 2 pencil. Yes, even timid little Bryce Carter had something of a barbaric nature. They just weren't done in his eyes until the point was like that of a spear.

He needed the sword to be like that.

She hadn't moved.

"Get up," he said again, glancing quickly around for something he could use as a whetstone. He was pretty sure that even a chunk of cement would do in a pinch. *You don't have time*, his own voice whispered through the dark spaces of his mind. Now that his senses were tuning back to their surroundings, he heard the groans that were hunger and not pain related.

Too many of the dead had survived.

"I said, get up," he growled, grabbing Victoria by the arm and pulling her to her feet.

"Get off me, freak!" She ripped her arm out of his grasp and then began jabbing him in the chest. "You think you can push me around? You think you're something special now, don't you? Let me tell you, you're not. You're no hero. This is all your fault. All these dead people; your fault. And Tessa is your fault, not mine. You knew we shouldn't have come down here. You said you had a bad feeling and yet you just walked us right into this!"

She wasn't wrong.

The realization didn't hit him like a slap it was more of a slow twist of an embedded knife. The only person he could claim to have saved in all of this was Maddy, while the list of people who had died because of his actions grew longer every second.

"I-I didn't mean for her to die."

"Do you think that matters? To Tessa? To me? To all of them?" Her voice was a perfect blend of ice and poison. It withered Bryce and he shrank back, turning so much into the old version of himself that the sword clattered from his fingers. He stared at the dull metal until Victoria hauled her hand back and slapped him across the cheek, leaving four blazing stripes on his face.

She grinned hatefully through her tears. It was as if she had triumphed over him by slapping him, and in a way she had. Her grief had become his guilt.

"You owe me a child," she hissed into his face. "You'll find my son. That's all that matters now. Swear it. Swear you'll do *everything* you can to find him."

He bowed his head, his eyes falling on the near useless sword. "I swear it. We'll go to the FBI field office first. He might be there."

"And if he's not?"

"I'll go look for him."

The FBI wouldn't need him, not if Maddy made it. Though they would have a handful with her. He knew her well enough to know that she had no intention of becoming a guinea pig for the government. Sure, she would let them have a little blood from time to time, but there was no way Maddy would allow herself to be housed in a little cage and watched all the live-long day.

The new Bryce wouldn't have either. Getting to the FBI had always been an excuse to get to safety, but that ship was going to sail without him. Maybe.

Victoria dropped to one knee to touch her daughter's leg one last time; he knelt as well, though only to pick up the sword. As he did, someone started to scream in the rubble. It was another brick to add to the guilt-load riding on his shoulders.

"Go with the others," he told her. "I'll catch up."

"But…" was all she could spit out before he was gone, dodging through the wreckage, racing past body after broken body, each one his fault. Not far into the mess, the darkness drew back slightly. Part of the roof of the tunnel had collapsed and Bryce could see a small patch of the city through a lattice of rebar. A building rising twenty stories right above them was being engulfed in a raging fire.

This horrifying scene was given only a glance. The fire wasn't his fault. The teenage girls trapped in one of the cars were, however.

Sixteen tons of concrete and rock had crushed the back half of the car, while the front half was canted into the air. This was the only thing that was keeping the girls alive. Zombies had been falling down from the street for the last few minutes, attracted by the smell of blood, and now a gang of them was trying to climb up to the girls.

Audrey Brooke, who was all of fourteen, was nursing a shattered arm. As the bones rubbed together, the pain was so great that she couldn't exhale without making a whimpering sound—it was driving the dead mad with desire.

Her friend, Barbi Doll Morales, was a year older, but was so covered in dust that she looked like an old woman. A minute before, she had pried her dad's long-handled framing hammer from his dead hand and was smashing grey fingers one at a time as the beasts piled up at them. Broken fingers were ignored and Barbi Doll was starting to get frantic when Bryce came flying into the crowd, his sword flashing in the meager light.

Had they been human or the sword actually sharp, his charge would've been a thing about which songs were written. Instead, the dead barely noticed him at first as he hacked at them with ugly two-handed strokes. There was little grace or skill to his attack. He used the sword more like an axe.

Half of them had their heads caved in by the dull blade before they even realized he was there. They turned on him; ten against one, but they were slow and with the ground broken beneath them and the twisted rails sprawled everywhere, they were more awkward than usual.

Still there were so many, and Bryce gave ground slowly, the sword going up and down, up and down, and the dark blood flying. He quickly discovered that any blow that wasn't aimed for the crown of the head was a waste of his energy. When he chopped at necks, he was lucky if the dull blade sunk in an inch, and when he slashed at the grasping hands, it had little effect. The zombie might lose a pinky or a thumb.

He fought among the rubble and the cars, always retreating. He fought until the canted subway car was lost in the darkness and by then, the newfound strength in his arms began to flag.

253

The ten zombies he had attacked were dead, but fifteen more had taken their place and he was starting to realize that *fifty* would take their place if the battle lasted much longer.

It was time to run.

With a last flashing swing of the sword, he darted into one of the subway cars, jumped through a blown-out window and ran through the maze of cars back to where Maddy was trying to help the girls who were still stuck, while Griff fought off more zombies with a short chunk of wood.

To Bryce, their roles had reversed. Griff, who was vulnerable to a scratch from the undead, was taller and stronger and could've caught the girls if they jumped the short distance. Maddy, who was fast becoming svelte, was quicker than ever and armed with a real weapon in the climbing axe. Unfortunately, there was no time for role-reversals.

There wasn't even time for Audrey Brooke to climb gingerly down, nursing her broken arm.

Bryce ran to the canted car and yelled to Barbi Doll Morales, "Jump!" His voice had deepened and there had grown within it a leadership quality that he had never known before. When he yelled the word *Jump!* it came out as more than just an order, it was a command with an imperative that it had to be followed.

Barbi Doll Morales jumped to Bryce's waiting arms. It was only a six-foot drop, but she topped a hundred and twenty pounds. He wasn't nearly strong enough to catch her and she pile-drived him into the ground.

"It's okay," Bryce groaned, ignoring the twinge in his back. He struggled to his feet. "I'm fine. You. It's your turn." Grimacing, he lifted his arms as if Audrey were a toddler at the playground.

Audrey backed away from the edge. They didn't understand the pain she was in. She could barely stand and her head swam. Dying was preferable to the pain.

All this was going through her head when Maddy climbed up into the car. Maddy thought they were running out of time, but when she glanced back, she saw that she was wrong; they were already out of time. From her vantage, she could see the zombies pouring down through the collapsed ceiling a dozen at a time.

"You have to jump!"

Audrey tried to back away, however Maddy wasn't going to allow that. The zombies were falling through the gap like sand in an hourglass. Time was flying.

Maddy grabbed the girl and hauled her to the edge. "Sit!" She pushed Audrey down, ignoring the girl as she cried out. "I'll lower her down by her coat," she said to Bryce. Audrey tried to squirm away, but Maddy put a knee in her back and shoved her off the edge.

One quick grunt escaped Maddy—the girl was surprisingly light, or she had grown surprisingly strong. Maddy liked to think it was the latter.

Because of her arm, Bryce caught her by the hips and lowered her easily down. "Hopefully you can run," Bryce said, picking up his sword. Barbi Doll was ready to run at that exact second. Her eyes were wild in her filthy grey face as she watched Griff swinging his hunk of wood in exaggerated circles as the dead closed in on all sides. "Get them moving," Bryce ordered and rushed to Griff's side.

"I don't know if I can," Audrey said in a whimper.

"Too late," Maddy told her and started dragging her along. The girl whined constantly, but Maddy had that ugly feeling growing in her again. Death and more death rode on the dark air. "Nothing new," she muttered. Death had been their constant companion and she was sure it would be until they got out of the city.

If we get out of the city.

There was that. It was beginning to feel impossible.

The three of them cleared the wreckage and caught up to a gaggle of men, women and children, most of whom were limping or swaying dangerously. They were making their slow way towards another tiny band of survivors, who were crouched down at the far side of the tunnel. Among them was sour-faced Wilkes, waving impatiently at Maddy.

"Where's Bryce? Never mind. He'll catch up. We got to move now. They're coming."

"No duh," Maddy snorted. They never stopped coming. But he was right. Maddy could see far down into the gloom to where dozens of shapeless, stumbling beings were heading their way along the one set of tracks not destroyed by the crash.

She hissed this new group along after Nichola who was at the front, her feet skipping sideways, eager to race out of there.

But she didn't run, and when the others caught up, she mingled with them, staying close to the front.

Of all of them there, she alone seemed to truly understand the concept of survival. She had the three basics down in her mind: flee, hide, fight. She even had the nuances: there was no need to be the fastest, she just couldn't be the slowest. Hiding didn't just mean cowering under a bed, it could mean hiding behind someone stronger…or weaker. Fighting was the last resort and if someone wanted to give their life up for hers, she'd let them.

Maddy hung back, her nerves mounting with every step. She hoped that her fear would dissipate when Bryce and Griff caught up…and it did. They came jogging up out of the dark, and for a brief second, she grinned, happy that they had made it unscathed. Then her fear crept back. It built inside of her until she grabbed Bryce's arm.

They didn't speak. She looked into his eyes and he knew her fear and felt it as she did.

Just like before, they were heading into more danger.

Chapter 40

Starving as usual, Bryce had been shoveling handfuls of lunchmeat down his gullet from his open pack when Maddy grabbed his arm, her nails digging into his flesh. He stopped and tried to peer ahead, his blue eyes dilated like a cat's. That's where the danger lay. There were easily two hundred zombies coming up behind, they were the known. It was the unknown that had her heart pounding.

And his as well, now.

"Something's going to happen," he whispered.

She rolled her eyes at him. "Yeah. The question is what do we do?"

"Um, we need to get out of here," he said. It was unhelpful to say the least, but the idea of stepping forward and leading was too much for him just then. The guilt of his failure still hung around his neck and this was made worse as Victoria kept looking back at him with the beginning of an accusation on her lips. He saw Tessa so clearly in the outlines of her face that it sent razors across his heart.

Maddy's eyes narrowed and Griff stared, seeing Bryce as he had been three days before: small, nervous, timid.

"Yeah and how do we do that?" Maddy asked.

Bryce shrugged, causing Maddy to scowl and ball her fist. Before she could punch him, Griff stepped between them. "We'll ask Jayson. He knows these tunnels like the back of his hand. He made it right?"

"No," they both said at once. The group was a shambling mound of dust, tears, blood and rags. In the dark, it was hard to pick one person out from the rest. But Jayson wasn't with them. His wine-marinated scent wasn't among the others. His body was more than likely a thin layer of jelly beneath one of the trains.

Griff looked back and forth along the dark tunnel. He could hear the moans and crazy laughter of the zombies coming up behind them. The sound sent a shiver down his back.

"We'll go on," he said. "Whatever's in front of us can't be as bad as what's coming behind. No train can get past all of that mess back there. Besides, as far as I can tell, we don't have a choice." He was unconvinced that either of them had any psychic abilities. So, what if they had been nervous about

257

coming down into the tunnels in the first place. It was a scary place to be. Being scared did not give someone ESP.

Whatever fear Griff and the others had diminished quickly. After only a couple hundred yards they could see the golden glow of a light. It was one of the sconces set on the tunnel wall and as they crept closer they could see that more of them were lit as well.

The ragged group was traveling in a sniffling, whimpering clump. Afraid to be heard, they had spoken little. Now they began whispering in excitement over the lights. After the terrifying crash and the hellish darkness, the lights represented a return to normalcy. They began to quicken their pace. Some at least. Those who were dragging mangled limbs were soon left further and further behind. Bryce and Maddy hung back with them.

"We have to do something," Maddy hissed.

"Like what?"

"Like something," Maddy shot back. "You're the one who used to always go on about your G.P.A."

School seemed like it was a hundred years ago, but that didn't mean he had forgotten how much he had crowed about his grades. He'd been like a peacock at the end of every semester. The memory made him feel like an idiot. The feeling was quickly swamped by the unsettling knowledge that with every step more of them would die.

With no idea what he was going to say or do, Bryce suddenly sprinted down the tracks, running to the head of the group. Putting his hands out, he stopped them. "We have to go back. Something bad is about to happen."

"Something bad?" a woman asked. Her features were obscured by the dust and grime clinging to her; the only thing that set her apart from the others was that she wore a man's yellow slicker over her winter coat. She had the insane idea that the zombie germs would slide right off the yellow vinyl. "Something like getting your face eaten off? Cuz that's what's gonna happen if we go back."

"Who are you guys?" a deep voice asked from within the crowd. A mountain of a man with cheeks like slabs of pork and three chins piled one on top of the other, pushed through. "You weren't on the train." His words came out slurry from a bloody mouth, and on closer inspection, Bryce could see he was missing almost all of his front teeth.

Sid, who had just finished the last of his whiskey and was eyeing the empty bottle unhappily, said, "We gotted run over by the train."

"Then you guys aren't a part of us," the lady in the slicker declared. Only the bloody-mouthed man nodded in agreement. Everyone else was still too shell-shocked to know who was who.

"It doesn't matter if we were on the train or not," Bryce told them. "We…none of us, can go on. What lies ahead of us is worse than what's behind us. If we go back, most of us will get past the zombies. The men will draw them to us on this track while the women and children escape along the other set. It's pretty simple and if we act…"

The mountain of a man spat at Bryce's feet. "Fuck that," he muttered and once more began heading for the golden lights. Most of the group began to move with him. "You're all going to die." It felt like a childish thing to say and the woman in the slicker responded in an equally childish manner by flipping him off with both hands.

"Ya think sometin's coming?" Sid asked before he tipped his bottle far back to get the last few drops of whiskey from it.

"Yep. Don't know what, but I have a guess."

"That crazy burnt chick?"

Bryce pictured her dragging her maimed body out of sight under the train, like a giant rat. She was out there, driven by hate and hunger, but had she gotten ahead of them so quickly? He wouldn't put it past her. Nodding he answered, "Her, maybe the other one. I'm not sure."

Sid looked ill. "They lived through all that?"

A shiver went up Bryce's back. "Yes. I saw the…" He had been about to say woman, but it was no woman. "I saw the burnt chick. She's hurt but that won't slow her down for long."

"Ya amember about that life debt ya owe me?" Sid eyed him close, looking for any sign that Bryce might try to weasel out of his obligation. Bryce nodded and Sid grinned. "That good. Ya seen what happens on *Star Trek* when people don't own up, right?"

Nerd as he was, Bryce had fallen in between the various *Star Trek* shows and had never watched a single episode, which was just as well since Sid was making things up concerning "life debts" as he went along. A few minutes before when they seemed to be moseying along nicely to the FBI, he'd been considering what sort of monetary value it might have.

"He owes me!" Victoria cried, shoving Sid back. "He owes me a child! I haven't forgotten and I never will."

"He owes me my life," Wilkes' last mercenary growled. He was barely holding on at this point. He kept blinking trying to focus his eyes and he had begun to feel a strange urge to sniff the people around him. He could smell their sweat and wanted to simply give a lick to their flesh. A strange thought kept running through his head: humans were the only animals that salted themselves.

The merc stumbled past Victoria who flinched back. "I'm in this mess because of you. You and her and him." He pointed vaguely in Maddy's direction. "You guys just shoulda said yes."

"Maybe," Bryce replied, without looking the merc in his darkening eyes. "Probably." If he had, none of them would be standing there, trapped in the dark tunnels. There was no getting around that painful truth.

"Ain't no maybe, probably," the merc insisted. "You did all this, you little shit. You don't say no to Daniel Magnus."

Victoria, with her hands covering her face, stepped up and shoved him away. "No one cares what you have to say. I want to hear from Bryce. He had a bad feeling when we came down here. We didn't listen to you and now look where we are. What's your feeling say now?"

"Not to go on."

"We can't go back," Nichola said. "There's a shit ton of 'em back there. You can hear 'em right?" The gibbering and the moaning was growing louder as they stood there.

"It doesn't matter," Victoria said. "Him and the fat…" Maddy was no longer the "fat chick." She was three inches taller and although she wasn't exactly slim, she was getting there fast. Victoria grimaced and amended her words to: "Him and her are different than us. They're changing and…and one of the changes is like ESP or something. We need to listen to his feelings."

Everyone stared. Bryce shrugged and said, "We shouldn't go on."

Nichola snorted, "That's it? We shouldn't go on? Fuck. Try a little harder. You know, search your feelings and all that shit."

"It doesn't work that way," Maddy snapped. "It just comes to us. It's not magic. There are no signs from the heavens that point…"

Far down the tunnel in front of them, the golden lights began to flicker, then they went out all at once. A second later a high, wailing scream ripped up the tunnel from behind them. Sid and Nichola looked concerned, but the rest of them clung to each other. They had heard that scream before and knew that it was coming from one of the weird little zombies that scouted for the demons.

"Okay, maybe this ESP stuff is real," Griff said, thankful that the dark hid the shaking in his hands. "We still need to do something and we need to do it now."

Again, everyone looked at Bryce, and that included Maddy, which was infuriating, but understandable. If he could look to someone else, he would have. *There's always God.* This would've been a laughable thought two days before. He had been a firm atheist, back when he had the world by the throat, back when he laughably thought he was the master of his own destiny.

Over the last forty-eight hours, he had begun to realize that God might be his only hope.

Of course, the city was strewn with the corpses of a million people, many of whom had believed the same thing. Were their deaths part of "God's plan, too?" Bryce couldn't know. He just knew he needed help. His own plan of going back and trying to fight through would result in at least half of them dying and that included himself.

For a brief moment, he looked up at the ceiling of the tunnel, wishing he knew a prayer that would help in this situation. As far as he knew zombies had been excluded from the Bible. With the dark, his eyes were wide open and it was in them that he felt the air around them move. It was less like a breath and more like a pulse...and there it was again. And again. "What is that?"

"What is what?" Griff asked, only to be shushed by Maddy.

She too was staring upwards as the pulsing grew. She put her hand on the damp wall. It vibrated under her hand like a car might under the influence of an over-sized stereo with the bass cranked to the max.

"Bombs," she whispered. The moment she said this, she heard the rumble of explosions. A second later, Bryce heard it as well. Two seconds after that, the others heard them too. Maddy turned her head, her eyes tracing invisible lines on the wall. "They're dropping west of us." The moment she said this she felt another change in the air—a tiny puff that built into layers. It was a plane heading their way and at great speed. "I think I know what's going to hap…"

The plane rocketed overhead, having released its payload of thousand-pound bombs seconds earlier. The bombers were targeting masses of the dead, and half a block from where Maddy stood with her eyes wide, hundreds of zombies were pouring down through one of the grates in the sidewalk. Dozens had already dropped down when the bomb struck with a brilliant, but hellish black and orange light.

In the tunnel, they were suddenly blinded as fire roared down the tracks. Framed against the fire was the group of limping refugees a hundred yards away. In front was the woman in the slicker. As the others turned and ran, she stood frozen as the flames swept right up to her. They melted her slicker and set her hair ablaze. Blind and screaming she fled, lighting the tunnel as the flames from the bombs winked out as quickly as they had come.

What came next was worse than the explosion and the fire. The roof of the tunnel began to collapse in a long wave as more bombs fell.

Everyone turned to run. Everyone but Bryce. He stood in their path, knowing that it was too late to run. They had missed their chance to run from this and now they were going to pay the price.

Chapter 41

Bryce grabbed Maddy and threw her bodily to the side where the tracks ran almost to the wall. Then he was sprinting along the rails, his nerve endings uselessly screaming to the point they felt electric. He was well past the need to sense danger, especially as he was racing *towards* where the ceiling was collapsing as more bombs hit.

"To the side!" he yelled, pushing faceless people to the wall as he ran past. He let his sword drop to give him more speed. He practically flew down the tracks, but he couldn't out-race the bombs. Just as he made up the gap between the two groups, there was a flash of white light as a blast of super-heated air roiled over him, whipping his hair back. It was hurricane in its force and it stopped him dead in his tracks. The next thing he knew a writhing creature plowed into him. It felt like a child and he shoved it at the wall and pushed on, fighting the blazing wind and the torrent of dust and debris it carried.

Three steps on, he found two people huddled on the tracks. He screamed for them to move and heaved them out of the way just as another bomb struck somewhere above them.

It felt like a hot hand crushed him down to the ground, which no longer felt solid as the earth beneath him lifted and undulated like a wave. This scared him more than the bombs and he knew it would be suicide to go on; he'd be lucky to save himself.

With the roof disintegrating above him, he started crawling over broken slabs of concrete heading in the direction he hoped the wall lay. In the swirling dust, he found a body. Alive or dead, there was no time to find out. He began dragging it along, only to come across another—this one's head was crushed beneath more concrete. He left it and kept going only to find yet another body; that of a child.

Feeling sick, he took the child in one arm and went back to pulling the other person to the shelter of the wall. It was ugly grey concrete, sticky with who knew what and smelled of piss. Still, it held up even as unnerving cracks ran along it as more explosions shook the ground. He huddled against it, shielding the two bodies with his own as bomb after bomb struck. The Air Force was releasing its arsenal on the city.

The five-hundred pounders had a distinctive *crack* to them and split the earth like a knife, while the thousand-pound bombs *fwoomped* into being and turned cement into ash in a blink. From where Bryce crouched in the darkness beneath the world, cluster munitions sounded like popcorn.

The last explosion defied all the rest in size and scope. It shook the ground for a minute straight and sucked the air from Bryce's lungs. He feared it had been a nuclear bomb and that with every breath he was breathing in radioactive fallout. If so, there was nothing that could be done.

Eventually, the earth stopped shaking, and Bryce pushed himself up, grimacing as he did. Somewhere along the way, he had lost a chunk of flesh from his left arm. Surprisingly, it wasn't bleeding nearly as badly as he expected and was already clotting. But there was blood all around him in an iron-smelling pool. Most of it came from the child he had saved. A falling rock had knocked him unconscious, while a second had nearly taken off his hand. It was hanging by a bit of flesh and a white line of tendon. From his torn arteries, dribbled the last of his blood. He had bled out with Bryce huddled over him, doing nothing.

"That's Ryan," Audrey Brooke said in a bone-weary voice. She was the other person Bryce had dragged away from the tracks. Blood tricked from her blonde hair and more stained her shoulder and ran down one arm. She had no idea why she was hurting or really where she was. The last thing she remembered were the lights going out. She knew Ryan, however.

"He lived in my building. Him and his mom and dad. He was a good kid. I babysat him a few times and he was really a good one. When you get a boy, you never know what you're going to get. But he was good." A tear worked its way through the grime on her cheek and dropped to her chest. "His mom was with him..." She tried to look around but a searing pain stopped her. "Did another train get us?"

"No. Bombs." Ignoring his own pain, he stood and dug his fists into the small of his back. There was diffused grey "light" that filtered down from the broken ceiling of the tunnel. Within it, he could see that a few others were getting to their feet as well. "Can you stand?"

Audrey twisted a little, grimaced in pain, and then slumped, looking down at herself in horror. "I can't feel my legs. Jesus. Mister, I can't feel my legs."

"No? Maybe it's a spasm or a pinched nerve." Bryce was grasping for straws as he knelt back down to inspect her wound. Gently he rolled her over and saw that the lower part of her coat was torn open and there was a cascade of tiny downy feathers. "There's no blood," he said, hoping this was a good sign. She was skinny and as he lifted her coat and shirt, he saw the ridges of her vertebrae clearly. They started off all in a line, neat as dominoes; however, at the base of her spine they were crushed and mangled.

To the right of her spine, in soft area beneath her ribs and above her hip, the flesh was so purple as to appear black. He touched it, and felt the warmth and knew that her kidney had been destroyed and that she was bleeding internally. A shiver racked him. She was going to die. Her only chance to live was if they crawled out of the rubble and found a hospital across the street with a fully equipped operating room ready to go and a surgical team on standby.

Without that, she would linger in excruciating pain for a few hours, if she wasn't eaten alive by the undead, that is.

Bryce wanted to make an excuse and leave as fast as he could. There was only one right thing to do with Audrey, but the thought of it was sickening. He lifted slightly, hoping to see Maddy, hoping she would be safe and sound…and ready to murder another young girl. But she was nowhere in sight and could be in trouble herself.

We're all in trouble, Bryce thought. The bombs had probably killed thousands of zombies, and also left millions untouched. They would come crawling over the destruction sooner rather later and when they found Audrey…

He swallowed loudly, took a shaky breath, and asked, "Is your mom or dad here with you?"

Her frightened eyes went glassy. "They never came home from work the other day. They left and I didn't come out of my room, and I didn't say good bye or nothing." Fat tears formed from nothing and fell onto her cheeks. "Is it bad?"

"Yeah." *It's so bad that there's nothing I can do about it but cave your head in with a rock.* He bit that back and wished himself out of the tunnel. He wanted to be anywhere else but right there.

She looked around at the remains of her world and the tears came harder and yet she didn't blubber and her chest didn't hitch. The numbness in her legs felt like it was spreading and that was a good thing in her mind. Maybe she would just fall asleep and wake up in heaven. That would be good.

But she wanted to live, too. She wanted to have her legs back. She wanted to run. She wanted to go back to when she was a kid when she was the terror of the neighborhood, racing around the cars stuck in traffic and laughing.

One look at Bryce killed the image. She saw the pain in his eyes; it had nothing to do with any real hurt.

"You can't save me?" He shook his head. "And I'm going to die?" His eyes slid away as he nodded. "No matter what?" This time his chin barely lifted. They were silent while all around them the tunnel filled with sounds: rocks crumbled and fell, dirt sifted down in a sighing rain, grunts and groans, and little cries of pain came from the darkness.

"They will be coming soon," he said. A part of him wished zombies would come creeping out of the thousands of new crevices right then. He would be forced to act without hesitation, without thought, without the guilt filling his insides.

She began to cry harder now and he realized that all he was doing was prolonging their misery.

"What do you want me to do?" he asked.

"Can you make it so it…so it doesn't hurt?"

Bryce was no expert at killing and for a moment his mind went to chemicals and poisons that supposedly induced a quick, painless death. They had none of these. He didn't even have his sword; it was lost somewhere in the rubble. All he had were his bare hands and some rocks.

Regardless, he nodded a vision coming to him: *He held a chunk of cement like a football as he cocked his arm back, but instead of throwing it, he slammed it…*

"Yeah," he said in a broken whisper. All the saliva in his mouth had dried up leaving a mucus paste. "Do…do you want to pray or something?" She nodded and turned away to stare at the wall. While she mumbled a convoluted prayer that seemed to meander over a score of topics, he found a chunk of cement. It was shaped somewhat like a football and when he picked it up, he was shocked by a moment of revulsion as his little vision came back to him.

When she had gone on for a minute and didn't seem like she was wrapping it up anytime soon, he touched her shoulder. "It's time."

The shoulder under his hand shook as she began crying harder. He waited, expecting her to give him permission, but she only cried. "Fuck," he whispered. He held the chunk of cement like a football as he cocked his arm back, but instead of throwing it, he…hesitated with it held high above her. Suddenly, it was Bryce the weakling holding the rock.

He was plenty strong enough to kill her; he simply lacked the internal strength to do what had to be done.

Audrey proved to be his superior. "Do it," she said. "Be quick."

Bryce the weakling slammed the rock down. And she did not die. Thankfully, she was knocked unconscious. He didn't know what he would've done if she had turned to look at him with a look of disdain. He lifted the rock again and brought down onto her temple with crushing force.

Or so he hoped.

He couldn't look at her. "I'm sorry." He didn't know who he was apologizing to exactly. It wasn't to God. It almost felt to Bryce that God was behind all of this, as if he were testing Bryce, personally.

"And I'm failing." He stumbled away from Audrey's corpse without looking back. There was no looking back; he was on the verge of vomiting and knew he would lose the dark stew churning in his stomach if he saw his handiwork. The rocks tumbled under his feet as he worked his way to where the tracks lay mostly buried. There he stood, bent over, gasping and the acid taste of his vomit was on his tongue when he spied something dull and metallic grey with in the rubble.

"My sword."

Taking the hilt and sliding it out with a ringing sound calmed his stomach amazingly—but he still didn't look back.

In front of him, his battered group was slowly climbing to where the tracks had once been. Every one of them sported new cuts and fresh bruises, all save Maddy, who was unmarked and the thirteen-year-old boy who had been too slow and had been crushed. His sneakered feet stuck out from beneath a strangely shallow pile of rocks. Just enough rocks to kill him had landed on him, and no more.

Bryce was still staring, when Griff said, "We have to help the wounded. We'll set up a triage down by the wall. Partner up. It'll make the work go…"

"Fuck that," Wilkes said, interrupting. "We have our group right here. I say we go on while we still can. Those fucking zombies will be here in no time and then what? What good will your little triage do you? Besides, they wanted to be their own group. I say screw 'em."

Sid shrugged at this, Nichola and the diseased merc nodded, Maddy looked too dazed to come to a decision and Victoria turned her face to Bryce. "What do your powers say?"

"I don't have powers, but it feels…" Dirty. Dishonorable. Immoral. "Wrong in some way." *More wrong than cracking open a girl's head like an egg? You know if we stay to help there'll be a lot more eggs to crack.* "Yeah," he muttered under his breath. Louder, he said, "I don't need powers to know we aren't safe here. At the same time, we lack, well everything to protect the weak. We should allow anyone who can walk to come with us."

"And everyone else?" Wilkes asked.

Bryce pictured himself kneeling in the gloom, a hand gripping his hoodie as he raised another rock. He squeezed his eyes shut and when he opened them again, it was to stare down the tunnel, into the darkness. "Zombies are coming. I'll take care of them. You guys figure things out."

Hefting his sword, he walked down the tracks. Someone would have to defend them. It was necessary for their survival, so why did it feel as though he was failing yet again?

Chapter 42

After the explosions, the dead were jarred into aimlessness. The air was thick with dust, disguising the scent of the survivors. Their ears, not great to begin with, rang with echoes from the explosions and in the shadows an injured person and a zombie looked a lot alike.

Bryce knew there would be a time limit on this period of inaction on their part and the weaker part of himself cried out to run while he could. The streets had to be far worse than the tunnels, and the zombies either blasted into bits or concussed into drooling manikins.

He could be at the Federal Plaza in ten minutes of hard running and then his living nightmare would be all over. It was such an alluring idea that he peeked back at the others. They were mere shapes nosing around the broken ground; they wouldn't notice him slink away.

A voice whispered up out of his soul asking, *What about Maddy?*

"Of course, I'd let her come. And Griff, too."

And what about your promise?

"Promise?" Even though it had only been made ten minutes before, he had already forgotten the promise he had made to Victoria. He pictured Tessa's mangled leg and suddenly he found he couldn't stand any longer. He dropped down on a rock with his sword across his knees.

"I want to be done with this," he said. Physically, he was still strong—hungry maybe, but still strong and able to go on. Mentally, he was exhausted by the endless running and fighting. Being surrounded by so much death was bringing him down.

Just then someone behind him cried out in misery. It was a cry from the soul and he knew someone had found a loved one crushed beneath a rock. His shoulders slumped, but only for a few seconds. He was not the only who had heard the sound. The dead were no longer so aimless.

A sigh drained from his chest, while he ran a finger over the sword. It was three and a half feet of dull steel and as such, it was only a step up from a heavy stick. He glanced around for something to use as a whetstone and realized he was sitting on a perfect rock. Kneeling next to the rock, he slid the blade across it at an angle. Using an entire rock like that felt strangely right. He was able to bring to bear the strength in his shoulders and back to really create friction.

But was it making the blade sharper? "It can't make it any duller," he said and slid the sword over the rock again. The metal let out a gritty sigh that caused the closest of the zombies to shift in his direction.

Bryce kept working until the thing was only feet away, then he leapt at the creature, aiming the now glittering edge of the blade at its neck. The result was disappointing. The zombie, a blank-eyed, ragged woman whose one arm was stretched out to him, was skinny. Her head should've popped right off and rolled down the craggy slope. Instead, the blade bit three-inches deep and lodged in her cervical spine.

The metal severed her spinal cord and she dropped in a revolting manner. It was as if her limbs had become soft rubber and she slithered into a pile at his feet. Working the blade back and forth freed it. He sighed and went back to the grindstone.

A minute later, the next zombie arrived, laboring over the rocks. It was a big, meaty creature and Bryce decided against testing the blade on it. Instead, he picked up a rock the size of his head and smashed it into the zombie's forehead, sending it sprawling backwards. It fell into more of the creatures, knocking a couple down.

A third came up a second later. It too was thick-necked, but that was okay since there were now a dozen zombies on his little hillock, plenty to choose from.

Fifty yards away, Maddy's eye caught the flash of metal and she paused as she was about to pull back a rock. Bryce was swinging a sword, hacking it into the skull of a charging zombie. Fear for him crept into her heart. There were so many of them! And for some unknown reason, he was letting them get too close.

"Does he want to die?" Sid asked. So far he had moved only a few rocks, picking them up and carrying them off into the dark. At the speed he worked, it would be a week before they uncovered all the bodies. He wasn't the only one whose heart wasn't in the task.

"Maybe," she told Sid. She wanted to go to Bryce's side and fight. She'd rather risk death than have to kill another innocent person.

Of the other group, only eight had been unhurt and standing when they came up. Together, they had quickly uncovered eleven other people; three of whom were dead and three more in the process of dying. Of the remaining five, only one couldn't walk.

Not far away, a woman sat next to her injured husband. She had found him deep beneath a pile of debris and had singlehandedly dug him free only to discover a huge hunk of his thigh had been ripped violently open. He couldn't put weight on the leg and at two-hundred and twenty pounds, he was far too big to carry through a city crawling with zombies. They all knew it.

"I'm staying with you," the woman kept saying to her man and by the fervent look in her eyes, she meant it.

No one knew what to say or do. They went back to digging with even less enthusiasm and, a minute later, when they uncovered the mountain of a man and discovered him to be crushed flat, the will of the searchers broke. There was only the question of what to do with the wounded man.

"I was against looking for them in the first place," Wilkes said and walked away, heading for where the rubble reached up to a hole in the ceiling of the tunnel.

"Just kill 'em," the diseased merc muttered. "It's all they deserve."

"We aren't going to kill anyone," someone in the darkness announced.

Nichola scoffed, "Then you can deal with them," and went to join Wilkes as he mounted the rubble. Victoria, Sid and a few others followed after.

Griff sighed. The long journey, along with the dust had aged him. He looked forty-five instead of twenty-eight. "We ask them what they want and we do our best to carry it out. That's what we would all want."

Of the five who were alive, two were unconscious and killed quickly, one asked to be killed, one couldn't make up her mind, and the last was the man with the injured thigh said, "Get her out of here and then kill me." His wife threw herself over him and blubbered. There was no time for this. Already Bryce was being forced back by the dead. He laid them out one after another, but always there were more.

Griff tried to haul the woman back, but she clung to her husband all the more fiercely, her long nails digging in. It was an ugly battle of wills that was won by the merc. He had found a railroad tie. It was a brute of a weapon handled by a brute of a man. "Get back, bitch!" he snarled, a second before swinging the hunk of wood at her husband's head.

No one had time to react, including the woman. The railroad tie smacked off her shoulder before glancing off the man's cheek, leaving a tarry gash. He grunted in pain, she screamed in anguish, and the merc swung the railroad tie a second time, again hitting her. Her arm took most of the blow, but her husband had his nose smashed, so that it was turned sideways.

The merc went to swing again and this time, Griff was able to pull the woman away before she was hit again. He wasn't able to turn her away quick enough, and she got to watch her husband get smashed a third time. Then Griff rolled her away and wrapped his arms around her head and squeezed. It looked as though he was trying to suffocate her, but in truth he was trying to drive out the sound of the railroad tie thudding again and again into her husband's skull.

"Enough!" Maddy screamed after the fourth hit. The murderous attack had taken her by surprise and left her flat-footed. Now she threw herself forward and grabbed the bloody hunk of wood as the merc brought it back for another strike. "Stop! You've done enough."

He stared down at the body, half in revulsion over what he had done and half in hunger over the freshness of the blood.

No one else looked at the deformed body. Stunned, they turned away and limped off. The rescue had ended in death.

Griff hauled the woman up, still crushing her in his arms. She sobbed against him as they followed the others. Only Maddy and the merc were left. In her hand was her climbing axe. Her hand grew damp around the handle as she eyed the back of his head…she targeted it. He was sick with the virus and had to be killed; the sooner the better. Because he was so big, she would have to be quick and precise, unflinching. Her hand went back.

"That was wrong," he said, confusion in his voice. "That was wrong and it was also right. It had to be done. Some things have to be done for the good of everyone." He turned and caught her with her axe raised. "It had to be done," he said again.

"Yeah," she answered, as her hand came down. He wasn't wrong. If he hadn't killed the man, who would've? Maddy had killed a girl who was halfway in the grave, but the man had been big and strong, still full of life. A broken leg shouldn't warrant the death penalty—Maddy wouldn't have been able to kill him.

Maybe Griff might've done it, and maybe not. He had no weapon, and perhaps that had been on purpose. You can't kill anyone without a weapon.

Had it not been for the merc they would all still be there, staring at each other waiting for someone else to do the right thing.

This was still flicking through her mind when he stepped towards her. She sucked in her breath, afraid that he was about to attack her, but he just walked past. For a fleeting moment she considered striking him down. *It has to be done!* That was a fact, but she hesitated, knowing how dishonorable it would be to attack him from behind. *But why did that suddenly matter,* she wondered.

When it came to honor, she felt hers fell within the normal range. She would never steal a penny from anyone but had no problem grossly "fudging" her taxes. She was kind to strangers, unless they were in a car then she had no problem verbally abusing them over the least traffic infraction, real or imagined. She would never strike a person unless provoked, that was true, but the merc was quickly becoming an un-person and his death had to happen sooner or later, so why did it matter if she…

"You coming?" the merc asked, breaking in on her thoughts. "Your boyfriend ain't gonna last much longer."

"He's not my boyfriend." He wasn't listening. His back was to her once more. Over his shoulder she could see Bryce flailing about with his sword, looking a lot like his old self. Actual combat was exhausting and this was doubly true of hand-to-hand. Against one opponent a fight was draining enough, against three or four at a time, it was a wonder he had lasted as long as he had.

"Bryce!" she called softly to him. "It's time to go."

He turned and she thought he would run, but the best he could manage was a staggering trot. It was faster than the dead, barely.

Maddy followed after the merc, who stumbled constantly over the loose rocks. He would send some tumbling at her; sometimes she could dodge them and sometimes she couldn't. She was good and bruised by the time Bryce caught up to her. His chest was heaving and he was speckled with dark blood.

The dead were closing in. They didn't care about bruised shins or broken knee caps. All they cared about was dragging Bryce down and filling their empty bellies with his warm flesh.

Maddy set her climbing axe among the rubble and picked up the largest rock she could throw. Two-handed, she lifted it up over her head, and then heaved it down into the upturned face of the closest zombie. With a satisfying crunch, its cranium was dented in five inches. It went toppling down to knock three others from their feet.

She plastered two more of the creatures before fighting her way almost to the top of the slope. When she was only feet away, the broken asphalt crumbled and she slid back a few feet. Afraid that one of the undead was close enough to grab her, she twisted around, ready to fight. They were having a worse time of it than she was and the closest was twenty-feet down.

There was little light in the tunnel, and yet her eyes picked out the body of the man the merc had killed. It lay sprawled in a pile of rocks. Seeing it made her feel unclean and weak. And wrong, as well. There had been a right thing to do in all of this and she had failed to find it.

A strong hand caught the strap of her pack and before she knew it she was being hauled into a new world.

The old world had been bad enough: People hiding in locked buildings, each one a weakly held fortress; abandoned streets empty save for the armies of the dead, and the tens of thousands of cold unmoving and unmovable cars; the strange quiet, broken only by a moaning wind. That world had been eerie, frightening and dangerous beyond belief.

Maddy stared about at this new world with her jaw hanging slack. The dark, shadowy street they had climbed up to didn't belong in New York. It belonged in some alternate universe where everything was backwards and nothing made sense.

"Is this shit Broadway?" Sid asked of the cratered smoking street.

Nichola shrugged. The street itself was unrecognizable. Warped and burnt pieces of cars were everywhere. Half a Tesla jutted from the second floor of the building across from them, while the remains of a bus leaned upright over them forming a surreal ceiling.

Every building in sight had been affected by the bombings. Gone were the sleek steel and glass monuments to a modern world. In their place were pillars of fire, sometimes rising fifty stories into the air. Those that weren't in flames bore craggy gaping wounds. Burning paper and shards of glass rained down from above, but this was a new hell and other things fell that had most of them turning away in horror.

People were jumping from some of the burning buildings.

The sound they made when they hit—like a head of rotting cabbage thrown on the floor—drained the energy and soul from the group. Maddy's knees trembled and if she'd had a pistol she might've stuck it in her mouth. She alone *knew* what was coming next. Her dream flowered into her mind. The white blast, the searing heat vaporizing the buildings, the nothingness that followed—all of it was set against almost this exact backdrop.

In her dream, the city was utterly dark, as if civilization itself had been extinguished. But just then there were still lights around them. Down a side street, orange neon glowed invitingly over a Japanese restaurant, high up in the untouched buildings frightened people peeked out of windows, and amazingly, despite the horrendous destruction, there was still a crosswalk sign working across from them. Its white light outlined a walking man.

There's still time, Maddy thought. Then, as if the very thought triggered it, the sign changed.

Its red light showed an angry red hand. It flashed at her, blinking out a countdown, and she *knew*.

Chapter 43

"What is it?" Bryce asked her.

Just like everyone else, Maddy had trembled and had gone pale seeing the bodies explode on impact with the street. However, the shudder that ran up her back a second later meant something else. She sensed something. His eyes were sharp and blue. Intensely blue, as if he were looking *into* her.

Do I tell him that we've fought all this way for nothing? she wondered. *That all this was a waste?*

She didn't know what he would do if she told him what was coming. The old Bryce would've given up. He had been just a normal person. Giving up sounded nice. Nice but wrong. "Nothing. It's just…nothing.

His eyes narrowed at the lie. He stepped closer, looking into her upturned face, trying to understand her new fear. It couldn't be danger. That was like sensing water while drowning in the middle of the ocean. They were surrounded by danger.

Zombies were still trying to clamber up from the subway tunnels behind them, and there were other half-alive corpses coming their way, struggling through the craters and the debris. Overhead in the night sky were bombers and more than one building in sight had collapsed.

But this feeling coming from her was different…it was worse…no, it was urgent. He felt the urgency coming off her like a fever.

It wasn't the demons doing this to her. Bryce took in a deep breath, drawing in more than just air around him. He breathed in something he couldn't articulate. It wasn't a smell or a taste. The closest thing to a name was one he couldn't give it. He refused. He was a scientist and the term *aura* was the furthest thing from science he could get.

Just the thought of it made him feel distinctly hippy-ish, and he had his own shudder.

Whatever the sense was, he trusted it. The two demons were not near, or if they were, their dark minds were not bent on killing him. But there was something out there. Bryce felt just an inkling of it, then it was gone, leaving a sensation akin to déjà vu.

"Behind ya," Sid said. Bryce glanced over his shoulder as one of the zombies emerged from the tunnel.

"Mine," the angry merc said and smashed the creature with his railroad tie. He grinned at the blood.

Sid rubbed his head as he eyed the zombie rolling back down into the darkness. A wicked hangover was just beginning to make itself felt and there was only one cure. "Maybe you can put that zombie killing to good use. Come on, I need a drink." While everyone else huddled in the street not knowing where to go or what to do, Sid and the merc tromped down the Japanese restaurant. He had a passion for sake and wearing silk kimonos over bare flesh. At the moment, he would settle for just the sake.

They passed Wilkes, who had been off by himself, hissing into a radio and looking angrier than usual. How the radio hadn't been destroyed after everything they had been through was a mystery even to him. He glared at the two men, but didn't try to stop them. The one was more interested in drinking than surviving and the other had no future. If they were both killed, it would be no skin off Wilkes' back.

Griff had sat down only to pour the rocks from his shoes. Now, he stood, grimacing as he shoved his knuckles into the small of his back. "We have to get moving. It can't be much further."

No one moved, except Nichola who had been run over by a train and had been buried alive without being so much as scratched. She was quite ready to ditch the walking wounded and get gone. This might be considered cold, but in her mind it was only a matter of basic math: if they all made it to the FBI building, her chances of getting one of the few spots on their choppers would be slimmer than if only a couple of them made it.

"It's like ten minutes from here," she lied. It was a fifteen-minute walk on a Sunday in late fall when all the tourists had gone home. With the streets blown to shit, people raining from the skies and zombies popping up out of the blue, there was no telling how long it would take the entire group. If it were just her and Bryce, like she wanted, they would be there in no time.

"Hold on," Wilkes said, hurrying over. "We need a new fucking plan. South is out of the question. We can't see it from here, but everything downtown has been obliterated worse than all this. So we're going to go west to the Hudson."

"Obliterated? How do you know?" Then Bryce heard the whirring of the drone. It was a different machine. This one was sleek and black. Bryce wondered if this was the cause of the odd feeling he'd been having.

Wilkes thrust the radio away. "Our guy got a visual. They bombed the crap out of the city to the south. There's nothing left. Our only choice now is to try to make it off the island, and the way I see it, the only way to do that is by boat. Supposedly, there's boats coming down the Hudson from upstate. If we can snag one of them we'll be in business."

"By snag, you mean steal," Griffin said.

"With you coming with us, *Agent*, it won't be stealing. We'll commandeer it. It'll be for the greater good. Right? We have to get these two to the proper authorities." He gestured towards Maddy and Bryce. "They're fucking medical marvels."

Nichola stepped forward, her chin set high. "And the rest of us? We getting on this boat?"

Wilkes looked down at her, pretty sure he had never seen her before. To him, she was just another stray they had picked up along the way. "If there's room, maybe. It all depends on how well you do following orders. You can start by handing over the bat."

Instead of putting it into his outstretched hand, she cocked it, ready to knock the shit out of him. "Get your own."

"Strike one," he said, dismissively. He looked around at the destroyed buildings. "We're going to need a bullhorn and a spotlight. Probably some…"

"We're not going with you," Victoria said, her voice strident and high. She pointed at Bryce. "Me and him are going to Federal Plaza. He promised to help me." She eyed Bryce hard, ready to jump down his throat if he even thought about trying to back out of their deal.

When Bryce nodded, Wilkes threw his hands in the air. "Are you kidding me? Look, Bryce, you don't get it. They described everything south of Canal Street as hell on earth. They bombed the fuck out of it. There's nothing there!"

"If that's the case, we'll figure things out then. But you can go get your boat. I bet a bunch of these people will go with you."

Wilkes' dark eyes glared at the battered group, most of whom wouldn't be able to stand on their own. "Shiiit," he drawled, stretching the word out so that every one of them got their own taste.

"I'm going south as well," Griff said. "My partner may be down there. And for all we know the field office may be untouched. If not, like you said, we figure things out."

"Your partner is fucking dead!" Wilkes snapped. "He and everyone…" In mid-sentence he raised a fist and shook it as he bit down on the torrent of curses that wanted to come pouring out of his mouth. Before they could, he turned and marched furiously off. He didn't go far, stopping at the side street Sid had taken. With his teeth clenched hard and his lips pressed into a snarl, the burly mercenary stared at the red neon sign until the words: *Kyoto Bowl!* burned a temporary imprint into his retinas.

He was staring when the power failed in Manhattan and the city went dark. His anger was extinguished as quickly as the neon sign and like everyone else in the group, he looked around in wonder and fear at being thrown back into the Stone Age in the blink of an eye. Behind him, there were gasps and a few of them cried out softly. They edged in closer to each other and the few with weapons held them tighter.

"Fucking children," Wilkes spat. Unlike them, he did not fear the dark or the things in it, except the demons that is.

The power outage should've been expected. The possibility had been in the back of his mind, simmering there, bubbling up little flashes of the cold dark city, almost exactly how he was seeing it now.

A sigh escaped him as he realized how worthless his promised million dollars was. At this point, a million dollars wouldn't get him a ham sandwich or a seat on a canoe. "It's always been worthless," he muttered, realizing that Magnus had known this was going to happen all along and had fucked him from the very start. "But I still have cards to play."

He also had allies who were not insubstantial. He still had employees working the drones and the communications. He had his government contacts dating back twenty years, people who owed him. And as much as Magnus had dicked him over, he claimed to be an honorable man. Maybe that really meant something.

"Or maybe not."

Magnus might turn a blind eye, and Wilkes' government contacts might go deaf and pretend not to hear his pleas, and his few remaining employees might grow a brain and realize just how screwed they were, and that every minute they spent sitting

279

in front of their computer screens was a minute in which they weren't making their own escape. This was Wilkes' reality.

He couldn't trust any of them.

It made him shudder to realize that here, right in front of him, were people he would have to trust. He looked over the beaten down group. Most of them were sheep and would deserve the slaughter that was coming to them. On the flip side there was Agent Griffin Meyers; he might be a goody two-shoes, but he also had an in with the FBI. And there was Bryce and Maddy.

If anything or anyone made him nervous, it was these two. The changes they were going through were unnatural and there was no telling where they would lead—his mind flashed to that horrible burnt creature. Was that the end result of this process? It was possible. His role in all of this had been to watch over Bryce and Maddy, to keep them safe. The million dollars hadn't blinded Wilkes, it had made him cautious and he had asked the obvious: "Safe from what?"

Magnus had given him the cryptic reply, "Maybe from themselves. We shall see, won't we?"

He hadn't known exactly what would happen and Wilkes had been paid an obscene amount of money to babysit a science experiment, one that was still in the process of unfolding. One that *seemed* good on the outside. They were growing stronger by the hour. And that was a good thing and would remain so, right up until it stopped being a good thing. The list of scientific failures that started as bright lights was long and frequently sickening. Edison killing his assistant with X-rays—Marie Curie dying of radiation poisoning, the Stanford Prison experiment in which normal college kids were turned into veritable Nazis within days.

Wilkes was going to have a front row view of this train wreck, if he lived long enough. He hated the idea of being defenseless and worse, he hated the idea of having to depend on others for his safety. There was no getting around it—just then he needed the group more than they needed him.

"What I need is a gun." A gun would more than even things out. A gun would put him back on top. Until he got one…he forced a grin onto his face and walked to the group.

"You guys want to see what it looks like down south?" he asked. "Then let's do it. Let's move. The quicker the better."

There was no quick with this group. Bryce insisted they wait for Sid, who came back bleary-eyed a minute later, clinking from the bottles stashed in his coat. He stumbled more than before, but even drunk, he wasn't the worst of them. Most of the others could barely plod along. Griff limped and frequently massaged his lower back. Victoria had turned numb and walked like the zombies pursuing them. Maddy was distracted and stared at the western skyline where the buildings thrust upward like black teeth. They were like shark teeth, sitting over-crowded, one on top of the other.

It was not an easy walk by any measure. The street was an obstacle course of death. One lady found out the hard way that some of the bomb craters had no bottom but opened into a black subterranean world—she slid into one, screamed and disappeared forever. The mountains of rubble were no better. They shifted and crumbled under their feet— one man ended up being impaled on rebar. Luckily for him, it tore through his thigh without hitting a major vessel and he lived. Of course he had to be helped along which slowed them down even more.

Every step was treacherous.

Many of the buildings on either side leaned dangerously over them, threatening to collapse at any moment. Then there were the zombies that would appear suddenly out of the dark. For the most part the group was unarmed, but they could throw rocks of which there were plenty around them. A shower of rocks would slow or stop a single zombie, but when two or more attacked Bryce would have to race to each threatened point.

Each of these problems had to be dealt with by the little company and each would stop their already aggravatingly slow progress.

Wilkes led but grew so frustrated by the frequent stops that it was all he could do to maintain his fake smile. Walking next to him, bat slung on her shoulder, Nichola didn't bother to spare anyone's feelings. Being nice for the sake of being nice felt like a luxury and she didn't whisper when she talked about leaving the "Dead weight" behind.

She thought she would be safe when they got to the Federal Plaza. According to his earpiece, Wilkes knew she was going to be in for a rude surprise.

Eventually, the street they were on bent southeast and the nearer skyscrapers could no longer hide what Wilkes knew: there was no going forward.

Giant mountains of near impenetrable black smoke, a thousand feet high, stretched from east to west as far as the eye could see. Here and there within the smoke were red-gold fires. Because so many of these were hundreds of feet in the air, they made it seem as if volcanoes were erupting in downtown Manhattan.

Nichola stepped back, her mouth open and her eyes unblinking. She hadn't been born when the towers fell in New York, but she had seen the videos. The smoke from the terrorist attack had engulfed the southern part of the city. It was night and with the smoke it was hard to see, but she guessed that the destruction wrought upon the city by the Air Force was a hundred times worse.

The group straggled up two or three at a time. Each of them were staggered by the sight. Some wept. Some collapsed in place and sat there, shaking their heads in disbelief.

Victoria walked past everyone, shaking her head, her face broken by misery. She whispered, "No, no, no, no. They're dead. They're all dead."

Bryce should've gone after her, but he lacked the energy to drag her back or the emotional strength to deal with her. Groaning, he eased onto the dented remains of a car. A bomb had turned its windshield to glass dust, and yet a pair of baby shoes still hung from the rearview mirror. They had once been pink but were now grey. He sagged, exhausted. His sword arm felt like it was filled with lead. He didn't know what to do or even think.

Maddy sat down next to him, staring like everyone else. "I don't remember this. That's good, right?"

"There's nothing good about this," Griff said, easing down next to her. "Nothing."

"There's one thing good," Wilkes said. "We can be done with this. I told you there was nothing left. Your fucking quest is over, Bryce. The lady's kid is dead, and I bet your partner is as well Agent Shit-brains, and if he ain't, he sure as hell isn't down there."

Chapter 44

When Victoria Deitch came wandering back, looking like she was sleep walking through the rubble, she did not make eye contact with Bryce. She said nothing to the others and stood apart from them. Her eyes were drawn upward, but not to heaven. It was to the tall buildings that her squinting gaze was drawn; to the jumpers.

Very few of them screamed. They were resigned to their fate. Her lips counted silently how long it took them to fall: four seconds from the roof of a twenty-story building. Four seconds of terror—she could handle that.

Bryce watched her, feeling her pain. It came off her in waves. No one else cared; they all had their own pain to deal with. They stared at nothing as their minds tried to come to grips with their losses and their wounds. Bryce felt the dull ache of guilt. He tried to force it away. "It's not my fault," he lied to himself.

"We go west," Wilkes said, hands on hips, staring around as if he were talking to a platoon instead of a group of broken castoffs. "The Holland Tunnel isn't far and it will be our second option if we have an issue getting a boat."

This wasn't exactly true, he just said it to appeal to the weak-willed among them. Without a gun, he would rather swim across the river than attempt the tunnel, especially since he knew it had been subject to numerous bomb attacks. The Governor of New Jersey had done everything in his power to cut links with the city. Judging by the glow of fires in the west, it hadn't done him any good.

The idea that the roof of the pitch-black tunnel could collapse with him in it freaked Wilkes out to no end. Drowning was not his greatest fear, in fact he had heard it wasn't a bad way to go, all things considered. However, the idea of drowning in utter darkness was appalling to him.

"We'll break into self-supporting teams. I'll be leading with…"

"Not any time soon," Bryce interrupted. Although he was drawing on the last of his reserves—he felt the exhaustion in the core of his bones—he knew the others were worse off. Some wouldn't be able to make it another block.

Wilkes tried to remain composed at what was more than insubordination. In this situation, he was being stabbed in the back. He could literally feel his blood pressure inching up; he could feel it in his neck which he was sure was swelling. "A word," he demanded walking so close to Bryce's jutting knees that he knocked them with his arm.

Bryce sighed and slid from the car.

He followed Wilkes to the other side of the street where Wilkes tried more intimidation tactics by standing over him in the gloom, almost within kissing distance. "You're a scientist, right?"

They both knew he was. "World-renowned," Bryce said. It was something of a dig at his own once super-inflated ego. A year ago he had done research on a paper concerning genetic splicing and although his part had been small, there had been enough big names attached to the project that the paper was cited as having been written by "world-renowned scientists." From then on, those three words were a permanent part of his bio, including on his Facebook page. They embarrassed him now.

"Then you know about critical mass," Wilkes stated. "I doubt a quarter of the population of this city has turned zombie. But every fucking hour more and more people turn. Soon, they'll be swarming the streets like fucking ants. Then what, smart guy? How do we escape when there are five or six million of them all over the fucking place?"

"Yeah, alright," Bryce said, knowing that although Wilkes' use of the word "soon" was deceptive, he wasn't entirely wrong. By morning, it could very well be death to be seen on the streets. Still they had six or seven hours before the sun rose and the group was in desperate need of a rest. "We need an hour and then we'll go."

"Half an hour."

Bryce looked over the group. A half hour would be short for most but too long for a few. He doubted they would be able to will themselves back to their feet if they stayed where they were for even a few more minutes. "An hour," Bryce insisted. "An hour or nothing."

Wilkes started to swell in indignation, which Bryce ignored. He looked around hoping to see a hospital or at least another pharmacy. The group needed any medical help they could find. New York seemed to have a pharmacy on every block, but there were none right around them.

Food was next on Bryce's mind. They were next to an oyster bar, which he turned his nose up at. In the last day, he had eaten ten monstrous sandwiches and had gone through six pounds of lunch meat, another five of cheese and a half gallon of mayo; he couldn't imagine lugging around forty pounds of what were essentially rocks to come away with a pound of slimy oyster mucus-meat.

Next door was a "European" furniture store. None of it looked European. The beds were beds, the dressers were all dull black, but otherwise looked like dressers. Like every other store in sight, its windows were blown out but its cage was down. His eyes swept across to the other side of the street where there was another New York favorite: a pizzeria. Bryce was all about pizza when it was fresh and hot. Pulled cold and smushed from his pack three hours from then was not something he was looking forward to.

Bryce's stomach rumbled when he saw a sign askew where the window had been: *Heroes Cold and Hot!*

Its cage was down but not completely intact. There were no parks in the area and yet a scorched park bench, having been hurled an unknown distance by an explosion, was embedded in the metal slats. The cage itself had held, but had been pulled from its runner on one side, just far enough for a small man to squeeze through.

"One hour," Bryce said again to Wilkes before crossing to the pizzeria, where he discovered he no longer fell into the small man category. He had to take off his filthy pack to force himself through, managing to catch the hood of his now ridiculously tight jacket on the metal. The cloth held him tight until, in fury, he tore it almost in half ripping into the store.

Tossing the remains aside, he went to the counter, laid his sword across it and leapt easily over. The owner of the pizzeria had taken the time to close up his shop properly and Bryce had to search through sticky, sauce-flecked cabinets before he found everything he needed. The zombies and the rumbling jets faded into the background as he began making a sandwich that was roughly the size of a newborn.

"Only you would be thinking of your stomach," Maddy said as she eased through the gap in the gate. It was an even tighter fit for her but once through, she looked down at her torn sweater with satisfaction instead of anger. For once in her life, her clothes had torn across her bust instead of her stomach.

Grinning, she turned and realized that Bryce was making the sandwich, half-naked. The grin faded away as she stared at his broad shoulders, and sculpted pecs, and his bulging biceps…

Her cheeks went past pink and right to a medium rare red. Quickly, she turned away. She didn't see Bryce that way. Or she shouldn't see Bryce that way. For as long as she had known him, he had been an annoying dweeb who wouldn't stop chattering in her ear—like a little brother. Yes, a brother, not this muscular, chisel-chinned *man*.

She picked up a menu and studied it in the non-light, forcing her eyes down at the useless words. "Wasn't there a television show called the Naked Chef? Did he really cook naked? Must've been dicey when he made bacon."

"Hmm, bacon," he mumbled. He hadn't thought of adding bacon to the sandwich, but now that the idea was planted in his head, he dropped down to sniff in the chilled cabinets. "Ah yes!" he whispered, plunking a plastic container on the knife-scarred breadboard. Excitement turned to disappointment when he opened it and found what appeared to be bacon-flavored cat food.

He shrugged. Bits of bacon were still better than no bacon at all, and he rained them down across the length of the sandwich. When he glanced up, he caught Maddy looking at him. For some reason she turned away.

"What's wrong? You okay?"

She was flushed and nervous. It seemed odd, though Bryce had to admit it was an improvement over how she had been acting since they fought their way from out of the tunnels. Unlike everyone else who acted like they were being born again, she had come out like a baby deer, timid and shy.

"Yeah, I'm good," she said, without looking him in the eye. She pointed vaguely behind her. "I…we, Griff that is, wanted to let you know that we're setting up across the street in the furniture store."

For Bryce, the intense dark was more of a soft grey light and he could see the outlines of people shuffling into the store. With the dust they looked wizened and bent with age. Even the children with them seemed ancient.

She had the same sensation, except hers came with the unpleasant thought: *They're all as old as they'll ever be.* "Wilkes said you demanded an hour to rest? We can't wait that long."

Bryce was just in the process of crushing down on the enormous sandwich to make it manageable. He looked like he was giving it CPR. Pausing in mid-compression, he saw her fear was just below the surface.

Why? Where was this fear coming from? It was different. Sharper, more specific. His exhaustion limited his curiosity to the one look. Letting out a sigh, he leaned back from the sandwich.

"If you rush them, you'll lose more than you save," he told her. Her eyes shifted away; she didn't believe him. Too tired to argue, he sat on a flour-dusted box and tore a huge chunk of the sandwich off with gleaming white teeth. "Needs pepper," he said around the bite. It needed pepper to be perfect. He was too tired to care about perfect and the pepper sat on the counter untouched.

"Them?" Maddy asked. "You're still going on?"

He took another bite before answering. "It depends on her. I made a promise, but…" He took another bite. "But I think she'll be reasonable. Hmm. Maybe reasonable isn't the right word. Accommodating. That's the word. She's starting to realize her kid's dead and there's nothing we can do about it. She'll probably kill herself soon." But not yet. Moving like an eighty-year-old, she had followed the others into the furniture store. Bryce sighed around another bite.

Maddy had no comment about Victoria. Killing herself seemed reasonable given the circumstances.

Besides, she'll be dead soon one way or the other, Maddy thought, her mind going to the fiery image from her dream.

As he ate, she struggled with the entire idea that she'd had a vision in her sleep. If she mentioned it, he would laugh at her and she would deserve it. Their spurts of ESP were completely explicable. Their intuition was likely the result of their subconscious picking up on clues that were otherwise overlooked. It was entirely possible they had caught the smallest scent of the demon before entering the tunnel, and it was this that had triggered their "something bad was about to happen," feeling. And the oncoming train must've signaled its looming presence through the rails themselves.

Yes, at the time it had felt like true precognition, when in reality, it was simply a response to external stimuli.

The dream could be explained away just as easily. The nuclear option had to be on the table. It would be foolish if it wasn't. And a dream was a valid expression of that concern. And yet, Maddy *knew* it was coming. She knew it in her bones. She knew it with every fiber of her being.

It made sense to tell Bryce, to warn him of the danger that was coming their way, except he would give her that look of his, the one that always made her feel as if she were his inferior. He had given her that look for years, all through school. Whenever they butted heads, which was always, out would come the look. Back then she kept ready-made insults and acid-hot retorts at the ready to spit back in his face to make the look dissolve. She had none of these this time.

Fortunately, there was no reason to tell him. The great smoke mountains to the south had made it unnecessary. He would go west and she would make sure he hurried. "I'll go talk to Victoria. I agree with your assessment, she's beyond the denial stage." She started to leave, but turned back suddenly. "Make me a sandwich, will you? Just make it like a third that size and no mayo."

"No mayo?" This seemed like sacrilege.

To her as well, however the thought of a layer of gelled fat on her meat made her newly shrunk stomach turn over. "No mayo."

She left him shaking his head. "No mayo?" he said again as his hands flew. He sawed open a new hoagie, layered two thirds of it with more mayo than ever and left the last third distressingly dry. Next he began to apply meat to the sandwich as if he were roofing a house. Now four types of cheese.

When he got to the cheddar, he began to hum, happily, thinking this sandwich would be even better than the last one. "The good half that..."

He stopped suddenly, a cold feeling sweeping him. The hair on his arms stood on end. Something was coming. "Or it's already here." Leaving the sandwich, he leapt over the counter, grabbing his sword as he did. There he stopped and closed his eyes. This allowed him to concentrate on his other senses; he heard the back door open with the tiniest of creaking sounds. He caught the scent of cologne; it was being used to mask the thing's real scent. He felt the tremor under foot; something big approached.

Bryce tensed, raising his sword, crouching, ready to spring. There in the darkness of the backroom was the demon, taller than ever.

Chapter 45

The desire to run swept over Bryce and before he could stop himself, he had taken three steps towards the broken metal gate. Only the realization that the demon would catch him as he was desperately trying to squeeze through the crack kept him from running away like a coward.

Spinning back around he caught the demon's white grin shining from its dark face. It was already laughing at him.

Furious at his cowardice, Bryce slashed the air with his sword, whipping it up and around so that it sat poised slightly above his head and parallel to the floor. It was a classic kung fu movie move and he couldn't have said why he did it.

"Come on," Bryce snarled.

Instead of attacking, the demon, which only appeared as the outline of a shadow, paused in the darkness. It stood thirty feet away in a long windowless hallway that smelled of sour cheese and mouse droppings, and from there it appraised Bryce before coming forward, slowly, step by step. Just as it entered the cluttered front room, Bryce saw that its eyes glowed silver.

That was new.

It also seemed to have grown at least three inches in the last couple of hours. It filled the doorway.

Against it, Bryce had little more than his sword. It was better than the hunk of wood he had laughably called a spear, but not a lot better. His eyes flicked to the blade poised over his head. It was crusty with old blood and there were nicks all along its edge; though edge was a word that was grossly abused in this case. Whatever sharpness he had managed to bring out of the blade was long gone.

The sword suddenly seemed wholly inadequate.

A second later, when the demon drew its own sword, Bryce realized that the sword was far worse than inadequate. It was useless.

The demon had its sword slung on its back. It was a huge blade, five feet in length and a hand's breadth in width near the hilt. It gleamed with silver fire. The sword boggled Bryce's mind. Where had it come from and how did a zombie come to have such a weapon when Bryce only had this pathetic hunk of…

Bryce sucked in his breath as he realized that this was not *his* demon.

It…no, *he* stepped fully into the room. He was no demon, at the same time he wasn't wholly a man. He was huge, just a few inches shy of seven feet. And he was strong, his shoulders were even more massive than the demon's. Stranger still, his eyes were metallic silver and his scent wasn't that of cologne as he had first thought. He was simply aromatic in a way that was beguiling and pleasant…and weird.

Everything about him was weird.

His flesh was a dark brown, which was normal, but it was utterly smooth, completely without wrinkles or blemishes. He had the skin of a baby. His shoulder length hair was straight and dark. It wasn't black though. It was a dark forest green. To add to all of this, he wore grey clothing: boots, pants, shirt and cloak.

He's wearing a cloak, Bryce thought. *Who the hell wear's a cloak?*

His clothes, including the cloak, were made of light silk and rippled as he moved. Like Bryce, he was unaffected by the cold night.

"Who are you?" Bryce asked, sounding both rude and crude in his own ear.

"Who?" The question seemed to bring up old memories and he hesitated. "I am Fifteen-Zero-Three, but you may call me Grae-zier. I'm looking for Twenty-one-Six-One." His silver eyes glittered and Bryce read condescension in them. "You can't be him."

Bryce lowered his sword. "My name's Bryce. I don't know anyone named twenty-one whatever." Was Wilkes Twenty-one-Six-One? Was that his nickname or his call sign? Had this man been sent by Magnus to find him? If so, why? Bryce was afraid to ask, guessing that the answer wouldn't be good.

Grae-zier studied Bryce for an uncomfortably long time before he smiled. "I'm being foolish doubting him when he's proven correct time and again?"

"Magnus?"

"Of course, Magnus! He *knows*."

After a few seconds when Grae-zier didn't go on, Bryce sighed and asked, "He knows what, exactly?"

"Everything. Even about you and your defects. You're Twenty-one-Six-One. I thought you'd be more than this." He gestured at Bryce like he would a runty red-headed stepchild. "But you and that laughable excuse for a sword are perfect."

Bryce was suddenly embarrassed. Instead of sharpening his sword or even looking for a better weapon he had made a sandwich. The smell of the salami was strong on his fingers. Wiping them on his pants, he said, "I am perfect. Perfectly happy to never see Magnus again. Tell him that Bryce says to kiss his ass."

He had just started to turn to leave when he caught a flash of grey out of the corner of his eye. Instinctively he brought his sword up to block the blow he knew was slashing at him. His sword was truly pathetic and had Grae-zier really wanted to kill him, he could have.

Grae-zier destroyed Bryce's sword instead. The first strike with the great blade knocked the top six inches from the sword. The metal flew up into the air and was still going up when Grae-zier reversed the swing of his weapon and struck Bryce's sword a second time. Bryce blinked as the hunk of metal twirled towards his face. Before it could hit him and while he was still in mid-blink, Grac-zier snapped his blade back again.

In the space of a single second, he had hit Bryce's sword three times, reducing it to a stubby piece of pitted and bloody steel that could only be used now as an ugly butter knife.

"You would do well never to say another disrespectful word about Daniel Magnus again," Grae-zier growled. "And you would do well to realize that there are no more laws to protect you from your own stupidity."

Bryce could only glare in response and even that was pushing it. He was at Grae-zier's mercy. "What is it that you want from me?"

"You are to carry on southward and bring a message to the FBI. You are to explain to them that Magnus is their only hope. That he is the only hope that humanity has left."

"But he did this!" Bryce was a little sharp; a little too accusatory and Grae-zier's huge brown hand clenched into a fist. "That's what they're going to say," Bryce added quickly before he could be punched.

Grae-zier's hand relaxed. "They will say a lot of things. Some will be true, some not so true, and some will be lies. That is the way of humans, as *you* know." He made being human sound like an affliction. "Your job is to make them realize that the course they're on will be what destroys the human race for good."

"And what course is that?" It was a stupid question, but one he needed to ask. The idea of nukes being used had danced in and out of his consciousness for the last day. He hadn't had a dream like Maddy, but it was still an obvious chance.

"You don't know?" Doubt crossed over Grae-zier's heroic features. "I suppose I shouldn't be so surprised given how the twenty-one series is turning out so far." He shook his head to clear it and told Bryce what he already knew, "The government is planning on using nuclear weapons. They've deemed much of the northeast to be lost and will employ a scorched earth policy. *You* will continue south and *you* must stop them."

Bryce had expected him to say nukes, and that alone would have left him winded and shaken. He certainly hadn't expected to be told that the fate of millions of people depended on him. This stole his breath completely. He clutched his bare chest before collapsing onto a stool covered in cracked red vinyl. His eyes fell to the red, pink and white tablecloth. The checkered pattern blurred as he picked out individual grains of salt.

"I think you've got the wrong guy."

Grae-zier did not have the patience to be called wrong by the likes of Bryce. His metallic silver eyes narrowed. "You are Bryce Carter, Twenty-one Zero One. I don't have the wrong man."

"I'm him, I guess, but, but, but what you're asking is crazy. The FBI won't listen to someone like me. If you want them to listen, you should be the one to tell them!" The thought, suddenly so obvious, popped into his head. "They'll believe you and that's for certain. You're all…whatever you are."

"I am Grae-zier, one of the chosen. And I would go happily if that was Magnus' wish." He grinned suddenly. His teeth were perfectly white in his dark face. "I think I understand now why you were given this assignment in my place. You are changed but weak. I'm beginning to believe that what I perceived as a design flaw in the twenty-one series must've been Magnus' concept all along. Tell me, Bryce Carter, how would the government officials see me were I to deliver the message?"

It was an odd question. Wouldn't they see Grae-zier just as Bryce did: impossibly big, impossibly handsome, impossibly perfect?

Yes, of course they would *see* the obvious, but what would their reaction to Grae-zier be?

Grae-zier represented the unknown. "They'd be scared, though not like…" *Not like I was*, he had been about to say. "They'd be afraid that Magnus had created a superior race. A master race, if you will, one that wouldn't hesitate to enslave the rest of us. It's what they would do."

They'd be jealous as well. Grae-zier was different in a much, much better way. He made Bryce feel like a child. He made Bryce feel stupid and weak, and if he'd had a gun a moment before, he might have used it. The government had guns and they weren't used to being talked down to, something Grae-zier was guilty of. This sudden realization was something of a jolt. Grae-zier was not perfect. He was haughty, quick to anger, and condescending. He treated Bryce like a child and not in the way a father might, but like that of a loutish uncle.

If Grae-zier were to deliver Magnus' message, the nukes would fall for sure.

"I think I understand the situation," he said to Grae-zier.

"Unlikely. Still. I believe you will do what you have to, to keep them from using their nuclear weapons. Let them know that Magnus does have a vaccine for the plague. That is a fact."

It was a fact, Bryce read it quite clearly in his handsome face, but it also held an element of uncertainty in it. "He has a vaccine but hasn't used it yet, why? They'll ask."

Grae-zier stood back, tight-lipped.

Again, Bryce asked, "Why not?"

"I'm sure you'll come up with a plausible reason."

"Meaning you want me to lie for you?"

The silver eyes blazed with a light of their own and Grae-zier's knuckles stood out like a ridge of mountains as he gripped the hilt of his sword. For a moment Bryce thought Grae-zier was about to take his head off; however the man controlled his temper. "You will do what you have to keep them from using nukes. That is your mission."

"What if I can't?"

"Millions will die."

Bryce shifted uncomfortably on the cracked red vinyl. "They'll die anyway."

"Maybe." Grae-zier slid his sword away. "You do not have a full understanding of Daniel Magnus. He is far seeing. He knows what cannot be known. Trust in that and your fears will be diminished." Grae-zier's enormous hand came down on Bryce's shoulder. "Be strong and do not tarry."

He turned abruptly, causing his cloak to flare. Bryce jumped up. "Before you go. I need to know what this is all about. You and me and…" He bit back on Maddy's name. It felt wiser to leave her out of this. "And all this. What series are you talking about? What did Magnus do to us?"

Grae-zier took his time answering. "He gave us a gift. Inside each of us is greatness that's been locked away in our genetic structure since the dawn of time. Magnus has discovered a way to bring it out. With each successive series of tests, he strives to recreate more of God's original creation. I am of the Fifteen series. Sometimes the advances are greater, other times smaller. Sometimes there are no changes at all…or there are backwards steps. There was great hope with the Twenty-one series."

"Was?"

"Like I said, sometimes there were backwards steps." He gestured at Bryce: Exhibit A for his example of genetic mistakes. "At least you're alive."

After everything he had gone through, Bryce did feel lucky to be alive, though he was sure Grae-zier was suggesting more. "Meaning what?"

Grae-zier's eyes shifted away. From what little Bryce knew of him, he wouldn't lie, but he might leave out important details if he felt there was a need. In this case he came right out and said, "So far, the trial has not gone well. Of sixty-two volunteers, only you and the woman with you have managed to survive."

"Sixty dead?" Bryce clutched his chest, wondering if he was even then on the verge of a massive heart attack or a stroke. He wanted to ask how the others died but a new thought struck him. "And where do you get off calling us volunteers? We didn't volunteer for anything. We woke up in a hospital with people thinking we overdosed on drugs."

As Bryce should've expected, Grae-zier ignored this unpleasant reality. "Like I said, you are lucky. Use that luck to complete your mission. Remember, lives are at risk."

Again, he swung away, allowing his cloak to ripple in a wave behind him. Soundlessly, he disappeared down the corridor and was gone.

"My life is on the line," Bryce mumbled, gazing down at a little chunk of his sword. "Do you care about that?" He felt it was unlikely that Grae-zier cared at all. "He just doesn't want to be incinerated." A shiver went down his back as he pictured a nuke exploding over the city, vaporizing everything.

Chapter 46

Five minutes later, Bryce stepped into the dark interior of the furniture store. Even from inside, the "Europeanness" of the furniture escaped him, unless stiff, uncomfortable and pretentious equated to being European, he didn't see it.

He had spent the previous five minutes collecting himself and, just as importantly, finishing the sandwich he'd been making and filling his pack once again with more fixings. He had also found a t-shirt hanging from a hook in the bathroom. It was liberally decorated with pizza sauce stains down the front and the armpits were a grey yellow color. The shirt smelled pretty much like it looked.

The smell seemed to drift from his consciousness as new smells greeted him: Wilkes' last merc was fast losing his humanity. He was off in the corner by himself, chewing on one ragged thumbnail. A little closer, someone's bowel had ruptured. A man named Juan had been crushed, first by a train and then by a falling chunk of cement the size of a Shetland pony. He had doggedly kept up with the group but internal bleeding combined with undiagnosed diverticulitis had resulted in his large colon splitting open. He was shitting blood.

Maddy was not far away when Bryce walked in. She was holding a woman by the shoulders as a white-faced man pulled on the woman's right arm. The arm was badly broken, and the woman was unable to hold back a scream. The entire room stared, frozen in shock at the sound.

"Shut her up!" Wilkes barked.

Bryce was the closest. He leapt on her and clamped a hand over her mouth. "Look at me," he hissed, staring her in the face. "It'll be alright." It was an outrageous lie. An ugly shard of bone had torn up through her bicep and erupted through her flesh. The arm was bent and swollen up twice as large as its twin, and to make matters worse, the scream had stopped the man in mid-pull, thus prolonging her agony without helping to set the break.

It was not going to be alright. The lie stung his honor, which had been only a vague thing with little meaning the week before. It was no less vague now, and yet it had more meaning, though he knew not why. Worse than the lie was the useless pain they were causing the woman. Her pulse was thready despite the fact that her heart bounded. It was trying to make up for the lack of blood in her system.

She had left a red trail all the way from the wrecked train and now she was going into shock. Unfortunately, there was nothing he or any of them could do. She needed a surgeon to repair the shredded blood vessels and she needed a blood transfusion or at the least a gallon of IV fluids to stabilize her. After that she would need antibiotics, pain pills by the score, and a great deal of rest.

And all that was never going to happen. The best they could do was splint and bind her arm. It would be a stopgap measure; without surgery she would slowly bleed out or the shock would send her into cardiac arrest. One way or the other, she was going to die.

"It'll be alright," Bryce lied again. He knew it would be a mercy to kill her now. It would be an honorable thing to do. In spite of this, he could not kill her, not while there was still so much life in her eyes. That spark in her eyes was also a lie. It was like the last day of Indian Summer with a nor'easter barreling down; it was little more than an illusion.

What would Grae-zier do? he wondered. *Or Magnus?*

The answer to both came quickly. Magnus would snap his fingers and one of his faithful followers would smother the woman with a pillow. Grae-zier would cut her in two with his sword without blinking. He would not need to justify his actions to himself or the people around him. They were only human and not one of the "chosen."

"Let's consider a different approach," he suggested. "I say we should bind up the arm as is until we can get in a safer spot or a more defensible one. In the meantime, she needs as many pain pills as she can handle and some rest." He smiled down at her. "How's that sound?"

"Yeah. Please. Let's do that." The woman laid back trembling, her eyes staring at the ceiling.

Maddy raised an eyebrow. Something had changed about Bryce, she saw. Behind the smile and the calmly spun lie he was suddenly skittish and his sword was gone, replaced by a long, white-handled kitchen knife. And he smelled odd. It wasn't just the shirt, either. There was the strangest aroma around him.

"Where's Sid?" Bryce asked, trying to pretend he didn't see Maddy's searching inquisitive eyes on him.

Without looking, she gestured to the side. "In one of the recliners. My bet's that he's asleep already. Asleep or passed out."

He turned out to be somewhere between the two states, but managed to come alive enough to rifle through his pockets. He found four little plastic containers. "I can't read none that," he muttered, squinting at the letters in the dark, "but one 'dem should be like ty-nol with codeine. That'll knock her on her ass, 'specially she takes it with Jack."

When it came to getting high, Sid was generous. Abandoning his recliner, he went to the woman, saying, "It's da ice cream man. What's your flavor?"

Bryce turned away without comment. He surveyed the low-ceilinged room; there were people scattered on every bed, turning the sheets filthy, mostly with mud or tar, but frequently with blood. He counted forty-three of them; they were still picking up people.

"You want to tell me what's up?" Maddy asked.

"Not here."

She was not the only one who was aware of Bryce and who had tracked him as he came in. Nichola wasn't going to be left behind, Victoria had a promise to enforce, Wilkes had his wagon hitched to him, and Griff still had his mission. These four trailed the pair into the gloom of the sales office. Although it was glass-walled, not much light filtered this far back into the store.

"I met a man," he said. Thinking back on Grae-zier he had to pause to reconsider the word "man". Clearly Grae-zier was more than a man, and yet Bryce wasn't going to describe him in fawning terms. "Magnus sent him." Again, he paused, knowing that the others would need a moment.

Nichola was the first to speak. "Magnus? Daniel Magnus? And he sent someone to see *you*?"

Maddy cast a side eye at the young woman's disparaging tone and was about to snap at her; however, Wilkes put up a silencing hand and asked, "What did he want? Did he mention me? Is he sending in another team? Did he give you an evac point?"

Bryce grunted out a laugh. "I wish. No, he said some stuff that may or may not be true. He seems to think it is and that it might be, you know, soon. And I…might believe him." Although Bryce stumbled over this string of nearly incoherent words, Maddy had heard enough in his tone to know that her worst fear was no longer in the maybe category.

A shiver made her shoulders twitch. "When?" she asked

"When what?" Victoria demanded. "What stuff?"

"They're going to use nukes," Maddy answered. "I've known it since whenever it was we woke up. I dreamed it."

Griff scratched his head and grit sifted down to land on the shoulder of a brown coat he'd picked up somewhere. "You dreamed it? Okay, that's, that's whatever. Magnus didn't dream it though, right? He has evidence?"

"Of course, he has evidence," Wilkes said, talking over Bryce. "You think my security team was the only one working for him? He had dozens; all the big names. What I don't get is why he didn't contact me? And you know what else doesn't make sense? Why did Magnus send this guy to find you to tell you to go to the Feds? Why didn't Magnus have the guy just go himself?"

Maddy felt Bryce's hesitation.

"The guy…the man was different. He wasn't a good choice for something like this."

Wilkes gave a quick glance around before he stepped in close. "Was he a zombie? Or becoming one?"

"No. He was just different. Sort of like Maddy and me but more so."

"He's more of a freak?" Victoria asked. Maddy shot the blonde woman a hard look, but Victoria only shrugged. "What? You aren't normal. You said it yourself. Magnus did something to you. Something that wasn't right."

"Look, the man doesn't matter," Bryce practically shouted. "The government is going to nuke us. That is the takeaway here. Soooo, what do we do? Wilkes? Do you have contacts we can draw on? And better visuals? Maybe satellite photos? I was told to carry on southward."

Wilkes rolled his eyes. "South? Through that? Did this guy look out the fucking window?"

Griff waved his hands. "We are jumping to insane conclusions. The government is not going to nuke New York City. That's crazy."

This struck them all dumb for a long second until Nichola made a dismissive *tsk* sound. "You need to wake the fuck up. Of course, they will. You ever heard of Waco or that thing in Philadelphia. They dropped a big ass bomb on some people there." Everyone was nodding in agreement. "And if some guy who's got more ESP than these two thinks it's gonna happen, it's gonna happen."

"Did he say this was from some sort of vision?" Griff asked.

Bryce grimaced as he answered, "The man told me that Magnus was far-seeing and that he knows what cannot be known."

Griff rolled his eyes and looked as though he was going to go on a rant about ESP. Maddy jumped in quickly, making a capital T with her hands. "This is Daniel Magnus we're talking about. We all know he has a ton of lobbyists. He practically has the government in his back pocket and God only knows how many spies at his beck and call. So, if he's worried about nukes, we should be twice as worried. I'm going south."

"Me too," Bryce said, raising his hand. *He knows what cannot be known*, the words echoed in his head. "ESP or spies, I think we can trust him on this."

"I was going anyway," Griff said. He glanced at Wilkes. "What about you? You could be helping to save humanity." This was so close to how Grae-zier had described the mission that Bryce felt an odd tug from within. Was this confirmation of a vision? Judging by Wilkes' reaction: a sour look as he turned away, digging for his radio, he didn't think it was.

Bryce watched him go, feeling a little let down and oddly vulnerable. Although Wilkes' motives were purely selfish, he had still been something of an ally, and at great risk had helped to keep Bryce alive.

As much as he wanted Wilkes to join them, he needed most of the others in the store to stay put. They would be a drag on them, slowing them down, making them more vulnerable. Speed and secrecy were their greatest hope.

"We may want everyone else to stay put," he said, speaking in general, though his eyes strayed to Nichola and Victoria. He hoped one of them would step up and act as leader of the group he wanted to leave behind. "You'll need to find a better place to hole-up, one that's more defensible."

Nichola leaned back from him. "I know you're not talking to me because I'm going, too. There's no way I'm staying with these guys. They're…" An entire host of adjectives sprang to mind; none of them were good. "They're unlucky." It was the least objectionable and truly the most accurate word she could come up with.

Victoria, who felt like she was the unluckiest of them all, said, "I'm going one way or the other. My husband and son are at the plaza. If the FBI is still alive then they are too. I know it in my veins."

So much for that. Bryce hoped his disappointment didn't show. "Do we invite anyone else?"

There were a few younger, stronger men in the group who were relatively unhurt. However, they were corralling families, and Griff voiced his fear that they would demand that their wives and kids came too. Their journey would revert back to a parade of the walking wounded in no time.

"We have to tell someone we're leaving," Maddy said. "It wouldn't be right to just up and go. Maybe Sid? People seem to like him." This was agreed to but Sid was passed out in one of the beds, clutching a bottle Johnnie Walker Black like it was a teddy bear. Maddy went to talk to Michelle Jones, a young mother of two. Maddy liked her because she had smart, wary eyes and had kept her children, a boy and a girl in line.

While she was gone, Bryce dug through the backrooms in search of a better weapon and came up with a hickory-handled ten-pound sledgehammer. With so much weight on one end, it was an awkward weapon. For Bryce who was in an equally awkward stage, the hammer was a little too short to use two-handed, but it was also a little too heavy to use one-handed.

He also lacked the training or practice to wield it like he had the pipe or the sword. His wrists kept wanting to turn over like he was swinging a baseball bat and when that happened the weighted end twisted his wrists painfully. The first time he made the attempt, the hammer flew out of his hands to strike a partially built credenza with a loud crash.

Wilkes rushed in a second later, a hunk of a bed frame held over his head at the ready. He snorted, "Did it try to bite you?" Bryce said nothing to this. As he picked the hammer from the remains, Wilkes offered to trade, holding up the piece of wood he carried, "I'll give you this for that. It's lighter. More your speed."

It looked like it would crack in two if he used it on the wrong zombie. "I'll pass, thank you."

The perpetual bitter look on Wilkes' face drew away briefly and when it did, he looked younger, and frightened. "I'm not getting any more info on what's going on downtown," he admitted, his eyes pinned to the floor. "Nothing. The situation is fubar all the way. The comm channels are filled with guys screaming for help. Positions getting overrun. People turning into fucking zombies. Ammo going fast or already gone. Everyone begging to be evacuated. It's…it's fucked up."

Bryce didn't like the fear in Wilkes' eyes. If he was afraid, Bryce knew he should be trying to keep from wetting his pants. To take his mind off the looming fear, he tried another practice swing with the hammer; it still felt off. "I need to hit *something*. That's my problem." It wasn't like a sword that you could swish through the air.

"Are you listening to me?" Wilkes demanded, grabbing the hickory handle near the head. "The army is all over the place and at the same time they're nowhere."

"I get it. The situation is fucked up. It's why we're going south." Bryce yanked the hammer away and walked to where some plastic covered mattresses stood leaning upright against one wall. He hefted the hammer.

Before he could swing it, Wilkes slammed his open palm down on a desk that was three-quarters built. It went to pieces under his palm. He stared at the wreckage. "This feels like some sort of metaphor. Or maybe it's a sign. You think it's a sign?"

"Nope," Bryce answered, paused with the hammer cocked and ready. "The idea of seeing the future is scary. Are we going to get killed trying to stop what only might happen? Will we cause it to happen by rushing into that cloud? Are we just deluding ourselves and all this ESP stuff is just a load of garbage?" He kept trying to tell himself it was garbage and yet he still felt the guilt of having gone into that subway tunnel to begin with.

"Maybe we should forget the future," he said and took a mighty swing at the mattresses. It was like swinging at a soft trampoline. The head sank a foot deep and then rebounded with almost equal force. Bryce found himself flying back, trailing after the hammer, an idiotic look on his face.

The next second, he was lying on the dusty floor.

Across from him Wilkes was staring as if he had just opened a birthday present and found a stripper inside. Then he threw his head back and laughed until his face was red and tears streamed down his cheeks.

Chapter 47

"I knew it," Wilkes said, his chest hitching. "I got the ESP. I saw it happen in my head…the hammer… and then…" He had to grab his sides as the laughter felt like it was on the verge of bursting out of him.

Griff came in a little later and Bryce was still lying on the cement with his arm outstretched. By then, he was laughing too.

"You missed it!" Wilkes cried in a high-pitched voice. He could barely breathe and he was so red in the face that with his laugh-squinting eyes, he looked a little like a pig. A crying pig. "He…he…he…" That was the most he could get out for some time and for a few minutes after that, he would chortle out of the blue and then sigh, happily.

"Are we ready?" Griff asked the small group as Maddy, the last, filtered in.

"Not quite," Bryce said. There was one too many of them and at the sight, and the smell of the angry merc, Bryce lost the last of his laughter. The man's eyes were red and furious; his lips kept lifting in a snarl. It was a wonder he could keep from attacking them. "One of the wounded has to be uh, dealt with."

Griff frowned, missing what Bryce was trying to say. "We don't have time for any of that. We've handed out a ton of pain meds. It should be good." Maddy gave him a tight-lipped smile and shook her head. Wilkes had stopped laughing and now he turned away. Nichola went to inspect the mattresses.

The merc look confused at the hold-up. "We gotta kill one? Then let's go. What are we waiting for?"

"Kill?" Griff asked. "Oh, right. I get it. Yes, we should kill it. Bryce?" Griff had a table leg, which was weak; Wilkes the length of wood, also weak; Maddy had her climbing axe stuck down in a sagging belt loop, and Nichola had her bat. Victoria had no weapon at all.

The hammer made sense as the weapon of choice to those who hadn't seen him make a fool of himself. His shoulders slumped. "Yeah, I guess. Let's kill it," he said this last bit to the merc. "After you." The big man went stomping off, a bit of drool at the corner of his mouth, his bleary red eyes hard on the door. Inside him, the excitement to kill brewed and bubbled, close to boiling over. Just giving in to it was changing him faster.

The smell coming up from his pores turned Bryce's stomach but it also hardened his resolve. "We'll make it quick," he told the merc. "Painless."

"Zombies don't feel pain," the merc growled. His own pain was cresting inside his skull. It was like there were a thousand fire ants biting and biting. "And they don't deserve painless anything. I'd torture all of 'em if I…"

He didn't see Bryce hurry up and swing the heavy hammer two-handed. He didn't feel it, either. The metal head sunk three inches deep and the merc ceased being angry in a blink.

"Shit," Bryce muttered. A strange hatred spiked inside him. It was hatred for the merc, and stupid people who got themselves infected, and weak people who couldn't step up when killing had to be done. He hated those hiding and those who wouldn't fight. If they came out of their apartments en masse the apocalypse would be over in two days.

In short, the sick feeling in the pit of his stomach was hatred for people and that hatred extended to himself. It got worse as he had to work the hammer back and forth to get it free. With each movement, forward and back, there was a crunchy sound like thick eggshell cracking.

Maddy heard every crunch as well as the slurpy, sucking noise the metal made when Bryce finally got it free. The infected brain was already dark and gooey…and the smell! It was akin to rancid milk, but with a copper tang. With a hand over her mouth, she hurried for the short hallway that ended in a back exit. It opened onto an alley where she took a deep gasping breath—and began choking.

The wind had turned north and now the smoke from a hundred fires was pouring along the streets. It had a chemical stench that was better than the past-due brain smell; however, under that was the hideous aroma of roasting flesh.

"This is insane," Wilkes said, stepping out into the dark cloud. With it being night on top of the smoke, he couldn't see ten feet. Something monstrous roared overhead; a bomber? A sleek grey fighter? Or was it an ICBM with a payload of nukes? It was impossible to say. "How are we supposed to get anywhere in this?" Earlier, he had found black sheets to replace the rags he'd been wearing over his street clothes and now he pulled the cloth over his nose making him look like a Bedouin.

Behind him, the others were gagging in the hall.

"We push through," Bryce said. After the appalling stench of the merc's brain, the smoke wasn't so bad to him.

He had started off alone when Nichola said, "Hold on. I'm gonna get some sheets, too. The smell…Just wait for me, K?" The others went back for sheets, too even Maddy. After her first gagging breath, she hadn't been able to control her breathing. Each gulp of air had brought with it a horrible taste and she was somewhere between hyperventilating and vomiting.

Wilkes had remained. "You understand that the FBI in New York isn't linked to the White House, right?"

"I'm sure they have a way to call," Bryce said. Even with just his dark eyes showing, Bryce could read Wilkes' thoughts. They hadn't strayed far in the last hour. "Trust me, I wish we could get a boat. That would be the dream." He could picture it: a sailing yacht, eighty feet at the waterline, crisply white with enormous baby blue silk sails. He had never sailed before, but didn't think it would be hard to learn.

"The only problem is where would we go? You think when the missiles fly we'll be able to outrun the radiation? You think they'll stop with New York? You've seen the news. The dead are everywhere and once the government starts using nukes, it won't end. Pressing a button is so much easier and safer than coming out and actually fighting."

Wilkes muttered into his rags, "That's exactly why I say we're wasting our time. Trust me, I know how the government works. Washington is filled with yes-men and lobbyists and people living high on the hog. It's a mean, selfish town. They don't care about you and me. They don't care about this country or doing the right thing. All they care about is themselves and you can bet your ass that half of them have already taken off running."

Bryce gazed up at the smoke, his mind harkening back to Grae-Zier and his curled lip. Wilkes could've been describing him. The half-man half-god had nothing but contempt for Bryce and viewed humanity as little more than sheep. "Then we make it about them, whoever's left," Bryce said. "We have to sell them on the idea that a vaccine is the only way they'll live."

"That won't work. The decision makers will be in a bunker somewhere. They'll think they're safe."

"We'll tell them that the disease is airborne, and it might be, for all we know." It was half a lie and even that felt slimy.

305

Slimy was fine with Wilkes. "If they think Magnus has some way of targeting them, it might work. I wouldn't put it past him to have his own missiles." Wilkes grinned. "He's got everything else."

The others were filtering back and Bryce didn't get an opportunity to ask what Wilkes meant by "everything else." It sounded ominous.

"By twos," Griff said. He had a black sheet pulled around his shoulders so that his head looked like it was floating in the darkness. "Wilkes and I in front. Victoria and Nichola in the middle. Bryce and Maddy have the rear. Keep your eyes up and out. If we keep quiet and we move quick, we'll be there in no time."

He didn't wait for questions. Pulling his sheet up like a cowl, he started off down the alley, moving with a panther's lithe grace. Next to him, Wilkes had a limping gait, making him look like a bear with a peg leg. The two women in front of Bryce were shadows, silent and crouched. The loudest of all of them was Maddy who was still fighting her stomach.

Still, she could barely be heard. Hammer-like explosions were making the smoke around them puff in and out so that it looked like the buildings were breathing.

"Maybe ya wants a little drink?" It was Sid Pitts. He had come staggering up from behind. His footfalls quiet compared to the explosions, his whiskey scent blown away from them by the gentle wind.

Startled, Bryce's heart spazzed oddly in his chest at Sid's words. He was half-turned with the hammer cocked, before he realized who it was. It was an effort to hide his look of disappointment at having the man following after them again like a stray dog that had been given a scratch behind the ears.

Sid took one look at the hammer and broke down laughing. By some miracle, he had managed to rebound and was back within the perfect range of inebriation.

Wilkes came rushing back. He pushed Nichola aside and stared down at Sid in anger. "Shut the fool up, and get him out of here."

Inexplicably, Sid carried a pillow instead of a weapon, though in this case it came in handy as he laughed into it. "I sorry," he said in between chortles, grinning merrily at Wilkes. "You jus' look like a nun or one them burka A-rabs. It's an improvement on being a Nazi"

"A Nazi?" Wilkes snarled.

With his bleary eyes and the pillow, Sid didn't see the punch coming. Bryce saw it before it happened: the twitch in Wilkes' eye, the gritting of his teeth, the slight drop in his left shoulder, the shift in his weight, and then the obvious balling of his fist.

Bryce was moving before Wilkes and caught his fist as he was cocking his elbow.

"Don't," Bryce said. "There's no reason to hurt anyone over words."

"Especially when they're true," Maddy added. "I'm just saying you scowl too much. You're like the poster-boy for the patriarchy."

Wilkes scowled all the harder right up until he yanked his fist away. "You think I look like the poster-boy for the patriarchy? What about you two?" He turned on Victoria and Nichola. "You ladies think that, too?" They both shrugged, not wanting to answer honestly and be dragged into the argument. Wilkes grinned at the lack of a response. "You know what I say? Fuck the patriarchy. Equal rights for all. We've had men leading this whole time. I say it's time for the women to step up."

He bowed while making a sweeping gesture to the opening of the alley. "Go on. No more oppression, I promise. In fact, I apologize for oppressing you. And I apologize on behalf of my men. I'm sure they'd apologize themselves if they hadn't died saving your whining asses." He straightened and waited for someone to say or do something. No one budged.

Normally Maddy would've ripped into the man, but she felt stupid for having mentioned the patriarchy in the first place. It wasn't the time or place—and probably wouldn't be for years to come. She was sure that the apocalypse had turned many social issues on their heads. There probably wasn't a racist left in the country. Skin color meant nothing when people were getting their faces chewed off.

Sexism, on the other hand, was reverting back a thousand years in front of her eyes, and it wasn't all a bad thing. In a battle for their lives, people fell into two categories: the weak and the strong. Overwhelmingly, women fell into the first category. And it wasn't just physically, either. In the last few days, the link between the physical and the mental had never been stronger. The correlation between physical strength and the outward displays of courage were so strong as to be taken as fact. The opposite was true as well. The more physically weak a person was, the more likely they would 1: show timidness in the face of threats, and 2: be a woman.

This didn't mean women had no value or should be disregarded, it meant that for women to keep the respect they had fought so hard to garner, they would have to step up and fill niches that were valuable to the group or the society they were a part of.

It was wishful thinking to believe otherwise, but the onus was on women to be taken seriously, not on men.

"No, you're right," Maddy said. "I will take the lead." She saw Bryce and Griff open their mouths to protest; she stopped them with a hand. "No. It makes sense. Griff is injured and Bryce is exhausted."

Griff swung the table leg in an easy arc. "I'm just a little stiff."

"And I'm good," Bryce said. "I just needed a few minutes rest." His eyes told a different story as did his reaction to Sid's appearance. He had been truly shocked, while she hadn't been. She had maybe a half-second of forewarning, which suggested that Bryce's exhaustion was worse than he was letting on.

She slid her ice axe from her belt. "No, I'll go first. I have the best night eyes of any of us." And the best sense of smell and hearing. She pointed to Griff. "Keep close enough to see me. No closer. We all good?" Everyone nodded, except Wilkes who hid his surprise at her reaction behind a half-shrug.

Without any more talk, she went off alone into the smoke. The streets to the south weren't quiet and empty. They were dangerous, every step of them. Zombies roamed the smoke, sometimes steps away, at other times they went unseen, but were heard by their gibbering laughter or soft moans.

As she went, her heart, which was still racing at close to ninety beats a minute, jumped up to one-twenty. Her hands shook and her breath was quick and too light to grasp. The air zipped in and out of her, and suddenly her thoughts of proving herself for all womanhood seemed to go right out the window.

She had to look back to calm her nerves. Griff was right where she knew he'd be, twenty steps away. He wasn't exactly quiet. When the bombs weren't thundering, she could hear the scrape of his fancy shoes, or his whispered curses when he'd turn an ankle on the unstable rocks. Seeing him helped and she turned south once more, every nerve on edge.

The first zombie passed ten feet in front of her not long after. It went up the side of a crater, paused so that she could only see its piss and blood covered shoes, and then fell down into the pit, disappearing from sight.

A second one came by within sight of the crater. She ducked down next to a yellow Prius and it went by, missing her by an arms' length. It was slow, wobbling worse than Griff. She counted to twenty before it was out of sight, and the moment it was, she realized that she should have killed it. What if it turned around and stumbled into Victoria, and what if she screamed and what if they were charged by a hundred of them?

There was no excuse not to have killed it either. It had been small… "A woman," she realized. A small, broken twig of a zombie and she had been right there. Maddy vowed to kill the next one and was put to the test right away. This one was bigger, standing just a few steps away from the obvious path through the destruction. *Be smart. Skirt around it and find a path…* "No," she whispered, under her breath.

No. The smart move would be to kill it silently and march on—it would be smart *only* if she could kill it silently. One blow. One quick strike. One quick swing of her…she was procrastinating, because *What if?* The what-ifs raced through her mind and formed a useless pile in her consciousness for her to pick over. She was stuck in neutral for so long that she heard Griff coming up from behind. That got her moving and not completely because his presence was about to bring a hurricane of trouble down on them.

It was also because he was simply there. Griff was a big athletic man, trained to kill, but unlike Wilkes, he was gentle and honorable as well. He wouldn't leave her if she got in trouble. His presence was a comfort. It was a wonderful feeling to know he was there and she felt a new warmth, right up until she realized that she was being a pathetic weak little nothing. She had cowered until a man showed up—Wilkes would've laughed, and he would've been right to.

Chapter 48

I'm not weak, she told herself. *I don't need Griff to do this.*

Despite this, she still didn't move. *I am woman, hear me roar;* the phrase she had repeated in college more time than she cared to remember was now an embarrassment as it rang through her mind. When had she ever roared? Once, she and dozens of others had screeched through a bullhorn trying to drown out the first amendment rights of a speaker she didn't agree with.

She remembered feeling so empowered, so brave, so virtuous standing up to him. In retrospect, what had been virtuous about two-hundred people screaming death threats at a bookish, nervous little man with an unfortunate little chin and a blob of a nose? Nothing. And where was the bravery? He'd been a guest speaker, not a dean or a professor. Screaming at him had been entirely without repercussion.

It was a bit of a shock to realize that her one brave act hadn't been brave at all. It had been vanity on her part and the bullhorn had only broadcast her own fear. She had been afraid that other people would hear the man and believe him and his outrageous point of view—in other words, she was afraid that she and the others around her wouldn't be able to counter his ideas in a fair and open debate.

The clarity at which these memories and thoughts buzzed through her mind was astonishing…and equaled to more procrastination!

Before she could remember more, reconsider, or rationalize another thought, she forced herself forward, advancing on the creature, her lips pursed and her right arm raised. It was facing her, but its eyes were blank and staring off to her right. "Quick, quick, quick," she whispered as she darted forward. With each step, the horror of the creature solidified in the smoke. It had been a man who had left his apartment two days before with a luxuriant brown beard that hung to the center of his chest, and a perfectly round knob of a man-bun sitting atop its head. The beard was now tangled in dried blood and straggly bits of flesh. The bun was unchanged and just as pathetic as it had been.

The rest of the creature was covered in tacky black blood that glistened, catching the bit of light that made it through the smoke.

Five feet from it, Maddy's foot kicked a broken piece of cement and the zombie began what felt like a slow-motion turn, its black eyes coming to center on her, its huge hands coming up to grab her filthy sweater as she rushed in. Close, closer; they were almost chest to chest when she swung the axe down with everything she had.

Its breath was pure sewage that washed over her just as the spike of the axe penetrated the top of its head and sunk five inches deep. The feeling that ran up the metal and into her hand was decidedly disgusting. It was like cracking a giant soft-boiled egg.

A flash of surprise broke briefly over its slaggy dead face, then its eyes rolled down in their sockets and it began to collapse as every muscle in its body went limp. Maddy considered trying to lay the beast down quietly. Two-hundred pounds of dead flesh and bones was about a hundred pounds too much for her and it fell with a soft thud.

Even before it thudded over, the axe handle was yanked from her hand and for a moment she was defenseless and she crouched, her eyes up and out as Griff had suggested. There were other zombies around, their moans drifting through the smoke. None were close. She bent to retrieve her axe and worked the pick back and forth. It was like unclogging a toilet, but in reverse. The moment the spike was free a vile black porridge squirted from the hole.

A groan escaped her.

"What is it?" Griff asked as he materialized out of the smoke. Further away, Wilkes faced to the right, his ears tracking another of the creatures.

"Nothing," Maddy whispered, wiping the spike on a strange mishmash of clothing that seemed to fill a nearby car. It was doorless on the side closest to her and it appeared that the bomb which had taken the doors and melted all four tires, had also exploded the suitcases inside. There were singed clothes from one end of it to the other.

"You should give me a little more room," she suggested, hitching up her pants. They had been tight two hours before; now they were in need of a belt. "You know, stay back a bit farther." She glanced into the car and happily saw a thin brown belt.

He stared as she worked the belt around her now much thinner waist. "If you're too far, I won't be able to provide back up."

The fear that had kept her paralyzed was gone—she had roared. She had stood alone and unaided, and had slain a beast, one on one. If felt more than just good, it felt fantastic. "Just another twenty feet or so. I'll let you know if I need you."

Already the others were close, stumbling through the dark. She patted Griff on his strong shoulder and left him. Now, instead of groping through the dark like a lost soul searching for light, she stalked on silent feet. For the first time, she realized that the dark was her ally. Except for smell, the average human had keener senses than zombies, and Maddy's senses were far greater than any human.

She had the next zombie she came across dialed in from forty feet away. Its moan was baby-soft and its step light. Maddy expected a female zombie but was surprised to find it was a teenage boy. It was more surprised when she suddenly appeared on its left. It looked blankly at her for the brief instant before the ice axe crashed into its head. Again, she had used too much force and had to wiggle the spike out.

"Lesson learned," she told herself. If she came across two, she couldn't waste time cranking out the pick when the second was right on her.

This problem came on her quicker than expected when she came across three at once. *Wait for the others*, a voice inside her said. A separate voice hissed, *Let them hear you roar!*

She teetered between the two before she sucked in a harsh breath and began angling around the cars. There were three shapes in the darkness but they were not together and they did not act with one mind. She killed the closer one without mercy or fanfare. It never saw her coming. In her excitement, she again struck too hard and the spike went as deep as it could. Pulling the curved metal out was not nearly as hard this time.

Her adrenaline was pumping like mad filling her arms and legs with nervous energy. When the thing flopped over, she stomped down on its head and ripped out the spike just as the second zombie attacked. Stumbling over the uneven ground, it lunged at her and grabbed the top part of her left arm in a sharp-nailed grip. Instinct made her lean back, while a lack of training had her attempting an attack with the spike while she was far too close.

The strike was all wrist and the bloody tip penetrated half an inch. Not even close to kill depth, and now its teeth were driving in at her neck. She could do nothing but slam the ice axe into its mouth. At the same time, a rock under her foot tilted and she was falling back with the creature on top of her.

Cat-quick, she jerked and spun so that they both landed on their sides. Neither felt the pain of the rocks digging into their flesh. The second they hit the ground, she was already moving, pushing off with an elbow and shoving it back with her opposite hand. Just like that, she was on top. She had lost her grip on the axe and it had disappeared, but her hand found a rock and she used it to smash the thing's forehead in.

One more blow finished the job. It was all she had time for as the third plowed into her. It was faster than the others; that didn't make it any smarter. It crushed her into the rocks, but its momentum carried it over her and it lost flesh from its nose as the ground stopped it.

Again, she was faster and twisted out from beneath it as it was still trying to get to its knees. A glint of metal caught her eye. The ice axe! She snatched it up and embedded it deep, once more as far as it could go.

"Hmm," she said, her lips pursed and pushed to the side in dissatisfaction. Although the creature was dead, she gave its head another *thwack!* This time she pulled back right at the end. That was better. She gave the other bodies a few more practice swings until she had the speed and timing down. The right depth called for a reversal of the downward sweep just at the point of impact. This arrested the point of the spike an inch and a half deep.

"Uh, you having fun?" Griff asked. She had heard him coming and hadn't given it a second thought. Now she froze and glanced back over her shoulder at his puzzled look.

"I'm just getting the hang of this." She straightened and tried to appear normal. Having just been locked in mortal combat with three zombies, all of which were bigger than her, it took more than pushing a stray curl of brown hair from her face. Her arms were bleeding, there was bright zombie blood on her shirt and the ice axe, and there was a look of triumph in her eyes.

Even with the blood and the dirt, Griff was surprised to find her alluring. It wasn't just that she was taller, far slimmer and fast becoming beautiful, she also radiated a new-found confidence that had nothing of her old smugness associated with it. He was still somewhat awestruck at this when, with a last ghostly smile, she disappeared back into the smoke.

313

She left him not as Maddy Whitmore, PhD, but as Maddy Whitmore, *Zombie Killer* and it felt good. She moved quicker, now filled with confidence. There was no reason to go slow. There was no reason to size up every one of the creatures and formulate plans or lines of attack.

In the dark, she was more than a match for those she came across. Like they were breadcrumbs, she left a string of bodies for the others to follow, and with each kill, her confidence grew. Then she smelled talc and fear. It was just a whiff beneath the chemical smoke, the endless zombies, and the new stench of decay that was beginning to rise up from the city streets.

Maddy pictured an older woman. Was she lost in the smoke? Was she trying to escape the city? Was she… A new scent: guava shampoo but with earthy undertones. It made no sense until she heard a whining sound—the woman was out walking her dog.

"In this?" Maddy had never been fond of dogs and generally avoided them at all costs. They were too needy and worse, they were a distraction, something that her former regimented life could not have borne. In the middle of an apocalypse they seem like even more of a nuisance. How would you feed them? How do you keep them from barking? And if they manage to help fight off zombies, how do you keep them from tracking infected blood everywhere? "No, thank you."

It seemed to Maddy that her best bet was to hunker down and wait for the lady and the dog to move along. She didn't hunker so much as she slid her ass up onto the hood of a Jaguar. Beneath the dust and the dents, she could see the gleam of paint and could smell the layers of wax. It had been someone's baby once. Now it was just another corpse. While sitting on the Jag, she ate the sandwich Bryce had made for her, and as she did she grew steadily more nervous.

The dog had not moved and its whining had not varied. The scent of the woman remained unchanged as well.

As the last of the sandwich disappeared into Maddy's cheek, she picked up her axe and slipped to her right. Her steps were light and placed with care so that she came within sight of the lady and not even her dog was the wiser. The woman was indeed old. She had the shape and color of a marshmallow, and the soft consistency of one as well. However much she looked like a marshmallow, she was glazed like a doughnut with fear sweat.

Biting into the soft folds of her neck was an extension cord. It ran up to a signal light but was just long enough that if she stayed perched on her toes she would keep from being strangled to death. Her hands were free and she had her fingers curled up beneath the cord. No matter how hard she tried, Maddy saw there'd be no pulling it over her head.

Maddy took an involuntary step forward, drawn by the terror in the woman's eyes and the sudden burning anger in her own heart. Someone had left the woman like this. Someone cruel and hateful.

Someone or some thing.

The thought stopped her. Where was the dog? Why was it unseen? It could've been trapped in the rubble. The same person who'd done this could've done anything to the dog. But the whine wasn't one of pain. It was fear. The dog was afraid and now Maddy was too.

She couldn't smell the demon, but she *knew* it was here somewhere.

Chapter 49

The cold sensation of *knowing* swept her. She could try to deny it all she wanted, but it was fact. A trap had been set. It had not been set for just anyone. It had been set purposely across their line of march, which meant it had been set to capture, or more likely, kill her and Bryce.

Subconsciously, her knees bent and she slunk low, her new finely tuned senses reaching out like fingers. Her blue eyes, now sharper than humanly possible, searched the shadows and found nothing, her ears, better than a fox's listened beneath the explosions and the ever-present crackling of fire, and heard only the dog and the woman's harsh breathing. Even her sense of smell failed to pinpoint a source of danger.

The walking dead and their stench permeated the air. On this last part of their journey, Maddy had been able to narrow down the closer scents or those that had unique signatures, but in this case, there was nothing that stood out.

And yet she knew the demon was there.

"But which one?" As she pictured the fire-burnt magenta-headed one a shiver went up her back. When the insidious image of the black demon came next, she felt small and weak, just as she used to, and she wanted to scamper away and hide.

"Where's the roar now?" she asked herself.

Her roar was locked in her throat, but that didn't mean she was like she had been, all fluff and bluff. She was deadly now… just not stupid. As much as she wanted to help the woman, she slunk down and away, and in seconds was dashing back the way she had come.

When she had asked Griff to give her more room, she expected him to be ten yards further away than before, instead, he and the others were a full seventy yards away, moving in a clump. Everyone was hitting the wall of exhaustion. The stress of fighting through such a deadly environment for hours on end was piling up on their shoulders and a few of them were bent at the waist as if they were hauling hundred-pound sacks of rice.

Griff limped and dripped with sweat. Wilkes stumbled and cursed. Sid had lost his peak and felt terrible all over. Victoria walked in a pain-filled exhausted stupor, still moving only because she was driven by the need to find her family. Nichola was the freshest; she was also the youngest and had spent most of the last couple of days sitting at home watching TV.

Bryce was slowly recuperating from the non-stop fighting he had endured, but for him it was two steps forward and one back as he was still protecting the little group from the zombies that had caught their scent and were coming up behind. At first there hadn't been many, but over the last few blocks they were coming hot and heavy, crowding the group.

He found the hammer to be a great tool for killing. A direct hit would turn a human head to mush. Even a glancing blow was usually enough to drop one of the beasts. But the weapon was so heavy. His arms and shoulders ached, and his legs quivered. He needed a moment of rest and something to eat. It made no sense, but he was desperately hungry again.

When Maddy came hurrying back, it took only one look and he got the same queer sensation of knowing again. He could sense the danger and the nearness of the demon, but that didn't stop him from slumping down on a broken curb and pulling out one of his sandwiches. The danger was close, but he had time for a bite.

As he ate, he only half-listened as Maddy explained what she had seen. The rest of his attention was reaching outward for the demon. Searching for it in a way that felt a lot like listening. He even had his head cocked as if trying to pinpoint the location of a cricket that had scampered into his house and was hiding under the oven. The only thing he could pick up was the old lady's fear. It was a heavy thing that came in slow pulses, like a heart that had to gather itself before each beat.

Were those pulses covering the demon? Hiding it?

It was close, he was sure of that, but not so close that he could pick up its scent. "Or it's masking its scent," he muttered around the sandwich.

Wilkes gave him a tired look. "All the more reason to go around. It makes no sense to walk into a trap when we're this close." He pointed south where the smoke was now being blown off to their left. His finger centered on a building not more than two blocks away. The buildings here were of a white granite, wide and stout. Many were on fire and the destruction just in front of them was greater than ever; however, there were buildings further south that stood untouched in all the devastation.

"The government's been protecting their own," Wilkes intoned with deep satisfaction as he gazed at them. In his eyes, this was the way it was supposed to be. A functioning government had to be protected even above its citizens.

As cold as his words were, everyone perked up. Their journey hadn't been in vain and at least there seemed to be some sort of plan in place to protect a small part of the city.

"So, we're going around?" Nichola made this more of a statement than a question. "I have a better idea. I know a dozen ways we can go *through*. I come down here all the time and in winter I cut right through half these buildings to stay out of the cold." She rubbed her hands together which Bryce thought was to emphasize her point. In reality, she was just cold. Everyone was, except for Maddy and Bryce. For them it was only cool, and yet Maddy shivered.

"We shouldn't," Maddy said. "The woman needs our help." No one said a word to this and none would meet her eyes.

Even Bryce. He wanted to help this strange woman, only they were finally within sight of their destination and he was overcome by a moment of weakness. Not just physically, but spiritually as well. He was bone tired and the sight of the Federal Plaza standing intact left him with a childish desire. He wanted to run into the building and throw his arms around the nearest adult and cry.

The desire was far from heroic…but when had he ever been a hero? He wanted to go back to being just Bryce, a person no one had ever turned to when the chips were down. He was more than ready to leave the responsibility for saving strangers or the world in someone else's hands.

However, the woman's terrible fear was too much. That pulse beat on his psyche—just as the demon hoped it would. It had set the woman there as a trap. But why so obvious? Why would it give Bryce a…

There was a scraping behind them; more zombies. Bryce slumped, his back curving into a worn-down hunch.

"I'll get that," Maddy said.

Griff pushed himself up. "No. You've done enough for now." His chivalry was as appreciated as it was misplaced. He could be infected by the slightest scratch, while she figured she and Bryce were immune.

"It's a small one," she told him, striding forward quickly. It was actually more of a medium-sized zombie; a few inches shy of six-foot but gangly and lopsided as it was missing an arm. It reached with its lone arm, making it an easy kill for Maddy. She grabbed the arm, which was thrust in her face, and yanked it towards her.

The zombie was already forward balanced and now it fell with its mouth open wide. It lost its front teeth when it hit rock and seemed surprised that it wasn't chewing on flesh. It died with that surprised look on its face, as Maddy's ice axe came down and turned off its lights. Everyone wore the same disgusted look as she worked the spike free.

"I could've gotten…" Griff started to say.

Wilkes rode right over him, "No one cares. It's dead. The plan raised by Nichola is a good one. She'll lead this time." He had been about to add that he would go second, but the talk of demons unnerved him. A flash image of the magenta-headed horror bearing down on him made his heart stutter. The she-demon had taken the brunt of a subway train right to the grill and was still kicking. "Bryce will go second and watch her back."

Nichola had looked alarmed at the idea of taking point, but Wilkes had guessed correctly that she would feel safe with Bryce near her.

Bryce had other plans. He let out a long sigh. "You guys will go around. I will free the woman and deal with the demon." He could only hope it hadn't healed all the way and that his hammer would give him the edge. As much as he wanted to deny it, within him had sprouted a tiny seedling of heroism—thankfully, it was as yet too small to overcome common sense. If things didn't go well, or if the demon was all the way healed, he would run. When it came to the demon, running would always be an option.

Before Maddy could say anything, Bryce added, "I'll go alone. This will be its last chance to stop us and with it focused on me, you guys should be able to get through."

"Is it trying to stop us? Is that what it's trying to do?" Victoria asked.

This was a question that Bryce couldn't begin to answer. He had no idea why the demons were stalking them.

Yes, you do. This was a whisper that came from deep within him. He wanted to argue against it, but it would be arguing a lie. Magnus had changed him so that now Bryce was one of the Chosen. The demon was his counterpoint.

The run of the mill zombies were the unwanted, the discarded, the wretched huddled masses that Magnus did not feel worthy of life. Ruling them were the demons; they were the princes of the undead world. Were they anomalies? Or had they been created specifically by Magnus to challenge his elite chosen ones.

Knowing Magnus, Bryce figured they had been. Boxers always lose their edge when they're not challenged and even Olympians grow soft when they sit too long at the banquet table. The demon had been created to do away with the weak among the Chosen.

"It's trying to stop me," Bryce answered. *It's trying to kill me*. This was the weakness inside him talking. Weak or not, it wasn't wrong.

"Then we take it on together," Maddy insisted. "That's the only thing that makes sense."

Griff nodded solemnly. No one else agreed, not even Bryce. "It makes so much sense that the demon thought of it, too. He won't be alone." This should've been obvious, but he only just realized it. The zombies would surround him the second he approached the old lady. They would charge in a ring and force him to fight harder than ever. They'd wear him down so that when the demon joined the fight, even injured he'd be more than a match for Bryce.

Don't do it. The weak voice again. *Go around. Forget the old lady. She's dead already and you know it*.

His eyes fell to the heavy, long-handled sledgehammer. It was a man's weapon. It wasn't made for a weakling. Going around was what a weak man would do. Griff wanted to fight. There was doubt and fear in his eyes, but he would do the right thing. He was no weakling. He had honor, and he would die with his honor intact if he came with Bryce.

"I'll go alone," Bryce said, without taking his eyes from the hammer.

"You can't win this fight alone," Griff said through lips pressed thin. This wasn't just a protest for the sake of being heard. He wanted to stand by Bryce's side.

"It's not a fight any of us can win," Bryce remarked, mostly to the hammer. "Winning is not the purpose. Holding their attention so the rest of you can get through is why I'll go. Alone. Another person with me would just mean…" *Another death*.

Silence reigned among them as they stared at the ground. No one said a word until Sid Pitts let out a low rumbling burp and made a face as if the burp had brought up something green.

"Then it's settled," Wilkes said. Groaning, he got to his feet. They all did. No one but Maddy thought there was any reason for more discussion on the matter.

"Hold on! I'm…"

"Going with the others," Bryce said, speaking over her. "We have to prove that Magnus has a vaccine. You and I are the only real proof of that. One of us has to get through."

She sucked in a breath to argue the point. It was second nature to her, after all, only she knew he was right.

"Ah shit," she whispered. It made sense that someone drew off the demon and it made sense that it would be Bryce. Of the rest of them only Griff could realistically challenge the demon, except the demon didn't want him. The trap wasn't for him.

She found she couldn't look at Bryce and didn't know what to say to him. It was astonishing, but she suddenly realized that she had feelings for him. Even before he had "changed", he had changed. Back in Magnus' conference room, days before, he had risked everything for her. He had been called gallant by Magnus and she remembered almost laughing at the idea. Bryce Carter, gallant? That would've been a joke back in their college days. There was no laughter in her now. There were tears that wanted to come pouring out of her. She held them back, knowing that although Bryce was now actually gallant, he was also newly so.

Tears could undercut him. They could weaken his resolve, and freeing the old lady and taking on the demon was all but impossible already.

They stared at each other and she knew she had to say something. "Be smart," she ended up saying.

He barked out a laugh. "If I was smart, I'd run the other way."

Then came an awkward silence with everyone watching. She felt she should do something, kiss him perhaps, but what if he didn't want to be kissed by her? What if his feelings for her hadn't changed at all? What if he still found her mouthy, bossy and annoying?

While all this was going through her head, he reached and grabbed her hand. He gave it a warm squeeze. "You be smart. Get through and keep the bombs from falling. Unless…" He broke off, his face twitching from a smile to a grimace.

"Unless what? There's no way we can allow them to nuke New York City."

"There's one way. If they have a real plan. A workable plan to contain all this. If they do then I say fuck Magnus. Let it happen. I trust a properly aimed nuke over Magnus."

Griff came up out of the gloom. "We have to go. The others are getting restless." He nodded once to Bryce and then paused to give them time for a hug or some other sentiment. Again, the two could only lock eyes. Maddy allowed Griff to pull her away.

"I'll give you three minutes," Bryce whispered to them through the smoke. He sighed when they were gone, wishing he had said something more to Maddy. The way she had looked at him had been very much a surprise. "I think she likes me," he said, fishing sandwich fixings from his backpack.

No. That was impossible. She had always been his sworn enemy, though she had clearly grown to… "Tolerate me? No, it's more than that. She does like me, she just doesn't like me, like me." With that out of the way, he concentrated on his sandwich and tried to ignore the shaking in his hands.

His death lurked somewhere in the dark smoke.

That didn't stop him from finishing his sandwich. It took him only eight heroic bites and when done, he felt better with his full belly; stronger than ever, but nowhere near as strong as the demon. Its strength was so fantastic that even with it not in sight, Bryce got a queer thrill up his back.

"I've stopped it twice," he told himself. *You've gotten lucky twice.* "And maybe I will again. Third time's the charm."

For you or for the demon?

He ignored that and, after a deep breath in which the trembling in his chest intensified, he strode forward, gripping the hammer by the neck. His steps were feather-light and somehow, despite the rubble underfoot, he ghosted along in near perfect silence.

As he went, the fear-scent of the old lady intensified and as it did his own fear was replaced by an unpleasant sensation of disgust and embarrassment. The sweat that made his brow shine was a source of shame and he used the cleanest part of his filthy shirt to wipe it away. His disgust was for the old woman. Her weakness cut across him, reminding him of the fear he felt when he first saw the zombies. He had wanted to cry.

Everything had changed since then. The world was crumbling around him and mankind was failing, and yet he himself had grown. He was powerful now and growing stronger by the minute. His minutes were numbered; however, and he did not dawdle to draw them out.

There was the old lady just as Maddy had described, except now there was blood dripping down from her neck. The cord was biting deep as her legs gave out on her. Bryce ran forward, leaping onto the hood of a barely recognizable Mini Cooper.

He stopped steps away from the woman, his hammer at the ready, his senses perfectly attuned with his surroundings. He was able to tune out his own quick breathing and the woman's frantic whispered pleas to save her. His entire body was a spring, ready for the demon's attack. Ready.

Ready.

However, the demon did not attack. A minute went by and still there was nothing to sense except his own growing realization that the demon was far more devious than Bryce had given him credit for. The old lady was not the bait. In a sense, she was little more than a hunk of stone in a river, diverting the water.

Bryce had not walked into the trap. Maddy and the others had.

Chapter 50

Just as the realization struck him, Bryce heard a muffled scream. He knew that screamer. It was Victoria.

A picture formed in an instant: his friends slipping through a maze of a building, filled with dark corridors and black doorways where anything could be hidden. Eyes began to gleam in the shadows; hundreds of them.

Sudden frantic fear gripped him and before he knew it, he spun on the hood of the car, ready to race west.

A single whispered word stopped him.

"Please." It was the old lady. The word echoed in his mind and he only just realized that she had been begging nonstop since he had appeared in front of her. He had no time to spare for her. Every second counted for Victoria and the others; they were the ones in true danger.

"Please help me." The words cut into him.

She was weak and terrified; he couldn't leave her like this. It went against something newly sprung up inside him and he leapt at her from the Mini Cooper, drawing the knife from his belt loop in midair. One slash freed her.

Her knees buckled and he caught her before she fell completely. Setting her back on her feet, he spoke quickly, his face an inch from hers, "Go south to the Federal Plaza. Find the FBI. Agent Plinkett. Tell him Magnus has a cure. Go!"

"But..."

He left her and her whining behind. He ran west to the sound of shouts. *One of you has got to get through!* the weak voice screamed in his head, trying to stop him. He had said these exact words to Maddy only minutes before. They had been true then and were just as true now. *Then turn around!*

Perhaps he would have except that voice did not care about saving New York, all it cared about was getting to safety. "No." It was the safety of cowering in some giant building, protected by federal agents while others died—while his friends died.

The city will be turned to ash. Millions will die.

Somehow, he doubted that. Magnus was too smart to let that happen. There was no way he would rely on a nobody like Bryce Carter. No, he would cover his bets and Bryce was sure there were secondary assets in place. Either that or Bryce was the secondary asset. "Or the third or fourth." Besides, he had sent the old lady on. For now that would have to be good enough.

Ignoring the weakness inside himself, he kept running towards the sound of battle, which was the only direction in which a man should run.

A block to the west, he saw the remains of one of the squat white granite buildings. This one took up the entire block, or at least it had. Half of it was a ruin. The other half was crawling with the dead. They were going through windows and smashing through the front doors by the dozen. A side door remained locked and was holding against four that were using their bare fists to club it down.

Bryce was on them in an instant bringing a hurricane of violence. The heavy hammer struck twice, killing the first two before the other two even knew he was there. The third grabbed his arm and pulled him close, too close for a proper swing with the hammer, but not too close to smash in its teeth with the end of the handle. Brain dead as it was, it didn't notice its missing teeth, however the crashing blow knocked it back and it tripped over one of the cooling bodies.

The fourth attacked Bryce teeth first. Like humans, zombies really were not built like wolves. They needed their prey held down or stationary to get within proper biting distance. Bryce jerked back and the teeth snapped shut an inch from his cheek. As he continued to fall back, he brought the hammer around one-handed, holding it by the neck. The weighted, blood-stained head smashed into the jaw of the creature, knocking its mandible out of joint and sending it reeling down the steps. This gave Bryce enough room to swing the hammer properly this time. With his arms extended and putting his back into the swing, he whizzed the hammer around. The metal head was a black blur before it blasted the zombie's head open, spraying blood and curdled brain in an ugly rain.

He struck with such force that the head of the hammer carried through tissue and bone. Bryce used the energy in the hammer to bring it around and up again, and as he did, he stepped forward and smashed the other zombie into the wall.

It hit with such force that when it fell it left a greasy smear behind.

The creature was still sliding down the wall when Bryce rushed to the door. Finding it locked, he raised the hammer once more and brought it down in a short swift arc, crushing the door handle with a single swing. The metal fell away, but that didn't open the door. The hammer went up again and now the dreadful fear that he was already too late lent him even more strength. DOOM! DOOM! DOOM! He pounded the door, warping the metal with each strike until the bolt broke, then he was inside and racing for the stairs, following the stench of the dead.

His senses were firing on all cylinders and he could pinpoint where his people were fighting for their lives. They were retreating upwards and were already on the third level. The stairs flew beneath him, three at a time, under his long strides and in a second, he came to the first of the dead struggling upwards. It had one leg and half an arm—he didn't bother to kill it.

The next had been a short venomous woman in life and she made for an extra mean little zombie, fast with needle-sharp teeth. Bryce caught her around the throat as she tried to disembowel him with those teeth. She was both small and light, so he was able to pick her up one-handed and slam her into the wall with such force that the back of her head left a hole in the drywall. Her legs went out from under her—her skull had been crushed by the blow.

Once more, Bryce was moving before she fell. A flight up, he came on more of the dead fighting their way upwards.

Only this time there was a baker's dozen ahead of him. Their focus was on a door being held by Sid Pitts and Nichola. The door itself was hanging by a single hinge, and the two were being forced slowly back into a dark hallway. They were desperate. Nichola was making a high whining sound in the back of her throat as she swung her bat. She had an ineffectual wide grip so that she looked like a baseball player from the turn of the last century. The bat thumped into the beasts, knocking out teeth, marking them up and cracking bones, but not killing them.

Sid seemed to have lost his bottles and in their place he had found a length of bent metal. It had been sheared from something larger and one end had a jagged spear-like tip. He was jabbing it at the creatures, shredding their flesh, tearing open their eyes. Again, he wasn't delivering killing blows and as more of the sickening beasts made it to the landing, his problems mounted.

No one noticed Bryce as he came up from behind. His hammer wreaked an awful slaughter, and the blood ran slick on the stairs by the time he killed the last between him and Sid.

"*They* are here!" Sid's dark eyes were wide and wild; his sanity was on the verge of disintegrating. "We have to get out of here!" He tried to push past Bryce and flee down the stairs.

Bryce grabbed his arm. After two days of non-stop growing, they were of equal size, but Bryce was stronger. "Stop." The command held Sid in place as much as the iron grip on his arm. "Both demons?"

Sid nodded staring into Bryce's ice-blue eyes.

The demons had come out of nowhere with only a moment's warning from Maddy. They had been waiting in the dark like horrid spiders. The simile was especially true of the burnt one. One of its legs trailed uselessly, but that didn't stop it from slithering forward on its three other limbs. It shouldn't have been so fast and if Maddy hadn't screamed, it would've pulled Sid down into the dark.

By the slimmest of margins, they had been able to dart into an office suite and slam the door. From there on it had been nonstop fighting and running. Every time they thought they had found a way out, one of the demons would be there with a swarm of zombies.

"Where's Maddy?" Bryce asked. From the sounds of it there were two other doors being attacked.

"Last I saw she was at the stairs by the elevator. You go straight down the hall and to the left."

Bryce still had a hold of the man's arm. "*We'll* go straight down the hall," he said and began dragging him along. When he saw Nichola sneaking a look down the stairs, past the thirteen corpses, he barked, "You're coming, too." She followed meekly, still gripping the bat.

The hall was lit from without; a building across the street was covered in flames and the orange light slipped through the cracks of doors along one side. All light ended at the entrance to the stairs where Maddy and Victoria were battling fiercely against a mob of the dead. Maddy had her ice axe and was hacking at the heads of the zombies as each climbed over the mound of bodies in the doorway. Victoria had a length of bright aluminum, three feet long. It ended in a flat sign that read "No Entrance." She swatted the zombies in the face with it, making a comical *prannng* sound with each hit.

Neither weapon was really suited for a raging fight like this. Maddy's was for quick kills and one-on-one battles. Victoria's was only meant for a movie set where the guy gets the girl in the end after a series of hilarious misunderstandings.

"Step back!" Bryce ordered.

327

Both women leapt back just as he swept between them, charging shoulder first. He plowed into the pile, knocking two of the creatures back and crushing the head of a third with a swing of his hammer. Then he stood on the mound of bodies and played a sickening game of King of the Mountain.

The creatures came at him one or two at a time and he destroyed them in the same manner.

Then there was a pause in the attack. Inexplicably, the zombies drew away and there was silence broken only by his rasping breath. Suddenly Bryce felt the cold like he hadn't in days.

"It's her," Maddy said in a whisper.

Down the stairs, the darkness seemed to gather and even the zombies shied from it. That alone was terrifying. And they were right to fear. The female demon approached, bringing with it a stench that had multiplied in its harshness. It was so overpowering that Bryce felt ill and the strength went from his legs.

He stepped back from the mound and felt Maddy's hand on his back. Her hand was strangely warm and he could feel its entire outline. When he looked back, their eyes locked, and the stink of the demon was either driven away or in his connection to Maddy he was able to ignore it.

Maddy's mouth came open and her lips formed the beginning of a word, however nothing came out. She wanted to say something supportive, something to help him, but her mind was overcome by the cold dark terror coming up at them.

Bryce found his voice after taking a gulp of the foul air. "Get the others. I cleared a way out. Sid will show you." He was shaking and the words came out short and sharp.

Again, she wanted to say something, but Sid was already dragging her away. Bryce gave her a last strangled smile before stepping back up onto the mound of bodies filling the doorway. The demon was a flight down. She was hunched to the side, favoring her good leg. Despite the hunch, he saw she had grown larger and was now half a foot taller and sixty pounds heavier than when he had first seen her. Still, she was injured.

It meant he had a chance.

"Come on," he said, hoping to sound tougher than he felt. He laid the bloody handle of the hammer on his shoulder. "I don't have all night. And neither do you. You remember what nukes are? There are nuclear missiles heading this way."

Her face, burned and horrid, gave away nothing.

She stared for a moment before reaching out a long flabby arm and snagging one of the cringing zombies. With a shove it came at Bryce. Her ploy was obvious; she was going to try to tire him out. It wasn't a bad idea, but there were only so many zombies near her and he still held a commanding position above her and them.

Bryce killed the zombie with a single swing. The next as well. Two more died before he mocked her. "I'm starting to think you're afraid of little ol' me."

She smiled at this and Bryce felt the weak shiver again. Her teeth were jagged and broken. They were like spear points and stuck down in them were hunks of human flesh.

"If you're not afraid," Bryce said, trying to rally, "then come on." When he shook his hammer at her, the smile widened even more and suddenly Bryce realized that she had no intention of fighting him, at least not yet. She was simply keeping his attention fixed on her. The why of it was obvious.

He was standing in a trap within a trap.

Chapter 51

Maddy trailed after Sid and Nichola, feeling that something was wrong, that they were hurrying the wrong way and yet the hall they were racing down was the only one that wasn't shrouded in smoke and free of the zombies.

It was almost inviting.

She stopped in her tracks. Her mind had been so focused on what she was leaving behind that she hadn't considered what lay in front of her.

"They're down there on the left," Nichola said.

"They?"

Sid half-turned. "They'll come on their own. Or…or they'll find their own way out."

"They?" Maddy asked again as Sid started marching on again, faster now. Her mind was being pulled in too many directions and it was a second before she remembered Griff and Wilkes. "Hold on. Sid. Hold on." He was quick-marching past another corridor, down which a fight was raging. Maddy paused to look down it as the other two went on towards the stairwell they'd been guarding minutes earlier.

Griff was down there. She could smell his particular scent above that of Wilkes or the zombies. It was a virile, manly scent that made her think of the forest.

"We have to get them," Maddy said. Neither of them stopped. "Hey!" This stopped them. She hurried to them. "We have to let them know we're leaving." *Leaving Bryce alone to die.* The thought made her feel useless again. *Where's my roar?*

"We nothing," Sid said. "There are fucking demons and zombies all over the fucking place, so if you want them, then you go get them." He turned and her hand shot out in a blur grabbing him. A jerk and a hard shrug failed to yank her hand from his coat.

Without taking her eyes from him, Maddy said, "Nichola, get them. I'll keep Sid from running out on us."

Sid wasn't the only one who wanted to run out on the entire scene. Nichola hadn't signed on for any of this and she didn't owe any of them a thing. Not even Bryce. "Me? Fine. WILLLLLKKES!"

Maddy glared through the scream. Nichola only shrugged which had Maddy stomping off for the corridor. "You two better hope…" she started to say over her shoulder when she caught the scent of the demon, fresher now. Nearer. Her head spun as she searched for the vile...

"Sid." She pointed behind him at the great black beast. Its flesh, once a beautiful velvety ebony was marred and torn. The train had crushed all the bones in its left arm and tore half its face away—and yet, here it was, nearly as dangerous as ever. It was certainly more malignant than ever. It exuded evil, the force of which froze Sid in place as the demon loomed.

"Sid!"

The scream from Maddy jarred him into action. He stabbed at the demon with his twisted hunk of metal. It was a weak and obvious attack. The demon slapped the makeshift spear aside and then grabbed Sid by the throat, slamming him so hard into the wall that he went half into it and sagged there, stunned, long enough for the demon to take his spear and slam it into his body. It pierced the rags he wore, front and back, so that he was pinned to the wall like a bug.

Nichola was the next closest and had been shocked by the creature into a torpid state. She was slow to run, but once she got moving, she raced with a sprinter's speed, her own rags flapping behind her. The demon was faster and it ran her down. It played with its food and reached out its good arm and tripped her.

She went down in a spazzing, screaming ball, thinking the demon would be on her in a flash. What she didn't know was that Maddy had followed after them both, running faster than she had ever in her life—but not with much stealth. She had her axe ready for the killing stroke when the demon suddenly turned on her. Her lack of experience in fighting caused her to hesitate instead of continuing the swing.

There was no hesitation in the monster. As it turned, it brought its fist around and landed a crushing blow to her midsection, not just knocking her back, but sending her reeling with her entire respiratory system seized up. Unable to scream she fell back, waving the ice axe uselessly in front of her. Then she was on her back with the demon looming over her.

"STOP!" The command roared out of Bryce's throat and for a second everything stopped in obedience. Even the zombies stopped their endless moaning.

Bryce and the demon stared at each other over Maddy's hitching body. Uselessly, he held the hammer at the ready. The demon had its own power and the fear that it exuded swept over the man, holding him in place. Useless seconds were wasted as he tried to overcome his fear. The demon stood, and Bryce was still trying to raise the hammer when the demon leapt at him. This broke the spell. He darted back and finally got the hammer up.

"Behind you!" It was Griff. He and Wilkes had come running at Nichola's scream, hoping that someone had found a way past the zombies. His warning to Bryce came just in time. The magenta-headed fiend was scuttling up from behind, looking like some hideous cross between a woman and a crab.

Bryce was caught between the two demons, each more than his equal, physically that is. Mentally, now that he had shrugged off the worst of the fear, he should've been their superior. Unfortunately, mental acumen wasn't going to get him out of the situation. A convenient door might, however. Just a few feet away was a door with the odd word: Muphidian set in a small plaque at eye height. If it was locked, he would be a dead man, torn to pieces even as he rattled the knob.

But it wasn't locked and the door opened under his hand. In front of him was a reception room with a desk off to the side and a long hall directly opposite from him where he could see the beginning of a cubicle farm.

He locked the door and raced for the narrow lane between the cubicle walls just as the door cracked in two behind him. His demon and stomped it with a bare foot. One more kick and it would come down.

"Come on, you little bitch," Bryce yelled. He backed away as the demon smashed through the door, shoulder first. It stumbled over the broken pieces, giving Bryce more time to retreat. The only chance the others had was if the demons followed him into the maze of cubicles. He had just reached the first when the building was rocked by an explosion. Everything around him went stark white as if a lightning bolt had struck at his feet. *This is it*, was the last thought he had before the building jumped and spun around him.

It wasn't a nuclear blast like he had assumed. It was only a thousand-pound laser-guided bomb that could turn stone to dust and melt steel. It struck just close enough to suck the air from his lungs and send him flying into darkness.

Sometime later, he had no idea how much later, he found himself blinking dust from his eyes with his head ringing. Like the goo in lava-lamps, thoughts formed with dreadful slowness and seemed to changed even as he tried to make sense of them.

Slowly, the dust settled enough for him to see that he was in one of the office cubicles, lying on one of the flimsy walls.

His weight had bent it in two and he felt like the filling of a taco. Groaning, he struggled out. The first thing he noticed was that his hammer was missing. The second was that blood was dribbling down his forehead and there was a searing pain in his left thigh.

Pushing through the smoke and debris, he hurried as best he could back the way he had come. As he crawled through the remnants of the building, he searched for his hammer or anything that could be used as a weapon. There was nothing besides chunks of concrete. It was better than nothing, and taking a chunk in each hand, he felt as if he were some sort of caveman as he emerged back into what was left of the hallway.

It ended in a jagged drop off a few steps to his right. There was only an immense crater where the dead no longer moaned and moved. Those that hadn't been blasted into pieces were crushed to black jelly. With the front of the building in ruins, his nightmare world was open around him and he had a wonderful view of the Federal Building. It stood out perfectly, an oasis amid the destruction. An American flag still flew high above.

Closer there were demons.

A grey dust-covered Maddy was swinging her ice axe drunkenly at the magenta-haired burnt demon. They fought in what was left of the hallway. It was a strange lurching fight as the floor was canted downward toward where the outer wall once stood. A slip would send them over the edge to a thirty-foot drop onto rock and rebar.

Further along the hallway, the building was more intact and that was where the demon stood against Griffin and Wilkes. Both men were injured and staggering around in the throes of exhaustion. They had been fighting for their lives at the north stairwell and now they were facing not just a demon, they were facing *the* demon.

"They're going to die," Bryce said, his voice soft and fuzzy.

Griffin saw him and shouted, "Run!" The agent was going to die. He'd known if for two straight days and now it was happening. He swung his table leg at the warped and wounded demon, putting everything he had behind it. Wounded or not, it was fast and deadly. It slid back, allowing the wood to whistle past it, then as Griffin stumbled, it seemed to fly forward, its left knee pointed directly at Griff's side.

The agent was overbalanced and too slow to recover. The knee hit him like a battering ram and stove in four ribs. Griff went flying back, the wind driven from his lungs.

Wilkes took his shot with his hunk of wood. He had seen the demon's speed and planned for it to leap back. The demon leapt inside the swing instead. As every baseball player knows, hitting with the inner third of the bat is basically useless, and against a demon, it was particularly so.

The wood thudded against its limp-hanging left arm. With a roar, the demon grabbed Wilkes one-handed, and slammed him against the wall as he had Sid Pitts, who was still pinned in place a few feet away. But Wilkes was not like Sid. He was a great bull of a man, tall, thick and strong. The demon was taller, thicker, stronger. It had only one working hand, however, and this gave Wilkes a fighting chance. He broke the thing's grip and in a flurry of kicks and punches drove it back.

Still, for all the damage he was doing, he might as well have been kicking and punching the side of an elephant. Ten seconds of this was all the demon would stand and after receiving a thudding roundhouse kick to its side, it darted in, faster than any of them thought possible. Strangely, it looked as though the demon was trying to hug Wilkes, but when it stepped back, its mouth was filled with red flesh, and there was blood shooting out from an outrageous gaping wound in Wilkes' neck.

Wilkes was paper-white as his knees buckled. This brought a bloody grin to the demon's face. He turned the smile towards Bryce before casually turning to look down at Griff, who was still gasping.

"No!" Bryce yelled.

He had been stunned by the explosion and then by the violence in front of him. Now he was racing along the uneven hallway, rocks in hand. They were stupid weapons, but all he had. Between him and the demon was an exhausted, out-of-her-depth Maddy and the gnarly she-demon. He had no time to deal with her. He headed for her all the same; she reared up like a viper and grinned in anticipation, thinking he would have to get within reach of her to use the rocks.

In this she was wrong. Cocking his arm, he hurled one of the rocks at her from a distance of five feet. There was no missing from that range. Still, she spoiled his killing throw by jerking away. The rock—four pounds of concrete—struck her on the side of the face and exploded. The demon's face was crushed inward by the force of the impact. Her jaw broke in three places, teeth shot from their sockets, and her orbital bone was turned to dust.

But the she-demon was not dead.

"Finish her!" Bryce cried to Maddy as he ran past. He couldn't waste another second. The demon had picked up the length of wood dropped by Wilkes and was advancing on Griff who was balled into the fetal position and unable to uncurl. Before Bryce reached it, the demon slammed the wood down, breaking it in two; both with ragged points.

It used one on Griff. Raising the wood, it stabbed down just as Bryce let fly with the second rock. The concrete hit a split second before the wood drove into the agent. Bryce was further away and his accuracy suffered. The rock hit the demon on the shoulder and did little damage, however, it did keep the spear of wood from going through Griff's liver and out the other side of his body. Instead it tore through flesh and muscle, and shredded his intestines.

Griff would've screamed if he had any breath.

In disbelief, he touched the wood sticking from him and as he did the world went grey around him. Through this growing haze he saw Bryce attack the demon empty handed and for the first few seconds the human held the upper hand. His fists were pale blurs as they pounded home. He fought with desperation. Everything was against him, including time. There was no telling when the nukes would arrive and wipe the city from the earth. And what of Griff? How long could he survive with a hunk of wood sticking from his belly?

And Maddy, how long could she hold out against the she-demon? They were going back and forth; the demon fighting tooth and nail; Maddy swinging the shining ice axe. It rose and fell as she hacked and hacked and hacked.

Bryce didn't even have time to watch that. His demon had caught hold of his stained white shirt, pivoted and slung Bryce twenty feet down the hall. It hurt. His elbows lost flesh and his shoulders took the brunt. He even struck his head and the blood flowed even more.

Slowly Bryce got to his feet as Maddy's axe finally scored a real hit. The she-demon's face was a bloody wreck, punctured ten times and it was still coming. The eleventh drove into its right eye and nearly got to its brain. Maddy tried to dig it in deeper, but the angle was odd and it meant staying in close where the creature could get her hands on her. Flinging out a huge flabby arm, it slapped away Maddy's hand and now the woman was defenseless and still too close!

Dread filled her and she tried to run, but the demon was so fast. It caught Maddy's hair and pulled her down by it.

Maddy fought back as best she could. She kicked and clawed which only seemed to encourage the demon. Its misshapen face, more hideous than ever, grinned down at her, drooling, uncaring about the pick of the ice axe in its eye.

Its great weight was too much for Maddy and she was pressed to the ground, barely able to breathe, and with her hands pinned, she was helpless. The demon opened its horror of a mouth and went to eat Maddy face. Panic filled the woman as she could do nothing except scream high and shrill.

The agonized sound struck Bryce, further weakening him. He had failed in every way. His friends were all dead or dying, and the city would be reduced to ashes any time.

By any measure of intelligence, the smart thing to do was to run away. Alone, he might make it to the FBI. Alone, he had a chance to survive. And wasn't that the name of the game? All his life the concept of survival of the fittest had been drilled into his head, and here it was in black and white. Stay and die. Run and live.

He took a step back and the demon grunted. Its face was a slaggy, broken mess from the train, still it was able to communicate utter contempt. It made Bryce feel weak and pathetic. It made Bryce feel like himself again…and he didn't like it. He turned back to the demon.

Chapter 52

Bryce turned from being Bryce Carter, PhD the egotistical, smarmy little shit who had the bad habit of pointing out the flaws in other people while ignoring his own. That person had been an infrequent but poor lover, a fair-weather friend and a backstabbing colleague. He also never bought pickles because he could rarely get the lids off and felt that this alone exposed his inherent weakness.

The Bryce who turned to confront the demon was certainly taller and more manly. Pickle jars no longer frightened him, but was he any better of a person?

"A little." He had tried and he had fought, and he wasn't running away. That was something.

He advanced on the demon, who nodded. Respect from an evil, soulless creature should've meant nothing and yet Bryce nodded back. In a way, they were both victims of Daniel Magnus. And they were both warriors. Like it or not, the demon had helped make him one.

The nodding was it for the preliminaries and the demon rushed at Bryce moving faster than the human eye could easily follow. Bryce's eyes were no longer simply human. With the light from the fires slipping through the smoke, Bryce saw the demon well enough; close on seven feet tall, two-hundred and eighty pounds of muscle, its left arm swung uselessly, and it favored its right leg.

During the train crash, something had happened to its left knee and it was only just healed, and perhaps it wasn't entirely so. Bryce decided in that split second, he would go for that knee. It would slow the creature down, giving Bryce a chance.

The demon went for a straight killing punch with its massive right hand. If it landed, Bryce's head would be turned around, his chin, or what was left of it, pointed back the way he had come. Right before impact, he dropped low, lashing out for the knee in something of low-altitude flying side kick. The fist skimmed off the top of his head, while his foot struck the demon's knee squarely.

The shock of the impact ran from Bryce's foot all the way up his leg and nearly popped the head of his femur out of its hip socket. The demon crashed over Bryce who felt like he was being run over by a small truck. He went tumbling and rolling backwards.

337

Had it even felt its knee crack in two? Bryce doubted it and he struggled to get to his feet before the demon could. The creature hadn't even tried. It had one good hand and one good leg. It half crawled, half dragged itself along, its nails ripping into the cracked tile floor.

Bryce was too slow and it was too quick.

It latched a huge hand onto his ankle and yanked him from his feet. Then, as if Bryce weighed nothing, it reeled him in. Bryce had both hands and one foot free, and he began kicking the demon square in the face. Although it lost teeth and had its nose bent sideways, the demon took the punishment long enough to drag Bryce under it, where his kicks were useless. Bryce then fought with his fists, landing heavy blows with each hand. He had never punched so hard in his life. The blows knocked even more teeth from the demon's gaping mouth which only meant that Bryce's death would be that much slower.

Then the demon planted his bad knee on Bryce's left arm and that was it for the fight. It could rain down punches with its good hand and Bryce was in no position to do much. Instinctively, and disgustingly, he grabbed the demon and pulled him close like a baby chimp clinging to its mother's breast. Keeping close was the only way to keep from being pulverized by that fist.

Baby chimps didn't win many fights for a reason. The demon reached down and pried Bryce away from it. Thinking, he'd just reattach, Bryce tried to nuzzle in again only to see the demon's elbow flying down at him. The elbow almost turned off his lights permanently. By the barest of margins, Bryce ducked into it and still saw stars when it hit.

Desperately, he grabbed inward again and again the demon went to pry him away, but that was when he heard something rushing at them.

It wasn't a someone. Who would it have been? Wilkes and Sid Pitts were dead, and Griff was beyond the ability to rush anywhere. Nichola was young still, and a fighter, but her energies were for her benefit alone, while Victoria's were for her family.

No, only another zombie would dare to run at a demon. But the steps were nimble and light.

The demon heard them as well, and looked up giving Bryce a second to see what was coming: a furious, bloody-faced Maddy Whitmore. Despite being pinned, she had slain her demon and hadn't needed hands to do it, either. With the spike of the ice axe in its eye, Maddy had slammed her forehead into the hammer end as hard as she could.

She had gouged her forehead deeply but had managed to pierce the thing's brain, sending the pick into the soft black sludge. The she-demon went spastic, shaking screeching and jitterbugging on the ground, nearly crushing Maddy in the process. She had squirmed beneath the hideous corpse, yanked out her axe and was now flying at the demon, thinking she had a free shot, thinking she could kill it and save Bryce.

She thought wrong.

It yanked its hand from Bryce's grip and shot out a long arm, grabbing Maddy around the throat just as she swung the axe. Her arms were short and the spike breezed an inch from its face. She went to swing again; however, the demon squeezed its massive hand and Maddy went stiff, her face going purple in an instant. She dropped the ice axe and grabbed the hand with both of hers. In vain she pulled at the black fingers. It was like trying to pull the root of a tree from the earth.

Beneath them, Bryce thrust out an arm and groped for the ice axe with a desperate hand. Just as Maddy sucked in her last breath, his hand found the handle. But even with the ice axe in his hand, the demon was safe from an instant kill.

The demon's heart was protected by a belt of muscle three inches thick and rib bones that were strong as stone. Its neck was stout as a bull's and the thin bones of its temple were impossible to get to with its arm in the way. With a quick death out of the question, Bryce aimed for the carotid artery that ran along the side of the creature's Adam's apple.

He missed, hitting the thing's larynx instead. Rather than pulling the spike right out, he pushed up savagely on the end of the handle in a prying motion, causing the spike to tear outward, ripping through the cartilage and gaping the wound. He swung again and the spike sunk three inches deep. Again, he applied pressure to the end and again the spike began to tear through the thing's throat. This time there was a spray of blood and he could feel the pulse of the great heart run down the metal.

Bryce was determined to carve out the thing's throat...but only if Maddy could last a few more seconds.

She went limp a moment later, just as Bryce brought the ice axe back for a third time. Maddy fell as the demon let her go and slammed its hand down on the axe pinning it to the tile. Bryce tried to lift it but it was like trying to lift a car. A second later, the demon ripped it from his hand.

The axe was no longer his or Maddy's weapon. It was the demon's. And chimping it in close was no longer an option, if it ever was. No one would save him now if he clung to the demon's breast. Maddy was unmoving and even if she were to suddenly spring up, she was weaponless.

Bryce was stuck fighting a superior being with only the pathetic implements God had supplied: hands, feet, teeth. Biting wouldn't work. Sure, there was a gaping hole in the thing's neck, but already the demon was rearing back, protecting its neck from a bite. Bryce was in no position to kick and now, with its larynx destroyed, even a throat punch was basically useless.

He tried anyway. He grabbed the creature's ear with his left hand and slammed his fist into its throat as hard as he could. This elicited nothing, not even a grunt. The only sound was the scrape of axe coming off the tile.

Bryce's fist came away wet and red. It had slid into the wound where, for an instant, he had felt the thing's pulse once more. The artery was so close he could touch it…and if he could touch it, he could rip it out. Forming his fingers into a flat plane he jabbed once more into the thing's neck, this time aiming for penetration.

The gaping wound was odd and ugly, with muscle and tendon overlapping or hanging like spare lines off a blimp. His fingers slid between all of this until he felt the artery. It was there, bleeding, making everything slippery, which only meant Bryce would have to get as firm a grip as possible. His hand crunched down into a fist and there was something definitely alive within the tissue, something alive and pulsing.

Only then did the demon realized his danger. It swung the axe at the same moment Bryce pulled his hand back with all his strength. The spike of the axe parted his ribs, just below his liver, missing it by half an inch.

Bryce didn't feel it. He was still pulling a handful of meat from the demon's throat. None of it ripped out in a big chunk. Instead it stretched like taffy. The carotid, a slimy red hose stretched and stretched as the demon paused as it was pulling the axe out for another strike. Then all at once, the great vessel split and a gout of blood sprayed over Bryce. The thing's heart blasted out another pulse a second later.

Realization came over the demon. It was going to die and for just a moment it hesitated as if it were an actual thinking person. Then its desire to kill overcame even its own onrushing death and it pulled the spike from Bryce's body. It slid out like it had been greased. The demon was surprised when he lifted the axe and found that Bryce was clinging to its wrist. Bryce had realized that he could do no more damage to the thing's throat and had grabbed hold of the creature's wrist.

The demon had essentially pulled him free and now Bryce staggered back, suddenly feeling the deep ache in his side. It hurt to move and every breath sent fire into his body. The demon stood as well as it could, blood jetting from its neck. Maddy lay unconscious between them. Her chest rose rhythmically. Bryce knew that if he backed away, the demon would kill her with its last remaining seconds.

Bryce stepped forward and stood over her, barehanded against the demon.

Chapter 53

Maddy had been drunk exactly four times in her life and she woke in that crumbling building feeling exactly like she'd been pounding gin fizzes all night. Her entire body ached, though it was mostly her throat that had her attention. For a moment she didn't know why, then she remembered the demon's iron grip. Her hand went to her throat as she sat up.

The demon was there, lying in an immense pool of blood. She was suddenly terrified to move, afraid that it was only sleeping and that if she made a sound, it would jump up and eat her.

Seconds ticked away before she gained control of her fear. The demons were dead. She remembered killing the she-demon by slamming her forehead into the hammer end of ice axe. Its blood had poured over her...

Maddy's stomach turned over. She had killed the one demon, but what had killed the big one? "Bryce?" she whispered. There was no answer and she pushed herself to her feet. She saw his feet first. The sneakers he had put on hours before were already splitting at the seams. The rest of him was no better.

His clothes were torn in places and shredded in others. There was blood all over him, some red and wet, some black and stinking of the demon. His arms had deep holes in them that bled sluggishly, and the ice axe stuck from his chest.

"Shit! Oh God, Bryce." She wobbled to him and found the axe was buried in the upper part of his chest near his left shoulder. She touched it gently and he groaned. Leaning over him, she hissed, "Bryce! Hey. Are you okay?"

His blue eyes fluttered open. "Wha...what happened," he asked, thickly.

"I don't know." She almost said, *I think we won*, but she could see Griff lying on his side, a hunk of wood sticking up out of him and Sid pinned to the wall. This wasn't a win. "How'd you kill the demon?"

He remembered flashes of the final fight. The demon was slow and grew slower, and yet even at the end it was still strong. They had battled back and forth over Maddy's body, neither giving an inch. Bryce couldn't, knowing that the demon would kill her if he gave it a second of respite. He had gotten the worst of the fight. The demon had hacked with the axe, aiming for

Bryce's face in its fury. Bryce could do nothing but throw an arm up time and again as he ducked to the side. He had been slashed and stabbed over and over and in the end he had taken the spike to his chest and had gone reeling back.

The demon stood looking from Bryce to Maddy, unable to make up its dimming mind which to kill and right then, in its moment of triumph, time caught up with it. With every beat of its black heart, a half quart of blood had come shooting out. The last of its blood drained from its body and it died standing.

This was all Bryce remembered. "It just sort of died," he whispered. "Help me." He pointed to her ice axe. Worried he would faint when she pulled it out, he closed his eyes. If felt distinctly unnatural coming out, like he was losing a part of himself.

The hole in his chest filled with blood and for some reason reminded Maddy of a toilet backing up. When the rising blood reached the level of his chest, she hoped it would stop, but it spilled right over. "Hold on," she said, and tore away the cleanest part of her sweater. It wasn't enough to properly bandage him with, so she shoved the end of the cloth down into the hole with her finger.

With dull eyes he looked down at the wound and then shrugged. "Good enough. Can you help me up?"

"Maybe you should…"

"We can't stay. There's no time." He looked like he was having trouble staying conscious just lying there, and yet he was right. Time hung over them, brooding darker than the sky.

She struggled him to his feet, and once there he felt much better. He was even hungry again, but had lost his pack somewhere along the way. Vaguely, he remembered shrugging it off at some point, though inside or out, he couldn't remember.

They checked Griff and were surprised to find him alive. "Still here," he whispered, still unable to unclench from around the hunk of wood that impaled him. Part of this was mental; he was sure his guts would spew out if he unballed and that frightened him more than anything. The pain wouldn't let him either way, and even if he could've straightened, he couldn't have walked.

And what was the point?

There wasn't a hospital awaiting him at the Federal Building and if there were, surgery would've been a waste one way or another. The length of wood had been covered in zombie blood when the demon had driven it into him. He was infected and for him the world was ending, nuke or no nuke.

When he mentioned this, neither seemed surprised. They glanced at each other, briefly and looked away. His scent was already going bad.

"We still need you," Maddy said after a moment. "You still have a duty."

"Yeah," he said, the word drifting listlessly from him. He had to save the world, or help to, at least. But he couldn't, not with what was essentially a two-by-four sticking out of him. He pointed at the wood and then turned away, closing his eyes.

Bryce was stiff and slow, and pulling the stake from Griff would require one quick yank. It fell to Maddy to pull the wood free and stuff the hole with a bit of rag from Sid's corpse. He had fought the least, run the most and was the cleanest. Recalling the ferret, he was carrying the first time she'd run into him, Maddy sighed taking the rag from his body.

Griff went into a shaking fit when she pulled the board from him and she thought he would die right there. Somehow, it passed, but for a long while he was in a stupor that resembled something of a pre-coma.

"We're going to have to drag him," Bryce said.

We turned out to mean Maddy. Using the strips of sheets Sid and Wilkes had draped themselves in, Bryce fashioned something of a drag sling that he wrapped around Griff's torso and shoulders, but when he tried to pull the big agent, blood began seeping from the many holes in his body and he turned pale.

Maddy worried that she would be too small to pull him, only she was no longer as small as she had been, and she found that she could pull him along the tile floor easier than expected. Going down the stairs was also easy—for her. For Griff it was akin to torture and he broke under the pain and wept soft tears. Bryce and Maddy pretended not to notice.

Things did not get any easier outside the building. The ground was broken and clogged with cars and corpses and great jutting hunks of concrete.

Bryce could not stand Griff's pain and so swallowed his own so he could help Maddy. They dragged the agent for two blocks until they were at the feet of the Federal Building where there were mounds and piles of corpses everywhere. It looked as though an army of zombies had attacked the building and had been repulsed after hours of fighting.

The building itself was perfectly intact and although it was dark, Bryce and Maddy could see people hunkered down behind the makeshift barriers that ringed it. It was a wall of sorts made from stacked office furniture; couches and desks for the most part, but also refrigerators, computers and more cubicle walls.

Hauling Griff along, they came to what they thought was the front. Two soldiers standing on a desk peeked over the cubicle wall at them.

"Mandatory quarantine is in back," one said. "It's eight hours. And it doesn't look like your friend can wait that long."

"None of us can," Maddy told him. "The city's going to be nuked any time."

"Daniel Magnus visited you, too?" the soldier asked, making Bryce blink. Had the old lady won through? Or Nichola or Victoria? The two had disappeared during the fight. Or maybe all three had come...

The second soldier cut across his thoughts with a grunted laugh, "Did he come to you in a dream?"

Bryce's fist balled, opening up one of his recent wounds. "No. We had a meeting with him three days ago, in which he tried to recruit us. And five hours ago, I met with one of his men who confirmed that nukes are targeting the city right now. If you don't believe me, this is one of your guys." He pointed at Griff. "This is FBI Agent Griffin Meyers. He can corroborate all of this."

Griff nodded and fished out his badge and ID. In a barely heard whisper, he asked, "Did Agent Plinkett make it back? Forties, balding. Looks like an old baby in a trench-coat?"

"Yeah," the first soldier answered. "He came in yesterday afternoon with some refugees. He raised a stink about being stuck in quarantine. It's mandatory," he added, just in case the agent thought he'd be able to skate past on an injury.

"We don't care about that," Bryce said, his exasperation showing. They'd been fighting for their lives for two days and now they had a couple of schmucks barring their way? "Go get him. Now." This last was a command and it wiped away the lingering smile from the second soldier. It was a good thing it had, too. Injured or not, Bryce had been itching to smack it away.

The second soldier took off at a jog leaving them to squat in the dark, just on the verge of safety. They said little, each worrying over Griff. He was slowly dying and there was nothing they could do.

"Do you have any morphine?" Maddy finally asked the remaining soldier.

"I think so."

"When your friend comes back, you'll go find out." Again, this was not a suggestion and the man nodded.

Plinkett came at a run, seconds later. The guard tried to stop him from jumping the fence, but the agent wouldn't listen and he clambered over. "Shit. God. Shit," he said as he knelt down next to Griff. "What happened?" The baby in a trench coat had aged and at the sight of his partner he aged another ten years.

"Demon," Griff whispered.

Deeper lines furrowed Plinkett's already furrowed brow. "A zombie got you? Do you think you're infected?"

"It was a demon. They're worse. And yeah, I'm infected." Griff paused as his own words sunk in. His shoulder twitched as he shoved the thought aside. "But we heard it straight from one of Magnus' men that nukes are going to be used."

Plinkett's smile dipped. This little thing was enough for Maddy and Bryce to know that Plinkett knew about the nukes and not from Magnus. He leaned in closer and whispered, "It's not something we're spreading around just yet." And that too, spoke volumes. They weren't telling the rank and file meaning they didn't have an evac plan in place.

"Magnus has a cure," Bryce told him. "The President should know this before he launches."

"Magnus lies a lot," Plinkett muttered, not taking his eyes from his partner.

"That's true enough, but Maddy and I are proof that he's not lying about this."

Plinkett turned to stare at Bryce. His eyes opened wide and then his head whipped around and he stared at Maddy. "It's you. It's both of you. You…you…you…"

"We changed," Bryce explained. "Magnus did it. This was what he did to us. He also made us immune to the zombie virus. We've both been drenched in their blood and we're fine. We're more than fine. You have to get the President to understand this. We are proof that Magnus has…" He glanced at Maddy. He hadn't told her yet of the sixty others who had died during the Serum-21 trial. "That Magnus has made a vaccine, of sorts."

Had they been there, the "of sorts" would've been enough of a lie to make Grae-zier raise an eyebrow and the demon laugh. It felt greasy and Bryce wiped his lips in an obvious tell. Plinkett didn't notice, but Maddy shot him a look; she kept quiet, however.

"I'll go see what the man in charge thinks. I wouldn't get your hopes up, though. It's the Ambassador to the UN and he's been fucked in the head all day; acting like some sort of sultan. Supposedly, we have one more Black Hawk coming and he's been selling seats to the highest bidder. One man offered his ten-year-old daughter to him. You know, in that way."

"Did he say yes?" Maddy demanded, her eyes flashing.

Plinkett dropped his chin, unable to look at her. He'd been fighting the dead on and off since he came out of quarantine but he had heard rumors. "All I know is she'll be on the chopper."

It said a lot about the man and none of it good. A man like that wouldn't easily give up a seat on the last helicopter to leave New York. Each represented a fortune and what did Bryce or Maddy have? The promise of a maybe?

"If he won't let us on," Bryce said, "have him call the President. See if he'll get him to postpone the attack by a day."

"I'll try," Plinkett promised. He shot away, racing past the two guards and into the building. It was fifteen stories up to the top floor and he was gasping and sweating by the time he made it. He was known by the senior agents and the military people who waited in the dark. They let him in without a word and he had yet to catch his breath when he found the Ambassador, still in a perfectly pressed suit of navy blue.

He was a heavy, jowly man with ripe wet lips and deep bags under his eyes. Those eyes only narrowed as Plinkett blared out his story, starting with Bryce's surveillance five days before. When he was done, the Ambassador surveyed the room. It was dead quiet and every eye was on him. None of them were slated to live; a Black Hawk could only hold so many people.

"I will talk to the President," he announced. Sighs of relief greeted him as he stood and walked into a back office. Once there, he gazed out the window, ignoring the satellite phone that sat on the desk, dark and black like the rest of the city. He knew Magnus. They'd been involved in many a twisted scheme together and every time the Ambassador had come out with the short end of the stick. Yes, he had made money on these schemes, but Magnus had always made more—he always managed to come out on top.

"But not this time."

Maybe a vaccine would work and maybe it wouldn't. Maybe they could be reproduced in sufficient numbers in time, and maybe not. Nuclear missiles were much more cut and dried. They would cauterize this little problem and the world would carry on.

The Ambassador forced his wet lips into a grin and hurried back out into the main room. "The President's willing to delay the attack!" he cried. A cheer went up. "He's giving us an extra two hours only. If these two uh, specimen don't turn into one of *them*, you'll be in the clear and I'll send the chopper back for more of you."

Watching them shaking hands and clapping each other on the back turned the Ambassador's fake grin into a real one. In two hours, they'd be dead, fried in the blink of an eye, but until then they'd at least be happy. And that was something.

As Plinkett spun around and ran back to spring the good news on Bryce and Maddy, the Ambassador turned to his aide. "Have our chosen passengers wait up on the roof. Keep them together and keep them from talking to anyone. And don't mention any of this." *We don't want them thinking they can back out on our deals now.*

When the man left, the Ambassador walked back into the office and picked up the sat phone. He squinted in at the contraption until he saw the battery compartment.

Sliding the battery out, he hefted it in his hand. It was surprisingly bulky and heavy. Figuring it would mar the perfect press of his Armani suit he tossed it into a planter on the way out the door.

"Dead in the blink of an eye. It's practically a gift."

The End

Author's Note:

Thank you so much for reading The Culling. I certainly hoped that you enjoyed it. If so, you'll be happy to know that a sequel is already in the works. While you're waiting, may I suggest another book of mine: <u>Dead-Eye Hunt</u>. It's a story set 150 years after the apocalypse where zombies hide in the midst of the over-crowded slum-states of New York and Boston. Their existence is denied by the corrupt governments, who are afraid of what will happen if the word gets out. Dead Eye Hunters, gritty men with few moral qualms about anything at all, track them down for the bounties paid. Yes, it's a lot of fun!

I've just started writing the second book in the series. There is a way for you to read it chapter by chapter, before anyone else! All you have to do is go to my Patreon page (<u>Here</u>) and support my writing. The tier levels are exceedingly generous with freebies running from autographed books, video podcasts, free Audible books, signed T-shirts, and swag of all sorts. At a high enough tier, you will even get to meet me in person as I take you and three friends out to dinner.

Patreon is a great way to help support me so I don't have to go back into the coal mines…back into the dark.

Another way to help is to write a review of this book on Amazon and/or on your own Facebook page. The review is the most practical and inexpensive form of advertisement an independent author has available to get his work known. I would greatly appreciate it.

PS If you are interested in autographed copies of my books, souvenir posters of the covers, Apocalypse T-shirts and other awesome Swag, please visit my website at https://www.petemeredith1.com

PPS: I need to thank a number of people for their help in bringing you this book. My beta readers Joanna Niederer, Monica Turner, Michelle Heeder, Roseann Powell, Shamus McGuigan, Amanda Peterman, Stefanie Foller, Victoria Haugan and Christine Beckman—Thanks so much!

PPPS: I will attach the first few chapters of Dead Eye Hunt below to wet your whistle.

Dead Eye Hunt:

Chapter 1

Manhattan
June 3rd, 2161

The girl was trying to pass herself off as a vamp. The flesh of her throat and the high mounds of her partially exposed breasts were so white that he could see the blue veins pulsing beneath. She had midnight-black hair that sat piled on her head in braided coils. They wound in ever-tightening circles, a foot in height and made her seem taller than she was. Her teeth were unnaturally white. They were the sort of white that only money could buy.

Her clothes were expensive as well: the boots that went up to mid-thigh were real leather, and the bone corset was trimmed with ivory and silver. The long, elbow-length gloves: one snowy white, the other rich burgundy, were silk.

She even had the half-lidded, haughty, slightly bored-with-life gaze of a vamp.

But now that she was only inches away, Mack-D wasn't fooled. Beneath the smell of 5th Avenue gin wafting from her breath was the sharp odor of syn-mint, which was normal enough at street level, but down below where the sun's light could never reach, no self-respecting vampire would touch synthetic anything.

With difficulty, Mack-D kept his disappointment in check. Sucking the blood from a vamp was a Dead-eye's wet dream.

"Welcome to the outside world," he said, calmer now that he knew she wasn't real. A minute before, his heart had been pounding at the sight of her and his stomach was roaring louder than the music vibrating through the walls. Still, vamp or not, he had to fight the urge to latch onto her right there and drain her dry. He was hungry after all.

It was a mortal hunger, and endless pain that he would take to his grave.

"The outshide?" she replied, slurring in a gin-mumble. "Oh right. I was slummin' it. But now, I gotta go home. Where's the shtreet?" She had taken the wrong door out of the club and now she found herself in a piss-smelling alley, eyeing a slag. And a big slag at that. She had to pitch her head well back to look into his tattooed face. As she did, the first touch of fear began to burn its way through the gin.

Mack-D could smell fear rising off her. He sucked it in deep, his nostrils flaring, his brilliant blue eyes almost closing as his lust and excitement mounted again. The blood was richer when they were afraid, and the flesh sweeter. The animal in him could barely be contained by what was left of the thinking man he had been. He held back. His filthy nails dug into the flesh of his palm, but he held back.

"I can take you home," he blurted out. Her fear spiked at the unexpected and unwanted offer. Her fear smelled like shaved brass and, as he breathed it in, saliva flooded his mouth. *No!* He couldn't give in to temptation. If he killed her now, draining her, eating his way into her heart, he wouldn't be able to stop. He'd be seen and the damned taxmen would be called. He didn't care about the police, they were lazy and could be bribed to look away from anything. But if they called in a hunter, his only chance would be to flee over the wall. Hunters never stopped. Never.

"It's okay," he said to her, holding up his large, filthy hands palms out so that she wouldn't see the black blood beneath his nails. "You don't have to be afraid. I'm a thumper here. You know, a bouncer. We provide security."

"I ammm shecure. Just get outta my way, 'n I'll be fine."

She tried to push past, and he took her by the arm. Now he smelled the cheap lye soap beneath her expensive perfume.

"Hold on a moment. Taking you home is part of the package. You know, the service we provide for our exclusive clients. You are exclusive, aren't you?" He was guessing that exclusive was the right word. Or should he have said premium? It had taken him hours to come up with this idea and to memorize his lines. Now, he waited, not sure what she would do, but fully prepared to crack her on the back of the head.

"Yeah. Yeah I'm 'sclusive. You got a limo or sumtin?"

Limo, limo, limo, he ran the word through his slowly disintegrating vocabulary and came up blank. "Uh, yeah. We have all sorts of limos. The best limos. My limo is *exclusive*."

"Really? But you're a slag."

Sudden fury swept Mack-D. *I ain't no slag!* he seethed inside, wishing he could chew her curled lip right off her face. It was true that he looked like the spitting image of a slag. His face was scrawled with tattoos in a desperate attempt to hide the pockmarks that were deep as small craters, and the scars that ran like ravines, and the strange snake-like scales that kept peeling from his throat. It was getting progressively worse, but he was no slag. Radiation poisoning wasn't his problem. In fact, other than his endless hunger, Mack-D would say he had no problems.

That was the best part about being a Dead-eye. Before he had been infected, he had been nothing more than balding Michael McDonald, a complete nobody. The day he was infected was the day he stopped worrying about bills, and work, and the missus complaining about the apartment, or what the neighbors thought of his drinking. He didn't care if his kids had their indentured licenses sold to one of the horrible Mandarin sweat shops that worked them until their fingers bled or until the toxins built up in their systems so much that they slagged out and became no better than trogs.

He didn't even care about the fallout that filled the air or the industrial toxins in the water. None of that mattered because it couldn't hurt him now. Very little could hurt him anymore and when he did get hurt, he healed in hours. They left scars but they were no consequence to Mack-D.

But he couldn't exactly say that to the girl, could he? "It ain't my limo. It's the company's." He held his breath, hoping she wouldn't ask: which company? The company he worked for melted down trash and strained out the good parts. As far as he knew, there were no limos at the plant. There was only a horrible stench that made the real slags go green beneath their tattoos.

"Oh, ho-kay," she said, falling into him. It was another sign that she was a fake. Even drunk, a high-box vamp wouldn't touch a slag. "Where's the limo?"

"It's close," he said, pointing.

She didn't like what she saw of the alley: the trash, the long oily puddle that ran straight down the middle, the over-flowing dumpsters, the dingy, grey panel van. At least beyond the van was the street. The real street. Behind her the alley was shadow-black as it wormed into the warren of a mid-center block. There was no telling what was back there. Even in Manhattan, a mid-center block was dangerous for an unarmed girl who didn't belong.

Mack-D led her up the alley, his hand on her tightening as he neared the van; she would try to run. Drunk or not, she was not going to go quietly. God, how he wished he could let her go, so she could scream and run for her life. He never felt more alive than when they screamed. It was always so primal. It was at that moment that they truly became prey and he became the hunter. Everything before that, the tears as they lay trussed up in the van, the begging, the same insipid questions—*What are you going to do to me?* It was all just foreplay.

She edged away from the van as they came close, not wanting to get her clothes dirty. He stopped her. "Hold on." He wanted to add more, maybe a reason why she should wait calmly while he opened the side door, but no reason came to him, as he fumbled with the latch. It was such a simple thing: lift and pull, and yet his left hand was missing two fingers and had become less reliable as he gradually lost dexterity.

"Hey, what're you doing?" she whispered, fear beginning to cut through the gin. "This isn't a…" Mack-D finally got the door open. The back of the van was windowless and dark as sin. She surprised him by not screaming. "No," she whispered, sobering quickly. His grip on her arm was like steel. He was hulking and outrageously strong. She was thin and shaking.

"Yeah. Get in."

Before she knew it, she was pushed inside, barking her shin against something hard and unforgiving. Everything inside the van was like that. She was twisted about and pushed down onto an uneven layer of rigid metal. "Please, wait," she whispered. "I-I'm rich. My f-father will pay good money for me. Just don't hurt me, please."

He was already hurting her. Mack-D had bent her arms behind her back at a severe angle and held her pinned face-down on the metal as he struggled to get the length of nylon rope from his pocket. "Why would I want money? Can't very well take a trip, can I?" He pictured himself on a white sand beach, sipping some sort of fruity cocktail and turning grey in the sun.

"Then what are you going to do with me?" She sucked in a sharp breath as he began trussing her up, looping and knotting the rope. It seemed to go on forever. In her mind he was creating the most elaborate knot ever tied. In reality, he couldn't manage more than a series of granny-knots, though he made up for their simplicity by tying the knots as tight as he could.

"What I want to do is eat you. I'm going to hang you upside down and slit you wide open and drink straight from your throat." He was bent over her, drooling down her neck. His hot breath smelled like an open sewer. She screamed, and it was all he could do not to tear into her beautiful flesh. "But not yet," he said, balling a fist as he fought for control. The screams had to stop and the fist was a convenient tool. One shot to the back of the head and she went face-first into the scraps of rusting iron.

She woke sometime later, just as the van was slipping beneath the skin of the earth. She was too frightened to move. Like a child, she hoped that if she just lay there, he would forget about her. Then his groping hand found her thigh.

"Too skinny," he muttered, giving it a pinch and a poke, like someone assessing a piece of poultry.

Tears came then. Silent tears.

The van chugged out a trail of black smoke as it entered the labyrinth of tunnels below the city. It took too many turns to count, still the girl was hopeful she would recognize one of the reflective signs that sometimes hung across the top of the roadway. Hope died a quick death as Mack-D swung into one of the unlit passages that branched from the main road.

Down they went into unrelenting darkness. There were no signs down here, no traffic, no pedestrians hurrying home. The road narrowed until the van filled the shaft.

"We're almost there," Mack-D told her. "Fourth left. There's number three." He slowed, looking for the turn. It always came up so suddenly when driving. When he saw it, he let out a long breath. He took the turn and stopped in front of a wall of solid iron that was splashed with graffiti. It was then that the girl began to realize she would never see the sun again.

Although she had been calling herself Allegro Albarossa all night, her real name was Christina Grimmett, and she was most definitely not rich. The fancy clothes she had on were the cast-offs of her employer, Ashley Tinsley. *She* was a true vampire. She was so rich that she only wore an outfit once before having it burned. Were she to be seen in the same outfit twice she would likely hang herself, and donating her clothes was something she could not contemplate. What if, God forbid, some lesser creature was seen wearing *her* outfit?

Christina had stolen the outfit piece by piece and now realized it was wrong and that this was her punishment. She began to blubber which made him grin.

"You can scream if you want," Mack-D told her, as he slipped out of the van. They both knew screaming was useless now. The earth would swallow it just as it had swallowed her.

She struggled up, realizing that he left the van running. Here was her chance—but to do what? He was working a heavy key into a slot, and the door or the gate or whatever it was, would be open in seconds. She would never be able to get the rope off her in time and even if she could, she didn't think she could back out of there without crashing.

Then a thought made its way through her rising panic: *Maybe I don't back out. Maybe I crash on purpose.* Her captor was framed between the headlights. All she had to do was get in the front seat, somehow get the van in gear, and slam on the gas. With her hands tied behind her back, it seemed impossible. Still, she had to try.

Squirming, she threw her torso into the passenger seat and then kicked her legs around to the driver's side. The plan failed at that point. Somehow, she got her crooked arm caught up on the gear shift jutting from the center console—and she couldn't get it off! To make matters worse, as she fought to free herself, her knee banged the horn and it let out a single tired honk, like a dying goose.

Mack-D reacted slowly to the sound. He turned and stared through the filmed-over windshield at Christina, his dulled mind unable to comprehend what she was doing. This gave her an extra few seconds to try to jerk her body off the gear shifter, but all she managed to do was mush the shifter into reverse. With a wailing shriek, the van ground backward against the tunnel wall. Desperately, Christina tried again, bucking as hard as she could.

The van jerked hard as it slipped into drive and then began to roll forward at an achingly slow pace. There should have been plenty of time for Mack-D to do something, but he only stared into the headlights as the van crawled up to him at a steady six-miles-an-hour. He seemed mesmerized by the lights, and to her amazement and grim satisfaction, the van crushed him into the iron wall. He let out a blast of air as his chest took the brunt of the blow and for a moment, he hung his head.

"Ha!" Christina shrieked. "That's what you get! That's what you..." What she saw when he lifted his chin choked her words off. At first, she thought one of his eyes had popped out and was sitting on the stunted hood of the van. Then she saw that it was only a contact lens and what she took for a gaping hole in his face was actually his real eye. It was black and wet as oil.

"No," she whispered, finally understanding what he was. "Dead-eye." It was one of them. One of the undead.

Her mind reeled. There hadn't been a zombie seen east of Jersey since before she was born, and yet here was one grinning at her, black blood dribbling from between its teeth.

She had to escape and not just from the beast, she had to get out of the city altogether. If people found out that there were zombies in New York, there'd be a panic. She'd be in a race for the harbor against ten million people. With a head start, she might beat most of them there, but could she beat the bombers or the missiles?

In Ottawa, it had taken only a pack of fourteen Dead-eyes for that city to be wiped off the map. That too was before Christina's time, but they say the city still glowed at night from all the radiation.

Desperation lent her strength. She heaved herself over the shifter but as she tried to roll over, she nudged it with her hip and shoved it once more into reverse. Back went the van, freeing Mack-D. A scream built inside her as she watched his black grin grow wide as he walked around to the driver's window.

"Yes. Scream for me," he said, climbing in, his face dark with hideous pleasure.

She did more than scream and he loved every second of it.

Chapter 2

It was only four and already the day was growing dark, not that it had been all that bright to begin with. A sunny day in New York was a rarity and Cole didn't like them. They weren't natural. A sunny day made him feel exposed. No, Cole preferred the anonymity of a dismal wet day.

The ugly clouds had been pissing out rain since noon. Not in torrents as it sometimes did, but in spurts, and now the streets were slick with muck.

New York had its own brand of mud. For the most part it was made up of human shit and ash that drifted in from the cratered remains of Newark. There was also a good deal of rat turd in the muck, and industrial waste sometimes made it fancy with prisms of obscene-smelling rainbows. Finally, corpses added their own special tang to the mix—the "daily" pickups had ceased being daily when Cole was a boy, and now a body might sit in the gutter for days before anyone came by to dispose of it.

Cole hunched broad shoulders against the rain and watched his prey as he finally left the Mandarin joint off 6th. Cole had never been to one of these joints where lunch wasn't a ten minute, eat-while-you-stand affair. If he lingered any longer than that he always had some tiny, wrinkled raisin give him the stink-eye and tell him, "Go way. You order more food or go way."

But the sick bastard Cole was after had been in the joint for three hours. Cole absolutely hated waiting like that. It made him antsy. Standing around doing nothing made his muscles stiff. He liked to be loose and ready for anything. In New York you had to be ready, or you could very well end up as just another bloated corpse, stripped bare-ass, maggots doing the funky jive in your hair, and rats tunneling into your bowels.

In this case, the waiting was meaningful.

There was no way a Mandarin was going to let some slick hang out in his shop all afternoon unless a deal was being made. Cole just hoped it was his kind of deal. He wouldn't have blinked an eye if the slick was trying to move uptown ice, or mule that had been spun-up in a Rican's toilet. People threw away their lives all the livelong day and that was on them.

But if 'ol Santino was buying up large amounts of syn-ope, well that would be quite telling. Dead-eyes needed to be on downers twenty-four-seven or they'd go monster. Near-lethal doses of opioids kept their rage in check and dulled the hunger for blood.

As always, the question was whether Santino Grimmett was a Dead-eye at all. There was a depressingly good chance that he was just a run-of-the-mill murdering psychopath. Cole hoped to God he wasn't. There was no money in it. Putting down a Dead-eye would net him ten-large. Killing an un-convicted psycho could very well lead to a prison sentence. Cole's predecessor was turning dusty in some black hole in the ground because he had offed a human.

Cole had to run a fine line. If he was too quick on the trigger, he faced prison, if he wasn't quick enough, he would end up like so many hunters: recycled out of a rat's ass.

The career of a hunter was generally short and violent. Still, the money was good. It kept the lights on and the booze flowing…barely. Things had been tight for Cole, and he was probably the only person in the world who wanted Santino to be a Dead-eye.

As the slick moved into the crowd, Cole trailed after, watching him closely as he trudged north. In this light, Cole's hazel eyes were as grey as the rain, though it was hard to tell as they were at squints as he looked for the smallest clues. Santino moved slowly, almost aimlessly, while all around him the faceless crowds hurried to get home and dry. Was the syn-ope kicking in? Were his neurons black with the virus and his brains drowned in a sick goo?

Or was he depressed because he had stabbed his wife of twenty years, butchered her remains and stuffed her different parts in his freezer? Of course, it could have been that he was tripping balls. It was hard to tell. Judging a person from behind by the way he held his shoulders was far from an exact science. Still, something was wrong with him. Something made him stand out.

Unlike the hundreds of people pushing along with him, he didn't duck his head as he passed through a grey curtain of water falling from a second-level catwalk. And he didn't seem to care when he angled off the sidewalk and his foot came down in the ghastly muck that everyone else avoided. He was also the only person who didn't glance nervously around as he crossed the unmarked boundary into Red Dog territory.

Even Cole let his eyes slip off his mark. A half dozen young morons with poorly concealed handguns lounged on an awning-covered stoop. They thought they were tough. Cole thought they looked like targets.

The pedestrians went stiff as they passed, holding their heads straight, while canting their eyes far to the right. All except for Santino. He moved like a sleepwalker and passed by without a challenge.

Cole was a different story. As much as he tried, sometimes he didn't blend in. He not only had a certain air of danger about him, but he also stood a head taller than most of the people in the crowd. The poly-leather black coat that hung to mid-thigh might have been expensive; and maybe the narrow tie, a black stripe down his white shirt made him look like an office worker, and everyone knew they had money.

At the same time, his black boots were worn and he had the partially inked face of a man who was slowly becoming a slag.

Two of the braver toughs came off the stoop and strode into his way, wanting a closer look. "We got a sidewalk fee here," the taller of the two said, giving a what-can-you-do shrug. The Red Dogs claimed they were pure breed Irish but in reality, they let in any pasty-faced wanker as long as he had a freckle or two. This one had a spray of them across a girly little nose. "I'm afraid we're gon' hafta charge you ten."

They also affected an annoying Irish brogue. They weren't alone in this habit. The Rastas acted like they were from Jamaica instead of from Jamaica, Queens, the Ricans called everyone "Ese," and Cole couldn't go to an Italian restaurant with a slick without wanting to punch him in the face. Rigatoni became ri-gahTONEY. And the damned Mandarins acted like they were fresh off the boat but there wasn't a one of them whose family hadn't been here for six generations.

Normally, Cole had little patience for this sort of thing. Just then he had even less. "Ten?"

"Each. In cash, o' course." The bigger one cast a quick glance at his companion, who wasn't going to be a Red Dog much longer. Cole was tall enough to see the slag building up in his thinning, greased hair and behind his ear. His eyes were already a bit dull.

"I could do fifteen," Cole said, pulling back his coat, showing off the 10mm Crown on his belt. The aluminum alloy winked silver in the low light. The gun was literally worth any three of the Red Dogs, and they stared as if they were looking at a diamond of the same size. They blinked back into the moment when Cole dropped his big hand down on the grip.

The leader started to draw in a long breath, which would end with him going for his gun. Judging by the bulge beneath his brown corduroy jacket, Cole figured it was one of the ludicrous .44 caliber Eagle knock-offs that were all the rage. Because of its size, it wasn't a weapon designed for a quick draw.

"Maybe you should rethink this," Cole advised. "I'd hate to waste a bullet killing you."

"There's six of us," the Dog answered, losing his accent in his attempt to sound tough.

They were teens who probably hadn't ever fired more than five rounds with their over-sized guns. The damned things were made of composite plastic and had a habit of cracking after a few shots. After thirty they could explode. To make matters worse, their eight-inch barrels were overly-light and with the rounds in the grip, the guns were completely unbalanced.

Cole wondered if any of them could hit the broadside of a barn. "I'm not too worried," he said. And he wasn't. The kid's right hand was frozen about a foot away from his body. When he tried to reach for his gun, it would be mechanically stiff and slow. His friend had been so cock-sure that he had walked up with his hands behind his back. He might as well be handcuffed.

"You and your little puppy friend are the only ones I need to kill. Once you're stretched out, the others'll run inside crying for daddy."

"Maybe," the Dog said, trying to sound tough. "Or maybe there are a whole mess of us and one of us will get you."

Cole glanced up at the building. Like so much of New York, its windows were bricked over in an attempt to keep out the acid fog, the fallout, and what the previous governor had called "heavy particulate airflows." It was the PC way of saying industrial contamination that made the southern wind smell like metaled rot. When it came in thick, it turned the sky the color of an old bruise and had been known to asphyxiate infants in their cribs.

"But you'll still be dead," Cole said, flicking his eyes back at the Dog. He was about to go on when they heard a sharp whistle from up the street. Two stoops up, a gaggle of money-honeys pulled their skirts lower as they scurried inside.

"Taxmen," one of the Red Dogs warned in a hissing whisper.

The lead Dog pulled his coat tight around his meager chest, doing little to hide his gun as a patrol of four police officers came strolling up the block. Like all taxmen they were tall and strapping to begin with, but looked even bigger decked out in their body armor. Beneath the plates of grey metal, they wore urban camo, and in their hands, they carried the scaled-down Forino version of the old Colt M4. They looked more like soldiers than policemen.

"We already paid our taxes, officer," the lead Dog said, raising his hands. "We pay Manua every month, rain or shine."

"That's Lieutenant Manua to you," one of the officers shot back. "And those taxes only cover everyday activities. This doesn't seem all that conventional. It looks to me like you boys were about to throw down right in the middle of the street. You know the governor frowns on a dozen people getting gunned down in broad daylight. And when he frowns on it, I frown… holy shit."

Cole grimaced at being recognized. He knew this officer all too well. "Bruce, it's good to see you," he lied.

Sergeant Bruce Hamilton laughed. "Look fellas, it's the White Knight himself, Cole Younger. How's the back? Not bothering you too much, I hope." Four years earlier, they had been on the same squad right up until Hamilton had "accidentally" shot him in the back.

"Better than new. Look, I'd love to reminisce about old times…"

Hamilton spoke over him, "You turning slag on me?" He pointed with his rifle at Cole's tattoos. They were a cheap blue-green. The four on the left were stylized hammers; on the right were six skulls suggesting he was part of the "Sledge" gang. "If so, I can put you out of your misery. That last bullet was just a warning. We both know I could've killed you."

Cole didn't have time for Hamilton and his hooked nose and thin greasy blond hair. With every minute Santino was plodding further out of reach. And yet this was the first time Cole had seen Hamilton in those four years. "You act like shooting a friend in the back is some kind of accomplishment. If you had taken me on, face to face, I could understand that cocky smile of yours, *taxman*."

At the word, Hamilton sneered. "Keep telling yourself that, Cole. I warned you. I told you it was going to happen if you didn't play ball. It's something I never understood about you. All you needed to do was take a little here and a little there, and maybe turn a blind eye every once in a while. If you had, you probably would've made lieutenant by now. Instead, you're one of the little people."

He laughed aloud, but then something caught his eye. Stepping closer, he used his rifle to push back Cole's trench coat. "And what's this? I thought you knew that packing heat out on the street is illegal. Got a license?"

There was no need to answer. One of the other police officers snatched the Crown while a third took his wallet. "Says here he's a bounty hunter. His license is up to date." The officer sounded disappointed. Bounty hunters held an odd position within society: not quite cop, not quite one of the little people that made up the masses. They couldn't be "taxed" while on the job.

"Ain't no bounty going to cover this," the other officer said, sighting down the length of the Crown, carelessly pointing it at a young woman who was hurrying by holding her child's hand in a crushing grip.

No *normal* bounty would ever cover the cost of the gun. So far, Cole's highest bounty had been fifty dollars for bringing in a serial rapist. The Dead-eyes were another story altogether, one that he couldn't ever mention.

The fact that they were in the city at all was deemed classified. If he mentioned them even in a drunken ramble, he would be liquidated. His body would be dissolved in a vat of acid and his name expunged from every record in the city. Each new recruit was given the same speech, the same warning, and had to watch the same video of some idiot who had talked. He had been lowered into the vat slowly, toes first. The grainy video ran for twenty-nine excruciating minutes.

"Some bounties pay better than others," Cole said, holding his hand out for the gun. "I doubt I'll get rich, but it's honest work, unlike what I used to do." The officer had been about to hand over the pistol, but stopped at the jab.

Hamilton laughed and slapped Cole on the back with stinging force. "As always, Cole, you're a damn hoot. That mouth of yours is going to get you killed some day, and hell, that day might just be today." He nodded to the other officers to give him back his belongings. As Cole holstered the Crown, Hamilton pointed up at the tenement. "Is your bounty up there? If so, have at it. You know I'd love to help you out but whoa, look at the time. Me and the boys are on our mandated break."

The gang of Red Dogs backed up a few steps suddenly looking uncomfortable and confused, not knowing whether they were about to be attacked or they were expected to attack a man with an entire squad of policemen watching.

Cole solved the problem for them. "Boys," he said with a nod to them, and then took off at a loping run. Behind him, Hamilton and his men shouted a few insults. Cole didn't care what they said. They were criminals themselves. It's what happened when no one policed the police.

Snagging Dead-eyes was far more important and far more honest—just as long as he didn't kill a human in the process.

After two blocks, the rain began to come down harder than before. It was a cold rain and tasted like dirty pennies. That was usually a bad sign. It meant it was coming in from the west. Cole slid his hood from the back of his coat and pulled it down in what was almost a useless gesture. A hood wasn't going to do jack if he was showering in radioactive water. "The sirens aren't going off," he told himself, and kept going, slowing down at every side street and alley he came to. If Santino took any one of them, he could disappear forever.

It was only after another couple of blocks that Cole realized where Santino was going. He was going home. For the last week, Santino had been hiding out in a flophouse in the village, but like so many criminals before him, he was drawn to the scene of his crime.

Santino's apartment was seven blocks away and Cole figured he could be there in minutes, only just then the klaxons started to sound.

"Shit!" he hissed. The klaxons were far worse than the sirens. It meant a Cat-2 radioactive cloud was coming in. "Or it's already here." The sensors set up on the Jersey side of the Hudson were always breaking down; the smart thing to do was to get inside as fast as he could. "But when am I ever smart," he muttered, pulling out a small emergency mask. He slapped it on and kept running straight down the street, which had gone from annoyingly crowded to deserted in seconds. Even the few taxi cabs that sometimes still prowled the streets were nowhere in sight.

It was like he was the last person left in the city. It was unnerving, but at least the empty streets made sprinting easier, and he ran like his life depended on it. By the time he made it to the building he was reeling from the run and from trying to suck air in through the mask.

Yanking it off, he laid it over the rail of the stairs, and then stood half-bent, gasping and staring around. The interior of the building was cleaner than most and as dim as all of them. Only the vamps could afford to properly light a stairwell or to run an elevator.

Santino lived on the seventh floor; a long climb after the run. Cole sucked in a deep breath and started up. His eyes had yet to get used to the dark and he kicked something after only the fourth step; and at eye level was another small lump. Although his mind immediately thought: *trash*, he hesitated. Trash was usually kicked to the side and these two objects were in the center of the staircase.

The first was a single high-heeled shoe, a spray of white plastic beads gleamed dully up at him from the toe. The other item was a purse. It hadn't been discarded, it had been dropped. He was just fishing the wallet from it, when he heard a thud, a scraping noise and a muffled shout. All of this came from below him.

Like practically every building, its foundation extended deep into the earth. There would be basements and subbasements. Sometimes there were proper tunnels that led to the subways. Other times there were hand-dug warrens and dens where squatting slags lived and died like roaches. They were dangerous places and frequently slumlords chose to brick off a shaft rather than trying to evict the poor creatures. It was efficient, but the smell of their rotting bodies would linger for months.

Cole did not relish the idea of going down to look and tried to tell himself that the thud and the dropped purse weren't necessarily connected. Only he knew better. Dead-eyes were vermin. They liked the dark, and they especially liked to feed in the dark.

Santino had probably surprised the woman who owned the purse. Caught alone, she would have been easy prey and maybe the temptation had been too much for him.

"Son of a bitch," Cole whispered, easing the Crown from its holster, and slipping down the stairwell, hurrying as fast as he dared. Syn-ope wasn't the only thing Santino might have picked up at the Mandarin Joint. Mandarins would sell a person anything as long as the price was right. Santino might be armed to the teeth.

The level below the street was made up of more apartments. Sub-gardens they were called, and Cole couldn't stand them. It was like living in a prison. The air in them never moved.

The next level down was where the darkness took on a physical quality. It sucked in around him. Cole carried a slide-light for the Crown and clicked it in place beneath the barrel. It gave off a timid light which the darkness greedily ate up after only a few yards. Still, it was enough to show him that the level had been designed for storage and at one time it had been filled with metal cages. The metal had been sold for scrap decades before and all that remained were rectangular rust outlines on the dusty floor.

Within the dust was a confusion of tracks. The shoeless prints stood out to Cole. They seemed so small, as if a child had been taken and not a woman.

Because the darkness was so thick, the subbasement had an endless quality to it and Cole suddenly felt the need to run to catch up with Santino and his victim. He raced along in their tracks and came up on them in a back corner, where they grappled together on a low mound just in front of a hand-dug tunnel that sloped away into an even deeper darkness.

"Let her go!" Cole bellowed.

Santino was a big man, almost as big as Cole, which made it a wonder that the woman hadn't already been dragged down into the hole. It was hard to describe her since all Cole saw of her was a wild mane of blonde hair whipping about as she fought like mad, clinging desperately to a gun they were both holding.

"I said drop it! I'll shoot if…"

Suddenly, Santino was flying at Cole with outstretched arms, his hands going for Cole's throat. With no idea where the woman was, Cole couldn't risk shooting. Instead, he threw himself backward, twisting his torso at the same time, so Santino passed over him, his nails scraping over Cole's poly-leather coat. They both fell and then got to their knees at the same time.

"Wait!" Santino hissed, holding out a hand that was dripping with black blood.

Seeing the blood was all the proof Cole needed. He fired twice from a distance of three feet, sending Santino's head back with such force that his neck broke. One shot struck just off the center line of his forehead and the next took out one of his dark eyes.

Cole wasn't taking any chances. In his line of work, he could never afford to take chances. He got to his feet and came to stand over the man and pumped two more into his head.

"That'll be ten-thousand dollars, please," he said, grinning. With a happy sigh, he spun his flashlight around at the darkened subbasement. "Ma'am? Are you okay? Hello?" She wasn't just gone. She was *infected* and gone. "Sad," Cole muttered.

He wasn't really sad. It was hard to be sad when he had just bagged a Dead-eye and had another on the hook. He'd let her stew in her juices for a day or two and then swing by and break the bad news. *No, that ain't the flu you got, girly. Sorry, but I got to pop you.*

Chapter 3

The free coffee wasn't worth the wait. The coffee beans were synthetic, meaning they weren't really beans at all, and the brew only tasted vaguely like coffee. Overall, there was more of a tinny, bleach flavor and Cole made a face every time he took a sip.

The brown fluid kept him awake and that's all that mattered. He needed to babysit his bounties because *things* had a way of happening when the government was involved. Bodies got misplaced, paperwork was lost, and checks could come back missing a zero or two. He had spent his entire adult life working for the city government and there was always a mistake and never one in his favor.

For the tenth time that night, he glanced over his report, making sure the wording was correct. It was important that the woman had: "*…entered the building because of the alarm warning.*"

Hunters were supposed to keep to their own territories, however the big bosses cared little for nuance as long as the job got done. If word got out that the woman in his report lived in the building, Cole would have his hands full keeping the others away. That's why he added: "*Dropped purse appeared fancy, with steel or silver clasp.*"

In the dark, he hadn't noticed any clasp and guessed that it had been a button job. This area had been a middle-class neighborhood and the women couldn't afford metal clasps or even faux leather. He paused, trying to remember the feel of the purse when he'd picked it up. It had been heavier than expected and maybe a bit larger than average. But was it faux leather?

"Don't matter," he muttered, as he wrote in: "*Dropped faux-leather purse appeared fancy…*"

He was just thinking about embellishing the shoes when his boss came in looking more haggard than usual. This was saying something since he always looked haggard. Cole wondered, and not for the first time, if he had slipped out of his mom's puss tired and scraggy with little baby jowls and a pinched angry look. Right away, Cole noticed that he wasn't carrying any of the green envelopes that always held his check.

"What gives?"

"You fucked up, Cole. Get in here."

Lieutenant Joshua Lloyd's office was in a constant state of dishevelment. His desk creaked under a mound of reports, while along the wall, the drawers of his four filing cabinets were so stuffed with files that none of them could close. Even the lone couch across from his desk was upholstered in paper a foot deep. When Lloyd slipped behind his desk, he seemed to meld into the mess.

The only chair in the room, besides the one under Lloyd's wide rump, held another stack of papers, that were topped by an ancient *Air-o-lux* box fan that was older than Cole and Lloyd put together. It was held together by tape and wire.

Cole didn't want to sit. "I didn't fuck nothin' up. It's not my fault the skirt took off. And I don't blame her either. And yes, I went after her, but she went out in a Cat-2 for fuck's sake. You don't pay me enough to run out in the middle of a Cat-2."

"The girl isn't the problem. It's Santino." Out of habit, he glanced toward his door to make sure it was shut. "He wasn't a Dead-eye."

"What the hell are you talking about? Of course, he was. I saw the black blood, Lloyd."

"It was dark. You said so yourself. Blood looks black in the dark."

"It wasn't dark when the recovery team got there." Though it had been a two-hour wait and congealed blood did darken over time… "No, it was black. I saw it. Damn it, Lloyd! What kind of shit is this? I want to talk to the recovery team. I want to see their damned notes."

Lloyd sat back shaking his head, making his limp hair move more than the *Air-o-lux* ever did. "You know what their job is. They're there to destroy evidence, not to preserve it. Do you really want to bring them in on this? It's their man who ran the tests. All he's going to say is that Santino was a *human* and that you plugged him four times, twice execution style. Son, you're just lucky this happened out of sight."

Cole heard the threat and had to grind his teeth on an entire string of curses. "There was a girl. He took her down into that…"

"Yes, the recovery team saw the bare print. It's why you're not being charged. Santino was a murderer, we all know it. But God, Cole! If he'd been just a regular guy…" He shook his head again, letting Cole know he would have been strung up for killing him.

"If he was a murderer, wouldn't there be some sort of bounty?"

Lloyd muttered, "Unconvicted murderer. Look, I'm not trying to dick you on this one. Santino's in the morgue. You can see for yourself. What's left of his brain is as pink as my balls."

"I will look, thank you," Cole said stiffly, doing his best to rein in his anger. Ten-thousand had just gone out the fucking window. Twenty-thousand, if he counted the girl. Furious he started to storm from the office and was halfway out the door when Lloyd called him back. "By the way, your paint's running. You should fix that."

Crap! One more expense he couldn't afford. His tats weren't real; they were squid-ink henna and usually lasted a few months if he was careful. The recovery team had been less than careful. Everything in the basement and the stairs leading down to it had been bleached and scrubbed, and that included Cole. Nine hours later and his clothes were still damp.

Without his tattoos, he looked exactly like a cop pretending he wasn't one. "This day just keeps getting better and better," he groused as he stomped down the stairs to the third subbasement. As always, the morgue was like a hothouse, and as always, the smell was enough to turn a hard man like Cole green beneath his smeared tattoos.

The morgue worked like a production line. The bodies were even placed on a conveyor belt. At the first station, they were stripped and any "valuables" placed in a single small bag. Those items not deemed valuable—a highly subjective term—were divvied up among the crew at the end of their shift. At the next stop, the body was printed. At the next, it was photographed from every possible angle. The actual autopsy came next. A difficult case might take all of five minutes. Santino probably took less than one. At the next stop, whatever notes that had been written were typed in triplicate.

After that, the body was sent to be mulched.

Cole caught up with Santino as he was rumbling down the line to the mulcher. He possessed no authority in the morgue except his voice, his steel fists and the fact that he would obviously use them if he had to. Three reasons that were good enough for the techs who got paid hourly and didn't mind the break, short as it was. There wasn't much reason to look any further than the holes in Santino's head. The brain was clean, as were his eyes.

"Fucking human," he whispered.

Mumbling more curses, Cole stormed from the morgue and then up out of the station, stopping on the crumbling steps outside. He thought about going back to his apartment, but it was a thirty-minute walk. He'd been planning to take a cab, but without the bounty he couldn't even afford to spring for the train, and that was seventy cents.

What was at home, anyway? Nothing. His apartment was cold and virtually empty. Other than a few old suits, a mattress and some bags of boil and eat ramen, he possessed next to nothing. Except pawn tickets that is. Over the last year he had collected enough of them to cover his walls. His phone was dead because he hadn't been able to pay the bill, and the electric would go any day.

His luck had been on a downward spiral and he hadn't picked up a decent bounty in months. And now he'd lost two in one night.

"I need a drink," he muttered, glancing around. There wasn't much to see. The sun was coming up in all its glory and somewhere people were enjoying it, they just weren't enjoying it in New York. The night mists were turning to a grey drizzle and the ghostly skyscrapers were beginning to solidify…more or less. Many of them weren't exactly solid. They were dying, crumbling monuments to an old world.

Cole was still staring up when someone pushed him.

"Get your ass off the steps, slag." It was a police officer, bringing in a stick-thin money-honey, in a see-through red dress that matched her contact lenses. She was twitchy, coming down from riding the Rican Mule. All in all, she looked as though she had been pulled from a gutter.

Normally, Cole would have knocked the beat cop's teeth in and strolled away before he had the chance to come to, only just then, Cole was the one who felt beat down.

The cop and the honey swept by and he stared after them. If she hadn't already, she was going to lose the cash she had made that night from renting out her body. Cole didn't want to know what her daddy was going to do to her. New age pimps were rarely kind.

"But that's not my problem," Cole said, repeating the New York mantra. His problem was that damned slick. Cole couldn't get him out of his head, and he knew that even if he went home, he wouldn't be able to sleep. There were too many loose ends, too many questions without answers. If Santino wasn't a Dead-eye, why on earth had he chopped up his wife and stuck her in a freezer?

"He could have buried her in the basement. It's what I would have done if I was just an everyday murderer. But why would an average killer take out her heart?" It was the wife's missing heart that had brought Cole in on the case. "I need to see the report on *her*," he decided, turning on his heel and following the cop.

Since computers had gone the way of the dinosaur a hundred years before Cole was born, every report generated in the police station was eventually sent to the "Hall of Records." If there had ever been an actual hall it had been buried under paper ages ago. Now the "hall" consisted of the top ten floors of the immense building.

It was a world unto its own.

The hall and the mole-like people who worked there had their own rules and worked on their own timeline. If a record took a week to be found, then it took a week, and no amount of bitching would ever move them along faster. If an officer was of a high enough rank, the moles could be threatened to produce reports quicker, and, like everyone else, they loved a bribe, and a good one could produce amazing results.

Cole had no money and less authority than anyone in the building, except maybe the honey.

He tried turning on the charm, however his smeared slag impersonation made his smile pathetic and the little person behind the counter—he couldn't tell if it was a man or a woman behind the thick spectacles—only turned up a sneer at the attempt, before squinting through the quarter-inch lenses.

"Hmm," he/she said. "A special? This early? It's going to be a while." The mole gestured to the waiting room, which was empty. It was always empty. A half day spent in the Records Hall waiting room was equivalent to six years on the outside. Still, there was a couch of sorts. It had been a cloth-neoprene mesh forty years before, now it was apparently made of tape. It could have been made of brick and Cole would have still slept on it.

Four hours passed in a blink and he was deep in a chaotic dream in which he was running through miles of barely lit tunnels when he heard: "Mr. Younger." Cole cracked an eye and found himself staring at the oldest person he had ever seen. It was a woman half his height, stooped, wrinkled and so dusty that her white hair looked grey. She wore a faded pale peach blouse from the turn of the century that was tucked into an equally faded blue skirt. Apparently, she used the waist band of the dress as a bra.

It was not a sight to wake up to.

He sat up, quickly, thinking that she might rap his knuckles with a ruler and admonish him for having his feet up on the couch. "Yes…ma'am. That's me. I'm Cole Younger."

"That wasn't in question. I know who you are. You're a bounty hunter." She sighed and shook her head. "Follow me."

Cole stood, noticing for the first time that the lights in the Records Hall had been dimmed and that the place looked deserted. As the building was windowless, there was no way to tell if it was night or day. He guessed it was night and was surprised that it wasn't even noon. "Where is everyone?"

"On a break," was all she said as she waddled along, watching her feet. He had to take achingly slow steps to stay abreast of her as they passed, with glacial slowness, through towering stacks of files each twice his height. They were so tall that he wondered how the diminutive clerks reached the higher ones. The moles hired their own people and it was obvious that men of Cole's stature need not apply. Or people of his age either, for that matter. The moles had an eternal quality to them. There was never a "new" person. Each of them looked as if they had always worked there and always would, long after Cole was mulched.

"In here." They had come to a door made of actual wood with a doorknob that was real brass. The knob was the only thing in the Records Hall that wasn't filmed with grey dust. It actually gleamed. The old woman reached out a spotted hand for it, again so slowly that Cole felt himself catching up to her in age.

"Let me." He opened the door, noting the stenciled name:
Joanna Niederer
Director

"Joanna or should I call you Director Niederer?" Unlike Lloyd's office, Joanna's was well lit and fastidiously clean. The walls were painted a stark white and empty of pictures. The floor was softly carpeted in white. The only real color was the desk and the two chairs that sat on either side of it. Again, they were of real wood and in perfect condition. Cole didn't feel clean enough to sit in the one on his side of the desk. What was more surprising than the wood and the cleanliness, was that there wasn't a single piece of paper in the room. He had expected her office to be a smaller, messier version of the Records Hall itself.

The director eased herself into her chair so slowly that she made all the sound of dust settling. "You can call me Jo."

He liked Director Niederer better. It seemed fitting. "Sure, Jo. Was something wrong with the form?" Other than maybe changing a lightbulb for her, it was the only reason he could think of why he was there.

"Of course, there was!" she snapped. "This is a special, and not just any special. It's a *special*, special." He wasn't following her and it showed on his face. "A special record usually involves a special person or a special case. You still don't get it, do you? Sorry to burst your bubble, but we're not all special. Yes, that talking butterfly my granddaughter watches on tv has got it all wrong."

Although she had the smell of a grandmother, Cole could not picture Jo ever being young enough to have a child herself.

"*Everyone* has a record, even the mega-rich douchebags you kids call Vampires. They are the special ones. If you're a famous person, or a mob boss, or a politician you're considered a special. But this is a *special* special. Your kind of special."

Cole only stared at her, refusing to acknowledge the obvious. She sighed tiredly and sat back. "Yes. I'm talking about a zombie. A Dead-eye." Jo pulled out a folder from her desk drawer and slid it over. "See the reference number. It starts with a 6. That means it's a special. The following 13 means it's either a *special* special, or it's tied to one. In this case, it's the latter."

"Tied to Mrs Grimmett?" Cole asked, sliding into the chair as he scanned the report. "She wasn't a…one of them. I don't see any sign of the infection. Her white count is within normal ranges. Was it changed?"

"No. She was only tied to the case. Take a look at her injuries."

Cole was still reading and said, almost absently, "Injuries? The cause of death was blunt trauma to the back of the head." When he glanced up, he found Jo had managed to summon the energy to cock a furry white eyebrow at him. Once more he felt as though she were about to rap his knuckles. His answer was incorrect. He looked again at the photos. "Her heart was taken out post-mortem. The lack of bleeding along the…wait."

He looked again at the notes. "Her blood volume was three ounces? Oh God. She was bled, wasn't she?" He saw it now. The jagged cut that took off her head had disguised the deep incisions on either side of her throat.

"Yes. It's a *special* special and you don't just come here demanding to see the notes on one of these. *You* of all people should know this. People talk, even my people, maybe even especially my people. I know it's hard to imagine, but this isn't the most exciting job and whenever any special comes up it becomes the stuff of gossip. And talk of actual specials is the last thing we need."

"I agree. May I take this?" he asked, holding up the file.

She scoffed, rolling her eyes. "Are you kidding me? No one takes my files."

It didn't matter. He had leads. Perhaps Santino wasn't a Dead-eye, but the blood he had taken from his wife was a lead. Had he sold it at the Mandarin joint? Or maybe at the flop house, or maybe...

He stood, his mind in a whirl and was about to leave when he stopped abruptly. "What did you mean by 'you of all people?' Did Lieutenant Lloyd say anything about me?"

"No. I've just read your file is all." From her drawer, she pulled another file, this one an inch and a half thick.

Cole grimaced at in disgust. There were probably horror stories about him in the file. The force needed to justify taking his meager pension and cutting his insurance off while he'd been recuperating in the hospital. "Don't believe everything you read," he told her.

Chapter 4

Unless you had a torture rack, a soundproof room and a lot of time to kill, breaking a Mandarin was next to impossible. Even the wrinkled-up grannies would only glare ferociously, cursing you and all your unborn children in every language they knew.

They could be bought, however. For the right price, they would sell out that very same granny. Unfortunately, Cole didn't have the money. He had just a few pawnable items left and only the Crown would get him anywhere near enough cash to move the Mandarin to give up info on a customer peddling blood. People bought and sold everything under the sun in New York, but blood was one of those items that raised flags, and for good reason.

Cole could see the reason from his apartment window when he raised his lead shutter. Jersey was a brown wasteland across the polluted waters of the Hudson. It was the edge of the *Zone* where a hundred million Dead-eyes had been incinerated a century and a half before. People had short memories for most things, but not with zombies. Everyone knew about their insatiable hunger for clean blood, and even a Mandarin would hesitate to sell it—unless the price was right.

With the smeared tats washed from his face and wearing his best long coat, Cole entered the Mandarin joint at just after one. He was immediately assaulted by the aroma of three-day old fish. Beneath that was the pervasive, cloying smell of fried food. Every Mandarin joint smelled like this.

There were fifteen or so customers; most at the standing tables in the center of the room. Two Mandarin families were sprawled out in a pair of booths in the back. They were all rather nondescript to Cole. It was another story with the wait-staff. They eyeballed a couple of almost-slags as if they were on the verge of becoming full-blown trogs in the middle of their Pho. The lone black man had it worse. The waiter wouldn't come near him. He passed in a wide circle around the man and when he dropped off his plate, he left it at the far end of the table.

To Cole's left was a counter where he could order seaweed noodles thirteen different ways, hot soup five ways, and "fish" either fried crispy or fried limp.

"We pay ah taxes, taxman," the lady behind the counter said, right away. "We pay on time." She spoke in the clipped tones of a recent immigrant. There was no such thing as a recent immigrant to New York. People paid good money to get smuggled out of the city, not into it.

"I'm not here to shake you down. I'm not even a cop. I'm here for a bite and maybe a chat. What's fresh?"

Because of the way Mandarins were, he judged her age to be somewhere between twenty and sixty. She wore her black hair short in front—razor sharp bangs sat high up on her forehead—and long in the back, reminding Cole of a silken mullet. Her eyes had been squinty to begin with, but at the mention of a "talk," they practically disappeared.

"It all fwesh." She cocked a thumb behind her at a filthy plexiglass aquarium where three fish of indeterminate species floated in some sort of fluid that was so grey and murky that Cole didn't know if it still qualified as actual water. As the fish weren't belly-up, he supposed that they weren't dead yet. Then again, they weren't alive like fish were meant to be; they only existed.

"You make insult, you go," the woman added.

"No one's insulting anyone. I'll have the number two." A quarter for soggy seaweed, a couple of old carrots and bits of "fish" bobbing about in the soup. He'd had worse. He ate slowly, ignoring the glaring counter girl. The black man had left, leaving Cole as public enemy number one.

It was an hour before a stunted little man slipped into the booth across from him. By his attire and the grease glazing his pockmarked face, he was a cook. By the way he studied Cole with dark, intelligent eyes, Cole knew he was much more than that. "You Uncle Wu?" The neon sign above the joint's door read *Uncle Wu's Happy Fish.*

"It's just Wu. You buyin' or sellin'?" He had no accent whatsoever.

"Buying. Syn-ope. I'm looking for maybe a kilogram." Moving a kilogram meant jail time and yet the man's expression didn't change.

"Twenty-two hundred, up front," he replied quickly, wasting no time. "Delivery: a quarter a day for four days."

It was too much. "Fifteen-hundred. All tonight. And I might need more tomorrow."

Wu's reaction, a tiny shift of his chin, was significant. He was interested. "Eighteen hundred for tonight. Short notice and all. If you give me more notice, I can shave some of that off for tomorrow."

"This is my notice. Thirty-two hundred for two kilos. I'll pay half tonight, half in the morning."

Instead of replying, Wu studied Cole for a long, uncomfortable minute. The entire time Cole was forced to sit there, a placid, simpleton's smile on his face. Finally, Wu said, "I need ID." Cole had never heard of a dealer asking for ID, and he sat back with what must have been a stunned expression on his face. Wu's flat, emotionless look had not changed since he had slid across from Cole. "I have friends on the force. I need to make sure you're legit."

In this case, "legit" meant being a criminal. To most of the police force, Cole was the worst sort of criminal. He slid over his ID. Wu took it and disappeared for a full hour. It took all of Cole's patience to sit in the sticky booth with the counter girl unrelentlessly sneering at him. The only time she took a break was when she sneered at a young girl with a bad case of slag who came slouching in. All the tattoos in the world weren't going to cover up the rot eating away her nose.

"The taxmen don't like you much," Wu said, coming to stand at the end of the table. He almost smiled. "That means I like you even more. Sixteen-hundred tonight. Order the number thirteen to go. Pay in cash and go. Simple." He didn't offer to shake hands.

"One other thing," Cole said just as Wu started to leave. "I need some clean blood." Wu's eyes narrowed slightly, otherwise his face might have been made out of wood for all it moved. "Not much. A few quarts every other day maybe."

"I don't move that stuff," Wu replied.

Now it was Cole's turn to remain still. He forced himself to count to forty in his head before speaking. "You will for the right price." Blood and Syn-ope; the implications were obvious.

"Maybe. Wait here."

Once again, he went into the backroom and once again Cole was kept waiting. He figured it would be another interminable wait, but Wu was back in only fifteen minutes. "I have a call in," he told Cole.

"Will it be long?"

"No."

Then why did you come out? To keep an eye on me? Cole's eyes flicked to the counter girl. Her sneer was gone. She was standing very still. The stagnant, grease-stinking air had become thicker than it had been. Had the alley door been shut? Cole suddenly felt trapped, both in the booth and in the restaurant.

"Have a seat while you wait," Cole suggested.

Wu's head turned toward the back. "No, I have soup on the fire and I..." Cole's left hand was below the table, the flimsy, wobbly, light table. He heaved one end up and smashed it into Wu's surprised face. The Mandarin fell back as Cole leapt to his feet, his right hand sliding into the long black trench, going for his gun.

The counter girl was no poker player, but God she was fast. She reached beneath the register and hauled out a cheap scattergun. The tip of the sawed-off barrel struck the register, giving Cole a split second to drop down and to the left, close to where Wu was scrabbling out from beneath the table. The girl hesitated, afraid she'd hit both Cole and Wu.

In that split second, Cole had the Crown out and fired, aiming purposely to miss her. With the force looking for any reason to sink him, he'd be facing a murder charge if he actually shot her. He shot the aquarium instead. Three hundred gallons of brackish, toilet-stinking water exploded out, washing over the tiny slip of a girl and throwing her off her feet.

Her scattergun went off with a deafening roar, taking out two ceiling tiles and a light fixture. Before the glass was done raining down, Cole was flying out through the kitchen. A knife was thrown his way, missing his ear by inches. The cook who'd thrown it reached for a second, but then lifted his hands as Cole aimed his gun at his face. "Where's the back exit?" Then he saw it and raced on, glaring at a skinny teen with a wisp of black hair on his lip. He had picked up a bowl of near-boiling pho and had been thinking of throwing it at Cole. Instead it sloshed on his already stained wife-beater, making him shriek.

Cole slammed through the back door, sending a pack of rats squealing beneath the battered trashcans they'd been feeding from. Hard, cold rain slashed his face, momentarily blinding him and nearly sending him into the back of a delivery van that was up on blocks. In the next second, he was racing down the alley, the sound of police sirens cutting through the storm.

He took a quick right, then his first left, and immediately slowed, throwing his hood over his head to blend in with the rest of the afternoon crowd as it plodded dully about its business. Cole's business was staying out of jail long enough to figure out how Santino and Wu were connected.

As he walked, Cole ran over the timeline: Santino kills his wife and drains her dry. Sometime in the next few days, the wife is reported missing by a sister and Santino runs. Cole is given his ticket, tracks him to the flophouse and then to Wu's. Santino dies half an hour later in the basement of his building.

"He attacked the skirt to drain her," Cole muttered, "and right in his own building, too. Talk about stupid." He stopped in the middle of the sidewalk, trying to remember what Santino's slag numbers were. Sometimes the slag built up more on the inside than the outside, and every slag eventually turned into a moron.

An armored police car trundled slowly up from behind. Cole recognized it by the crunching sound its wire mesh tires made. "Shit," he whispered as it began to slow. When it pulled up abreast of him, he didn't wait for the window to be cranked down; he turned and raced to his right. There was no alley to duck into, there was only a series of stoops, each leading to its own tenement building.

With no time to be picky, he rushed for the nearest, taking the stairs three at a time.

"Stop!"

The one word was all the warning Cole could expect. The police could now legally shoot him if he failed to comply, something he had no intention of doing. He was through the door like a shot and found himself in a small vestibule that once held rows of mailboxes on either side of the front door. They were long gone. And so too was the door that led to the rest of the building. It and its frame had been stripped away, leaving a gaping hole that opened onto a long dim hall.

Running up one side of the hall was a flight of warped "poly-granite" stairs. There was no actual granite in the formed rubber, and neither were they very hard. Each step sagged under his weight as he went up at full speed. Behind him a cop had just charged into the building. He paused long enough to jerk out his .480 service piece, which fired a huge slug that could turn a man inside out. They could defeat body armor and car doors with ease, and it was said they could penetrate an engine block, if that was ever needed.

Cole felt his back tingle on the last few steps, expecting the bullet that would send his spinal column shooting out through his belly. The shot never came. He blended in so well with the darkened stairwell that the officer couldn't line up a good shot in the split second he had Cole in his sights.

The officer followed Cole up the stairs, losing ground with every step. He was carting around thirty pounds worth of body armor and another ten in equipment. The man was something of a juggernaut, built for power, not for speed. But he didn't need to be especially fast. All he had to do was get a clear shot and that would be that.

Cole wasn't going to allow the cop the opportunity. With his life on the line, he ran at a full sprint up a third flight before speeding down the hall. This hall was even darker than the ones below and Cole was only a distant shadow by the time the cop made it to the third floor.

Cole was only steps from the far end of the hall and another flight of stairs when thunder exploded behind him. It was followed immediately by a *crack!* as the bullet tore through the plaster wall in front of him. Then he was on the stairs, leaping down them seven, eight at a time. Down he went until he was at street level and, without pausing, he burst into the alley, knowing that if he was unlucky, he would charge right into one of the onrushing police cars he could hear screaming into the neighborhood.

He knew that he was hated, but when he saw a cruiser turn down the alley and plow into a slow-moving slag, he realized they weren't thinking about taking him alive.

The driver of the car stopped, rolled down his window and looked back at the slag bleeding in the street. Cole saw that it was Bruce Hamilton driving. "You heard the siren, didn't you?" Bruce yelled at the slag. "Next time, stay out of the damned street." By the time he turned back, Cole was across the alley and slipping between two buildings. There was barely room to move sideways and smack dab in the middle was a mound of trash, taller than he was.

There was no climbing it, but with the walls so close he was able to put his back to one and shimmy up and over. Dropping down on the other side, he froze. Not fifty feet away was another police car, shining a light through the driving rain. The narrow passage was shadowed to begin with, but with the rain, it seemed like night, and Cole slunk down low hoping to blend in.

The beam of light passed only a foot over the top of him and stopped. A curse was just taking shape in his mouth when he heard a low, hungry moan behind him. He cast a look over his shoulder and found himself staring at a grey…thing. It had made a burrow of sorts in the trash and was now emerging, flashing broken, yellowed teeth in black gums, and when the spotlight hit it, the angry moan became one of pain. Immediately, Cole's mind screamed: *Dead-eye!* and he dug for his gun.

Before he could get the gun from its holster, the creature hissed, "Go way," breathing the hideous stench of death over Cole, causing him to shudder.

It wasn't a Dead-eye. A Dead-eye as grey as this one would have attacked without hesitation. No, this was a trog. A trog was what happened to a person when the slag building up in them hit a runaway point. Half of its face had rotted away, as had four of its fingers. The rest of his body was covered in lesions and boils. There was no telling what sort of insidious tumors were growing inside him.

Trogs rarely ventured out of their pits beneath the earth where they lived out the remainder of their shortened lives. If the police hadn't been searching for Cole, they would have killed it without hesitation, citing a "quality of life" law that had been in place since the bombs fell.

Just then a trog was low priority and the light passed on. "Sorry," Cole said, backing away from the thing. He still had his hand on his gun and was thinking about using it if the trog came any closer. They carried every disease known to man. "I'm leaving, just relax."

"Go way." It pointed half a finger toward the street.

Cole backed away from it until he saw it crawl back into its mound. Then he turned and hurried on, glad for the rain washing down on him. When he got to the street, he saw a police car half a block down. Despite the short distance, he breathed a sigh of relief, glad to have gotten away from the trog without being touched. "I'd kill myself before I ever got that bad," he muttered, stuffing his hands down into his pockets and turning away from the police.

After five blocks Cole felt that he was in the clear and he cut across town to the only place he was likely to pick up any leads: Santino's apartment. The small lobby was just as dark as it had been the day before and this time, Cole wasn't going to take any chances. He had his gun tucked in his coat pocket as he mounted the stairs on cat's feet.

He took the seven stories slow, stopping only to ask the one woman he passed about Santino. The man's trench coat she wore hid whatever form she had, but Cole could see that she was well past her prime and crabby about it. The frown lines running down her cheeks were now permanent.

"Never heard of him," she muttered and tried to push past. Cole showed her a picture. "Nope," she said after barely a glance.

"Look again. It's important."

She jerked her wrist out of his grasp. "And so is getting my shopping done before another Cat-2 comes in. Now, get out of my way." She went stumping down the stairs in oversized boots that matched the coat.

Cursing her, he went up to the seventh floor and paused before stepping into a windowless hallway. Evenly spaced along the ceiling were nine light fixtures; only three were working and the light they emitted equaled to a few candles. They barely gave off enough light to form a shadow among the shadows. While he waited for his eyes to grow accustomed to the dark, he listened: two doors to his left a woman was nagging her husband about his job. In the apartment next to it, a baby was wailing while Station 3 played the annoying *Busy Bee* show. Another television was blaring some soap: "I've always loved you, Rhett!" A man's rasping snore could be heard from behind another door.

Once his eyes had adjusted to the near black, Cole crept past these doors and their living occupants and came to apartment 714. Out of habit, he put his ear to the door. It was eerily quiet inside. After giving the knob a single twist, he broke out his set of lock-picks. The lock in the door was ancient and the tumblers were practically begging to turn. The door opened into a cramped two-bedroom apartment that was almost as dark as the hallway. Light trickled in from a crack along the edge of a lead-shuttered window.

In front of him was a living room with two couches; one threadbare and the other still wrapped in plastic. They were canted toward a big box television that sprouted bunny antenna three feet long. Past the living room and to the right was a narrow dining room that held an eight-foot long table with four high-backed chairs. Although they appeared to be made of wood, they were hardened plastic.

A single door in the dining room led to the kitchen, while another in the living room went to the two bedrooms and the apartment's only bathroom. At first glance, there was nothing special about the place. There was no suggestion that a Dead-eye had ever lived there—or a murderer for that matter. He had expected there to be a smell of death in the apartment. Instead there was only stale air and a whiff of cologne, it was a scent he knew.

He sucked in his breath as a cold barrel touched the side of his neck.

"Sorry, Cole."

Fictional works by Peter Meredith:

A Perfect America
Infinite Reality: Daggerland Online Novel 1
Infinite Assassins: Daggerland Online Novel 2
Generation Z
Generation Z: The Queen of the Dead
Generation Z: The Queen of War
Generation Z: The Queen Unthroned
Generation Z: The Queen Enslaved
The Sacrificial Daughter
The Apocalypse Crusade War of the Undead: Day One
The Apocalypse Crusade War of the Undead: Day Two
The Apocalypse Crusade War of the Undead Day Three
The Apocalypse Crusade War of the Undead Day Four
The Apocalypse Crusade War of the Undead Day Five
The Horror of the Shade: Trilogy of the Void 1
An Illusion of Hell: Trilogy of the Void 2
Hell Blade: Trilogy of the Void 3
The Punished
Sprite
The Blood Lure The Hidden Land Novel 1
The King's Trap The Hidden Land Novel 2
To Ensnare a Queen The Hidden Land Novel 3
Dead Eye Hunt
Dead Eye Hunt: Into the Rad Lands
The Apocalypse: The Undead World Novel 1
The Apocalypse Survivors: The Undead World Novel 2
The Apocalypse Outcasts: The Undead World Novel 3
The Apocalypse Fugitives: The Undead World Novel 4
The Apocalypse Renegades: The Undead World Novel 5
The Apocalypse Exile: The Undead World Novel 6
The Apocalypse War: The Undead World Novel 7
The Apocalypse Executioner: The Undead World Novel 8
The Apocalypse Revenge: The Undead World Novel 9
The Apocalypse Sacrifice: The Undead World 10
The Edge of Hell: Gods of the Undead Book One
The Edge of Temptation: Gods of the Undead Book Two
Tales from the Butcher's Block

www.ingramcontent.com/pod-product-compliance
Lightning Source LLC
Chambersburg PA
CBHW070359260626
47161CB00001B/194